I0761611
Cavallon
THE SLANT SEA
THE INTERLANDS
The Crown River
(Marro)

THE EVERLASTING

OTHER BOOKS BY ALIX E. HARROW

Starling House

The Once and Future Witches

The Ten Thousand Doors of January

FRACTURED FABLES NOVELLAS

A Spindle Splintered

A Mirror Mended

THE EVERLASTING

ALIX E. HARROW

TOR PUBLISHING GROUP :: NEW YORK

This is a work of fiction. All of the characters, organizations, and events portrayed in this novel are either products of the author's imagination or are used fictitiously.

THE EVERLASTING

Interior illustrations and endpaper art by Alice Cao

A Tor Book
Published by Tom Doherty Associates / Tor Publishing Group
120 Broadway
New York, NY 10271

www.torpublishinggroup.com

EU Representative: Macmillan Publishers Ireland Ltd, 1st Floor, The Liffey Trust Centre,
117–126 Sheriff Street Upper, Dublin 1, DO1 YC43

The Library of Congress Cataloging-in-Publication Data is available upon request.

ISBN 978-1-250-79908-1 (hardcover)
ISBN 978-1-250-79910-4 (ebook)

First Edition: 2025

Printed in the United States of America

10 9 8 7 6 5

For Nick, again and always

Again and again, even though we know love's landscape
and the little churchyard with its lamenting names
and the terrible reticent gorge in which the others
end: again and again the two of us walk out together
under the ancient trees, lay ourselves down again and again
among the flowers, and look up into the sky.

—"Again and again, even though we know
love's landscape" from *Uncollected Poems*
by Rainer Maria Rilke,
translated by Edward Snow

THE FIRST DEATH OF UNA EVERLASTING

UNA AND THE YEW

t begins where it ends: beneath the yew tree.

The yew stands in the wood like a great queen grown old, limbs wracked with age, head bowed by the weight of her crown. In the gnarled grain of her trunk there is a woman's face, with weeping cankers for eyes, and in her heartwood there is a sword driven so deep that only the hilt is still visible. You already know the name of that sword, I think; who doesn't?

They say time runs strangely, beneath the yew. They say many things are lost there, among the tangled roots: years, hearts, lives. But they say, too, that some things are found: fates and fortunes, beginnings and endings.

And, once, a child. You know her name, too, or at least one of them.

She was still pink and toothless when the woodcutter found her, and he fretted. He needn't have; she grew quickly and well, as wild things do.

As a child she was all mischief, her fingertips stained with yewberries, her hair light and fey as dandelion down. As a girl she turned solemn, studying the woods as a saint would study the word. From them, she learned everything.

She learned to run as the stag runs and to be still as the goshawk is still; to stalk and to swim, to wrestle and to whistle; to vanish so thoroughly her own father could not find her and to kill so cleanly she left nothing but a tuft of fur, the metal scent of entrails.

She was strong, and arrogant in her strength. She was a young lion, a child-king, a lord of the wild woods.

And yet, she was no one at all. She was nothing, daughter of nothing, heir to nothing. Just another of the numberless, featureless small folk of Dominion, whose name would not be forgotten only because no one ever learned it in the first place. She would die a heathen death, unchristened and unshriven, so that even God would not remember her.

But then came her twelfth winter, and the Brigand Prince.

She was away when it happened. Perhaps she was stealing feathers for her fletching or pulling the hide from a hare. What matters is that she was far enough from her father's cottage that she did not hear the ring of iron-shod hooves, or the screams.

When she returned to the cottage the fire was cold, and her father was dead.

They had taken everything—the sow, the salt box, the pair of axes her father kept above the hearth—so she went to the yew.

She wrapped her hands around the hilt of the sword that had waited there for so long that the bark had boiled and knotted around the blade.

There were whispers about that sword, even then, but she hadn't heard them. She hadn't heard the tales of an ancient blade that neither dulled nor shattered nor rusted but remained whole and shining. She hadn't heard the prophecy that said it would be drawn only in the country's darkest hour, by her rightwise champion.

She only knew that her father was dead, and that the hilt in her hand felt like the clasp of an old friend.

And so—full of grief and fresh-born fury—she drew the sword from the yew.

She overtook the Brigand Prince and his men that very night, tracking them through new-fallen snow, and found them while they sat sated and dozing around their fire, beards shining with pig fat. She might have slit their throats in silence—she had learned to be silent as the fox is silent—but she was arrogant, and she was angry, so she called out to them first. She allowed them to scrabble blades from sheaths, spears from saddles.

And then she fell among them: a wolf now, a shrike, a terrible reaping.

When she was through, and the woods were quiet, the snow was no longer white.

That is how the queen—who was not yet the queen but only a king's daughter taken captive by the Brigand Prince—first saw her: a wet, red girl in the center of a wet, red circle, her wrists bent beneath the weight of a blade that had not been borne in a hundred years and a hundred more.

The queen-who-was-not-yet-queen rose and went to her, and the girl trembled, because the woman was so beautiful and gentle, and because the girl had killed those men so easily, almost joyfully. Her own body felt sharp and unwieldy, like a knife without a hilt.

The queen asked, 'Who are you?'

And the girl answered, 'No one.'

The queen asked, 'To whom do you belong?'

And the girl answered, with grief, 'No one.'

The queen knelt low. She stroked the girl's hair, heedless of the stain it left on her palm, and the girl felt her terror washed away beneath that touch. She thought she would not mind being a knife, so long as it was this hand that wielded her.

'Then,' said the queen-who-was-not-yet-queen, 'will you be mine?'

'Yes,' the girl whispered, and meant it with all her young and shattered heart.

So the woman—who would be queen very soon, for what is a queen but an ambition pursued—took the sword from the girl's hand and bid her kneel. She asked the girl if she would swear by her good right arm, and by her left, and by her life and death to serve no master save her queen, and she touched the blade once to each of the girl's shoulders and to the back of her bowed head.

The girl said, three times, 'I swear it.'

'Then rise, Sir Una,' said the queen, because the name meant *only*, and already she could tell there would never be another like her.

Over the years Una gathered more names. She became the Queen's Champion, the Red Knight, the Virgin Saint, the Drawn Blade of Dominion. She became Sir Una Everlasting, hero and paragon, arcing through history like a bright-tailed comet.

She became a legend.

Most legends are lies, pretty stories meant to keep the children quiet on long winter evenings. But I, who rode so many miles at her side and slept so many nights at her feet—I, who was her shadow while she lived and her echo ever after—am no liar.

I will not waste too much time with those stories that have already been told and retold, traded like coins in every hall and tavern. Everyone has heard the tale of Una and the False Kings, and the Winning of the Crown, and the First Crusade, which brought all of Dominion into the light of the Savior. Everyone knows how her legend began, beneath the yew.

But gather close, all true hearts of Dominion—

And I will tell you how it ends.

—*Excerpted from* The Death of Una Everlasting,
translated by Owen Mallory

Received 8-17

Attn: Prof Owen Mallory

WOULD BE THE FIND OF THE CENTURY WERE IT NOT A CROCK OF SHIT WHICH OF COURSE IT IS

Prof Gilda Sawbridge

Sent 8-17

Attn: Prof Gilda Sawbridge

ANALYSIS SUGGESTS IT IS AT LEAST A VERY OLD CROCK OF SHIT MAAM

Owen Mallory

Received 8-17

Attn: Prof Owen Mallory

DONT MAAM ME YOU [REDACTED] I PAID A PENNY FOR THAT WORD THE [REDACTED] FASCISTS BETTER NOT CENSOR IT MEET ME AT THE STATION TOMORROW

Prof Gilda Sawbridge

Received 8-18

Attn: Prof Owen Mallory

WHERE THE [REDACTED] ARE YOU MALLORY? IF IT WAS MY COMMENT ABOUT THE FASCISTS I WAS ONLY JOKING GOD SAVE OUR BOYS IN RED ETC

Prof Gilda Sawbridge

Received 8-20

Attn: Mallory

WELL GOOD LUCK OUT THERE BOY TAKE GOOD NOTES FOR ME DONT KNOW WHERE YOUVE GONE OR WHY BUT I KNOW YOULL COME BACK EVENTUALLY AS YOU HAVE SIX OVERDUE BOOKS

Gil

1

SEVERAL YEARS AFTER the war, during the mid-afternoon hour I generally put aside to fantasize about setting fire to my manuscript and disappearing into the countryside to raise goats, I received a book in the post.

This was not, in itself, remarkable; most members of the Cantford College Department of History received so many books in the post that their offices had been overtaken by a series of architecturally unsound towers, which would collapse if anyone exhaled too aggressively in their presence.

But this particular book was different, because this particular book did not—according to every archaeologist, historian, medievalist, linguist, antiquarian, archivist, and even most of the conspiracy theorists I had ever consulted—exist.

True, I may have harbored certain fantasies that I would one day prove them all wrong. I may have pictured myself unlocking a long-lost vault or descending into a catacomb, perhaps holding a torch aloft and whispering, to no one in particular, *By Jove, I've found it.*

But I was not in a vault or a catacomb.

I was sitting at my very ordinary desk in my very ordinary office, which the department had granted me only last term, in the manner of people who have been feeding a stray for so long they might as well name it. Outside the sky was a very ordinary late-summer blue.

And I was holding in my hands the single greatest historical discovery of the century, or possibly the millennium.

I wanted to weep. I wanted to laugh. I wanted most of all to open the book and run the tips of my fingers over the pages, to prove that it was real and so was I. (I was prevented by a vestigial but powerful fear of the college archivist, who kept thumbscrews in her desk specifically for people who touched old paper without washing their hands first.)

Instead, I whispered, somewhat hysterically, "By Jove, I've—"

"Mallory, old boy?"

A moneyed, overloud voice, a tread like a parade march: This could only be Jeremy Harrison, the other lecturer in my subfield.

As was my long custom in every stressful situation, I panicked. I wrapped the parcel paper back around the book, fumbled with the top drawer of my desk, which always jammed when it was damp, which it always was, and, in the end, stuffed the book down my shirtfront and hunched my shoulders to hide the lump.

This was sheer professional avarice, I'm afraid: There was only one endowed faculty position in Middle Dominion Studies. Harrison wanted it with the indefatigable passion of someone who thought admiration and wealth were his birthright; I wanted it with the indefatigable passion of someone who had never experienced either and would eat bullets for a taste.

Whoever discovered this book—the book whose corners were presently digging into my ribs—would have more than a taste.

"There you are." Harrison rounded the corner and slouched against the doorframe, looking as usual like an escapee from a painting of a fox hunt. "How's the book coming?" He asked this question two or three times a week, because he was at heart a bastard who reveled in the suffering of others.

"Fine. Wonderful." My voice was a thin rasp, unpleasantly high. I tried not to resent it; the field surgeon had told me I was lucky I had a voice at all, or, indeed, a pulse. "But I was just leaving, actually, excuse me." I stood, still hunched, scuttling around my desk in the manner of an arthritic crab.

"Of course, of course. Far be it from me to stand between a war hero and his duty," Harrison said, solicitously and hatefully. The Everlasting Medal of Valor was the only thing I had ever achieved that Harrison hadn't. I longed to rub his face in it but, as the whole thing was a complete fucking farce, never quite could.

I produced a hoarse *ha, ha* and ran for it, like the coward I always was and always would be.

I waited until I was on the train back to my flat—still bent nearly in half, as if I were smuggling an infant or suffering from an intestinal complaint—before extracting the parcel from my shirt.

There was no return address on the wrapping, no stamp of origin. Just my name, *Owen Mallory,* and the address of the campus mail room written in an unremarkable hand. I should have been at least mildly concerned that the entire thing was an elaborate hoax designed by Harrison to embarrass me, but all I felt was a rising, heady relief. As if the whole of my life up till now had been a sort of dreary, shameful churning, like dog-paddling, which would be redeemed by everything that happened next.

I peeled back the paper.

The book was bound in rich red heartwood, cut against the grain so that the rings of the tree were visible, rippling outward. The spine was affixed by a series of clever bronze hinges, cerulean with age, and a familiar, circular symbol had been burned deeply into the wood, stained with soot or wine-root. I traced it with one shaking fingertip.

An underfed boy of seven or eight was seated beside me, watching me in the frank, unashamed way that young people watch the unwell. He had an extravagance of eyelashes, which gave him the wistful, sleepy look of someone woken mid-dream.

I found myself opening the book, pointing to the title page. "Can you read this?"

The boy recoiled a little from the sound of my voice. Then, warily, as if I were mad or, worse, intending to teach him something: "No, sir."

"Don't worry, few people could." Middle Mothertongue bore a frustratingly faint resemblance to our modern language, but it had always come easily to me, like a childhood dialect I'd not quite forgotten. I closed the book and tapped the cover. "And what does this look like to you? This symbol?"

He bent to study it obediently. His hair—an unfortunate, Gallish shade of red—was still fine enough to form a babyish snarl at the nape of his neck.

"A lizard," he declared, eventually. "Or a dragon, maybe, chewing up its own tail." He spent the rest of the ride offering suggestions for the improvement of the design (blood, teeth, blood dripping from teeth, et cetera), gesturing enthusiastically. His wrists were spattered with hot pink scars, as from welding sparks or ash. The munitions factories ran on twenty-four-hour shifts these days, and there weren't enough grown men and women to work them.

The train dinged. I stood, and the boy nodded amiably at the book. "What's it called?"

I swayed, teetering on the edge of the thing that would transform me from *no one* into *someone*. It felt momentous, fateful, even. As if you had watched over me—haunted me, guided me, saved me thrice over—solely so that I could be here, now, with your name on my tongue.

The boy was waiting with his long dreamer's lashes tipped up to me. Would there be another war by the time he was old enough to enlist? Would it be your story—newly published, perhaps leatherbound, with my name in small print on the title page—that sent him to the front? Something swelled painfully in my chest at the thought; pride, I decided.

I leaned closer and told the boy the five words he couldn't read, that I could, as easily as if I'd written them myself: "*The Death of Una Everlasting.*"

Before I stepped off the train, I dug a coin from my wallet and tossed it to him. He caught it in one small, scarred hand.

2

I WAS BORN not quite ten centuries after your death; the first time you saved my life, I was nine.

It was between the wars, when my father and I lived in a narrow gray row house in the narrow gray village of Queenswald, in the part of the country that had once been a fathomless green wood but was now nothing but bald hills and pit mines.

I woke that morning and listened, as I did every morning, for the gentle engine of my father's snoring. The house was silent, so I laced up my boots and slipped out the door.

It wasn't far to the tavern, but it was dark and cold, and I did not like the dark or the cold. I also did not like locked doors, large dogs, the sound of gunfire, or the sight of blood. I was aware that these were girlish, humiliating tendencies that made the other boys laugh at me, but they would have laughed anyway, I think. Partly it was my looks—my hair and eyes were nearly black, and my skin had a suspiciously Hinterlander undercurrent, beery gold even in winter—and partly it was everything else about me.

I had slim shoulders, thick spectacles, a fine singing voice, neat handwriting, a subscription to the lending library, and the best marks in class; my shins were always a little too long for my trousers and I cried easily, sometimes for no reason. I was a walking flinch. An open invitation for other boys—bolder, louder boys, with ruddy pink cheeks and trousers that fit—to knock their shoulders purposefully against mine as they passed.

But those boys were still sleeping at this hour. Everyone was, save the barkeep, and she was inexplicably fond of my father and me. By the time I knocked she was wiping down tables with her youngest daughter propped on one hip.

"By the fire," she said, and I nodded.

My father was slumped over the hearth like laundry that had fallen from the drying rack. It took several minutes to get him conscious, and another several to get him vertical. He mumbled things to me as we navigated the empty chairs, nice things, like *there's my boy* and *thank you* and *sorry, sorry.* I knew my father often behaved shamefully—knew he drank too much and said too much and refused to sing the anthem on national holidays—but he was never unkind, so I'd decided I didn't mind the rest.

The barkeep set a basket on the counter as we passed. She was always slipping me things, leftover pies and hand-me-down sweaters. I knew this, too, was shameful, but her pies were very good and my father was always between jobs or about to be, so I'd decided it was another thing I didn't mind.

I took the basket. My father stumbled.

The barkeep's daughter looked at him with her big blue eyes and her perfect yellow curls—like an advertisement for Dominion's Own soap, like my exact opposite—and said, with the eerie mimicry of a child repeating words they've heard but don't understand, "Fucking coward."

I'd heard it before, along with words like *turncoat, traitor,* and sometimes *deserter,* although Queenswald was awfully far from the desert.

But that morning I felt my father cringe away from the word and understood for the first time that it was true. That my father was something even more shameful than being a drunk or a radical, something so awful that the stink of it followed him everywhere and sank into everything he loved, including—and this I saw in the mute pity of the barkeep's face, the way she scolded her daughter—me.

And so I left my father there in the tavern, still drunk, still saying nice things, and ran away.

It still wasn't fully light, and the muddy streets had frozen overnight into alien figurations, which reached for my ankles and twisted. I tripped and crashed into a woman wearing a fine wool coat. She was very nice about it, bending to help gather the scattered contents of the barkeep's basket while I fumbled for my spectacles. She smelled like summer, sweet and flowery.

"Poor thing," she said, as she handed me back the basket, and I thanked her, hot-faced with shame.

Running away, I decided, was more of a spiritual state than a specific speed, so I walked. I walked until the hunched shoulders of the houses gave way to sheepfolds and frostbitten hills, and the street became a narrow track that became nothing at all.

I walked until I reached the grove.

No one much liked the grove. Later I would learn that it was the last remnant of the Queen's Wood, the great green shroud that had once run all the way to the sea. But most of the trees had been turned into ships a century ago, the last time we'd gone to war against the Hinterlands, and now all that remained were a few ghostly acres.

It seemed larger, to me. The air beneath the trees was very still, and the branches seemed to catch all the ordinary sounds of Queenswald—the coal trains and carts, the lambs and schoolchildren and the bitter wet wind that blew all winter—and turn them away, so that stepping into the woods was like slipping under the surface of a lake.

Every now and then someone would announce that it was high time they cleared the land, and the young men would be hassled outside with axes and saws. They only ever made it through the slender new growth at the edges; any farther and the men would begin to complain that their blades, freshly sharpened, were going dull, and their good ash handles were turning spongy with rot. They would return home, defeated, and no one would mention the woods again for a year or two.

For this, I was grateful. Everywhere I went I was plagued by the sweaty sense that I was in the way or underfoot, unwanted, ill-fitting, missish—but not here. Here, I was neither my father's son nor a foreigner but only myself.

The only other person I'd ever met in the woods was a girl a little older than me, a proud and feral creature I'd met one day after I'd fallen and scraped both knees bloody. She was my superior in every subject that mattered—climbing, running, spitting, rock-throwing, fighting with sticks—but I didn't mind. She liked to win, and I liked to watch her, and afterward I liked to lie next to her among the tiny white flowers that covered the grove every summer.

Last winter she'd stopped coming. I asked after her everywhere, but no one seemed to know where she'd gone, or even to have heard of a girl by the name of ███, and eventually I had concluded, with a new and grown-up sadness, that I'd made her up.

I headed now to the very middle of the woods. She used to wait for me there, beneath an old yew so vast and so misshapen it no longer looked much like a tree, but like some secret organ of the earth itself, exposed. We liked to find patterns in the grain of the trunk: a dragon, a crown, a woman's tortured face. In spring the sap would run from her eyes like tears.

It was even quieter than usual, beneath the yew. So quiet I thought maybe I wouldn't run away, after all. Maybe I would just tuck myself down among the roots, cradled by dead needles and worms, and disappear.

They wouldn't look for me for very long. My father would want to, but he wouldn't go this far into the grove, being a fucking coward, and in a few months those little white flowers would cover me over, and the name Owen Mallory would be wiped clean from the world, as if it had never been.

That sounded rather grand and tragic, so I settled myself between the roots and waited to disappear.

It was hungry work, I found. By the time the sun had fully risen I'd decided maybe I ought to eat whatever the barkeep had slipped me, as a last meal. I opened the basket.

That's when I first saw the book.

Not *the* book, of course, but *a* book: thin pages, already brittle; a cloth cover, moth-chewed; illustrations printed so cheaply the colors didn't line up properly with the drawings, so that each figure appeared to be haunted by his own merry ghost. None of the barkeep's baskets had ever included a book before.

The title was written in an elaborate, curlicued font that was supposed to look medieval: *The Legend of Una Everlasting.* And then, in smaller serif print: *A Children's Retelling of the Classic Tragedy!* And, even smaller: *Look inside for a complete listing of titles in the Little Soldiers National Heritage Series.*

I sat there beneath the yew and read your story for the first time.

It was not, I would realize only when I was much older, a particularly good adaptation. The author had sprinkled *thou*s and *forsooth*s with a criminal disregard for syntax, and the illustrator had an unwholesome fascination with decapitation. All the messy loose ends of the Everlasting Cycle—the result of centuries of iterations and variations—had been pruned away in favor of a morality tale with all the subtlety and nuance of a nursery rhyme.

But the story itself shone through the prose like sunlight: a nameless child who became a knight; a knight who went to war and became a champion; a champion who slew the last dragon and found the lost grail and became a legend. It was a story of chivalry and courage, where good and evil were neatly labeled, and one always vanquished the other.

And when I turned the final page, there you were: Sir Una Everlasting.

They'd laid you out in full armor but for a helm, mailed fists still curled around your hilt, as if you kept some vigil even in death. Your hair was a startling, fluorescent yellow, which spilled like melted butter over the edge of your bier, and your face was the pure white of the page beneath. There were flowers tucked all around you: tiny, colorless roses, I thought, though the artist had no particular botanical skill.

I thought you were the saddest and most beautiful thing I had ever seen, like a dead angel. I looked for a long time at the bright line of the sword along your sternum, at the solemn shape of your mouth.

I looked at you for so long and so well that I felt something inside me shifting, irrevocably. It was like dying or being born, or being hit very hard on the head. It was like falling in love. (This was another thing I would only realize when I was much older.)

The longer I looked, the more ashamed I felt.

Sir Una Everlasting—you—had never run from anything. You hadn't disappeared from the world—you had burned your name into its surface, carved it so deeply into the stone of history that it was still legible a thousand years later. You had died, yes, but only because you had found something worth dying for. You had been born poor, but no one had ever called you a *poor thing.*

If I turned the book sideways, I could read the letters inscribed on your blade: *Erxa Dominus.*

For Dominion.

Perhaps if my father had read your stories as a boy, he would not have grown up to be a traitor and a turncoat; perhaps he would have served with honor and come home with a pension instead of just a bad hip and a motherless child.

And perhaps—despite my reservations about gunfire and bloodshed—it was not too late for me.

Here I was visited by a somewhat confused daydream of myself returning to Queenswald in triumph—being swept up, adored, admired. The ruddy-cheeked boys would clap me on the back and my father would sober up and *you* would be there, somehow, glowing faintly with holy light. You would take my hand and guide me down to lie beside you on your bier.

I repacked the basket, fingers clumsy with cold, and went straight home.

My father didn't even look up when the door closed behind me. He behaved, in fact, as if no time had passed at all, as if the whole world had held its breath while I sat beneath the yew in the heart of the grove that was all that was left of the deep wild woods.

I lingered, wanting him to ask where I'd gone and why I'd come back. If he had, I would have answered, somewhat theatrically: *For Dominion.*

But I would have meant: *For you.*

The second time you saved me, I was twenty-three, and we were losing the war.

The Sunday papers printed fresh maps each week, with squiggly red lines to show how far our troops had retreated, how much territory was still held by the Hinterlanders. They used to list the casualties by name over the wireless, but they'd stopped after a group of dissidents broke into Chancellor Gladwell's bedroom and wrote the names of the dead on his walls in gory red paint (I'd told myself the red spatters on my father's cuffs were coincidental).

Now the evening radio hour was reserved for the Minister of War. Every night she addressed the nation, begging every concerned citizen to tighten their belts, every able hand to take up arms. She recalled our past triumphs against worse odds: Were we not the sons and daughters of Queen Yvanne the First, who united the whole of Dominion and brought the Savior's light to every hollow and dale? Had we not stood against the Hinterlands for centuries, bloodied but never beaten? Surely our nerve would not fail now, on the very cusp of peace?

There had been murmurs and jokes and a run of extremely nasty cartoons when the Chancellor had named a woman as Minister of War, but her speeches were very good, and they left me restless and guilty.

Now, as I walked toward campus, I caught edged looks and suspicious glances, blond heads bent together, muttering. People wondered, perhaps, where I had gotten my dark eyes and hair, and why I hadn't been detained with the other enemy aliens and foreign suspects. Or perhaps they only wondered why a healthy young man was walking down the street with library books tucked under one arm while their own sons were bleeding or killing or rotting in the Hinterlands.

I wanted to point at my spectacles, which were so thick the lenses had to be specially ordered; I wanted to tell them I was from Queenswald, actually, and did not have to register as an alien; I wanted to wave my transcript at them, which had earned me a fellowship at Cantford College and an exemption from the draft; I wanted, with a dispassionate sincerity I hadn't felt since I was nine years old, to disappear.

I turned down an alley, hunched with loathing—and there you were again.

For one wild moment I felt everything shift around me, the city street dissolving into moss, the chill gray light going softly green. My mouth was full of the clean taste of winter and my heart was, for some reason, breaking.

Then I blinked and discovered that I was staring at a poster pasted to the alley wall.

The poster version of you was similar to the one in *The Legend of Una Everlasting.* You were still armored, and your hair was still an unlikely, over-saturated yellow. But you were alive now, caught mid-battle, an angel gone to war. Valiance—the sword you pulled from the yew, the blade that built Dominion—was held dead level in your hands, pointing straight out at my chest. Behind you, legions of Hinterlanders skulked in the shadows. Their faces—leering, animal-like, with eyes so dark they appeared to have no sclera at all—bore no resemblance to my own, or to any human face I have ever seen.

Neither did you, really: Your features were perfectly symmetrical, your cheeks marked by two circles of maidenly pink. Your cloak swirled Dominion-red behind you, and there was a faint halo around your head.

Only your eyes seemed real. The expression in them was exactly right, I thought: grave and proud, faintly contemptuous, as if you were asking for help but very much expecting to do everything yourself. Just their color, a floral and frivolous blue, was incorrect.

The caption read: DOMINION NEEDS YOU!

I looked at the poster for a long time. At you, who were everything I wasn't and everything I wanted.

Then I turned around and walked straight to the recruitment office. I cheated on the eye exam, lied baldly about my exercise regimen, signed several forms, shook two hands, and then I was an enlisted man.

Three weeks later I was at the front. I'd had to return my library books by mail, at a cost I didn't like to contemplate.

The third time you saved me, I was twenty-six, and we were winning the war.

It was harder to tell the difference between winning and losing, from the front. I had found that both states involved an enormous amount of marching and suffering, endless days spent eating shitty tins of beans, and endless nights spent praying to God you got to eat one more shitty tin of beans and wishing you'd said a proper goodbye to your father.

I hadn't even spoken to him before I shipped out. I'd posted a brief, slightly nasty letter explaining that my country called in her hour of need and that I, unlike certain others, was not afraid to do my duty (I was). In reply I had received a single telegram which read, when decoded: WOULD PREFER TO DISOWN YOU IN PERSON SO DONT DIE LOVE DAD.

I hadn't died.

True, the first time we charged enemy lines I had puked from sheer terror, and when it was over, I had wept, helplessly and hard, like a child—

But I hadn't died.

After the weeping had subsided to irregular hiccups, Colonel Drayton had taken me aside. "It's like swimming," he'd said, with the pride of someone delivering a line they've written themselves. "You drown, the first time. But the next one will be easier."

The next one had not been easier.

It had in fact been infinitely harder because I knew then how a bullet sounds when it hits bone, how intestines feel beneath a boot, how desperately and cravenly I did not want to die, no matter how noble the cause.

I had begun to cry before the order was even given, that time, and survived only because I turned out to be—to the bafflement of my commanding officers, myself, and everyone who'd ever met me—the best shot in the 2nd Battalion.

There was no rational explanation for it. My vision was terrible and my reflexes were worse; at school I had been chosen for teams only when every other option was exhausted, including younger siblings and girls.

And yet: The rifle settled so sweetly to my shoulder, and the revolver lay so tenderly in my palm. The motions of loading, firing, reloading—the fall of the hammer and the kick as the bullet left the barrel—all of it was like a clapping game I'd learned as a child. I'd forgotten the words, but my muscles remembered the rhythm.

I didn't even have to aim. I only lifted my arm and pulled the trigger and my enemies fell like bottles at a carnival game, and later I would vomit until I couldn't anymore.

I was not well-liked in the battalion. There had been a rash of ugly jokes early on, which Colonel Drayton quashed, somewhat clumsily. (Drayton was a liberal, which meant he thought boys of every race and class ought to be allowed to die for their country.) Then there had been an awkward encounter on sentry duty, where I'd been obliged to tell another private, politely, that I didn't fuck men, and he'd said *neither do I!* with confusing venom. The others had pointedly ignored me, since then.

But after that second battle they regarded me with sullen hostility, as if they suspected me of playing an elaborate trick on them. After the fourth battle, when it was clear the shaking and crying were not an act, they accepted me. Not as a fellow soldier or even, really, a fellow man—but as a sort of embarrassing lucky charm, like an unwashed sock or the foot of a dead animal, which they carried along against their better judgment.

They carried me far—across the whole of the Hinterlands. We waded through waist-deep fields of grain, which we left trampled and soiled, and crossed rivers whose names we changed to make them easier to pronounce. In the papers, the maps turned triumphal red in our wake.

Colonel Drayton's speeches grew longer and more florid. He discovered at some point that I'd studied history and badgered me for poignant details.

"Boys," he would begin, and several of the men would pull out their pencils, because there were running bets on the number of times he would address us as *boys, my boys, lads, sonny Jims,* and *buckos.*

"Let me tell you of the dark days before Queen Yvanne, back when Dominion was nothing but a hilly backwater ruled by petty kings and squabbling tribes. The Norns of the southern marsh, the savage Hyllmen, the Gallish with their heathen temples all painted up like fast women. All of them mired in filth and darkness, beset by famine and pestilence—even dragons! That's right, sonny Jims!" (Pencils would scratch.) "The devil's own creatures, pale as ghosts, huge as houses!

"Yes, nasty business all around, lads." (More scratching; some soft cursing.) "Until a young girl pulled a sword from a tree. Until a queen rose to power and sent her champion out to bring peace and prosperity to the land. And then there was only one crown, one God, and one nation. And that nation was called Dominion."

Here he would smile with a sort of rugged paternal pride. "For a thousand years, we've held fast. Despite treachery and idolatry, despite foreigners and radicals worrying at our heels. Despite even these damned Hinterlanders—who slew the Virgin Saint herself, who despise our very way of life!" He shook his head, dolefully. "How many times have we gone to war with them, and settled for sniveling treaties, slick promises from soft-handed diplomats? Not this time, buckos! This time let us have victory or death! Let us, gathered here"—I could never tell if he was faking it, or if he was genuinely choking with tears—"Let *us* be the Last Crusade, my boys! For crown and country!" (There was a separate tally for this phrase, which the Colonel deployed at least once a day despite the fact that no one had actually worn the crown for a century or so, as Dominion was now a republic.)

A beat or two would pass while everyone ran the numbers, followed by perfunctory applause and furtive shuffling, as a great deal of cigarettes and pornography changed hands.

Then we would string up flags and pose for photographs in front of whatever little village we'd liberated for crown and country.

I had formed the idea, from the little newsreels that played before films at the theater, that the new citizens of Dominion would applaud as we passed, weeping with gratitude and tossing fistfuls of poppy petals, but they only watched us, silently, with eyes like thrown stones.

Every now and then they approached me, speaking rapidly in one of the many languages of the Hinterlands: Shvalic in the east or Merrish in the south, or the musical, gapless speech of the Roving Folk, who lived everywhere, on horseback. But I would shake my head—only the Mothertongue was taught in Dominion schools—and they would recoil, as from a stick that had turned out to be a snake.

I wondered if I really looked so much like them. If the mother my father never mentioned had been one of them, some nameless Hinterlander girl he met during the last campaign. If she was even now standing in the crowd, watching me through the gaps between rifles.

I tried not to look at the townspeople, after that.

My sleep suffered. My dreams became torturous circles, looping back over the same battles again and again, with slight, disquieting variations, interrupted only by the anxious grinding of my own molars. In the morning my hands shook so badly that I struggled to tie my own laces or button my own coat, although they were always perfectly steady when I raised my revolver. I thought often of my father, not with my usual pity or disgust, but with a treacherous, wormy sympathy.

"Think of your girl back home," Colonel Drayton advised, cliché-ly. I thought of flaxen hair, of mailed fists, and eyes like judgment day. My breathing eased.

Drayton clapped me on the back very hard and said, "See, lad? It's all worth it."

I found myself repeating those words like a prayer. I believed them, or at least believed that I believed them—until we reached the southern coast.

Our enemies had fallen back and back until there was nowhere else to fall back to. The ones who would surrender had surrendered; what remained were the ones who never would. Who no longer hoped for victory or mercy, but only blood.

They were dug in now among the dunes, waiting for us. We might have starved them out or waited for the fleet to fire on them from the seaward side. But the public was tiring of the war, and Colonel Drayton had been asked to provide a decisive victory. So there we were in the pale dawn: running the leather straps of our holsters over our shoulders, affixing our service knives to our belts, laughing in the urgent, overloud way of young men who can taste their own deaths in the backs of their mouths.

I snapped my revolver into its holster—a Saint Sinclair Mark III, finest product of the finest army in the world, accurate to thirty paces—and looked out at the shadowed figures waiting for us in the dunes. Within an hour or two they'd all be dead, along with most of the men beside me.

I couldn't see, suddenly, how it could possibly be worth it. How lowering, after all this marching, to discover I was still my father's son.

They found me six hours later with my throat half cut, so that my breath bubbled obscenely through my trachea. Poor Colonel Drayton lay beside me, service knife still gripped in one cold hand, and a neat black hole burrowed directly between his eyes.

The following week was a grim haze of needles and stitches and medics with distant, resigned expressions. Someone turned on a wireless so we could hear Minister Rolfe's speech, thanking us for our noble and worthy sacrifices in the name of crown and country. I laughed, and it was such an unpleasant sound that they sedated me. The fever set in some time that night, and I thought, with no small amount of irony, that I might die for my country after all.

And then I dreamed of you.

I'd dreamed of you many times, as a boy and after, but you were always two-dimensional, a character from a storybook rather than a person.

Now you were so real I could see the lines tanned into the corners of your eyes, hear the wet rattle of your breath. Your teeth were filmed with blood.

"Owen," you said, and your voice was deep and cool as still water, "come back to me."

Then you said, "Please," and that cool voice caught and hung on the word, and I thought I would do anything at all—live or die or burn in hell—if you asked it of me.

In the dream, I answered you. The medics told me later it was the first word I'd spoken since the dunes, the first time any of them thought I might live.

I said, "Always."

The fever burned out within a week, but the dreams lingered.

They were almost always of you, though you did not speak again. I saw you kneeling, head bowed so that your hair parted in two bright wings around the back of your neck. I saw you astride a rangy blood bay, the two of you moving in eerie, perfect synchrony, like a single animal. I saw you by firelight and leaf-light, moonlight and sunlight and, once, bizarrely, by the spectral, electric blue of a searchlight.

Sometimes, of course, my dreams were merely the senseless, anxious dreams of a coward: looking for my father and not finding him; trying to hold a pen with curled, blackened fingers; calling out the names of two children I'd never met and knowing they wouldn't answer.

Sometimes, too, I dreamed of home: the long gray summers of Queenswald, when mold bloomed overnight and moss burst green between every cobblestone; the quiet winter evenings with my father, both of us reading, nearly content; those eager spring mornings in the grove, waiting for ███ beneath the yew.

That's where I went when they finally let me out of the hospital. I took the train straight from Cavallon to Queenswald. An elderly, jowly man offered me his seat, which puzzled me until I recalled that I was still wearing my red service jacket, with the Everlasting Medal of Honor gleaming dishonestly on my chest. Other passengers regarded me with fond, vaguely paternal expressions, rather like the ones in my childhood vision. I found they made me a little sick, now.

I walked from the station past my father's house and up into the hills. I went to the place where I first saw you, which was the last place anything had made sense.

But the grove was gone.

During the war the land had finally been cleared, and the entire hilltop given over to pasture. There were a few stumps and thickets left, but of my favorite tree—that great and ancient yew in the heart of the woods—there was nothing at all. Even the roots had been dug out, so that all that remained was an indentation in the earth surrounded by tiny white flowers, like a plundered grave.

For once, I did not weep.

I only knelt for a while in the place where the woods had once been, but were no longer, until I understood what every person understands eventually: that I had left home and could never return to it, and that there would never be a time when I did not miss it.

Yet still, I lingered. You had come to me three times, I thought; why not a fourth?

I whispered your name; nothing answered me but the bitter wet wind, which blew hard across the bare hills.

I picked a fistful of those little white flowers before I left. Then I stood, damp-kneed and dry-eyed, and went down to the tavern. My father wasn't there, but the barkeep told me she would save the dragonscales for him.

I asked, "The what?"

She nodded at the flowers hanging limply from my hand. "Dragonscales, my mother always called them."

"Ah," I said. I looked them up later; they're also called ulla flowers, which means *many,* in Middle Mothertongue, because they're so common as to be considered weeds.

I tucked the flowers obediently into a little jam jar and thanked the barkeep, who kissed me on the cheek and told me my father had worried himself sick, which I did not imagine was distinguishable from drinking himself sick.

Then I walked to the village post office, where I mailed a letter to my old adviser apologizing for going to war in the middle of term and begging to be readmitted to the Cantford Department of History.

If you would not come to me, I thought, I would go to you.

Professor Sawbridge's reply arrived four days later, so heavily redacted that it was mostly prepositions and conjunctions. (Gilda Sawbridge had a low opinion of the government and a high temper, which tended to upset the censors. It also upset the Cantford Board of Fellows, her students, the other faculty, and me, but, as she was the most acclaimed archaeologist of her generation, we all did our best to overlook it.)

Tucked in the envelope alongside the letter was a formal notice of acceptance on school letterhead. At the top, Sawbridge had written: *Don't make me regret it.*

I returned to Cantford campus the following week. In our first meeting, I told Professor Sawbridge that I'd chosen a specialization: the folkloric traditions of Middle Dominion.

She propped her glasses on top of her head and gave me her full attention. I've never been vivisected, but I imagine it feels very much like receiving Gilda Sawbridge's full attention.

Eventually she said, without looking away, "Too broad."

"I intend to focus on the Everlasting Cycle, our founding mythological—"

"It's played out."

"It's patriotic."

"Please, I've just had breakfast," she said, without inflection.

"I wonder that you, of all people, could fail to appreciate the need for further study of Una Everlasting." This, I thought, was clever of me: Sawbridge was the only female professor in the whole of Cantford. "Her story tells us that a woman might take up arms as well as a man. That she might fight, even lead—"

"So long as she dies before she starts wondering why she can't vote, divorce, or open a bank account. Do not patronize me, Mallory." This, too, was delivered flatly. "Now tell me honestly: Why?"

I answered, softly, "*Erxa Dominus*, ma'am."

It was a good line, well delivered, and even a little true. I had failed my country on the field, but still hoped to serve it better on the page. To earn the medal I could hardly stand to look at, to finally become—despite my embarrassing origins and even more embarrassing father—a true son of Dominion. I imagined myself standing proudly behind lecterns and oaken desks, beyond all reproach and suspicion, unassailable at last.

But beneath all that, of course, there was another reason, which I could not say aloud.

Professor Sawbridge looked at me some more. She looked at my hands, which were shaking again, and at my throat, which I kept hidden behind tightly buttoned collars. She looked at my eyes, and perhaps she saw something of that last, unspoken reason there.

She said, on a sigh that made her book towers wobble dangerously, "Good luck."

I left the office that day feeling like a hound let off the leash, permitted at last to give chase.

In the years that followed, there was nothing but the hunt. I ignored the papers and wireless speeches and my father's pamphlets. I ignored everything—save you.

You led me into archives and private collections, libraries and museums, ancient ruins and family vaults. I excelled at the chase—I had a better-than-average memory and an eye for detail, and a mind that clicked obediently along like a series of bright brass gears. But it was like hunting in a hall of mirrors; I caught glimpses of bright armor or pale hair, but when I reached out, I touched nothing but glass.

I read and re-read every accounting of your story—Lazamon's shambling anthology of legends, Marie de Meulan's romantic verses, Montmer's *Historica*—but all of them were third- or fourth-hand, history watered down into mere hearsay. Most of the authors claimed to have based their versions on *The Death of Una Everlasting*—a true accounting of your adventures as written by an anonymous traveling companion—but, as there was no evidence that such a text had ever existed, most modern historians saw this as a bid for legitimacy rather than a fact.

My undergraduate work was therefore little more than an echo's echo. My papers were all reinterpretations of reinterpretations, dissections of lines that had already been dissected a hundred times before. It was received well enough—I graduated with the second-highest marks in the history of the department, after Sawbridge herself, and my article on the grail as a metonym for nationhood had been quoted in the *Times*—but Professor Sawbridge was not fooled. ("You are clever enough to convince the swine that you are giving them pearls," she observed, idly. "Alas, alack! I am not a pig.")

My current manuscript—*An Everlasting Legacy: A Survey of Modern Translations*—was supposed to earn me the Middle Dominion Faculty Fellow title, the respect of my peers, and a living wage. But it was so anemic and derivative that even the swine (the other faculty) were beginning to entertain doubts. They muttered often about the benefits of fresh air, and more than once I'd heard the words *extended leave* floating ghoulishly down the hall. Though I had nowhere else to go—I wasn't even sure I could crawl back home, after the things my father and I had said to one another during our last fight—I was on the verge of agreeing with them.

Until I received that book in the post, and you saved me for the fourth time.

3

I BARELY TOUCHED the book, that first day.

I simply crouched in my flat above the butcher shop and smoked an entire pack of Lucky Stars, lighting each cigarette from the butt of the last. It was a habit I'd picked up during the war and continued on doctor's orders for my weak disposition, and also because it was the only way to overpower the meaty, battlefield smell of the butcher shop below.

I moved the book from my bedside to the desk and back again. I performed a series of tests—not on the book, but on myself: writing out my whereabouts for the last three days to ensure there were no odd gaps, reciting every monarch of Dominion from Yvanne up to the republic, pinching myself quite hard, et cetera. I had suffered some little disturbances after the war—forgetting things that had happened only the day before, or remembering things which had never happened, or confusing dreams for memories—but my mind seemed to be in perfect order now.

I went to bed early and lay tense and unsleeping for several hours.

At two or three in the morning I said, aloud, "God, enough," slipped on a pair of cotton gloves, and opened the book. I translated the first sentence:

It begins where it ends: beneath the yew tree.

A surprising peace moved through me as I wrote the words, an almost mechanical satisfaction, as of a key turning smoothly in a lock. I returned to bed and slept well. I dreamed, and my dreams were all of you.

The second and third days I spent examining the book as an archaeological object, striving for some semblance of objectivity.

It was not at all uncommon for unscrupulous or excitable persons to "discover" artifacts related to Una Everlasting. Every old tree in every old village was the one from which you first pulled Valiance; every rusted shield was the one you wore on your left arm, a white dragon upon a red field. Just last week Professor Sawbridge had been called away to investigate a vault beneath the ruins of Cavallon Keep, which might have been your final resting place.

I extracted tiny samples of ink and studied the grain of the wood beneath my strongest magnifying glass. I took meticulous, if inconclusive, notes. *Ink is oak gall, hand-lettered—rate of decay indicates early period. Pages are wood pulp. Parchment or vellum would have been more typical.*

On the fourth day I opened the book again and worked through the first six pages, and forgot all my fussy, doubtful notes. Yes, the paper was anachronistic. Yes, the binding was unusual, perhaps even unique. But the words themselves rang in my head like church bells, and I came to believe that whoever had written them had truly known you, not only as a hero or a saint, but as a living woman.

It was the way he described you, the casual familiarity of it, and the way he sometimes forgot the grander quest in favor of odd, quiet moments of intimacy. But most of all it was the way he mourned you. Grief rose from every page like turpentine, burning the back of my throat.

On the fifth day I made copies of my translated pages and mailed them to Professor Sawbridge, who was still away supervising the excavation of the burial vault.

On the sixth day Professor Sawbridge and I exchanged a series of telegrams, in which she called me a rude name, committed light treason, and cast aspersions on the veracity of the text. I knew she was at least intrigued, however, because she was taking the early train back to campus, and the only thing she hated more than her country was getting out of bed before ten o'clock.

On the seventh day, I went out for cigarettes and milk. The sun was far too hot and the air was far too fresh, moving around me in great unsettling billows, tugging at my sleeves.

When I returned, with relief, to the stale dark of my flat, the book was gone.

In its place there was a crisp white card, bearing no name, but only an address.

I had never flourished in a crisis. I was one of God's natural ditherers, much given to the wringing of hands and the writing of unhelpful lists. Since the war, I had added fits of weeping and melancholic stupors, and every now and then a wave of confused and violent memory that left me curled in a corner, shaking.

I did not dither now, though, nor wring my hands. I did compose a brief and unhelpful list (1. Report the theft of a nonexistent book to the police; 2. Search the room for clues, as they are always doing in novels; 3. Weeping fit??), but I did not even bother to write it down. My body was already moving, as if it had decided on a course of action without me.

I donned my old red service coat, then—after a moment's sweaty uncertainty—removed the coat, strapped my holstered Sinclair service revolver over my shoulder, and slipped the coat back over it. I tucked two packs of cigarettes into the breast pocket and left the flat with the white card clutched so tightly in my hand that the edges cut into my palm.

I showed the card to the cab driver, who read the address twice, gave me a suspicious, flinty look, then drove in silence to the very heart of Cavallon and deposited me on the steps of a building I'd never seen, but recognized nonetheless, because it was stamped on the back of every coin in the country: the capitol.

I exited the cab clumsily, blinded by the sheer volume of white marble. The air was thick and hot, as if it had been panted from a dog's mouth; I couldn't imagine, suddenly, why I'd worn my service jacket.

"Traitors, the lot of you." It was my driver, leaning one elbow out the window and enunciating very clearly, as if he'd been rehearsing during the drive.

I was not surprised by this statement. The war was over, but the occupation was proving messy and expensive, and there were plenty of people who were thrilled to find someone with brown eyes to blame for it. I also happened to be, by literal and legal definition, a traitor.

But then I saw the crowd gathered at the steps of the capitol, signs and banners waving, and felt a surge of embarrassment instead.

"Oh, no—I'm not with—" But the driver had already slipped back into traffic.

I turned quickly away from the crowd, hunching my shoulders. I comforted myself that treasonous chanting was probably quite diverting, and there was no reason any of them should notice a panicky scholar lurking nearby. And anyway, they might not even be affiliated with my father. Those radical organizations were always dividing and sub-dividing, as if their true purpose was not the downfall of tyranny but the invention of new acronyms.

"Owen? That you?"

I flinched, feeling like a boy caught sneaking out of the house, except that my father had never much cared where I went or when I came back.

I turned, sweating hard, and saw him limping gamely through the crowd, one arm raised.

"Well, if it isn't my favorite propagandist," my father said, and smiled at me.

It was such a good smile—sincere but a little roguish, the bags beneath his eyes folding up like merry accordions, as if our last fight had never happened or wasn't worth remembering—that I muttered, "Hello, Dad." And then, more stiffly, "What's all this?"

"Ah," he scoffed, "some friends of mine. Just a little gathering."

"A gathering with slogans is called a protest, Dad."

The smile faded. Without it, my father looked more like what he was: old and tired and hungover, probably in a great deal of pain. He'd always been thin, but now he resembled the scraps one might save for a stray, all bone and gristle.

"That bloodthirsty tyrant—"

"Her title is *Minister Rolfe,* and as our first female Minister of War I think she deserves a certain degree of respect—"

"Oh-ho, does she show *respect* for the women who've died in her munitions factories—which she refuses to investigate, because they're owned by her nasty industrialist friends?" I often imagined my father would have made a good solicitor, if he hadn't taken up anarchy instead. "The union girls invited her to speak at one of their meetings and do you know what she called them? *Poison!*" My father shook his head. "She wants to be Chancellor, if you ask me. Thinks we'll all just go quietly along with it."

He added a scornful *ha!*, but the truth was that I'd spent the last several years going quietly along with it. It wasn't hard; I simply never read the papers or listened to the wireless or voted. I declined every invitation to veterans clubs and kept my Medal of Valor in my loose change jar. If it wasn't for the dreams and the shaking fits, I might have been able to pretend I'd had my throat slit in a terrible archival accident.

My father was still talking. "But I can tell you our pamphlet circulation is up two hundred percent! Not everyone wants to see their tax dollars support an illegal occupation. Not everyone was happy to waste their sons on a ridiculous war—"

"Some of us shed a lot of blood for that *ridiculous* war," I interrupted, in that especially priggish tone I seemed to reserve solely for my father. "Some of us fought for crown and country—"

"A country with colonies is called an empire, son."

We regarded one another unhappily for a little while. The chanting continued shamelessly on. The sun shone heartlessly down. I was very conscious of the strap of the holster beneath my coat, and the sheer insanity of bringing a weapon to the capitol of Dominion.

Eventually, my father offered, with gruff resignation, "There's extra signs, if you'd care to join us." Behind him two men were unrolling a long banner that read: *VETERANS AGAINST WAR!*

"I thought you were the Veterans for Peace."

"Don't you mention the VFP in my presence. Class traitors and sycophants, all of them." My father softened, leaning close. His breath rose in fumes between us. "What do you say, son?"

I looked at him, with his pinkish-white complexion and his hair the color of underbaked bread, and marveled that he had never truly noticed the difference between us. He didn't seem to understand that a man like me would never be wholly beyond suspicion, no matter how ardently loyal, while a man like him would never be wholly condemned, no matter how faithless. That I had always hated him, just a little, for the privilege of his deviance.

I answered, in my coldest Cantford drawl, "No, thank you."

My father would have said something else—I had never in my life gotten the last word—but someone touched my right elbow and said, "This way, sir," with the professional unobtrusiveness that I associated with spies or very good waiters.

"Excuse me," I said to my father, and turned away with profound relief.

His voice followed us into the building, asking why I wasn't angry and how I slept at night, and finally, plaintively, as we approached a nondescript door, "And why the hell are you wearing that coat? It's hot as the devil out."

The spy/waiter led me through the door, where I was handed off to an even more unobtrusive person, who took me through a series of hallways that ended in another door, which was attended by someone so masterfully unobtrusive they seemed to blend into the plaster.

They turned the knob and announced, deferentially, "Corporal Owen Mallory, ma'am."

I had a fleeting impression of wealth—velvet drapes, waxed parquet—before my eyes landed on a heavy desk and, sitting behind it, a woman.

I'd never seen her before in my life, but I had the brief, disorienting sense that I knew her. I knew the sleek brass of her hair, styled so perfectly it might have been strapped on, like a helmet. I knew the clear blue of her eyes and I knew—I *knew*—that voice: "Thank you for coming, Corporal Mallory."

It was the *thank you* that did it. Suddenly I was back in the field hospital after the dunes, listening to that voice thank me for my sacrifice to crown and country.

I froze two steps across the parquet, contorting into a panicked gesture somewhere between a salute and a bow. "Oh my God, ma'am—Minister Rolfe—"

A low laugh, which managed not to be mocking. "Call me Vivian. Sit down."

I settled myself, carefully not imagining what my father would say if he knew his son was on first-name terms with Vivian Rolfe.

She regarded me across the polished expanse of her desk. She was always perfectly composed in her speeches and appearances, no matter what the opposition said or did.

But now she looked a little harried. Two of her nails had been badly chewed, and the starch had gone out of her collar, so that it lay limp against her collarbones.

She set a slim cigarette between her lips and leaned minutely forward. An awkward beat passed before I fumbled the matchbook from my coat pocket and cupped a flame between us. The light settled in the hollows of her face, finding the skull beneath her skin. I couldn't tell how old she was.

She exhaled a long white plume and said, pensively, "You'd think it would have been enough. There were losses, to be sure, but we won. Our oldest enemy, thrown down! If I were a man, he'd be crowning me by now."

"Ma'am?" I offered, intelligently.

She cut me a wry, pitying look. "Chancellor Gladwell has asked for my resignation. I *made* that boy—does he think he would have been reelected without a war?—but now they're whining about the budget and the cost of reconstruction, and they've found just the woman to blame."

"Oh," I said. In the silence, the faint sound of chanting could be heard from the window.

Vivian rubbed her temples. "And those bastards simply *refuse* to *shut up*." I tried not to blink, because I'd read somewhere that blinking was a sign of guilt. She added, wistfully, "I'd have them rounded up like cattle, if I could."

The dispassion in her voice sent a chill over my scalp. My father had so far suffered no worse than a ritualistic series of arrests and fines, but suddenly I could imagine his body splayed on the capitol steps, the butt of a rifle raised above him. I made a mental note to remind him to start using a more difficult cipher for his letters and pamphlets.

Vivian tapped her cigarette twice on the lip of an ashtray. "But nothing is ever handed to us, is it, Corporal Mallory? This country may not believe in me anymore"—a self-deprecating laugh, only slightly bitter—"but I'll be damned if I stop believing in it."

"Ma'am?" I said again.

Vivian rolled her neck from side to side, and when she looked at me again a subtle transformation had taken place. Her spine had stiffened and her shoulders moved back, so that the points of her jacket drew a perfect line in the air. All the irony and weariness had leached from her face and left behind a quiet, earnest zeal. She looked both younger and much older.

When she spoke again, it was in the flowing, modulated voice I heard on the radio. "Our country is at a crossroads. Finally, after centuries of strife, we stand as Yvanne imagined us: a nation united, at peace. But peace is a fragile, fleeting thing. It must be protected, fought for, defended against all threats, native and foreign alike—and I fear we have grown weak."

I felt I ought to nod, so I did.

"I don't refer only to the obvious dissidents—at least they care, in their misguided way, about the future of the nation. It's the disinterested, the doubtful. It's the empty pews in our churches and the apathy in our schools. The young people who don't know where we came from or what we fought for. We've forgotten—as a nation, as a people—who we are."

All of these were lines from her speeches, which left me with the sweaty, trapped feeling that I was the only person in the audience of a one-woman play. I wished, passionately, that I'd taken off my coat.

But then Vivian pulled something heavy from a drawer and set in on the desk between us with the muted clack of wood on wood, and I forgot about my coat.

A book. *The* book. I leaned toward it, pulled by whatever secret gravity had sent it to me in the first place.

"I read your article about the grail. Brilliant work." (When Professor Sawbridge had read that article, she'd sighed for a long time and said: *You may be a patriot or a historian, Mallory, but not both.*) "You argued that a nation is not a boundary on a map or a flag on a pole, but only a story we tell about ourselves."

"Yes, ma'am."

"It's a hell of a story, isn't it?" One of Vivian's fingers, long and delicate, touched the cover. It was not a reverent or thrilled touch, but the casual, possessive gesture of a reader to her favorite book. "Honor. Courage. Tragedy. The villains cast down, the hero triumphant, the rightful queen restored. And yet, it fades. The people forget. It's time we remind them."

She traced the circle of the device on the cover and then, abruptly, slid the book several inches toward me. "You have served your country well, Owen Mallory." She met my eyes and her voice fell nearly to a whisper. "Are you the man who will save it?"

Some latent desire in me—to kneel, to surrender myself to some grander purpose—to erase the ignominy of my origins and earn my place at last in the grand tradition of Dominion—unfurled inside me. Vivian Rolfe looked at me so steadily and for so long that I felt the light contract around us, so that I imagined the shadow of a crown on her brow, felt the phantom weight of a blade on my shoulders.

I nodded, because I had an awful certainty that if I spoke my voice would be choked with tears.

"I knew you were." The warmth in her voice, the absolute certainty—as if she was not at all surprised by my answer—sent a flush of pleasure through me.

"It was you, wasn't it?" I sounded boyish, overeager. "Who discovered the book."

She dipped her head in grave approval. "We've been excavating the ruins of Cavallon Keep for years now. A few weeks ago, we found a vault, and in the vault was a locked chest, and inside the chest . . . Well." I hoped the archaeologist had gotten to say *By Jove* at least once. Vivian continued, "Can you imagine? People have been searching for centuries, scouring every crypt and castle, and only now—in Dominion's darkest hour!—does it reveal itself. It's providence. Fate. The hand of the Savior Himself, I sometimes think."

"And then you . . . mailed it to me?"

Her expression turned indulgent. "Forgive my little test. If you had gone to the press, or tried to sell it—but you didn't. You kept it secret, treasured it, labored over it. That's how I knew you were the right man to tell Una's story."

A new and delicious sense of my own significance filled me. I'd never been picked first for anything in my life, and now the Minister of War—or at least, the former Minister of War—had chosen me to translate the greatest historical artifact in Dominion's history. Visions of honorary degrees and book tours danced in my head; becoming the Middle Dominion Faculty Fellow; Harrison combusting from pure envy; my father clapping me on the back and saying, *You've changed my mind about everything, I'm so sorry for my decades of embarrassing radicalism.*

"I—I'll try, ma'am."

"Excellent! Go ahead then, no time like the present. Get in touch when you finish your translation." Vivian ground her cigarette into the tray and reached for a letter opener, as if our conversation was over.

I stood clumsily, dizzy with awe. "Yes, ma'am." My hands shook as badly as they had in the war, as if they were approaching a battlefield instead of a book.

The cover was cool and smooth as stone. I felt Vivian's eyes on me again, perhaps wondering why I lingered. But a strange anxiety gripped me, a sense that some trick was being pulled. I opened the book carefully, praying the college archivist never found out.

And then I went very still. I wet my lips twice before I could speak. "The pages." I cringed from the hoarse whistle of my voice. "The pages are—"

"Blank? Yes." Vivian spoke lightly, with humor, twirling the letter opener in her fingers. The point glinted.

I had the sudden, inexplicable urge to hit her. For a moment I saw it so clearly in my mind—saw my knuckles splitting against her perfect white canine, blood overfilling her mouth and sheeting down her chin—that I recoiled from myself.

"Why," I asked, swallowing, "are they blank?"

She leaned over the desk, smiling peacefully. Beneath the tang of cigarette smoke, I smelled something sweet and a little familiar, like summer flowers. "Because you haven't written them yet," she said, and then she stabbed the letter opener through the back of my left hand.

I did not scream. My vocal cords were too knotted and scarred to produce anything louder than an eerie, breathy howl, like the keen of a dog. I tugged dumbly at my hand, but the letter opener had sunk into the pages below, pinning it there.

Vivian leaned closer. Her expression was still peaceful, perhaps even sympathetic. "Your country needs you, Corporal."

I watched with a sense of unreality as my blood spread over the empty paper like a red map, an empire in bloom. I looked quickly away, but something had gone wrong with my vision.

Everything in the room felt translucent, impermanent, as if the paint of the world was fading and peeling away in great strips.

I closed my eyes. I smelled pine and snow, now, instead of flowers.

Vivian's voice came to me from very far away, softly urgent. "She needs you, Owen."

4

WINTER SUNLIGHT, THIN and crosshatched. Air so fresh it burned in the lungs, like gunpowder. Branches circled all around, bowed low with frost.

I concluded—reluctantly, against all reason—that I was no longer in the office of Vivian Rolfe.

I was in the woods, with one hand pressed tight to the trunk of a tree so huge it seemed built rather than grown, a cathedral of bark and sap.

Despite my cowardly and flinchful nature, I'd never actually fainted, and I did not faint then. But I found that my thoughts were coming slowly and effortfully, as if they were climbing a steep hill.

I thought: *It's summer.* But my breath rose in milky clouds and my sweat had chilled to a gelid film beneath my coat. It was cold—the deep, rheumatic cold of midwinter—and I did not like the cold.

I thought: *I don't know where I am.* But I did. I knew the muscled shape of the bark beneath my hand and the striations of light that fell between the needles. I knew the brilliance of the berries hanging like red bells from the branches and the weight of the air on my eardrums, hushed and heavy.

This was the grove, *my* grove, though I'd been miles and miles away from Queenswald. This was the old tree, *my* tree—the one I had run to as a boy, which had been my castle, my refuge, my only-good-place—though it had been cut down years ago.

I thought: *What's that awful sound?* A pitiful, sniveling whimpering. I took a breath and the sound stopped, and then I thought: *Oh.*

I looked at my left hand, which I had so far carefully avoided, and saw Vivian's letter opener—actually a slim, sharp knife—still buried between my second and third knuckles. The pain immediately tripled, as if it had been waiting for my attention.

Unsteadily, praying I didn't choose this moment to faint for the first time, I braced myself against the tree and used my right hand to draw out the blade. I made a mess of it, of course—my damn hands were shaking again—and was relieved there was no one around to hear the sounds I made.

I leaned against the great trunk of the tree, waiting for the tremors to recede. My thoughts now were loud but inscrutable, like the static between radio stations or the noise of a crowd. It was easier to make sense of my body: My hand hurt. My feet were cold. The skin on the back of my neck was tight and prickling, as if—

As if someone was watching me.

I turned slowly. Something drew a bright, stinging line from the hollow beneath my ear to the column of my throat.

The tip of a sword. It came to rest over the knot of my larynx. I swallowed and felt my flesh part easily, almost eagerly, like the skin of an overripe plum.

My eyes moved up the blade, refusing to make sense of the whole, seeing only scattered details. The long, long edge of the blade, sharpened almost to invisibility; lettering etched into the surface, illegible at this angle; the hilt braced crosswise on a mailed forearm. A cloak the color of a picked scab hanging from a truly vast pair of shoulders, capped in shining, scarred metal.

And, above everything: A face that I knew better than my own.

A face I had seen in penny papers and fine oil paintings, in terrible street theater and political cartoons and every night in my dreams. A face I had feared and coveted and envied since I was nine years old.

Later, I would wonder how I was so sure, because none of those artists had done you justice.

They had shied from the sheer scale of you, narrowing the great sweep of your shoulders, tapering your wrists and waist. They had made your face smooth and poreless, forever youthful, when in truth it was pocked and wind-burnt, with heavy lines carved between the brows. Your hair was not the sulfuric yellow of a Saint of Dominion, but the stark white of a snapped bone. A thick welt of scar fell through your left brow and into the eye beneath it, so that the pupil was misshapen, elongated into a black tear.

You did not look like any kind of angel. Yet still, I knew you.

"Una," I said, and could not imagine why I'd addressed you so informally. I tried again, voice cracking. "Sir Una Everlasting."

Your eyes—not blue, never blue, but a dark, resinous gold, like burnt sap—did not flicker. You spoke, but it took several moments for me to parse the words. I'd rarely heard Middle Mothertongue spoken aloud, and I was distracted by the sound of your voice, deep and cool and familiar.

You said, "Drop the knife." And then, "Drop the damn knife, boy."

I tried—although privately I thought thirty was a decade past the time when anyone was pleased to be called *boy*—but my hand was so far away from my body, and so hard to see through the narrowing tunnel of my vision.

It was only when my cheek hit the earth, the wire of my spectacles biting into the bridge of my nose, that I realized I had—for the first time in my life—fainted.

My last, petulant thought was that my father had been wrong: It was the perfect weather for my service coat, after all.

The next time I opened my eyes, I was somewhere else again. This, I thought, would quickly grow tiresome.

I was indoors now, rather than out, but the line between the two seemed uncomfortably thin. Starlight fell through ragged thatch. One of the walls had sloughed away, revealing bare wattle. Coals hissed on a dirt floor, smoky and sullen.

And crouched across from me, regarding the coals with a vexed expression, was the founding myth of my nation. I'd thought I imagined you.

But you sat as any soldier might on a long night's watch: straight spined, red-eyed, a little grim. The armor was mostly missing now, except for the pauldrons capping those immense shoulders, the straps crossing over the quilted wool of your chest. Your hair was half loosed, hanging over your collar in a rough white skein. At your temples I could see the faint tarnish of true silver.

It unsettled me greatly, that tiny, pedestrian evidence of your mortality. You had always been ageless and hale in my mind, like one of those creatures preserved perfectly in amber at the peak of its health. Now you looked dangerously exposed, vulnerable to the ordinary violence of time in a way that made my chest constrict.

I looked at your hands instead. Broad and veined, scarred so thickly in some places the skin tugged the fingers at odd angles. I watched the play of firelight over the knots of your knuckles, and all the questions I'd been trying not to ask myself—where was I, when was I, had I gone finally, fantastically mad, et cetera—fell away. I have always liked your hands.

You looked sharply up at me. You were already frowning—a stern, weary expression you'd worn often enough to wear a deep furrow between your brows—but now you scowled.

"Something amuses you?" you asked, which caused me to become aware that I was smiling, somewhat doltishly.

I stopped. "No. My apologies."

I sat up, discovering that stiff, rank furs had been piled over me, and that my hand had been bound roughly with linen. I flexed it once and sucked air between my teeth.

"Do you write with the sinister hand?" The question suggested concern, but your voice was flat and gray as gunmetal.

"What? Oh." I switched to Middle Mothertongue, the words welling up easily. "I'm right-handed. I'll be fine."

"A shame," you said, coldly.

I looked up in time to see you move. It was a fluid, muscular gesture, almost too fast to follow, which resulted in something arcing over the coals toward me. I fumbled the catch and had to scrabble to keep it out of the fire: the book, again.

My hand spasmed around it. The last time I'd touched this book I'd been flattered, then frightened, then stabbed and transported—here. (I was too clever not to know where—and when—*here* was, but too much of a coward to let myself think the words.)

You were watching me closely with those mismatched eyes. When you were not moving you were inhumanly still, as if you had been carved rather than born. "How did you find me? I would swear no one tracked me from Cavallon Keep." Still that chilly, taut voice. I had the worrisome impression of a fraying leash.

"No," I said carefully, "I did not track you from the Keep."

"You are geweth, then?"

"Pardon?"

"Then *how*?" Another thread or two snapped in your voice. "How far must I run before I am free of you? When I go to Hell, shall scribes and bards wait at the gates like carrion birds?"

"I'm not a bard or a scribe. If that helps."

Your brows went flat. You looked pointedly at the book in my arms. "I am no great scholar, boy, but I recognize my own device."

"Ah." My hand spasmed again on the cover. I wondered if you had opened the cover, and if you were literate enough to read the title. "I can see how you would think—but it's not—well, I suppose it *is,* but—"

"All my life men like you have followed me." You were dangling now by a single thread. "Hounding me, lapping up the blood and begging for more. You have turned all my graves into glory, all my carnage into pretty songs they sing at court."

"That's very . . . vivid, but I'm telling you I'm not—"

The leash snapped. Suddenly you were on your feet and that enormous bastard of a blade—the most famous sword in the whole of history, the sword every child in Dominion had pretended to wield, swishing sticks at nothing—was back at my throat. The hilt was long enough for at least one-and-a-half hands, but you held it steadily in one, tendons corded around your wrist. It occurred to me, with a queer shiver, that you must have carried me from the yew to this cottage, and that you wouldn't have found it difficult at all.

The point of the sword dipped lower, settling in the scarred hollow between my collarbones. And yet, your expression was not angry, after all. It was—lost. Bewildered. Afraid, almost, as if you were a stranger to yourself. I felt I'd seen that look before, though I couldn't say where.

"Liar," you said. "I know your face. I know your voice. I've seen you at court, or the tourneys, watching me—but no more. I'm finished." There was a sheen over the sap of your eyes, and I thought you would probably kill me rather than let me see you cry.

I should have been terrified, reaching for the revolver at my hip—but I wasn't. I was perfectly calm, as if I'd seen this play before and already knew my character survived.

I resettled my spectacles. They were bent slightly out of shape. "Listen to me. I am not a bard or a scribe. I am Lance Corporal Owen Mallory of the 2nd Battalion, a shit soldier and a decent historian. I was sent here from"—I paused there, lingering in this last moment of sanity and order—"the distant future, to record your story and—somewhat indirectly, I suppose—save Dominion."

"Oh," you said, after a pause. You sounded strangely contrite. "I beg pardon. You are mad."

You sheathed your sword with another of those inhumanly quick gestures and did not speak to me the rest of the night, no matter what I said or did.

The next time I woke the fire was dead and the sky was pale. I wasn't sure whether the sun ever properly rose here, or if it merely slunk, catlike, between the branches.

There was frost in my hair and on the lenses of my spectacles. My throat was raw. I'd talked and talked to you, while the coals rusted into ash and the stars brightened, and you had ignored me politely, as you would ignore a drunk or a street-corner preacher. Sometime in the blue hours before dawn I'd given up, tucking myself sullenly back under the bad-smelling furs. I had fallen asleep watching your face, baffled and irritated and strangely, childishly content.

I was alone, now.

I scrabbled out from under the furs and ducked beneath the sagging lintel. I was no longer within sight of the yew but in a nearby clearing that—in my boyhood—had contained nothing but brambles and goosegrass. Now there was the cottage behind me, which already had one foot firmly in the grave, and an enormous blood-bay gelding, which had at least three.

He reminded me of the skeletons they displayed in the Royal Museum, or a tarp draped over a stack of chairs. His spine protruded tumorously from his back, and his muzzle was the color of dust, or dull knives.

He fixed me with a rheumy eye and peeled back both lips, revealing teeth so long and yellow they might have been whittled from pine.

A voice said: "Be easy."

It was you, ducking beneath the horse's neck and running a palm over the ladder of his rib cage. You wore no armor now, but only plain wool beneath that scabrous cloak, which ought to have been a proud Dominion red, but was actually a middling, stained brown. "He's harmless."

"I'm sure," I said, and understood from your expression that you had not been speaking to me.

You spent another moment communing with your horse, or at least his remains, before crossing to a downed log and laying several limp, furred bodies over the wood. Your knife flashed and dipped, peeling them easy as apples.

I lit a cigarette before the smell of blood could reach me. I ought to ration them, but I'd already whimpered, fainted, and babbled in front of the nation's greatest hero, and I was rather hoping not to vomit, too. I slouched in the doorway and blew out a long stream of smoke, which rose, switchbacking into the sky. Your eyes followed it.

I twiddled the cigarette at you, obnoxiously. "Lucky Stars. Half sawdust, half tar, a testament to modern manufacturing. Uncommon in this era, I imagine."

I didn't know how well I was making myself understood. My mouth produced the odd vowels and archaic syntax of Middle Mothertongue with unnerving ease, as if it had been waiting in some unlit corner of my skull, but I wasn't sure dry condescension had been invented yet.

Apparently it had, because you made a sound that would be described as a snort in anyone who was not a mythic hero. The little corpses, now stripped pink, steamed faintly in your hands.

"What about these, then?" I tapped my spectacles, now slightly misshapen.

No response.

I fished around in my jacket and brandished the revolver at you, somewhat rashly. "How about this? It's called a *gun*. See the stamp, just here? The mark of a genuine Saint Sinclair, the finest munitions maker in Dominion." Still nothing. My voice rose a half octave, whistling through my macerated larynx. "It's a deadly modern weapon of war. If I pointed it at you, and pulled this little bit here, you would be dead before you could say 'anachronism.'"

You looked at the revolver briefly, with the tolerant curiosity of a parent being shown a snail shell or a shiny rock, then looked down again. You didn't say anything.

I put the gun away. "Test me, then. Ask me whatever you like. I know everything that's ever happened to you."

That got me a wry, sad smile. "Who doesn't?"

I have no real temper to speak of—I rarely raise my voice and frequently apologize to people who cut in front of me in queues—but I found a nervy anger rising in me. I had dedicated my life to the legend of Una Everlasting. It was you who sent me to war and you who brought me back, you who stalked my dreams and consumed my days.

And now here you were, the object of all my reverence: a weary, hard-weathered woman who would not even look at me.

I flicked ash forcefully over the threshold. "And do they know everything that *will* happen? Because I do."

Your hands went briefly still, fingers cradling an animal skull.

I pressed into the stillness. "Where are you in your story? You're not young, so you've already defeated the False Kings and won the crown for Yvanne. Some of the tales make mention of a 'great injury' during the First Crusade—was that your eye?" A hot, uneven glare that I interpreted as a *yes*. "So. You're hunting the last dragon, then, and the grail."

Now you looked away. You staked the animals neatly along the spine and nestled them into the coals of another sullen fire. "It is no secret," you said, after too long a pause to appear casual. "The Queen did command it so before the whole court."

"But then—what are you doing *here*? This isn't where you find it."

"And I suppose you, a madman, know where the last dragon dwells?" you drawled, removing all doubt about the existence of dry condescension.

"Yes," I answered promptly, and was pleased by the fractional widening of your eyes. "It was a subject of some debate—Lazamon's map was the only record, and he was famously unreliable—but they found the bones in Lysabet I's reign, and that settled it." I paused, eyes narrowing. "If you don't already know where it is . . . shouldn't you be out there looking?"

I felt as if the machine of my brain was finally grinding into motion again, after stalling out from sheer shock. Assuming I had truly fallen through time to the era of Una Everlasting and was not suffering a colorful mental breakdown—what were you doing in the woods outside of Queenswald, huddling in the remains of some poor peasant's hovel? In the ballads and books, you struck forth with pure heart and fiery eye, praying to the Savior to guide your feet true.

Your expression had not changed, but somehow—by the bend of your shoulders or the angle of your neck, by the way your eyes fled from mine—I *knew:* "You're not looking for it at all, are you. You've abandoned the quest." My voice was high, a hoarse accusation. "You can't. You're supposed to—you *must*—"

"Only one person has the ordering of me." Said sharply, with one lip peeled up to reveal the white tip of a tooth. "And she is not here."

"The queen, you mean." That nervy anger was sharpening, edged with disgust that felt outsized, misdirected. "The queen whose death would mean the end of Dominion. The queen who called for you—her champion, her right hand—as she lay dying?"

"And I answered, as I ever have!" You were on your feet, striding toward me, hands balled into red fists. I was taller than most men, but you stood head and shoulders over me, glaring down at me in a way that made my palms hot.

"Though I swore I would never again ride to battle, I rode out that very night, for her." Your voice was low and viperous. "Though I had put my sword aside, I took it up once more, for her. Though the hope of the grail is no more than the echo of an echo, the whisper of a whisper—I have scoured the countryside since midsummer. For *her*."

I did not retreat or look away, although I felt the force of your furious despair like a battering wind. I saw your eyes move to my throat, where my pulse beat fast and uneven.

Shame chased the wildness from your face. You took a deliberate step back. The muscles of your jaw rolled before you said, stiffly, "That is three times now I have frightened you. Forgive me. I sometimes—forget myself." You unclenched your hands with an effort so visible I expected to hear cartilage popping.

You continued evenly, almost formally, "I have searched, and I have failed. I came here because I had not returned to this place since"—a pause, a drawing up of your shoulders—"the day my fathers were slain. Though I have dreamed of it, these many years."

These sentences slotted into my mind like keys into locks. I badly wanted a pen and paper. *Ha,* I would write, and also *Eat it, Harrison,* because I was now the only living scholar who could definitively state the location of Una Everlasting's childhood home.

But there were other things I would not write down, like the wistful pang I felt at the idea that you and I had played beneath the branches of the same tree, separated only by a millennium. I would leave out the plural *fathers,* too, which had never been in the books or ballads, and which bewildered me; I'd had a vague conviction that homosexuality was a recent invention, symptomatic of modernity, or at least boarding schools.

And, of course, I would not mention the dreams; a courtesy, from one madman to another.

I prompted, carefully, "And why have you stayed?"

You were quiet for so long I thought you wouldn't answer. You busied yourself at the fire again, the flames hidden by the slab of your cloaked shoulders.

Then you said, "Because it is quiet here, where there is no one to bid me rise or kneel. Because I can sleep, at least some nights, and I am so damn tired." You pulled a charred body from the coals and studied it. "Because, for weeks now, I have butchered only animals."

That lost, fearful expression had returned to your face, as if you had been walking for a long time in a country you did not know under stars you could not name. As if you had forgotten where you had meant to go in the first place, and no longer believed it was worth it.

I knew, suddenly, where I'd seen that look before: in my father's eyes when he sobered up and in my own mirror every morning. It was the look of a coward, a turncoat, someone with a crack running down the center of them, so that all the honor and courage ran out and left nothing but shaky hands and bad dreams behind.

And I knew, too, why Vivian Rolfe had called me to her office. Why she had slipped her blade between my knuckles and sent me tumbling into the past. It wasn't because of my articles or my Medal of Valor or my uncommon grasp of dead languages.

I wasn't here to translate or transcribe your story; I was here to make sure there was a story to tell.

She needs you, Vivian had said.

You had lost your way. And I—who knew every turn and twist in your journey, every step you must and would take—was your compass.

I crouched at your left side, near enough that you turned your head sharply. I wondered if you had learned to guard your blind side yet, or if it still startled you, the way I was still taken unawares by the frailty of my voice.

I held myself motionless, palms loose, trying desperately to assemble the right words. I wished I could retire to my office for a week and return with a typewritten speech. I wished for the first time that I were more like my father, who never stuttered or second-guessed.

Eventually I began: "I know you don't believe me. I don't blame you, really. But imagine I was telling the truth. Imagine I really had seen Dominion nearly a thousand years from now—still strong, and growing stronger, all because of the foundation laid by you and Yvanne. Imagine I could tell you that all of this—the fighting and the killing, everything you've done—is worth it?" It was not possible to say the words without thinking of Colonel Drayton: of his big pink jowls and his big pink hands, the way he clapped us on the back as if we were choking on our dinners and the way he looked at me just before he died.

I dragged again on the cigarette, although it had burned down nearly to my knuckles.

I went on: "Every queen since Yvanne has worn the crown you won her. Every war since the First Crusade has been fought beneath your flag. The highest military decoration is named after *you,* for God's sake, and do you know what they call the very best and bravest soldiers, at the front? *Red knights.*" Technically the term only applied to men who died in battle, but I thought it might be poor taste to say so. "Now, you are legendary. One day, you will be a legend."

You looked away again, but not before I saw the hunger in you. That same burning, aching desire I'd felt as a boy, and again when I stood in Vivian's office—to matter, to make something good and great out of the pitiful meat of my life.

"Listen, I grew up not far from here. I was—still am—nobody. Nothing.

I was lonely and frightened and foreign, or foreign-looking, which is just as bad. But then I found you." I was glad for my thin, wisping voice, which disguised the tightening of my throat. "I read your stories—I mean, everyone does, but I read them over and over. And I found the courage I needed to serve my country."

I reached for the collar of my jacket, hands shaking, and folded it down so you could see the wreckage of my throat. It was not the handsome, dashing sort of scar that every soldier privately hopes for. It was fat and wormy, stretching the skin unevenly over my collarbone and knotting over my windpipe like a badly tied cravat.

The first civilian who'd seen the whole of it had gasped once before pressing her hands over her mouth. But her shock had transitioned quickly into fawning admiration, as if the scar were a medal I couldn't take off. She'd kissed it—sweetly, even eagerly—as if she had been appointed by the state to thank me for my sacrifice, and I'd escaped her flat seconds before the shaking fit began.

You did not gasp or fawn. You considered me steadily, like a woman who had both suffered and committed much worse. I experienced such a keen rush of gratitude that little spots danced briefly in my vision.

I blinked them away. "This was the price of my service. Of my loyalty." This was an absolute lie, but it was such a familiar lie by now that the words tripped out of my mouth like soldiers in a line. "But I swear to you: It was worth it."

And, for the first time, I thought maybe it was true. Maybe my whole life—my shame and my torment, my bad dreams and my pitiful manuscript—had been in service to this moment, when I recalled Una Everlasting to her duty.

"Please," I said, and you looked at me as if you, too, felt some grand design at work, the invisible thread of fate tugging you toward your destiny. Your eyes were a dark and lambent amber, without grain or variation. "We need you."

I reached, impulsively, for your bare hand.

I had time to think: *I should not have done that,* before I found myself looking up at you from the cold ground, your knee on my breastbone, your hands pinning my wrists on either side of my head.

There followed my first moment of real terror: that I might respond disgracefully. That you might notice. I twisted beneath you, suddenly frantic. "Let *go*—"

You threw yourself away from me and sat staring, breathing hard, so obviously horror-stricken that my pride suffered a slight injury. You climbed slowly to your feet. “Four times, now,” you said, almost to yourself.

Then, louder, “You may stay if you like. I will share my fire and food, in memory of my fathers, who let no one go cold or hungry in this wood. But do not touch me unawares, and do not go unarmed in my presence.”

You drew a slim knife—Vivian’s letter opener, which I had forgotten about entirely—and flicked it so that it buried itself point-first in the dirt, bare inches from my head.

I blinked at it. “Why?”

“So that you might feel . . . safe.” You looked at your own hands as you spoke, as if you mistrusted them. I did not think a letter opener, nor even a revolver, would greatly extend my life if you desired to end it, but I didn’t say so. I reached for the handle.

You nodded stiffly at my hand. “And tend to that. The blood will draw beasts.”

You turned and strode into the trees.

“It will come to you in a dream.” I threw the words at your back, a prophecy lobbed at an unwilling subject. “That’s what the stories say. God-the-Savior speaks to you in a dream, and you follow His word to the last dragon.”

You stopped but did not turn. “I have not dreamed since I came here.”

“You will,” I said.

5

DAYS PASSED, AND they were each the same.

I would wake alone. You would greet me with grim silence, and I would search your face for some sign of renewed faith or divine awe. Only your eyes changed, sinking deeper into their sockets; I suspected you of avoiding sleep.

Later you would hunt, or tend the bay, rubbing handfuls of dry grass over his scarred hide, speaking in the low, honeyed voice you reserved exclusively for him. I had learned not to approach you at these times. For an animal of his size (prehistoric) and age (also prehistoric), your horse moved very quickly, and still retained enough teeth to leave a crescent of yellowing bruises on the back of my arm.

You had said, quite harshly, "Stay away from him."

"It's alright, no real harm done," I'd said, and understood from your expression that, this time, you *had* been speaking to me.

I gave your horse a very wide berth thereafter, and did not miss the hopeful way he lifted his hind leg as I passed.

At first, I was afraid to wander out of sight of the hut, but I never got lost, or even slightly turned around. The land was familiar to me, though I had learned it as a boy, twenty years ago and a thousand years from now. I knew every slope and dale, every bare crag and narrow stream. I knew where the rabbits denned and where the yew stood, already ancient even here at the beginning of everything.

I sat among the roots sometimes, head tilted back against the tendons of the trunk, and understood why you ran here, when you ran. It was a place apart, a secret kept from the world: There were no queens or ministers beneath the yew, no wars or quests. There was only the slantwise light and the gently moving air and the wild, cold smell of the earth.

In the evenings we would huddle in the remains of the hut, talking softly. Or, at least, I would talk—asking questions or complaining about the cold or describing my attempts to brew oak-gall ink—and you would suffer in stoic silence.

Sometimes you would tend your tack or armor, working oil into the leather joints; sometimes you would lay your blade across your knees and polish the metal with long, even strokes. I would fall quiet, then. I liked to watch you—the easy competence of your hands, the pull of muscle in your wrists—and I liked to watch the sword.

There were so many stories about it: They said it could cleave stones and fell trees, that if it broke in battle it would appear whole and perfect again the next dawn, that it had been forged long before Dominion was born.

Horseshit, according to Professor Sawbridge. She'd become an archaeologist, she always said, because words lied and bones didn't. She'd shown us the actual swords she'd dug up from this era—rough, lumpen things, with horn hilts and bog-ore blades.

Yet: Here was Valiance, with a hilt cast wholly in metal, a grip wrapped in fine leather cording, and a blade of such pure, coruscant steel that it shone blue in the firelight.

After your work was done you would bank the coals and settle in the doorway to keep watch, your cloak pulled tight around your shoulders. The knot between your brows would ease then, and you would stare out at the star-pocked wood as if you would be content to live out the rest of your days here, in the dim margins of history.

I would feel restless then, almost guilty, and turn to the book instead.

My pen was a hollow reed, clumsily cut, and my ink was gummy brown, but the words came easier than I expected. Like the lines of a poem I'd memorized as a boy, or a story I had told before and would tell again.

UNA AND THE CROWN

They say that when the Brigand Prince dragged Yvanne into the woods, having stolen her from her father's lands, she was weeping.

They say that when Yvanne rode out of the woods, with the prince's head knocking wetly against her saddle, she was smiling.

They say the common people fell to their knees and pressed their brows to the earth as she passed, for they had long suffered under

the prince's tyranny, and the girl who rode with Yvanne—a wild and strange creature, with matted hair and a huge blade bound across her back—did not look down at them even once. She had eyes only for the queen-who-was-not-yet-queen but would be soon.

I could not say the truth of it; I did not know her, then. But I will tell it to you as it was told to me, much later.

Yvanne saw the tears of the peasants and knew it was time to claim her heritage, for Yvanne was of course descended from an ancient line of kings who had ruled the continent before it was divided by creed and tongue.

So Yvanne rode to the prince's seat at Cavallon and asked his people to swear new oaths to her service and to God-the-Savior. This they did gladly, because they saw Yvanne's grace and wisdom—and because some of them knew the name of the sword the girl carried across her back, and knew they bore witness to the birth of a new legend.

But there is no such thing as a bloodless birth.

Before they had even laid the anchor stone for the Queen's Keep, the first of the False Kings came calling.

He rode up the hill with ten knights at his back and demanded that Yvanne give up her title and bow before him.

'Certainly I will,' the queen said, 'if you can best my champion.'

The False King looked about him and saw no one but peasants and children, wielding staves and rusted axes. The only sword was held by a ragged girl wearing armor that did not fit her. The False King laughed.

They say he was still laughing when Valiance slid neatly between his ribs.

The second of the False Kings fell the same way, full of hubris, but the third was canny enough to be afraid. He held a tournament and offered a prize—his own weight in silver!—to the man who could best the Queen's Champion.

It was Ancel of Ulwin who won the tournament, who rode with the last of the False Kings to Cavallon and challenged the Red Knight to a duel. And, for the first time since she drew the sword from the yew, Una faced a worthy foe.

Ancel was young and fast and beautiful. He moved like a needle through cloth, diving and rising in a perfect rhythm. Una was taller and stronger, but for a long time, she could not best him. They fought until their lungs ached, until their blood had turned the earth to slick mud beneath their boots and their shadows stretched long at their backs.

Later, those who saw the fight would agree that Ancel was the best swordsman in the land. But in the end, he was only a man. What is a man, against a legend?

The end, when it came, came quickly. Valiance caught neatly beneath Ancel's cross guard and sent his blade flying from his hand. Una drew back for the final blow. Ancel closed his eyes.

And a voice called, softly, 'Mercy, my love.'

Una wrenched her sword aside at the last moment.

Ancel opened his eyes and beheld the queen, looking down at him with such gentility that his knees buckled.

Distantly he heard his False King braying, urging him to rise and fight, but Ancel found he did not care; nor did he care when the king's voice went abruptly quiet.

He cared only about the queen, smiling wryly down at him. 'Would you like to know why she won?' When Ancel did not answer, Yvanne went on, 'Because you fought for yourself. For glory, for silver. But she . . .' Her eyes found Una, who was cleaning the False King's blood from her blade. 'She fought for Dominion.'

Ancel asked, 'What is Dominion?'

Yvanne answered, 'One nation united under one God. One kingdom, from the Slant Sea to the Northern Fallows, prosperous and peaceful. Just a dream, for now, but one worth dying for.' She might have been a saint or a seer, she spoke with such perfect faith.

And Ancel, who had only ever served himself and other men who served themselves, felt an aching, helpless love take root in his chest.

Humbly, head bowed, he said, 'I know nothing of dreams, my lady, but I would fight for you.'

There was a considering pause. Then he felt the flat of a blade fall heavy on his right shoulder. 'Good enough,' said Yvanne, and she swore a second knight to her service.

Later, they would come to call him Ancel the Good, the Knight of Hearts, for he collected so many, though he took neither wife nor lover. Later, Ancel and Una would come to trust each other as brothers, fighting side by side for crown and country.

But as Una watched Ancel take his oath in the bloodied earth of the courtyard, she felt nothing but uneasy envy. The False Kings were cast down. Ancel had joined the court of Cavallon, and he would not be the last. What purpose, then, did she serve?

She went to the queen that very night and took Yvanne's soft white hands in hers. 'Tell me what else I may win you, lady. Only name it, and it will be yours.'

And the queen answered, as if she had been waiting for the question, 'A crown worthy of Dominion.'

The following morning, Sir Una rode out on her first quest. It would be three years before she returned.

She journeyed deep into the wild reaches of Dominion, chasing legends of a crown fit for her queen, and wherever she rode she left new stories in her wake. Some of these you have heard, I'm sure: the Duel of the Stone Keep, in which she bested Bodrow the Giant; the great dragon hunt, when all save one of those unnatural creatures were slain, and their ivory scales sewn into a white mantle for the queen; the Ballad of Morvain, in which a wicked sorceress beguiled Una for seven days and seven nights, until Una recited holy prayers and caused Morvain to forsake her sorcery and take the veil instead.

It is only the final story that matters, anyway, when Una took to the Slant Sea in a humble fisherman's boat.

She was following the tale of Sinclair, the Saint of Smiths, who had long ago crafted a crown of such surpassing beauty that he had buried it on a hidden isle rather than see it sit on an unworthy brow.

The smith had set his sons and their sons to guard it against the day a true champion would come to claim it.

At the time Una came to the isle, there were three brothers remaining. They had spent the whole of their lives training together, and the beach was pocked white with the bones of their enemies.

Una buried the brothers side by side in the sandy soil.

When she returned to Cavallon, Yvanne bent her head, and Una placed upon it the Crown of Dominion: a golden circlet, set with three rubies red as pigeon's blood. It fit her brow as if the Saint of Smiths had crafted it for her alone.

When Yvanne rose, Una said again, 'Tell me what else I may win you, my lady.'

And the queen answered, 'A kingdom worthy of this crown.'

The following morning, Sir Una rode out with Valiance in her hand and an army at her back, and made war on the world.

Later, they would name those bloody years the First Crusade. Historians would call it the beginning of Dominion, when the people were freed from the rule of petty lords and tyrants and united under one flag at last. The bards would sing of glorious battles against insurmountable odds, of desperate victories and tragic defeats and always, endlessly, of her: Sir Una, the Drawn Blade of Dominion, who fought so well and so long that her enemies ran from the meanest glimpse of her red-painted shield, the merest rumor of a pale-haired woman upon a blood-bay steed.

It was during that time that people began to believe she was not a woman at all, but a demon or an angel. They said no mortal could fight as she fought—perfectly, without pause, as if she knew the arc of each blow before it fell—or survive what she survived. More than once she was carried from the field, her sword shattered, her shield split; more than once the queen kept vigil at her champion's bedside. But always, Una rose again: her wounds healed, her blade whole and unmarked.

I cannot say the whole truth of it because she will not speak of those times, even to me. But I have seen the scars that run over every part of her, biting deep into muscle and tendon, and I can tell you with certainty that she is mortal.

And I can tell you what any map would: Una swept across the continent like a scouring wind. She took the salt marshes of the south from the Nornish heathens; she slew the Lords of Gall and had their idols defaced, the mark of the Savior scratched into their stone brows; she fought the Hyllmen last, those stubborn, savage kings of the Northern Fallows. She drove them behind the high walls of their Black Bastion, which had never before fallen to any invader. Una took it in only three days.

And when the battle was over, the dream of Dominion was true: one God, one flag, one nation.

Una returned to Cavallon in triumph, showered in rose petals and songs. And—though she was older now, and some of her wounds were the kind that never quite healed—she knelt again before the queen.

She said, 'Tell me what else I may win you, lady.'

The queen stroked her hair as if she were a girl again, and the Drawn Blade of Dominion closed her eyes, overcome with love. 'Rest now,' said the queen, and Una did as she was bade.

For a year and a day, she lived peacefully, giving herself to prayer and silence. The kingdom flourished and the joints of her armor grew stiff with rust.

Until the time came when the queen fell desperately ill. Yvanne, a woman of God, did not fear death—but she feared for Dominion, for the dream she had brought into the world. And so she called out—ah, so weakly!—for her champion.

There was one thing still left to be won.

***—Excerpted from* The Death of Una Everlasting,**
translated by Owen Mallory

I chewed at the splintered end of my pen. "Could you describe the scene for me, when Yvanne's messengers came to you?"

You paused in the act of adding wood to the fire. "I thought you knew everything that had ever happened to me."

"Well, I know *versions* of it. Your story has been—will be, I suppose—written down a dozen different ways, by a dozen different authors. Lazamon is the most complete and popular version, but it's also the most recent. My old adviser—uh, that's sort of like a liege lord, except instead of beheading you she can make you rewrite your thesis chapter—says the material evidence is even more contradictory and varied." I adjusted my spectacles, which had developed a tendency to list to the left. "Personally, I always liked the one where they find you at prayer, and you break your vow of silence to answer the summons. 'I would deny God before I deny my queen,' you say, and then—"

"I told them to fuck themselves." You settled the log on the coals and added, almost chattily, by your standards, "I was drunk as a dog, when they found me."

". . . Oh." I chewed my pen some more, and then wrote: *When the queen called, Sir Una answered, as she ever had.* There was no need, I thought, to burden the reader with unnecessary detail.

I wrapped the book carefully in a scrap of hide and burrowed under the furs, watching you. You sat very upright, but there were bruised hollows beneath your eyes, as if someone had pressed their thumbs hard into your face.

"Do you ever sleep?"

You shrugged. "Fire needs tending." I'd noticed by then that you were uneasy around the fire, approaching it reluctantly and feeding it warily, as if it were a dog that had bitten you once before.

But I didn't think it was the reason you never slept. "You don't want to dream, do you."

Another tectonic shrug, as if the earth itself rested on the bend of your shoulders.

I watched you for another few minutes. I thought of simply telling you where the dragon's bones were found, but I didn't think you would believe me. And even if you did—I had decided to believe in God as a very young man, mostly to annoy my father; I was not so faithful that I could turn down the chance for proof.

I crawled out from under the furs and crouched by the coals. "Let me mind the fire tonight."

Your eyes flicked to me, then back to the flames, uncertain. I reached—very slowly—for the stick you used as a poker, taking it from your hand without touching your skin. "Look, if you collapse from exhaustion, I will starve almost instantly. Or be murdered by brigands or, more likely, your horse. Surely even a madman deserves better."

I could tell I'd hit some deep-set nerve, some fundamental instinct that caused you to come when you were called, to serve when you were needed. Yet your queen needed you, and here you were, hiding where fate couldn't find you.

You didn't lie down, but you unbent enough to lean against the mud wall, swaddled in the muddy folds of your should-be-red cloak. Your eyes narrowed to dark gold slits.

You slept, eventually, brows low and knotted, as if you dreamed and did not like it.

I pulled the furs over you with a tenderness that was almost an apology, although I didn't know what I was sorry for.

Fate always finds you, in the end.

"How did you know?" Your voice woke me, trembling with some great emotion.

I tried to jerk upright in answer, but I'd fallen asleep in an awkward huddle beside the ashes of the fire, and my muscles had fossilized overnight. I made a feeble flopping motion instead. "Know what?" My voice sounded like two knives scraping together.

"The dream." You were breathing hard, air rushing through the bellows of your chest. "Last night I saw the dragon, dead before me. I saw the cup. And I heard a voice—a terrible voice. It said—"

"Cloven Hill." I had achieved an approximation of sitting up, but my neck seemed to have several extra angles in it. "The remains were discovered there by a shepherd's son who was looking for a lost lamb, apparently. The papers loved it. The skeleton hangs in the Royal Museum now, of course."

I managed to turn my head the five degrees necessary to look at you. Your face was so pale that the scars were a garish pink. That misshapen pupil was huge and black, almost spilling the bounds of your iris. "It's true, then." Nearly a whisper, full of awe. "You knew what would happen before it came to pass. You've come from . . . the future."

"I *did* mention it." I was rubbing my neck with one palm, to no effect at all, resisting the urge to whoop with awe and triumph only because I thought it might leave me permanently crippled.

You glanced at the corner of the hut where you kept your kit. A bright flash of silver winked beneath the leathers. I hadn't seen you fully armored since the day I arrived; it struck me now as strange that you'd been wearing it at all.

You said, "Tell me how it happens, then."

I wished I'd thought to rehearse in all these long, silent days. I wet my lips. "You follow God's voice north. You find the last dragon in its lair. The battle is long and bitter, but you prevail, and in the dragon's horde you find the grail. You carry it in triumph to your queen. And then . . ." The final twist, the heroic last stand. The tragedy.

In my undergraduate courses, I'd taught your death as a narrative tool, an elegant equation about honor and valor and the cost of nationhood. Now, looking into the burnt sap of your eyes, close enough to see the ordinary imperfections of your skin, it did not seem much like an equation.

But you had already strayed far from the path of your story; if I told you how it ended, you would never return to it. You would never slay the dragon or fetch the grail. The country would lose its first queen and its greatest hero, and I didn't think Dominion—fragile, freshly born—would survive the loss.

Your country needs you. Had Vivian Rolfe seen that version of the future, somehow? Was that what drove her, what gave her such a burning, unbending air of purpose—the terror of a world without you?

"And then?" you prompted, and I found that—though I was a coward and a deserter—I was not yet a traitor. I would not trade the past and future of an entire nation for one woman.

"And then," I said, "the queen is healed, and the kingdom prospers forevermore." It wasn't a lie.

You did not look comforted. "And afterward?" you pressed. "Does she—Yvanne said this was my last quest. Did she speak the truth?"

My mouth was full of acid, burning the back of my throat. "Yes," I said, and—God forgive me—that wasn't a lie, either. "This is your last quest."

For a moment, you didn't react at all. Your face was so perfectly still it might have been a painting or a sculpture, the symbol of a person rather than the thing itself. But your features softened suddenly, animating into an expression I'd never seen you wear. Not joy, but the hope of joy, like a lost sailor who hasn't yet seen land, but believes for the first time that he might.

The sight of it did something odd to my vision. For a moment I could see the way joy would look on your face when it finally arrived. I could see you laughing, head thrown back, throat long and unguarded. I could see a ripe berry popping between your teeth—juice running clear down your chin—my own hand reaching to wipe it away—

"Gather your things," you said, sharply. "We leave before noon."

My head jerked back, causing my neck to make a sound like a guitar string snapping. "Oh, thank *God*." And then, after a pause: "We?" I'd anticipated a lot of wheedling and pleading before you permitted me to come with you. I had several very compelling speeches worked up, including one on bended knee and one in verse.

But you were ignoring me, already bent over your work. I hurried to gather my few things before you changed your mind.

When the camp was cleared and the gelding saddled, you mounted with fluid certainty, as if you'd been mounting this same horse for ten thousand years and would do it for another ten thousand.

In the softened light of morning, I could almost imagine him as a noble steed, rather than a bad-tempered mummy. He pranced a little, as if he, too, felt the threads of the story pulling taut around us.

I was backing awkwardly out of the way, wondering grimly how many miles my shoes would survive, when your hand appeared in my vision. It remained there, cracked and callused, red knuckled in the cold, until I realized you were waiting for me to take it.

I had noticed by then the way you held yourself away from me, as if your body was a grenade with the pin half pulled. I wondered when you had last touched someone you did not intend to kill, if you even remembered how.

Yet still: There was your hand, waiting.

I eyed it. "Are you sure you—"

"Yes."

I eyed the gelding, who was rolling the bit in his jaw with a sound like bones in a meat grinder. "And you're sure *he*—"

"Yes."

"Why? I thought you despised bards and scribes. 'Carrion birds,' I think you called them."

You did not answer. Your hand did not waver.

I took it. I set one foot in the stirrup, and you hauled me up as if I weighed nothing at all. You settled me in the saddle in front of you, where one of the furs had been folded over the low pommel, so that my thighs lay over yours, my back against your chest. Your arms reached easily around me for the reins, which you hardly seemed to need. The long muscles of your legs tensed in some secret language spoken only between you and the gelding, and he turned northward.

And for the first time since I had lost the book, everything felt *right*. It was like an out-of-tune instrument finally ringing true, a poorly told tale finally making sense.

I was so overcome by it all—by the wild, fresh smell of the air and the heat of your body around mine, by the implausible fact that I was riding out on the last quest of Sir Una Everlasting, the Red Knight, in the name of Yvanne the First—that I almost didn't hear you when you finally answered my question.

"Because it was not God's voice I heard in my dream, boy," you said, and I felt your breath on the fine hairs at the back of my neck. "It was yours."

6

I MADE A dismaying discovery that day: A journey which takes only a few paragraphs in a book takes considerably longer on horseback. Especially if the horse is old enough to draw a pension, and the woods are thick enough that there are no straight or obvious routes, but only slim game trails that weave and curl among the trees.

After a long day spent either clinging grimly to the horse—who was not actually a horse, but a clever device for flaying the insides of one's thighs—or limping grimly alongside it, we had not even reached the edge of the Queen's Wood. I lay on my back that night, shivering and aching beneath my bad-smelling fur, trying not to whimper every time I moved my legs.

You rose before dawn the next morning to saddle the gelding, who scrubbed his jaw affectionately against your shoulder, apparently unbothered by a full day's hard travel bearing two riders. I approached, bowleggedly, and did not quite dodge the edge of his hoof as it descended on my left foot. By the time I was done cursing him and all his ancestors in the foulest language of the 2nd Battalion, you were mounted and waiting.

You reached out your hand. I took it. We rode on.

You seemed content to pass the hours in knightly silence, speaking only to suggest one of us walk for a while, but I found myself fidgeting after the first quarter hour. Eventually I gestured down at the gelding. "What's his name?"

Perhaps I would write it down in the book; perhaps with a little patriotic editing he could be transformed from what he was (a mean fossil) into what he ought to have been (a proud warhorse).

"He's no pet," you answered, as if you didn't feed him grain from your palm every evening. And then, in gruff apology, "He doesn't mean any real harm."

"Truly?" I could already feel my left foot ballooning gruesomely in my boot. "I have convincing evidence to the contrary."

"As do I." I made a doubtful noise, and felt you shrug behind me. "You're still breathing."

"Oh," I said.

Another hour or two passed. My vertebrae jostled against one another. The trees repeated themselves. I had the slightly hysterical thought that you might be riding in circles, just to torment me.

"How far is it to the Northern Fallows?"

"Far."

"How far to the edge of the wood?"

"Less far."

Was it blasphemous, I wondered, to swear at a saint? What if they hadn't been sainted yet? Instead, I observed, with forced cheer, "I've never seen anyone with hair quite like yours. That strange color—where does it come from?"

I felt you stiffen at my back. "Where does *your* hair come from, madman?"

I flushed. I knew my appearance must be odd to you—this was the old Dominion of Vivian Rolfe's speeches, free of foreigners—but I'd been hoping you didn't know what it meant. My answer was a weary one, learned by rote. "My father was born and raised in Dominion, I assure you."

There followed a somewhat baffled silence. Then: "I meant no offense. The geweth make their homes where they will."

"The—what?" It was the second time you'd used that word in reference to me.

Your bafflement deepened. "*Geweth.* Are there no Roving Folk in the future, save you?"

"Oh. No. Or yes, but they keep to the Hinterlands. And I'm not—that is, I suppose my mother may have been, but I never knew—"

You interrupted, mercifully, "I never knew my birth mother, either. And my fathers thought my hair—strange, as well." God, I was an ass. "Little Dragon, Father Foy called me."

"What else were you called? Before the queen found you, I mean."

"I don't remember," you answered, coolly, and would answer nothing else the rest of the day.

I spoke to myself, instead, and to your awful horse. I prophesied to him, speaking of the rosy future when everyone would ride streetcars and automobiles instead of horses, and all the nasty oversized nags would be turned into canned meat and boots. *Do you know what a knacker is?* I asked, and his ears swiveled back and forth, as if I were a gnat.

We left the Queen's Wood on the third morning. The sky opened like a cold gray sea around us, so vast that I had the dizzy sensation of falling upward into it. I found myself clutching at the horse's mane, fighting the sudden conviction that we should turn back. That we should remain forever in the shadow of the wood, safe and secret, rather than take a single step forward.

"Easy," you said, at my ear, and it was only then that I realized I was breathing in uneven, absurd gusts, that my muscles were seized and shivering. *God,* I thought, *not now.*

I said, "S-sorry. It'll pass." But if you answered, I couldn't hear it. My pulse was rushing in my ears as if I were back at the front, as if there were something terrible waiting just over the horizon.

I became aware, distantly, that you had dropped the reins. You bent yourself around me, your arms hard across my chest and ribs, your chin notched over my shoulder, your touch firm but careful, as if I were a cracked glass in danger of shattering. I could feel your heart against my spine. It beat steadily, sanely, a simple lesson mine couldn't seem to learn.

Another ragged breath, and another, and my muscles began to slacken. Shame arrived, then. That I had disgraced myself so thoroughly before the Drawn Blade of Dominion—that the Virgin Saint had been obliged to hold me so intimately and improperly—even now your left hand was wrapped around my hip, low enough that my pulse picked up for an entirely different and more sordid reason. Your thumb began to move in a manner you must have imagined was soothing.

I flinched upright, flushed and ashamed. "Sorry," I said.

Perhaps you'd spent enough time at war to see every kind of malady and madness, because you asked no questions. You only cleared your throat and said, "No need," in a strangely rough voice.

I spent the rest of the morning ridding myself of impious thoughts. It was difficult; in your innocence, you had not realized that your left hand was still on my hip.

It was colder, beyond the trees.

The wind rushed freely over the heather, landing like an open palm on my cheeks. My blisters wept and froze against my thighs.

You hardly seemed to notice the cold or the terrain or the long days in the saddle. It didn't strike me as toughness so much as an odd divide between you and your own flesh. As if your body was merely something you owned, like a sharp knife or a good pair of boots, which you might use hard and tend only when it showed signs of weakening.

You commented, irritably, that I was shivering, and I said, "Well, so are you." After a brief, surprised pause, you wrapped your matted brown cloak around both of us.

That night you made a fire, though the only fuel was willowy green brush. I fell asleep curled around the coals.

I was awoken by your voice. The fire had smoldered down to ash and smoke, and you were visible only by the lunar glow of your hair. You were twitching and thrashing, but I was sure you were still sleeping; awake, you would never have let me hear you weep.

I called your name, softly. You settled.

The second time you woke me, I had to shout before you fell quiet.

The third time, I crawled to your side. Your expression was desperate, so twisted with grief I felt my eyes sting in sympathy.

"Una," I said, softly.

Your eyes snapped open, wild, unseeing. Before I could say anything else, before I could blink or flinch, your hand was at my throat, thumb pressed into the hollow beneath my jaw, fingers wrapped around my neck.

I went still and oddly slack, as prey animals do in the mouths of wolves. I waited patiently as reason leaked back into your eyes, and your expression soured from grief into guilt, and then bitter fury.

Your hand spasmed away from my skin. You shoved yourself backward, away from me, clutching the cloak to your chest. "I told you not to come near me, boy," you said, roughly. "I could have *killed* you."

I rolled my jaw. I suspected you could have ripped out my trachea barehanded, but you hadn't even applied enough pressure to bruise. "You've called out twice in your sleep already tonight," I observed. "You haven't killed me yet."

"I still might," you said, with such sincerity that I retreated to my own side of the fire. Your shoulders unknotted, fractionally.

After a long silence, you said, with effort, "Forgive me. I dream often of things I would rather forget. Old battles. Old wounds." Then, a little defensively, "Many soldiers suffer so."

It hadn't been battle you were dreaming of, I was nearly certain. You hadn't yelled or cursed or screamed in terror. You had begged, in a voice like two halves of a heart scraping together.

But I said, as lightly as I could, "So I've heard," and resettled beneath the furs, head propped on the book.

You looked as if you might say something else, but your eyes fell to the book, and the scars pulled taut across your face. You said, harshly, "Keep to your own side of the fire," and turned your back to me.

I did as I was bade.

When you called out again—that night and on the nights that followed—I did not go to you. Sometimes I pressed my palms flat to my ears, so that I could not hear the words you said, over and over, in that funeral of a voice: *Please,* you begged, *come back.*

On the sixth day, we passed through our first township.

There had been a few sad clusters of cottages near the edge of the woods, occupied by nothing now but rooks and field mice. When I'd asked, you told me there had once been people who made their livelihood from the forest. Huntsmen and furriers, poor crofters who set their pigs loose in the loam, weavers who gathered woad and rue for their dyes. Even the Roving Folk sometimes summered there, when they were not wandering, trading horses and telling stories.

"But no one lives in the wood now?" I'd asked.

You'd answered, neutrally, "It's the Queen's Wood, now, and no one else's."

The homes ahead of us were not abandoned. Clean, white woodsmoke unfurled from every chimney, and the hum of human voices buzzed in my ears. I braced myself for gawking and muttering, perhaps worse—

But the town was not the uniform, idyllic portrait of old Dominion that was conjured by columnists and cartoonists. It looked more or less like any modern city, minus the sewer system. Children darted down the streets, laughing and jeering in languages I didn't know. A well-dressed man with dark skin led a pair of laden mules. There was even a Gallish temple on one corner, with finely painted alcoves for each of their forty gods, although most of the gods had been defaced.

I decided I would not mention any of this in the book. (An acerbic voice in my head noted that I was accumulating quite a list of things I was not mentioning; the voice sounded very much like Professor Sawbridge's.)

People did gawk—but not at me.

You wore no armor and rode with no complement. You had even covered your shield with old canvas—but still, they knew you. They knew you by your bone-colored hair and your broad shoulders, by the glint of armor in your saddlebags and by Valiance, hanging always at your side.

They knew you, and they watched you. They nudged one another and pointed, twittering like starlings. Except—they were not joyous or reverent. They did not greet you with cheers or thrown flowers or babies in need of blessing, as they would a hero. They did not even greet you with a hot meal or a spare bed, as they would a weary stranger.

They only watched, as if you were a thing apart from them, neither man nor woman but some third chimerical thing, as likely to break bread with them as a dragon or a lion.

You ignored the stares, or seemed to. I felt the way you shrank inward, tucking your elbows and ducking your head in a laughable attempt to make yourself ordinary. When you dismounted to buy grain from a ploughman you spoke softly, with your eyes averted; his hand shook as he took your coin.

When you turned toward a young woman bearing a basket of sooty griddle cakes, she backed away, her face so pale her freckles looked like pepper sprinkled on a dish of milk. From the saddle, I saw your shoulders sag.

"Wait, miss," I said, sliding awkwardly from the horse and stumbling on numb legs. "I'm starving, and she's a terrible cook." I could feel your glare on the back of my neck. I held my hand up behind me and, after a disapproving pause, you placed three small coins in my palm.

I pulled the girl a few steps down the lane, talking and gesturing.

Five minutes later, I returned to you with five griddle cakes and a half-full flagon of wine.

"And," I announced, in some triumph, "she says there's a bathhouse two streets north."

For a moment—during which I discovered how badly I longed for hot water and soap—you looked as if you might refuse. Then, with a short sigh, you tugged the horse north.

The bathhouse was a lime-washed building that smelled of lye and charcoal. The attendants—businesslike women with substantial shoulders and red-raw hands—led us to a low-ceilinged room with a vast tub in the middle. The water was scummy and grayish, tepid at best; I thought I might weep at the sight of it.

The attendants set a crumbly cake of soap on the sill, bobbed in matching curtsies, and turned away.

"Uh, pardon me, but where should—" I began, but the door snapped shut behind them.

I heard, at my back, the sound of a belt sliding through a buckle. I stood very still. There was the rush and thud of clothes hitting the floor. Then a faint splash, followed by a sigh of sheer pleasure, half stifled, which made the muscles of my stomach tighten unaccountably. Perhaps your body was not merely a tool, after all.

After a while you asked, in a languorous, amused voice I hardly recognized, "Did you seek a bath only for my sake? Was I so rank?"

You were, I reminded myself firmly, the Virgin Saint. You couldn't understand the temptations and impurities of the less chaste. I kept my back virtuously turned. "Do—do men and women not bathe separately?"

"They do."

I asked, haltingly but not entirely facetiously, "And are you—not a woman?"

A sharp sound, not quite a laugh. "Turn around and see." I did not; this, I thought, was the sort of behavior that ought to earn a man a medal.

Eventually you sighed a little. Water splashed. "A woman may not dress as I do, or bear arms, or carry any device that is not her husband's or father's. Yet I do these things, and I am not punished by church or crown—and so it is easier for most people if I am not a woman."

"Do you mind it?"

More splashing sounds, the rattle of soap on the ledge. "I couldn't say. Yvanne dresses me in fine gowns sometimes, for holy days and feasts. The first time I tripped over my own hem, and the whole court laughed and laughed. I am not sure which I prefer: To be taken for something I am not, or to fail at being what I am."

A weird shock went through me, as if I'd caught a glimpse of myself in a mirror I hadn't known was there: I knew what it was, to feel that you were doing a poor impression of what you were. I said, "I would not laugh at you."

"You would prefer me in a dress, then?" You asked it lightly, as a joke, but there was a bitter edge to your voice that made me turn.

Whatever I meant to say was instantly obliterated by the sight of your bare back: the pale streaks of scars, the ridged muscles on either side of your spine, the shadowed divots behind your shoulders. The white tangle of your hair falling over them, wet and soap-slick. You stretched, carelessly.

I looked away. My mouth was very dry. "I would prefer you—however you chose to be."

"No one chooses that, boy." You sounded so sad and so human that I had the wild urge to turn back around, to step closer—but no. You were Saint Una the Everlasting, and I would not profane you.

Instead, I left the room and waited in the hall. I struck up a conversation with one of the attendants, and by the time you emerged—fully dressed once more, no longer talkative or languorous—I had two new tales of the Red Knight to replace the memory of your bare skin.

I made a habit of collecting stories about you, after that.

I was good at it, talking to strangers, pulling gossip from them like twine from the spool. It was not unlike working in the archives: sifting through the various contradictory accounts, plucking threads from each tale and weaving them into a single whole.

I was less good at talking to you. But I found if I repeated what the villagers told me, you might be provoked into correcting them (*I had him disarmed in six moves, not three* or, fondly, *No, never. I'd wager Ancel started that rumor himself*), and in this way you, too, told me your story.

You told me of the Brigand Prince and the False Kings, of your first duel and of the happy fortnight you spent in Morvain's bed, beguiled by nothing other than her dimpled white thighs and clever hands. You were caught together, and Morvain was sent to the convent—where, you had heard, she was not altogether unhappy.

I fell silent for a little while after this last story, thinking of the chastity vows young girls sometimes took in the name of the Virgin Saint, and of the army nurse I'd known who was discharged for possession of unnatural literature, and of Professor Sawbridge's dictum that if the history you were reading wasn't filthy then someone had censored the good bits.

Thinking, too, of you: not as a symbol or a saint—pure, inviolate, beyond both desire and desiring—but as a human, with human appetites. I wondered a little wildly if you enjoyed men at all, or if you were like that army nurse I'd known.

I adjusted my collar, which had grown tight and overwarm, and found you watching me with something like amusement. "Have I shocked you?"

"No," I lied. "It's just—well, one expects a certain—from a saint—"

The amusement deepened. You said, "I promise you, I am no saint," in a low, wry voice which told me Morvain was neither your first nor your last such affair, and which cost me several hours of sleep that night.

The one subject you would not discuss was the Black Bastion. Of that battle—your grandest victory, which won the First Crusade and made Dominion the greatest nation of your time or mine—you would say nothing at all. You would only tighten your jaw and watch the fire, with something red and awful in your eyes.

I ducked my head and kept writing.

It was difficult work, transmuting all the dull indignities of travel—the gristly dinners and the grueling miles, the blisters and the stiff joints and pissing in ditches—into a tale to lift the hearts and minds of a nation. Line by line I made you—shattered and silent, half blind—into Sir Una Everlasting, hero of Dominion.

I could almost see her sometimes, a shining, heroic figure transposed over you. One day, I knew, she would replace you entirely, so that there would be no trace of you left at all.

At this thought I would be overtaken by a wash of inexplicable melancholy and put my work away.

But then, without the work, troubling thoughts would sometimes come to me. I might wonder if I'd ever return to my own time, or if I was lost here, like an arrow loosed into the past and never recovered. Or if dragons could really breathe fire hot enough to melt plate armor, and if you could truly face one alone.

Or, worse, I might imagine what came after the dragon. What was waiting for you at Cavallon Keep, and how you would look laid out on your bier.

At this thought my lungs would refuse to work properly and my hands would shake again, and my ears would fill with a sound like radio static.

You never remarked on such fits. You only folded yourself around me while I shuddered and panted, letting the heat of your skin soak into mine. It was an impersonal courtesy, a service rendered, but still: I lingered longer than I should have, afterward.

Forgive me—a coward so rarely feels safe.

The farther north we rode, the grayer and more miserable the villages became, until they did not resemble villages so much as wild outcroppings of huts, sprouting like pale mushrooms between the rocks. The people were bent and wind wracked, their faces hollowed in a way that made me think of the Hinterlander children who used to steal our empty bean tins in the war, running their fingers around the edges for the last drops of brine.

The whispers grew sharper, more vicious, and the stares grew colder. We did not speak of it, but you began to guide the gelding more often away from the road, along the gorse-eaten slopes and stone ridges.

But we couldn't avoid every village. In a narrow pass between two peaks, we came upon a place so desperately poor it was difficult to tell if it was a settlement or an encampment. Several of the structures were nothing but stacked rocks and goatskins, and the smoke that slunk from their roofs smelled of green wood and animal shit.

We had to lead the horse—blindfolded, to reduce civilian casualties—and pick our way through the churned mud between huts. I'd been planning to trade the fresh hare you'd tied over the saddlebow for some ale and a few more stories, but the expressions of the gathering villagers changed my mind. They did not whisper at all, but only stared, mute and hostile.

A stooped old man spat deliberately on the ground as we passed.

A bony young woman dumped her wash water so that it slopped over your boots, leaving them filmed with lye and grease.

A boy contrived to knock a cart of shriveled swedes directly into the path, so that the horse stumbled.

The villagers watched you avidly, but you did not scowl or recoil, or even break your stride.

They reminded me of the crowd I'd once seen in a lion-tamer's tent. The lion had been torpid and rheumatic, and the less dangerous it seemed the more vicious the crowd became, as if they were owed blood, and were determined to get it one way or another.

We were at the very edge of the village when a man approached at your back. He was thin and nearly bald, the flesh of his head covered in slick pink scars, as from fire.

The gelding tossed his head as he approached, nostrils wide, but you did not turn. The man spat something in a guttural language I didn't know, and I understood that he hated you. They all did.

Then he grabbed a fistful of your hair, and I thought, fervently: *You should not have done that.*

You stopped walking, chin jerked upward by the tug of your scalp.

There was a tiny pause, during which the reins slipped from your hand,

and your expression turned remote, as if you had gone away and left your body behind. It was the way you looked when you woke from your bad dreams, reaching for my throat, and I knew that very soon there would be a dead man in the street.

Some dark, subterranean part of me—the part of me that saw those dirty knuckles wrapped in the shine of your hair and wanted to put the entire godforsaken village to the torch and salt the ashes—didn't really mind.

But I thought you might. I should have grabbed your arm—but I hesitated, and then you were moving.

You were so damn fast. You had turned, blade drawn and lifted, already falling downward, by the time I shouted your name. "*Una!*"

You flinched. Not much, but enough to ruin the perfect arc of the blow. Instead of falling across the man's neck, Valiance fell at his wrist, with a sound like a hatchet into wet wood.

All of us—you and I, the scarred man, and the straggling villagers behind us—looked for a moment at the neat pink meat where his hand had been. The white stubs of his arm bones sheered cleanly away. Then the flood of red, and the wailing.

You watched, impassive, as he collapsed. The gelding reared, blind but bloodthirsty, and you made no move to catch the reins.

I said your name again, and you looked at me in a way that suggested there might still be a dead man in the street soon. Who was I to you, after all? A lost scribe, a slightly-above-average fortune-teller, a stray you dragged reluctantly along with you.

I didn't blink or step back. I only held your gaze, and held it, my fists clenched so tightly I felt my palm crack and bleed fresh.

Eventually something flickered in the depths of your eyes. Valiance hissed back into its sheath. You caught the gelding and quieted him. A pair of women came running to the man's side, tears running down their cheeks. One of them reached toward the hand—now sticking upright in the mud, as if someone were reaching up from under the earth—but drew back.

You watched them weeping with no expression at all. Then you turned your back on the village and walked on.

After a mile or so you paused and dropped to one knee, head bowed, hands cupped in the shape of a stirrup. I blinked down at you for several seconds before stepping gingerly into your palms. You lifted me into the saddle without effort but did not swing yourself up behind me. You walked instead, apparently too furious with me to bear my company.

It was a long way before we made camp that night.

Long after dark, after the horse had been rubbed down and fed hot mash, after the fire had worn itself down to shadow and ember, I offered, by way of apology, "Bastard."

You shrugged without looking at me.

I tried again. "It was—merciful of you. To spare him."

Your mouth twisted. "You would call it mercy, to take the right hand of the only hale man, in a family already hungry?" You shook your head once, sharply. "The only mercy I have ever shown is that I kill quickly, and I did not even grant him that."

"He shouldn't have touched you. None of them should have dared." The Drawn Blade of Dominion shouldn't have to hunch and duck among her countrymen, shrinking herself down to mortal proportions. I found myself gesticulating, restless and angry. "They should be grateful. They should be falling to their knees, crawling after you to apologize. They should—"

"Can't you bind that properly?" You pointed with your chin toward my hand, which was oozing again. "Come here."

I edged toward you around the fire. You reached out slowly, deliberately, as if giving me time to withdraw. I didn't.

You turned my wound carefully to the light, the crease deepening between your brows. My hands looked fragile in yours, long boned and ink stained against the cracked callus of your palms. I searched your face for contempt or derision, but found it curiously absent of all expression.

You began to unwind the bandage, with a sound like a boot being drawn out of deep mud. I turned my face hastily away.

I spoke to the low line of hills, their shape visible only by the absence of stars. "They should at least show you respect. They owe it to you, as—as citizens of Dominion."

"They were not born citizens of Dominion." You said it mildly, without reproach. "They were Hyllmen, once, and they did not come eagerly to the queen's banner. Even when they knew their cause was lost, they would not open the gates of the Black Bastion." I heard the click of your throat as you swallowed. "Those people lost their sons to the war, their gods to the Savior, their land to the crown. They'll turn to banditry soon, if they have not already, and then they will be hanged, and their children made into beggars."

You tossed the soiled bandage into the fire, eyes flashing red. "The cost of peace, she tells me. Sometimes I wonder whose peace she means."

You fell silent, dripping cold water into the mess of my palm and dabbing gently at it, wiping away blood and lymph. Your fingers were so thick with scars they were hard to the touch, like hand-shaped stones, and your motions were uncertain, as if you didn't trust yourself not to hurt me.

There was a prickling, restless sensation growing just beneath my skin. Anger, perhaps, because your speech had sounded very much like one of my father's, or fear, because it hadn't sounded untrue.

I took a bracing breath. "Still. Yvanne is the rightful queen. She's *their* queen—"

"And I am her drawn blade." The words came quick and bleak as the fall of an ax. "It was *I* who beheaded the False Kings, one by one, though they cried mercy. *I* who set the crown on her brow, with blood still crusted around the jewels. I who rode at the front, who struck first and last, who drew every border in red. Do you know what they call me, in the north? What that man called me before I crippled him?" Your lip curled, and I couldn't tell if the contempt was directed at them or yourself. "The Knight of Worms. Because I feed them so well."

You tore a strip of fresh linen with your teeth and spat it out. "They *should* fear me, boy." You bent over the work, hair falling to one side and baring the pale nape of your neck to me. "And so should you."

I watched you bind the fresh cloth around my hand—clumsily, gently, frowning hard—and thought maybe I would head back to the village and raze it after all. It was a shame, really, that I only had three shots.

You began to draw your hand away from mine, but I caught and held it instead. You looked up sharply, eyes dark as silt.

"Well," I said, enunciating very clearly. "I don't."

Your lips parted, and I saw again that phantom smile, berries bursting between sharp white teeth. I had never heard you laugh, but I knew then it would be low and rough and wild.

And I knew, too—from the subtle shift in the air between us, from the catch in your breath—that you were not like that army nurse I'd known, after all.

I permitted myself to imagine it, just for a moment. I would turn your hand palm up, press my lips to the soft, secret center of it. I would reach up and bury my fingers in your hair, pull you down to me. You would let me. Then you would let me go to my knees and give you what you wanted, for as long as you wanted it, until your thighs were slick and the line between your brows was finally gone, and afterward you would sleep deeply, without dreaming.

The images arrived with such vivid assurance, such fine-grained detail, that they felt more like memories than fantasies. You met my eyes and I felt myself tilting toward you, the woman I had wanted since before I knew how, the woman I was just now coming to want—

The woman I was leading to her death.

I recoiled.

You saw it. I watched the knowledge of that flinch move across your face like an early frost, killing whatever had been in bloom. It wasn't pain. It was closer to relief: You had wanted me to be afraid, and I was.

You pulled your hand away from mine and rubbed it hard against your hip. I watched in awful, cowardly silence as you wrapped your cloak around yourself and lay down with your back to me.

I stayed awake most of the night, sick with guilt and want. I smoked three Lucky Stars in a row, heedless of the waste, before I turned to the book.

The words came easily, pouring from the pen in a hot, spiteful rush. It was all lies, but what did I care? If I couldn't have you or heal you or save you—if I couldn't love you—then I would make all of Dominion love you, forever and ever.

UNA AND THE GRAIL

When the queen called, Sir Una answered, as she ever had.

She rode out that very night to seek the grail, the holy cup that had resurrected the Savior Himself, that would now pull Yvanne from the very edge of death.

But understand: In that time, the grail was less than a legend, less even than the meanest rumor. Only the most dogged priests spoke of it as any other than a holy gesture, and only the most foolish of men went looking for it. None of them found anything but their own graves.

But see now how God favors Dominion. To all those desperate, greedy grail-seekers, He had said nothing. To Una—whose heart never once faltered, whose faith never once wavered—He said two words: *Cloven Hill.*

Few people knew that place, then. It was not labeled on any map or mentioned in any myths; it was nothing but a low mountain far in the Northern Fallows, too lonely even for hermits, too barren even for goats.

But the queen's service had sent Sir Una to every corner of Dominion. She had walked the storm-bitten coasts and ridden down the white streets of Cavallon, chased her enemies through the north and slept in the cool shade of the western woods. She had eaten of every orchard and drunk of every beck, so that if you plucked her heart from her chest it would be a perfect map of the country, with blood for rivers and red muscle for mountains.

God no sooner spoke the words than Una saddled her horse. North she rode, as hard and fast as her loyal steed would carry her, stopping only when the falling light risked the horse. Then she wrapped herself in her woolen cloak and slept the deep, untroubled sleep of the faithful.

At dawn she rose with the sun and rode north.

Most often she took the secret ways of hinds and hares, or the dirt tracks of farmers and herdsmen. Only sometimes did she take to the great roads, veering between merchant carts and mule teams until someone saw the device on her shield, and the cry was taken up: *Make way! Make way for the Queen's Champion!*

Wherever she rode, the people of Dominion bowed low as she passed, and wept tears of awe and joy, and told their children and their children's children about the day the Red Knight rode through their village. Little girls tossed torn petals wherever she walked, and boys crossed stick-swords, and their mothers and fathers welcomed her into their homes.

For they knew what she had done for them, and they loved her for it.

—*Excerpted from* The Death of Una Everlasting,
translated by Owen Mallory

Six days later, you raised your arm and pointed over my shoulder at the horizon, where the shadow of a mountain now stood. The clouds clung thick and white to the ground, so that the mountain reared up like a broken molar from pale gums.

"There," you said.

I asked, "Are you sure?"

You did not bother to answer, and I did not bother to ask again. I knew, somehow, that you were right: We had come at last to Cloven Hill, where lay the grail, and the last dragon of Dominion.

7

I HAD READ and re-read every version of your battle with the last dragon. I could—and had, on several regrettable social occasions—recite Montmer's account in the original Middle Mothertongue.

It began: *It was there, in that burnt and barren place, where Una met the dragon, last of his kind.*

Cloven Hill was, to Montmer's credit, fairly barren. There were no towns or villages here, or even the lonely camps of shepherds or hunters. There was nothing but bare stone and wind-stunted pines, and the shifting clouds that kept the peaks partly obscured, like poorly kept secrets.

And yet: The earth was not scorched. The air was not sulfurous. An aura of dread did not blacken the skies. There were still slim gray foxes and white hares among the stones, and colorful bursts of lichen and juniper berries. It reminded me, inexplicably, of the Queen's Wood. It was the sheer wildness of the place, maybe, the sense that no mapmaker had ever written down its name, and no army had ever driven a flag into its dirt.

When the land turned steep, you made one of your subtle gestures to the horse and we halted beneath an alder. You dismounted and I slithered ungracefully after you. You caught me as you always did, hands braced patiently around my waist until I found my feet.

You spoke to the bay for a while, in that soft, private voice that made me wonder if you were lying about not naming him, before you loosed the bindings on the packs.

I didn't understand what you were doing until I caught the mirror gleam of metal.

You laid a vambrace against your left forearm and pulled the strap tight with your teeth. Knights were supposed to have fleets of servants to assist them, but it was clear you'd learned to manage alone.

I fished the second vambrace from the pile and held it ready.

After a sharp, inscrutable look, you set your arm carefully against the metal and permitted me to wrap the leather straps around it. I didn't have to ask which piece came next; my fingers already knew the shape of each greave and gauntlet, each strap and buckle. It fit you well, impossibly well, as if the iron had been poured like candle wax over your skin, and the metal was as fine as anything made in my century. (If I ever saw Sawbridge again, I would tell her plate armor had been worn much earlier than she claimed.)

Piece by piece I transmuted you from mortal to myth, from flesh into blinding, blue-white steel. If you wondered where I'd learned to play squire, you did not ask, and I was grateful; I had no good answer.

"Shield?" I asked, hefting it.

"Won't need it."

"Helm?"

"Don't have one." It was true that you were always bareheaded in the paintings and plays, but I found this suddenly and unbearably stupid. A single stray arrow, a lucky blow—

"The belt, boy," you said.

I had to reach both arms around your waist to fasten the belt, flushing slightly when my knuckles brushed the small of your back. I fumbled for Valiance, drawing it clumsily from its battered leather sheath. The light caught the blade and my breath stopped.

I'd never held it before. It took both hands, and the tip still bobbed and wobbled. I knew it was old—knew it had been in the yew for centuries before you drew it—but it looked fresh from the forge.

I ran my thumb up the flat of the blade. "Not so much as a dent or chip. Has it never failed you?"

Your answered evenly, without inflection, "Every tool fails, used hard enough."

"But—is it true—" I felt like a boy asking his priest if angels were real. "The damage disappears?"

You looked away, squinting up the mountainside. "I took a hammer to it once, after—" You stopped. Coughed. "Broke it into ten pieces and threw the shards into the sea." Your throat moved as you swallowed. "When I woke the next day, the hilt was in my hand, and the blade was whole and pure as the day I drew it from the yew."

You had been granted a true miracle—an unbreakable sword!—yet you would cast it away if you could. Your fate was laid out before you like a shining path, a tale so perfect it must have been written by the hand of God Himself, yet you would turn away from it.

If I let you.

I thrust the sword toward you, and you sheathed it at your hip, a quick iron whisper. You reached for your hair, twisting it carelessly into your collar, and I found myself saying, "Here, sit down."

You sat, strangely pliant. I knew as soon as I touched your hair that I'd made a mistake. The weight and texture of it—heavy and slick and tangled, like a thicket of silk—struck me as the sort of thing that might haunt a person, lingering like a wound and aching years later.

I braided it hastily, leaving long tendrils falling around your face and down across the metal of your shoulders.

With your back still turned to me, I said, "You'll win." I swept a wisp from your neck, tucking it into the braid. "Just—so you know, you will kill the dragon and find the grail. I've read all the stories."

A slight pause before you asked, "Then why do your hands shake?"

"Oh." My laugh was unconvincing, rusty sounding. I stepped away, trapping my treacherous hands beneath my elbows. "Because I'm an awful coward. Ask anyone."

You stood and gestured to your horrible horse. "There's grain for three days more. If he misbehaves"—you appeared to struggle briefly—"his name is Hen."

"I *knew* you were lying! But—*Hen*? Well, perhaps some things ought to be lost to history." Only then did I follow the implications of the instructions. My chest contracted. "You're leaving me here?"

Your brows crimped, bemused. "Yes."

"You can't slay a dragon alone!"

"Everything I have done, I have done alone." You said it without emotion, as a statement of fact. "I thought you'd read all the stories."

"But what if—look, just let me come with you. Please."

Your expression moved from bafflement to some harsh, taut emotion that made the muscles of your jaw roll. Eventually you said, roughly, "You make a poor coward, boy." You turned away and said, "Stay," as if I were a poorly trained puppy, worrying at your heels.

I watched you disappear into the clouds with something flailing behind my breastbone, a mad desire to shout after you: *Wait! Come back! It is not worth it!*

Instead, I wedged myself against a crag and opened the book in my lap. There are blotches on that page where the ink dripped and dried before I could think of anything to write.

Eventually I simply stole Montmer's opening line on the grounds that, technically, Montmer would be plagiarizing from me.

UNA AND THE LAST DRAGON

It was there, in that burnt and barren place, where Una met the dragon, last of his kind.

At one time, dragons had been the plague of Dominion. They lurked in deep woods and sea caves, on lonely mountaintops and beneath ancient keeps, sleeping among the bones of stray cattle and lost children. They were unlike every natural creature—they were not born and never died, but only persisted, a ceaseless hungering that was never sated.

The people of Dominion had lived in the fell shadow of that hunger for so many centuries that they no longer even dreamed of a different world. They sought shelter when the wind smelled of sulfur, and never wandered far off the edges of the map.

But Yvanne was not born to tolerate despair. The very day she was crowned she sent knights and armies to purge the land of dragons. They dug the beasts from their caverns and set fire to their forests. She did not make trophies of them, for her own glory, but had the carcasses burned three times, and their blackened bones ground and scattered over the farmlands. Only a few scales she kept, for her mantle.

By the time Sir Una rode north, all the dragons were dead, save one: the canniest and oldest of them, which lurked in the bleak mists of the Cloven Hill. It had taken many lives, over the centuries, including Galawin the Great, who—they said—had carried the grail with him from the Savior's resurrection.

When the last dragon heard again the clang of armor and the hiss of drawn steel, it rose from its lair like a demon loosed from hell. It smote the air with pale wings so vast they cast a pall over the sun itself.

Sir Una stood beneath it, atop the bones of all the heroes who had fallen before her, and all the simple folk of Dominion who had suffered beneath the dragon's tyranny for too long. Valiance was in her right hand and death was in her eye.

The dragon blew its brimstone breath down upon her. She caught the flame on her shield and bowed her head against it and, though the metal blistered her arm, though cinders burned her brow, she did not yield.

The fire faded. Una rose like the dawn.

The sight sent the dragon into a frenzy of fearful rage. 'Think you, a mere mortal, will defeat me?' it shrieked, and its voice was a torment, which peeled bark from trees and stripped moss from stones.

And then the battle began in earnest.

Three days and three nights they fought, and each dealt bitter wounds to the other. By dusk on the third day the mountain was gray with ash, and the stones were so hot they glowed dull orange. The dragon crawled now, its white wings in tatters. It bled, and where its blood fell it hissed faintly, and poisoned the earth, so that nothing would bloom in those places even a century later.

Una faced the dragon, her lungs choked with ash and sulfur, limping badly. Her armor was scorched black, and her hands were blistered with burns, and yet she smiled.

'I may be a mere mortal, dragon,' she said, 'but Dominion is everlasting.'

It is said that the heart of a dragon is so small—nothing but a bitter red seed hidden deep beneath vast ribs and iron scales—that no arrow may find it and no sword may pierce it.

But they had never seen a sword wielded by the Red Knight. Sir Una struck the great breast of that beast, and she struck true, as she ever had. Valiance pierced the dark heart of the last dragon, and the world was free of them forevermore.

This is how Sir Una received the last of all her names and titles. Everlasting, they called her, for she would be remembered for as long as Dominion lasted, and Dominion would never die.

—*Excerpted from* The Death of Una Everlasting,
translated by Owen Mallory

When I finished, I put away the reed pen and the oak-gall ink and the book. I paced. I sat. I waited. I felt slightly nauseous and rebuked myself for it.

Then from up the mountainside came a high, keening cry. It was an awful noise, like the scream of metal on metal, but it went on so long it resolved into a single, pure note. The note burrowed into me, becoming very nearly beautiful, so that when it finally ended, I felt as if something precious had been lost.

Silence followed.

I pelted uphill, breathing harshly, stumbling over stones and roots. I rounded a wiry stand of pine, heading into dense mist—

And slammed into something tall and unyielding, like the face of a cliff.

"*Una—*" I unpeeled my face from your cuirass and fell back, arms lifting and hovering on either side of your shoulders. "Are you alright?"

"Of course," you said, and you laughed. It sounded like a jar full of teeth being shaken.

You did *look* alright. Your armor was unscratched. There was a shallow scrape across your left temple because you still hadn't learned to guard your blind side, but the blood was already gummy, half dried.

But—your eyes. They'd been hollowed out, as if someone had broken into your skull and scraped it clean with the edge of a spoon. The echo of that eerie cry seemed to spread between us like a stain.

"And"—damn my wreck of a voice for breaking—"did you find—"

"Of course," you said again, coolly. You strode by me, shoving something hard into my belly as you passed.

I nearly dropped it, and when I looked at it properly, I nearly dropped it again. It was a small cup of purest gold, set with tiny red jewels: the grail of Dominion. The half-legendary blessed artifact that had resurrected the Savior Himself, that would save Queen Yvanne's life and the future of the nation itself.

I wriggled out of my coat and wrapped it tightly around the cup, lest the college archivist come charging down the mountainside, thumbscrews in hand.

By the time I caught up, you were already mounted. You waited in a clearing, just where the sun poured through the branches, running over the plates of your armor and pooling in your hair, so that you were haloed in hazy gold light. Your head was bowed as if in prayer, and one hand rested on your hilt.

I stood mute, while time twisted and sloughed around me.

I forgot you were scarred and plain and unchaste. I forgot you cried out sometimes in the night, as I did, and dreamed of a home you could never return to, as I did. I even forgot you were the sort of woman who named her horse Hen.

You were Una Everlasting, the Drawn Blade, the Red Knight, and I was a boy again, choked with that covetous tangle of desire and desire-to-become that had driven me to war and back again, to archives and libraries and finally here, through time itself, to the far side of history. My whole life existed only to bear witness to yours, and God! It was worth it.

Then the light shifted; the halo vanished. When you reached your hand down to me, I could see again the lines and hollows around your eyes, the rucked skin of scars and the freckles gone blurry with years in the sun.

I should have been able to breathe again, but could not.

You made an impatient, extremely human sound. I took your hand again, and we rode down the mountain together.

When the ground leveled, I asked, quietly enough that you could pretend not to have heard me if you chose, "Was it so terrible? The dragon?"

"No," you said, and then, after a long time, "it was a wild creature, and old—older than anything that ever was, I think, but it was not terrible. None of them ever were. They were"—the cool voice cracked, and I heard the grief running beneath it—"beautiful."

I clutched the grail hard to my stomach to remind myself that it was worth it, all of it: the cry on the mountain and the hateful faces of the villagers, your nightmares and mine, the blood we spilled and the scars we bore, and even the death of something wild and old and beautiful.

"But we ride now to the Keep," you said, into my silence. "And there the story ends." Such yearning in your voice, such relief, that for a moment I couldn't answer. I felt you stiffen behind me, wary, mistrusting.

So I said, "Yes," and it felt like sliding a knife between your ribs, or between my own, or as if there were no difference between the two. "The story ends there."

And this, too, I told myself, was worth it.

8

THE JOURNEY TO Cavallon is distorted in my memory.

I recall it—every bitter and aching mile—but it's like recalling a play I saw once as a young man. My own voice sounds rehearsed, stiff with portent. Your every gesture is an elegy. All the ordinary, unscripted labor of the road—tending the tack, skinning the kill, striking the flint, burying the offal—is lost to me, drowned by the bright lights of the stage.

But I remember the cold. The weather turned as we left the hills, the sky turning the bluish-white of a frostbitten finger. Each night we huddled miserably on either side of the wind-whipped fire, sleeping fitfully and shivering ourselves awake.

At these times I found myself watching you, remembering the heat of your hand around mine, thinking of all the obvious ways two people might drive away the cold.

But I was too much a coward to cross the fire without an invitation, and you did not invite me. You barely even spoke to me. You had drawn subtly away from me since the dragon. There were times I thought I saw something in your eyes—an anger that festered and wept, like a gut wound—but then you would look away, and it would be gone.

Eventually I resorted to blunt provocation.

"She must be truly something. Yvanne, I mean." I couldn't see your face as we rode, but I felt you flinch from her name. "Or perhaps the stories have exaggerated, and I'll be disappointed."

When you answered, the words came in bloody lumps, as if they'd been chewed and spat out. "She never misspeaks or missteps. She is never afraid, no matter the odds. She is never, ever taken by surprise, no matter how clever her enemy or how slippery her quarry. She is five—ten, a thousand—steps ahead of you or I or anyone I have ever met." And then, with unmistakable pride, "You won't be disappointed."

"You *do* love her."

You answered softly, with grief, "Always."

You didn't speak again until late that night when you said, "It'll get colder, before dawn. Might even snow." I nodded, miserably. You went on, "We fought the Hyllmen in winter, you know. At night we stripped bare and slept pressed together." Then, meeting my eyes, "I barely felt the cold."

You had a hectic, mean look on your face as you said it. A look that invited me, finally, to come across the fire, but guaranteed no gentle treatment if I did.

And oh, I was tempted. I flushed with heat, hungry to be handled as roughly as I deserved. To have something of you that would linger after your death, even if it were only teethmarks.

But if I touched you, and found only flesh—if I tasted you, and found only the ordinary bittersweetness of a wet cunt—then you would no longer be a legend to me, but only yourself.

I could kill a legend; I didn't know if I could kill you.

I'd hesitated too long. You'd turned away, wrapped in your cloak. I did not sleep that night, but curled around myself, face tucked into the collar of my jacket so that I could smell my own sour, unspent desire.

In the morning we rose and rode east, into the third act.

In my own era, Cavallon Keep was a ruin: a haunted tumble of stones gathered on the hill above the capitol, admired only by historians and bloodthirsty schoolchildren. Even I had only visited once, and hadn't lingered. The wind had whistled mournfully through the walls, and my hands had shaken too violently to take notes.

But here in the youth of the world—looking up at it from horseback, in the early dusk of winter—the Keep was a wonder. It seemed less a castle than a child's drawing of one: a perfectly symmetrical assemblage of turrets and towers. Curtain walls that met at ninety-degree angles. Battlements like the teeth of a zipper. And the size of it—ten times taller than even the great yew in the grove, a hundred times taller than any village church, built in less than a decade. It was said that any man who died in the quarry or on the scaffolding had his blood mixed into the mortar, and that it was counted a great honor. I wondered, a little queasily, how many men had been honored so.

At my back, I felt the muscles of your stomach tense. "The queen's colors are still raised," you said. "She yet lives." There was no inflection in your voice.

Indeed, the bright flag of Dominion snapped smartly in the wind. It was the only sound in the whole valley: No voices drifted down from the Keep, no figures walked the walls. The great gates stood open and waiting, like the gullet of a wolf.

And suddenly I could hardly breathe, suffocated by a grief that was both premature and a thousand years too late.

"Your armor," I said, buying time, knowing it wouldn't matter. "You should ride in full armor through the gates. It's—how it looks in all the paintings."

I expected you to scorn such vanity, but instead your muscles loosened at my back. "As you say."

My hands shook as I drew the straps of your armor tight. You sat on a low stone without being asked, offering me the tangle of your hair, and I closed my eyes as I drew my fingers through it. I would not braid it this time, but let it run loose and heavy down your back. I was picturing you as you're painted in Goletti's *Sir Una and the Grail,* or perhaps I was picturing you somewhere else, running young and barefoot between the trees—

"This will truly heal her, then?" I opened my eyes to find you studying the grail. It looked gaudy and absurd in your hand, like a stage prop.

I cleared my throat. "It will. She reigns for another thirty years and brings peace and prosperity to all of Dominion. And even centuries afterward, during our darkest times, it's that golden age that we remember, that we fight for." I clung childishly to my own words, trying to see you for what you were: a necessary tragedy, a single red knot in the grand tapestry of history.

You made a small, musing sound in your throat. "When she first fell ill, I thought: Perhaps there is a God, after all. Perhaps every sin is counted and gathered on a great scale. Perhaps everyone gets what they deserve."

I tried hard not to flinch. Who knew better than I how war could warp the mind, until you hated what you ought to love?

Somewhat at random, flailing for a distraction, I said, "I never asked—why were you armored, that first time I saw you in the woods? Must have had a devil of a time doing the buckles in the back."

You shrugged one shoulder, eyes slitted as if you did not mind the feel of my hands in your hair. Drowsily you answered, "So they would know me when they found me. I suppose even there, at the end of reason, I did not want to be forgotten."

My fingers stilled. There was a metallic ringing in my ears, like bullet casings on stone. "Pardon?"

You shrugged again, more forcefully. "I could see no other way out. I could not bear to serve her any longer, and I could not bear to let her die. I loved her too well, even then, even still. So I thought, I have taken so many lives. What's one more?"

I did flinch, then. Another of those lurid visions arrived, awful in its clarity: you, lying flat on the forest floor. Dead needles in your hair, dirt under your nails. Valiance growing from your sternum like a silver sapling.

I shoved my hands beneath my elbows to stop their shaking. "But you couldn't do it. You wouldn't have."

You turned slowly around on the stone, looking up at me with eyes gone oddly gentle. "I know what you want me to be. What you have made me, in your book. But you should know what I truly am." You closed your eyes then. The wind rose, lifting your hair, so that you spoke through a tangled white veil. "Had I been alone—had you not come when you did"—you were whispering now—"I would have done it."

I stood looking down at you, while the ringing went on and on in my ears.

Then, clumsily, numb fingered, I folded down the collar of my service jacket for the second time, baring the pink whorls of scar to the cold. Your eyes were still shut, so I took your hand carefully in mine—your eyes snapped open, hot and yellow—and brought it to my throat. I could feel nothing but a faint, faraway heat, like winter sun; the nerves there had been boiled away by the infection.

"I didn't get this from the enemy," I said, and for once my voice did not break. "The Hinterlanders had retreated to the southern beach. They couldn't win, but it was going to be—well. I couldn't face it. Threw down my rifle and turned around. My own commanding officer slit my throat."

Oh, the change that had come over Colonel Drayton's face as I dropped my rifle, as I transformed from one of his boys to one of his enemies. The bite of his knife into my neck. The clean black hole that appeared in his temple, by purest happenstance, by fate, and saved my life.

I lowered my voice, felt it thrum against your palm. "We are both of us deserters. Cowards, maybe. But when you ride through those gates, bearing the grail you won from the last dragon—it will all be wiped clean. Our doubts, our mistakes, will be forgotten."

You watched me closely, hungrily. "And what of our sins?"

They came to me one after the other: the Hinterlanders and their thrown-stone eyes; the Hyllman's hand standing upright in the mud; the cry of the last dragon as it died. And on and on—every soldier I'd shot, every enemy you'd fed to the worms—until the earth beneath my boots felt soft and foul, like grave dirt.

"Those, too," I said, desperately.

"You don't know the whole of it." Your pupils had eaten up the gold of your eyes, and some awful confession swam in the black. "You don't know what I've done. At the end, at the Black Bastion—"

"*It doesn't matter.*" Weeks of pestering and wheedling, and suddenly I was begging you not to tell me anything more. "In a thousand years, they will sing your name in the streets. They will raise their children on stories of brave Sir Una Everlasting, the Red Knight, who fought for crown and country. You may not have lived as a hero, but I swear: You will die as one. Just—" My voice split and bled. "Just do this last thing."

Your eyes fell closed again. "As you will," you said, and I let go of your wrist. There were thin pink bands where my fingers had been.

You mounted. For the first time, you did not reach your hand down to me.

I walked alongside you some of the way, one hand on the stirrup. Hen nipped me once, nastily and for no reason, and I let him. None of the stories said whether your horse outlived you.

We approached the gates, where no guard called out to us, no watchmen cried greeting—did you not wonder why?—and I fell back.

I watched you ride toward the bloody end of your story alone, as you always were, as you must be.

You passed beneath the stone arch and paused. You turned your face back to me. I caught the wry lift of your lips, that smile that was not a smile but only the premonition of one.

And that old weakness came over me, the fault line that had cracked wide during the war and healed poorly. A tremor began at the base of my spine and shivered through my limbs. My teeth clacked together.

For crown and country, I thought, numbly.

And then I thought: *It is not worth it.*

"Una!" I shouted, and God, let my voice not be too weak—let me not be too late—" 'Ware the archers!"

I knew before the words formed on my lips that I was too late. I heard the taut thrum of bowstrings, the whistle of fletching in the air, and knew no one could move fast enough.

But you could.

There was a sound like bullets hitting a tin can and then there were two arrows sprouting from your shield, held high to guard your face. The third arrow was lodged just above your left elbow, nestled in the slit between two plates of metal.

You didn't seem to notice. You swung low in the saddle, shield still raised, as the second volley found you. Hen screamed. Someone shouted orders. Boots clanged on stone.

I knew who they were: Hinterlanders, come to pay their respects to the fresh-made queen of Dominion. But instead of finding a monarch in the fullness of her power, they had found a dying woman and a worried court. They had waited and watched, drinking the queen's wine and eating the queen's bread, until someone had whispered to them that the famed Red Knight was gone away on a fool's quest.

The temptation had proved too great. The Hinterlanders had called for toast after toast—to the queen's health! to Dominion!—and waited till even the Queen's Guard was laughing and stupid with drink. It had been easy to take the Keep, then, and easy to lie in wait for the Red Knight's return.

Their plot would fail, of course. Valiance would cut them down, every one, and their corpses would be hung from the gates for the crows to pick clean, and their treachery would be remembered for a thousand years. When the Hinterlanders sued for peace during the war, Vivian Rolfe had laughed in their faces. Her answer had become famous, printed on posters and shouted in battle: *Dominion does not forget.*

Dominion would survive this. But you would not.

You would kneel before the queen one last time, pierced by a dozen arrows. You would lift the grail in one bloodied hand, head bowed, and the queen would touch your hair and say, *Rest now, my Red Knight.*

And the Drawn Blade of Dominion would die with a smile on her lips.

I was not aware of making a decision. But I found my feet moving, my hand reaching for the service revolver that rested warm and heavy against my breast. I crouched behind the low wall of the courtyard well, finger already hooked around the trigger.

You shouted, angrily, "Run, boy! Are you not a coward?"

I was. A brave man would have stood at the gates and let the past take its course, for the sake of the future. But I was too much a coward to watch you die, Una.

The archers were already notching arrows again on the curtain wall, taking aim. I counted three of them.

And for a moment I felt sure that the whole machine of the world, every birth and every death, every tick of every clock, had been designed to bring me here, now: with three bullets in my revolver and the best eye in the 2nd Battalion.

I looked at my hands and found them perfectly steady.

I aimed—except I never had to aim, I only had to fall away from myself and let my body move without me, like giving a horse its head. I fell into alignment, eye to arm to barrel, and all I had to do was pull the trigger.

Three shots, one after the other. Three bodies bursting on the stones of the courtyard, one after the other.

An odd silence, as if the entire Keep had been suspended in amber. The Hinterlander soldiers looked at the broken shapes of their archers. They looked at you, mounted upright once more, another arrow now sprouting from your back.

Then the Red Knight drew her blade, whose name was known before their mothers' mothers were born, and the silence was replaced by screaming.

It was the first time I'd seen you truly fight. I suppose I had grown used to the disappointing gap between myth and reality; I suppose I thought your skill had been embellished by time, exaggerated as all legends are.

It hadn't been. You fell among the Hinterlanders like a mad dog cut loose from its leash, like a scythe across dry wheat, like a weapon wearing the skin of a woman.

You did not fight cleanly or prettily; it was nothing like a dance. It was an annihilation, brutal and inexorable, and the only beauty was in the sheer fucking speed of it. You swung Valiance one-handed, quick as a cleaver, and if your enemies did not meet your blade they met the blunt edge of your shield, and when the shield was ripped from your arm, they met your mailed fist. You were Una Everlasting, and there was no surviving you.

I understood then why the villagers feared you, and why you feared yourself. I closed my eyes, like a child, so that I would not fear you, too.

When I opened them again, there was a fine spray of blood on the lenses of my spectacles, and hot, grassy breath on my face. It was Hen, still somehow alive—I supposed it was difficult to kill a cadaver—now nibbling delicately at my hair.

I knew a moment of true terror when I saw his empty saddle—but no.

There you were: alone in the awful silence, your hair slicked redly to your armor, still standing.

Still alive.

I thought, with a distant, obligatory panic: *Oh God, what have I done,* but all I truly felt was giddy, euphoric relief. More than relief—reprieve, as though it was my own life that had been spared.

I rested my head gratefully against Hen's jawbone. "Well done, old man." He nuzzled at my curls until he found my ear, which he bit. *Glue,* I whispered to him, eyes watering. *Great vats of it.*

By the time my eyes cleared, you were standing above me, one gauntleted hand extended. I took it, as I always did, and you hauled me to my feet.

I swayed a little, looking up at you through smeary glasses. There was a wet gobbet of something stuck to your cheekbone, steaming faintly in the cold. A bruise was blooming at one temple, and you were scowling down at me like the wrath of God. I thought how funny it was, how baffling, that I'd ever thought you unbeautiful.

You snarled, "I told you to run, boy!"

You seemed very upset, but you also seemed very alive, and so I found it impossible to stop smiling. I shrugged and gestured vaguely with my Saint Sinclair, which I was surprised to find still in my hand.

You looked at the revolver and then, eyes narrowing, at the fallen archers. Your face unsnarled, became still. "You killed them. With your—gone."

"My *gun,* a standard-issue Saint Sinclair six-shot, yes." I nodded, a little sloppily. I'd nearly forgotten this feeling—the drunken, clammy high that comes after battle, after the danger but before the vomiting. "It's the archers that get you, usually. Almost all the sources agree."

Your expression didn't change, but your eyes became a pair of coins, cold and yellow. "You knew, then. What awaited me here."

Guilt drew me back to earth as surely as an anchor around my ankle. I swallowed hard. "Yes. God, Una—" I experienced a moment of regret: If I'd let the archers get you, at least you wouldn't be standing there, looking at me like that, and my heart wouldn't be splitting in my chest. "I'm sorry. I should have told you. Or I shouldn't have, I don't know—this is how it ends, how it *has* to end. And now it's all wrong, I suppose, but—"

"You meant me to die." You said it quietly, almost to yourself. "And yet—you saved me." You were looking at me now with a kind of furious ambivalence, like a judge who couldn't decide if a criminal ought to be hanged or merely locked away in the madhouse. You asked, white-lipped, "Why?"

"I just—couldn't." I laughed, poorly. "The whole reason I was sent here in the first place—the one real duty I could have done for my country—and I couldn't do it." I looked down, spread my hands in another shrug. "Coward."

"Who first called you that, I wonder? But give me a name, and I will bring you his tongue." You sounded so annoyed, so alarmingly sincere, that I couldn't speak, or look up.

Then: the clank of your gauntlets hitting the cobbles. Your gloved hands on either side of my head, unhooking the spectacles carefully from my ears, reaching for the hem of my jacket. You rubbed the lenses in circles on the red wool until the blood flaked and fell away.

When it was done, you touched a knuckle to my chin, tilting my eyes back to yours. "To charge into battle, with neither shield nor mount, against terrible odds—to know the odds, and charge anyway—" You shook your head. You settled the spectacles back on my face, and your features came into sudden focus: the severe line between your brows, the faint flush over the bridge of your nose. "There is a word for someone like that, and it is not coward."

I suggested, a little thickly, "Traitor?" and wasn't entirely joking.

"Madman," you answered, and neither were you.

You turned to Hen, fussing over him as if he were a child with a scraped knee rather than a serial murderer with a saddle. He knocked his head against your chest and pawed fretfully at the ground as you drew the cup from his bags. You turned to face the Keep—and stumbled.

I'd never seen you stumble. It was only then that I remembered the arrows.

One, haft snapped, nestled in your left elbow. Another was buried in the gap between your backplate and chest, right at the bottom of your ribs.

God, what if it hit something vital? What if—even now, after I had overturned all of known history to keep you alive—the story wrenched itself true, and took you away?

"Saints, woman, don't—just come here." I took your wrist and hauled your arm across my shoulders, grunting a little under your weight. I expected you to protest, but instead you sagged into me, and shuddered hard.

I aimed us toward the front steps of the Keep, speaking in the same soothing nonsense-voice you used on the damn horse. I said stupid things, embarrassing things, like *You're alright, now* and *I've got you.* The shudders seemed to ease, so I kept going. My babble took us up the steps, through the door, into the shadows of Cavallon Keep.

I should have been fretting about the flow of time and the disruption of our national narrative, my failures as a soldier and historian, et cetera, but I wasn't.

Instead, I was listening to the sound of your breath moving in and out of your chest, over and over, as if it might go on forever, and thinking: *It was worth it.*

The Keep hummed and rattled as we passed through it, like an engine sputtering to life. Doors were unbarred. Bells were rung. Serving boys and soldiers ran past, calling to one another, and fine lords and ladies crept fearfully out of hiding, rushlights trembling in their hands.

In the time it took for my sight to adjust, there was a crowd gathered, and all of them were staring up at you with slack jaws. A few of them approached, their voices merging into a low, worshipful susurrus. You shook them off, as an injured lion would shake away flies.

You gestured wearily through an arched entranceway. The cup was in your hand, glinting richly. "There," you said. "She'll be waiting."

"Then she can keep waiting. You need a surgeon"—I recalled one of Sawbridge's lectures on medieval medical instruments and rates of infection—"or a place to lie down, maybe."

You didn't seem to hear me. You staggered on like a figure in a cuckoo clock, propelled by hidden gears to tell the same story over and over.

Through the archway was a high, vaulted hall, and at the end of the hall was a throne, and on the throne was a woman.

Even across the long hall, it was impossible to mistake the queen for anything but a dying woman. Her face was veiled, but the cloth was so fine it was possible to see the fragile bones of her face beneath it, the sunken pit of her mouth when she drew breath. Her hands lay like a pair of felled doves in her lap.

Yet she held herself upright on the throne, chin high. A vast dragonscale mantle flowed over her shoulders, the same eerie, irradiant white as your hair. A heavy crown sat on her brow, pinning the veil in place. I'd seen the Crown of Dominion before, in the Royal Museum. There, displayed on a fussy velvet pillow, it had looked gaudy, almost childish, like a piece of costume jewelry.

But here, in the shadowed hall, with the pigeon's blood rubies gleaming like eyes in the torchlight, it did not look childish. It looked like a legend, a thing forged by the Saint of Smiths and won by the Red Knight, which would be worn by every queen until the rise of the republic.

There were knights gathered on either side of the throne like iron wings. It took me a long beat to recognize them as the Queen's Guard—heroes, all of them, with ballads and legends of their own. But none of my comics or adventure novels had mentioned that Bodrow the Giant had Hinterlander blood, obvious even at this distance. And that must be Sir Gladwyn, beside him, with the winged lynx on his shield—but no portrait had ever given him silky black hair, or skin the color of oiled leather. It was with relief that my eyes landed on the man at the right of the throne: his hair a perfect, pure gold, his face so handsome it might have been cast from plaster. Ancel, the Knight of Hearts, the only swordsman whose skill rivaled yours.

You didn't seem to notice any of them. Every inch of you, the whole weight of your gaze, was for the woman on the throne.

I had still doubted, until then, that you loved her. But despite all your bitter words and bad dreams, all your talk of sin and regret—you looked at her like you would set your own neck in the noose, if she held the rope. It was beyond loyalty, closer to the sort of flayed, mad devotion you find in mistreated dogs.

Yvanne, First Queen of Dominion, said, "Sir Una," and the gathering crowd fell quiet, although her voice had been thin and weak.

You pulled away from me so quickly it was almost a flinch. I watched you stride toward the throne as if reeled in on a line, heedless of your wounds, heedless of the eyes on you. The hall was wholly silent now, but for the occasional, faint drip of your blood.

The crowd, which had parted before you, closed ranks in your wake, so that I had to shoulder my way through. If anyone took offense, I didn't see it; I couldn't look away from you.

You knelt when you reached the throne, ignoring the arrow still lodged in your rib cage. Your hair was a sticky red curtain, obscuring your face.

"And so," the queen said, in that deathbed voice, "you have returned to me at last."

"Yes, my queen." You said it to the flagstones.

"And you have slain the last dragon of Dominion."

"Yes, my queen."

"And you have brought me the lost grail, which they say restores all that time takes from us."

"Yes, my queen," you said, and raised the golden cup, face lifting for the first time, gazing up at your queen with that awful, doglike love. Yvanne reached out to stroke your brow with trembling fingers, and you closed your eyes, as a child would.

She took the grail. "Wine," she said, and a serving girl brought wine. "Pour," she said, and the girl poured.

Then the First Queen of Dominion lifted her veil just enough to reveal her mouth and bent her head to sip from the lost grail.

There was no heavenly choir, no blinding light, and yet: Yvanne's spine unbowed. Her chin lifted. She stood—smoothly, easily, as a person in the prime of life—and lifted her arms to her people. In a bold and ringing voice she said, "So long I have prayed for one thing and one thing only. And now, by the grace of God and Sir Una, I am given it: *time.*"

She lifted her veil fully back from her face. The crowd gasped, but I wasn't looking at the queen. I was looking at you, still kneeling, still breathing. You had survived the end of your own story.

Perhaps now you could rest. Slip away to the woods where you were raised and bury your sword beneath the yew. For a moment I could see you laughing, unarmored, lips stained with summer berries. You were watching someone, and you loved them—God, how you loved them—

But then, from the courtyard: an animal scream. Your shoulders jerked. The queen said, quietly but with feeling, "I hate that fucking horse."

And the Knight of Hearts drew his sword.

I would have warned you, but my voice—my treacherous, useless voice—snapped and broke beneath the strain, so that when I shouted nothing emerged but a hoarse rush of air. I would have shot him, but my three bullets were spent.

You would have seen the blow coming, but he was on your fucking blind side.

You were turning your gaze back up to the queen when his blade slid neatly, almost surgically, between the plates of your armor, through the great muscle of your body and out the other side.

You did not react, except—as Ancel drew his sword back out of your body with a wet, gristling sound—with a small, polite cough. The cough sprayed blood across the flagstones, painting a delicate arch on the hem of the queen's robes.

I thought, madly, wearily: *Not again.*

Someone yelled. Panic rippled through the crowd. They surged in every direction, forming a writhing wall of sweat-sour velvet and clawing hands. I shoved through them, aware that I was yelling your name over and over, my voice too thin and weak to rise above the noise.

Through the thrash of limbs, I saw you rise, unsteadily. I saw you turn. I tripped over someone's ankle and the next thing I saw was Valiance, bare and bright. You held it with two hands, now, your body bent around the wound, teeth bared.

Ancel faced you with an odd expression on his face, a tired camaraderie, as if the two of you were starting the same shift on the factory floor. Then he drew himself up—shoulders back, hair falling in glossy, angelic waves—and lifted his blade. His lips moved, but I couldn't make out the words.

You fought, then.

The Knight of Hearts might have been made by the Savior Himself as your opposite: He was light and glancing and lovely, a golden cat that struck and slipped away. Any single movement could have been painted in oil and hung in the hall, and it would have been the portrait of knighthood. It was difficult to imagine anyone defeating him, if only because it would have ruined the painting.

But he could not win against a dead woman. Blood was sheeting down your chin, bubbling pinkly from your nose. I could hear the whistling sound of your lung as it collapsed. You did not bother to protect yourself; you simply strode through the beautiful pattern of his sword work, ignoring the wounds that opened on your jaw, your right wrist, the soft underside of your thigh.

Your fist shattered the beautiful arch of his cheekbone. Your boot bent his knee inward, the angle obscene. Valiance split his clavicle with a sound like a tongue clucking, a damp snap, and lodged in his sternum.

The Knight of Hearts looked at you with chagrin, as if you had beaten him at cards, and as if he wasn't surprised. He fell, and you followed him.

Ancel hit the stones hard, with a graceless, meaty slap. But your head never touched the ground because I had finally pushed through the crowd.

We landed together in a bloody tangle, my arms clutched around you. "No, not again, not again—" I should have comforted you, told you how well you would be remembered, how long Dominion would love you, but instead I babbled uselessly over your body, spectacles askew, ruining the dignity of your death.

But you were not dying with dignity. You were not proud or peaceful; you were gasping for air, blue-lipped, wild-eyed, convulsing in my arms. Blood was pumping unevenly from the hole in your back, overfilling my palms.

I was aware, distantly, that people were moving around us. The queen was speaking again, the crowd was calming. History was striding on without us.

I didn't care.

"Owen," you said. Your pupils were black, frenzied, as if you were running fast through dark trees. "Come back for me, you have to come back—"

I slid my hands—and oh, they were so red and so wet—around your shoulders until I cradled your face. There were tears sliding toward the fine hair of your temples, running over my thumbs. I couldn't tell if they were mine or yours.

"Come back," you said again. "*Please.*" Your voice cracked on the word.

I didn't know what to say, but my mouth formed the word without me, easy as aiming a gun. "Always," I said. "Always."

Your body slackened. The muddy, clawing panic left your eyes. You said, your voice cool and even now, "Wait for me, beneath the yew tree."

And then you died.

Your eyes stared, emptily. Your blood turned cool and tacky on my hands.

At first, I felt nothing. Just a distant, disgusted weariness, as if I was back at the front opening another shitty tin of beans. *This again.*

Then that fault line inside me, the flaw that ran through my character like a vein of coal, split open. It tore right down the middle of me, and then—

I'm sorry. I don't remember the next part very well; I went away from myself, because it hurt too badly to stay.

It was a woman's voice that called me back. Not yours, but one I knew. It said, "Enough now, you'll hurt yourself." And then, "Just let go of her, there's a good man."

There was something incorrect about the voice, but I was still not quite returned to myself and couldn't place it.

"Get the body out of his sight—there, now. That's better, isn't it?"

I blinked, and found myself crouched on the stones, my arms empty. Three of my fingernails had been ripped away, leaving nothing but pink pulp. Perhaps that's why my hands were shaking so badly; perhaps that's where all the blood had come from.

Fine white skirts brushed my knees. Gentle fingers touched my face, tilting it upward, and I was sufficiently returned to myself to feel shame, that Queen Yvanne the First would see my coward's face covered in snot and tears.

She did not look ill anymore. Her veil was pulled back over her crown, and her cheeks were flushed, her skin taut.

She smiled down at me, and for a tilted, dizzy moment I was standing again in a dark-paneled office with a white card clutched in my hand. The back of my hand throbbed sharply, in memory.

I realized then what had been wrong about the voice: It had not spoken in Middle Mothertongue.

"Well done, Corporal Mallory," said Vivian Rolfe.

9

I WASN'T SHOCKED or dismayed. I wasn't anything, really, except tired, and a little chagrined, as if I had fallen for a rather cruel joke. I wanted to leave. I wanted to fall asleep, or wake up, or run away.

But the first queen who was also the former Minister of War, a paper doll of a woman switching from one costume to the next, looked down at me and said, quietly, “On your feet, Corporal.”

I stood up.

A flock of attendants descended, cooing and fretting as they shuffled me out of the hall. I followed them placidly, holding my hands out from my sides so they did not accidentally brush against my body.

We spiraled up one staircase and then another. They deposited me in a small, barren tower room and left.

It was cold. The windows were uncovered, and the wind licked through the room like a tongue, worming beneath the collar of my coat, tasting the ruined beds of my nails. There were logs stacked in the hearth, but it did not occur to me to search for a tinderbox, or even to button my coat. I would have had to use my hands, and I didn't want to use my hands.

The light fell. The tongue of the wind grew teeth and chewed at me. Snow spat through the windows, scudding over my boots.

Footsteps sounded sometimes on the other side of the door, and I called out, but it was difficult to speak through the chattering of my teeth. Once I managed to ask, “Where is she?”

A voice answered, soothingly, “Her Majesty will speak with you soon.”

I hadn't been asking about the queen.

Eventually, though, she arrived, sweeping into the room like the sun itself, orbited by attendants. They scurried to light the fire and pull the drapes, sending me furtive, appalled looks from the corners of their eyes, as if I were embarrassing myself somehow.

I recalled that people were supposed to bow before royalty, or was it kneel? I knelt. My knees cracked like frost underfoot.

The queen looked down at me with her hands folded gracefully at her waist, one atop the other. She murmured softly and the room emptied around us.

Her posture changed as soon as we were alone, loosening at the joints. She rolled her neck to either side and sat, wide kneed, patting the mattress beside her.

"At ease, Corporal." There was such dry good humor in her voice, such natural authority, that something in me eased, instinctively. I never missed the war, but I missed the sense that someone else, someone better and braver, held the reins of my life.

I rose and perched at the very edge of the bed.

"Sorry for hustling you offstage. It's just a delicate situation down there, at the moment. Half those bastards were planning coups of their own, before the Hinterlanders beat them to it." She shook her head. "They loved Yvanne, but love isn't enough, for a queen. If there's a woman on the throne, there are ten men trying to take it from her." At my silence, she prompted, gently, "I imagine you have questions."

I did—why is the (former) Minister of War dressed up as a medieval monarch, what the hell is going on, et cetera—but I found I didn't care much about the answers. I shrugged.

"I'm sorry for your loss," Vivian said. "If it matters—I can see why you loved her."

"I didn't—that is, I admired her very—"

Vivian continued before I could perjure myself further. "I knew how it would end. I'd read the stories, too. But I really thought, up until the end, that she'd done it." There was, I thought, real regret in her voice. "And then that little shit killed her. Ancel was in league with the Hinterlanders, as you may have guessed."

I suppose I had. I hadn't wanted to think about it, but my brain must have been ticking coldly along, picking at the torn edges of the story and stitching them into something new, as if I were taking notes in the archives.

"It was Ancel who told them my champion was away, who had the wine served unwatered, who urged me to accept their envoy in the first place. I suppose he had grown tired of his part in the story, and wanted more, and didn't care what it cost." She added, fretfully, almost maternally, "He always was jealous of her."

I shrugged again. My attention kept sliding off the surface of the conversation, falling into some lightless place.

Vivian studied me, sidelong. In a gentler voice, she asked, "Would you like to see her?"

I could not speak; I nodded.

There were vaults beneath the Keep, carved deep into the bedrock, where the air was still and cool. Normally I think they kept wine and meat down there, but now the chamber was empty but for a few stinking tallow candles, a stone table—and you.

In death, you looked more like your posters and paintings than you ever had in life. Your hair had been carefully washed and combed until it fell in long white sheets over the edge of the bier. Your armor had been scrubbed and polished so brightly that I could see my own face in the curve of your pauldron, bony and bespectacled. Your face had been caked with chalk, so that all the crags and scars were smoothed away. There were clownish pink circles drawn on both your cheeks, and tiny white ulla flowers tucked all around your corpse. They had a sweet, green scent, like spring.

I wanted, quite badly, to rip the flowers away from you. To rub my thumb between your brows until I found the knotted lines beneath the chalk—except I wouldn't want to touch you with these hands.

I fumbled for a cigarette instead. I dropped the match twice before Vivian plucked the cigarette from my shaking fingers and held it to a candle flame. She took a second one for herself.

We smoked for a time in silence. The candles spat. The air turned sickly fragrant, like meat and perfume.

Vivian said, "I know none of this is easy, Mallory, but I need you to understand why we're here, why *you're* here, particularly." Her tone had a clipped efficiency I associated with military commanders, or librarians. "The first time around, we lost the war."

A pause. I waited obediently for my brain to arrange the verbs and tenses in a way that made sense. When it didn't, I said, "Pardon?"

"I know you like a good story, so listen: Once upon a time there was a shitty little backwater country whose name everyone forgot on their geography quizzes. It wasn't so much a country, really, as a border drawn around a group of strangers, united by nothing more than a tax code. They had a noble history, but they had forgotten it. They had myths and legends, but they had buried them. So when war came—as it always does—they lost it. Badly."

She put the cigarette back between her lips. Her cheeks hollowed as she inhaled.

"Now, in this shitty country, there was a woman—yes, I'm talking about myself in third person, see what monarchy does to a person—who wanted better for her people. She listened to the stories they barely told anymore, of heroes and crowns and enchanted swords and so forth, and she went digging. She was looking for a weapon; she found a book."

From the heavy drape of her skirts, Vivian produced a book bound in polished wood, the hinges like moss creeping around the spine, your sigil burnt deep: a dragon, eating its own tail.

For the first time since it had arrived on my desk, I had forgotten the book existed. I supposed some unlucky servant had been sent to retrieve it from Hen's saddlebags. I wondered how many fingers it had cost them.

Vivian was rubbing her thumb over the cover. "I don't know who first made this, or when, so don't bother asking. But it's old, and it has an old magic to it, of the kind that died out before the dragons. I opened it and cut my finger on the page. I suppose you know what happened then."

I did.

"It's quite a shock, isn't it? I was in my study, and then I was here. Well, not *here,* but several floors above us, at the bedside of a dying woman." She tapped a little shower of ash to the floor. "She was beautiful, Mallory. Even on her deathbed, Yvanne was something to behold."

I felt a weird surge of relief at the sound of the name. A part of me had begun to fear it was all some terrible pantomime, that the oldest and most vital story of Dominion was nothing but sleight of hand. But Yvanne had truly lived, and so had you. I dragged again at my Lucky Star, trying not to let my fingers touch my lips.

Vivian went on, musingly, "She thought I was an angel, at first. And then, when I explained, she decided I was something better: a second chance. A way to outlive herself."

I had begun to see, unwillingly, where this monologue was headed, but my thoughts were slow, smoke swaddled.

"She could hardly draw breath, but she presented her case efficiently. She said there was too much left undone, that Dominion would not survive her passing. She said it wasn't her the people needed, but only the idea of her, and anyway we looked enough alike that her clothes would fit me." Vivian smiled fondly. "I refused, of course. I knew my history, even if no one else did: The grail was never found. Sir Una never returned. Yvanne's dream died with her."

"That's not—ah." In the stories I knew, you slew the dragon and saved the queen. But perhaps they'd been told differently, once. Perhaps there was a version where you'd lain down beneath the yew, after all, because I'd never arrived to stop you.

You'd said it yourself: *Had I been alone . . .* And then: *As you will.*

I swayed a little, suddenly dizzy; Vivian didn't notice. "But then I thought: What if the first queen had lived? What if Dominion had a stronger foundation, a better history? What if *this* was what I had been searching for?" She gestured at herself, the heavy drape of her skirts, the yellow gleam of her crown. "In order to have a future worth fighting for, you must have a past worth remembering."

It was a good line; the heartless scholar in me tucked it quietly away for the conclusion of my next article.

"It was easier than you'd think, to take her place. I carried her body up to the tower roof—her idea—and let the birds have their way with it. By the time her attendants returned, I was wearing her gown and veil, laying where she had lain. We really do look very much alike." Vivian had taken off the crown and was turning it in her hands, cigarette crooked expertly between two fingers. In the low candlelight the gold seemed sinuous, nearly alive. "I kept thinking someone would catch me, doubt me, demand I remove the veil—but no one did." A crooked smile, which revealed the point of her canine. "It's not bad, being queen."

I blinked smoke from my eyes. "But you looked so ill. When I saw you, in the throne room—"

"You see what you expect to see." She sounded apologetic, as if she were explaining to a child that the actors in the film were just pretending. "Even now, the court is convincing themselves that they misremembered my features over the long months of my sickness, or that the miracle of the grail changed them. As if a cup of wine could cure cancer."

I hadn't known, until that moment, that there was still a stubborn cinder of hope somewhere in the banked hearth of my chest. I wet my lips twice before I spoke. "So it's not—it isn't real. The grail can't—heal anyone."

The apology in her face turned to awful, stinging sympathy. "The cup is real enough. I'm sure it's the very same grail that Galawin carried three hundred years ago. But no one can cheat death, Mallory."

I imagined a boot stamping out that last, pitiful coal, leaving nothing but bitter ash. It filled my mouth, acrid and foul, so that when I spoke it all came pouring out. "It's all a lie, then. She killed the dragon and brought you the grail for nothing. She *died* for—" I bit my own tongue until I tasted salt.

Vivian held my gaze evenly. "No. I swear to you. Without her sacrifice—without the tragedy of Una Everlasting—none of this will matter. It won't do a damn thing for Dominion."

"What the hell do you—" But then, in a rush of cold certainty, I knew. "You've done this before. Differently."

A ripple across the surface of Vivian's face, as if something dark had swum close to the surface but not broken it. "It's true. The first time I came back, I didn't bother with all the . . . pageantry."

All those hard, cold miles we rode together. The scream of the dragon as it died. Your blood filling my palms, staining them, ruining them. *Pageantry.* My vision pulsed, redly.

Vivian continued, unconcerned, "No quest, no grail, no miracles. The queen was sick. The queen got better. What could be simpler? I uninvited the Hinterlanders, foiled a few assassination attempts, and ruled well in Yvanne's stead. I made treaties and trade agreements, held the borders, wrote charters, made speeches. I thought it would be enough." That dark thing swam up in her eyes again. "But it's never enough, simply to be competent. I was overthrown in less than three years, and Dominion fell with me. When I returned to my own era, I found a Dominion that was still divided, disillusioned, *weak.* For a king to hold the throne it takes skill, lucky genetics, good timing, and hard work; for a queen, it takes a fucking miracle." She strode closer to your bier. "It takes a *story.* And every story needs a hero."

I watched, with a hot spike of jealousy, as she leaned over you and stroked the hair tenderly from your brow. She traced your jawline with one fingernail, her expression odd, almost desirous. "She must have loved Yvanne very much, don't you think? As a mother, maybe. Make sure you put that in the book. And crucify Ancel for me, would you."

"The *book*?" Anger swelled like a tumor in my stomach, fatal, full of bile. "You want to turn this, turn *her*, into a fucking campaign ad? A tragedy you can tell on the radio?"

Vivian clucked her tongue. "This from the man who led her to the gallows in the name of—what? A byline? An endowed position?" She fisted her hand in your hair and gave your head a small shake. Your body had stiffened in death, so that your neck and shoulders moved together, like the joints of a cheap puppet. "Tell me. Was it worth it?"

Oh, I deserved that: I had buckled your armor myself. I had sent you through those gates, knowing what was waiting, though I could not now remember why.

I discovered I was kneeling again, panting hard, choking with guilt and grief and cancerous fury. My cigarette had fallen from my fingers. "Send me back again," I said, and for once my wreck of a voice suited me perfectly. "Let me change it. I won't let her go alone, this time. I'll slit Ancel's throat. Just let me try again."

"You think I hold the power here, but I don't." Vivian settled you back on the bier and arranged your hair, fussily. "You and I are serving something higher than ourselves, now. Neither of us chose where that book sent us. It took me to the queen just before she died, and it took you to Una just before she failed. Do you honestly think it was *chance*? Call it fate, call it the hand of God—this is how the story goes, and this is our part in it."

A little of that old, childish hunger—to be chosen, to matter, to earn my place in a country that didn't want me—rose up in me. I closed my eyes against it.

In the dark, I heard the approach of slippered feet. Vivian spoke in a near-whisper now, poisonous, inexorable, like one of those harpies who drove men mad with prophecy. "She dies, and they forget her. I've seen it. She becomes a footnote, a piece of trivia. And she wanted so badly to be remembered."

She pressed something heavy into my hands. "This is why you're here, Mallory. Dominion is nothing without Una Everlasting, and she is nothing without you."

I opened my eyes, blinking down at the book I'd always dreamed of finding. At my hands holding it, and the blood crusting in the beds of my nails.

"I don't—I don't understand," I said. "If we forgot her, then why do I remember her? If her story was never written down, how do I already know it? And why did I have to watch her—to know her—"

A vexed expression crossed Vivian's face, familiar to me from professors who did not appreciate interruptions to their lectures. "Because time travel is very fucking complicated, Corporal." She exhaled carefully, as if counting to five. "Because you were born a thousand years after all of this happened, in the aftermath of a choice you'd already made. Because the past becomes the present which becomes the past." A small, wry smile. "Her device was no accident, I think."

I traced the design on the cover of the book, my thumb circling the dragon over and over.

Vivian knelt before me and covered my hand with hers. Her fingers were very cold. "Understand me. Her death is worth nothing. It is meaningless. It is a *waste*—unless you make it matter."

I couldn't think of anything to say.

Eventually she stood. Her cigarette butt landed beside mine, and she ground it beneath one delicate toe. Her voice echoed back to me as she left, clear and hard as a rung bell: "If you loved her at all, Owen—make them remember her."

I lingered for a time in the vault, knees stiffening on the stone. I didn't weep or yell or tear my hair, but only watched the candlelight chase over your corpse.

I imagined this was how a saint must feel after a holy vision: as if a great curtain had been pulled aside, and the secret engine of the world revealed in all its vastness and cruelty. I didn't understand most of what Vivian had told me—the story looped and doubled back in my mind, cause and effect hopelessly tangled—but I understood that you and I were a pair of gears turning together in the belly of that engine.

You had to die, and I had to watch you, and then I had to wipe your blood from my hands and make sure it had been worth it.

Did I consider refusing? Did I imagine crawling to your bier and lying down beside you among the flowers, so that a thousand years from now they would find our bones so intermingled it would be impossible to tell which were mine and which were yours, and no one would care, because no one would know our names?

Of course. But I had sworn to you that your name would be remembered, and though I was a coward and a deserter, though I had broken every trust and faith, I found I could not break yours.

I pressed my lips to your brow before I left. Your skin was the same temperature as the air, so that I felt nothing but a slight pressure against my mouth.

In the tower room I found the fire blazing and a fresh-cut pen waiting beside a pot of ink. I sat down at the desk and did not rise again until dawn.

UNA AND THE BETRAYER

We come now to the end, and I find I do not want to tell it. I would finish the story here if I could: with Sir Una kneeling before her queen, sorely wounded but still breathing, the cup held high in triumph.

Yet I cannot. For evil days will come again to Dominion, and it will be the memory of Una Everlasting that lights our way. When our sons and daughters ask how she died, we will answer: bravely, for crown and country.

And when they ask what killed her, we will answer: treachery. And then we will say the name Ancel of Ulwin, Ancel the Betrayer, because Dominion does not forget.

Sir Ancel had loved his queen, once. But Yvanne had never loved him in return, or had loved him only with the generous, mothering love a queen has for her people. For Una, this love was enough: She was content to serve her queen, to stand by her side and sometimes brush her lips across the back of her fair hand. But Ancel—proud Ancel, beautiful Ancel—wanted more. His love withered and blackened on the vine, until all that remained were the bitter seeds.

When the queen fell ill, he reveled secretly in her suffering. Some said it was he who poisoned her in the first place, driven mad with longing. It was certainly he who welcomed the Hinterlanders and laid a trap with them for Sir Una.

But his trap failed. Ancel watched in an agony of jealousy as Sir Una threw open the castle doors, bloodied but not beaten, and knelt at the queen's feet. He watched Yvanne gaze down at her champion, the knight she loved first and best, and suddenly he could bear it no longer.

He drew his sword. No one saw, not even Sir Una. The most dangerous enemy is the one we trust enough to turn our backs on.

While she looked loyally up at the queen, Sir Ancel drove his blade through her body. Who can say what he might have done next? He might have struck down the queen herself. He might have burned Cavallon to the ground and smothered the dream of Dominion in its cradle.

But Sir Una had sworn to defend her country by her life and death, and she was not dead yet.

She stood, and drew steel, and the Knight of Hearts fought the Drawn Blade of Dominion once more. The battle was just as beautiful, just as long and glorious, as it had been all those years before, when they and their country were still young and unbloodied. But this time, when Ancel's sword flew from his hand, the queen did not cry mercy. Dominion has no mercy for traitors.

After, they threw his corpse in the midden, and the Knight of Hearts became the Knight of Worms, because in the end it was only the worms that loved him.

But the battle had drawn the very last of Sir Una's strength. She fell at Yvanne's feet.

The queen knelt on the floor, humble as a peasant, and took Una's head into her lap. Gently she touched her face and wept with love for the first and best of her knights.

But Sir Una did not weep. She smiled, perfectly at peace.

And as the last of her heart's blood stained the stones of Cavallon, two words left her lips: *Erxa Dominus.*

***—Excerpted from* The Death of Una Everlasting,**
translated by Owen Mallory

At sunrise a girl came to scrape the ashes from the hearth. I had the impression there had been others in the night, fetching candles and feeding the fire, scurrying like stagehands through the shadows, but I couldn't be certain. Only one thing had mattered to me, and now it was done, and all I wanted was to fall asleep or disappear, to excuse myself from reality like a man escaping a long and awful dinner party.

Instead, I said, "Bring the queen," in a voice like the wind over dead grass. The girl startled so badly she spilled ashes down her front. She looked from my face to the book in my hand; she hurried away.

I waited. My eyes hurt. My hands hurt. My back had given up hurting and stiffened into a shape like an italicized *C.* My stomach was full of a vague, acidic dread.

It was the last line that bothered me most. I don't know why. *The Death of Una Everlasting* was full of lies and omissions; what was one more?

Perhaps it was just pride. Perhaps I wanted the world to know that in your final moments you had not thought of crown and country, but of the wild green woods you loved best—and of me. *Wait for me, beneath the yew tree.*

"Quick work, Corporal." Vivian's voice made me flinch. I handed her the book with an aching, trembling hand.

I expected her to whisk it away, but she didn't. She pulled a chair up to the hearth and settled with the book in her lap. For a long time there was silence except for the hiss of coals and the rasp of pages turning.

I stared vacantly out the window, not thinking anything at all. My missing fingernails throbbed, fiercely.

When she finished, Vivian closed the book and said, softly, "It's well done, Owen." She gazed into the fire, stroking the spine with one thumb. The expression on her face made me want to turn away, politely, as I would turn away from a woman laying flowers on a grave. "Truly. Well done."

I didn't say anything.

Eventually I heard her draw a brisk, bracing sort of breath, stand, and stride toward me. She laid the book on the desk between us, and I was struck with a sudden, visceral memory of the last time we'd faced each other across those pages. My left hand spasmed.

"I think it's just what we needed. A little overwrought in places, but people will lap it up. And Ancel, my God! I couldn't have asked for a more thorough assassination if I'd given you a grenade. I don't know why I didn't think of it before now—every story needs a villain." Her voice was light now, her face polished so smooth that all the grief had slid off the surface. She stuck her hand across the desk. "Thank you, Corporal."

I took her hand with a feeling of deepening unreality, as if I might blink and find we'd never left her office in the first place, and everything in between had been a disturbing daydream. "Is it—will it be enough? Will they—" The sentence caught on the barbed wire of my throat and went down, thrashing.

Vivian softened, just slightly. "They'll remember her. I promise."

I swallowed several times, my hand shaking badly in hers. "As will I," I said, and that, too, was a promise. The world might remember you as I wrote you, but I would remember you as you were: hard and strange and silent, your hands bloodied and your soul sick with it. I would remember the line between your brows. I would remember that you were not beautiful, not really, but that the sight of you struck me as a hammer strikes hot iron, reordering my very atoms.

"As will I," I said again, thickly.

Vivian smiled fondly down at me. Then her grip tightened without warning, crushing my hand in hers until I cried out, until the crusted beds of my missing nails burst open and bled fresh.

Both of us watched a fat drop fall from my hand and splash, lavishly, across the open book.

Vivian's smile had not faltered. She said, "Oh, Mallory. You never do."

And time unraveled again.

THE SECOND DEATH OF UNA EVERLASTING

10

SEVERAL YEARS AFTER the war, during the mid-afternoon hour I generally put aside to fantasize about setting fire to my manuscript and disappearing into the countryside to raise goats, I received a book in the post.

(I wonder sometimes: What if I'd refused it? What if I'd let it sit on my desk, unopened, or set fire to it, or thrown it out the damned window? But of course I didn't. I never did.)

I tore away the wrapping. Observed your device carved into the cover and your name on the title page. Concluded unhappily that the doctors had been right about me, after all, and the pressures of academia had proved too taxing for my delicate mind.

They hadn't wanted to discharge me, even once the war was won. My throat had healed, and the infection eased, but I'd remained unwell, prone to odd anxieties and lapses of awareness. I would touch my own cheek and discover I'd been crying without knowing it. I would wake sometimes from a bad dream to discover I was standing at the sink, washing my hands over and over.

But, as I wasn't technically dying, they sent me home with several diagnoses, a recommendation to avoid crowds and loud noises, and the Everlasting Medal of Valor.

I'd found ways to lessen the frequency of my lapses, since my return. I avoided crowds and loud noises; I stayed out of the cold and slept with the lights on. I tacked a poster of you to the back of my office door, so that I could glance up from my work and remind myself that you were a figment, a fable, a stranger who'd died nine hundred years before I was born.

But perhaps I was getting worse again, because there I was, absolutely certain that I was holding a book which did not exist.

It was doing a very good impression of existing—I could feel the weight of the wood on my palms, smell the wintry scent of the pages, like woodsmoke and frost—but my body was no longer a reliable narrator. For example: Was I standing on thin carpeting, or deep loam? Was that ink smudged on my fingers, or did it glint red in the light?

"—you quite alright, Mallory?" The tone (irritable, becoming alarmed) suggested the speaker had asked before; the voice (a solicitous drawl, of the kind they teach at boarding schools) told me who it must be.

"Sorry, Harrison, just distracted." I set the book on my desk slightly too hard, provoking a small landslide of old term papers and library notices. I made a show of gathering them up again, keeping my hands obscured just in case it wasn't ink.

There was an expectant silence, which told me Harrison had asked another question. Probably about my manuscript, because he was, as I think I've mentioned before, a bastard.

"Oh, it's shit and you know it," I said, surprising us both. Our enmity was the type that was conducted through a pantomime of friendship. "Now if you'll excuse me, I was just leaving."

"Of course, of course. Mustn't push yourself too hard—doctor's orders, I'm sure," Harrison said, demonstrating that he, at least, had not abandoned the rules of engagement.

I shoved past him, book hidden in my armload of folders and notes, scurrying past Professor Sawbridge's office and out into the sodden heat of late summer.

On the train home, I sat beside a boy—redheaded, long lashed. About the age I was when I first read your story.

I showed him the book, softening the scrape of my voice as much as I was able. He couldn't read the title, but he could describe your sign on the cover—at length, with enthusiasm. Not a hallucination, then.

I stood when the train dinged. The boy nodded to the book. "What's it called?"

It occurred to me that, if I translated and published the book in my hands, he might one day read the title himself. Perhaps he would dream then of knights and swords and glory, as I had. Perhaps those dreams would send him to war—the next one, or the one after that—and perhaps he would come back broken, bent subtly out of true. As I had.

Something swelled painfully in my chest—guilt, I thought. "*The Death of*—" I began, but your name caught like a sob in my throat.

Before I stepped off the train I scrounged a few coins—too many—from my wallet and stuffed them awkwardly into his small, scarred hands.

I didn't touch the book, that first day.

I drew the curtains and went directly to bed, still in my slacks and undershirt, as I often did. The doctors had listed *fatigue* among my many symptoms, but I didn't sleep because I was tired; I slept because I dreamed, and every dream was of you.

They were not always pleasant. I saw you weeping and bleeding, killing and dying. I saw you on your knees and I saw you on your bier, and I woke with tears on my cheeks and a tremor in my hands.

But other times I saw you laughing, head thrown back. I saw you above me, beneath me, pink and urgent, and when I woke, I would touch myself before even opening my eyes, aching for a memory that never happened.

That night I saw you white-faced, blue lipped, a ghost of yourself. You told me to wait for you, but when I woke, I couldn't recall where.

I smoked two Lucky Stars. I drank a half pot of thin, acrid coffee. Then I opened the book.

Over the following week I fell into a sort of fever, translating without pausing to stretch or smoke, eating only when I felt myself flagging.

I decided very quickly that I disliked the author. His prose was stilted and portentous in a way that reminded me of narrators at the beginnings of films. And if he had truly ridden at your side, if he had stood in the court of Cavallon as you presented the grail to Yvanne—why hadn't he saved you? I concluded he was a fellow coward and could not forgive either of us.

But even a coward couldn't ruin a story like yours: the wild girl who became a knight; the knight who won her queen a crown and kingdom; the kingdom that would have fallen had it not been for the knight's love and loyalty. I wept with pride when you slew the Hinterlanders and clenched my teeth with fury at Sir Ancel's betrayal, though any child could have told you it was coming.

Ancel was the villain on every stage, the traitor in every political speech, the part no child wanted in the school play. Professor Sawbridge claimed there was contradictory material evidence of Ancel's character—a few old tapestries and trinkets that portrayed him as a chivalrous, noble figure—but her article on the subject had been quashed by the Ministry of War.

I mailed her the relevant pages of my translation, along with a note; her replies were apparently too crude to make it past the censors.

On the sixth or seventh day I went out for cigarettes and milk.

It was hot, and the mood on the streets was strange. Half the shops had locked their doors in the middle of the day, and people were gathered in nervy, whispering clumps.

At the corner-store counter a man spat on my boots and called me a word I won't repeat; from this I concluded there must have been unrest in the Hinterlands and made a mental note not to go out after dark. I was a proud son of Dominion, but—at night, when it was angry and drunk and no one was watching—Dominion would beat its children bloody.

It was a relief to return to the stale dark of my flat, and to the book.

But the book was gone. In its place there was a crisp white card, bearing no name, but only an address.

The city was even hotter now, and oddly quiet, like a held breath. It reminded me of that final morning before the dunes: hot and silent, full of hate.

The cabbie read the address on the card twice and spent the drive casting me narrow looks in the mirror. I wondered idly if it was my service jacket or my hair, or the fact that I hadn't bathed or shaved properly in several days.

Half an hour later I stood blinking and sweating on the white marble steps of the capitol building, where a crowd had gathered. It was as if someone had picked up the city and tilted it, so that all the pedestrians slid to the center. They were all shouting.

Behind me, the driver said, venomously, "Traitors, the lot of you."

In my ears, the noise of the crowd abruptly resolved itself into chants, of the kind I used to yell from my father's shoulders before I was old enough to understand that protests were futile, shameful affairs that got your scholarships taken away.

I staggered back toward the cab. "Oh, no—I'm not with—"

"Owen? That you?"

I closed my eyes in brief but profound agony. I did not see, but physically felt, the cabbie's nasty smile as he pulled away from the curb. I inhaled and exhaled twice before I faced my father.

He was moving as quickly as he could, shoving past his fellow protesters, limping badly. There was a disarming urgency on his face, as if our last conversation had never happened and all that mattered was that he reach me.

I pushed my spectacles farther up my nose, suddenly awkward after months of righteous silence. "Hello, Da—"

"Get out, boy! Get away!" He added a violent shooing gesture.

The last time I'd seen my father, in the Queenswald tavern, he'd called me a bootlicker and a child and asked how I could sleep with the blood of my countrymen on my hands. I'd said, stupidly, "What have I ever done to my countrymen?" before I understood that he hadn't been referring to Dominion. I wasn't truly surprised—I'd looked in a mirror—but I'd never asked about my mother, and he'd never told me, and that tiny sliver of doubt had been precious to me. He hadn't even apologized for taking it away.

And now, apparently, he still had nothing to say to me.

"Oh, I'm sorry," I said, with a condescension so insufferable that Harrison would have been jealous. "Did I interrupt you mid-chant? They're good, although I don't know that *chancellor* quite rhymes with *criminal*—"

"Go *now*—she's called out the fucking cavalry—got us good and kettled—"

Only then did I realize the chanting had been replaced by cries of alarm, a rising hum of fear. An officious voice was warbling through a bullhorn. I heard the phrases *immediate dispersal* and *failure to comply,* but there was suddenly nowhere to disperse to: Men in red jackets were pouring from the alleys, circling the building.

A brief and awful quiet fell over the crowd, which I recognized from the moments just before battle breaks loose. I looked down at my hands and found one of them was reaching for the revolver tucked in my coat. I clenched it into a fist instead.

Somewhere down at the front there was a sound like a brick on meat—and then war broke out.

I'd never been much of a soldier, unless I had a gun in my hand: I stood like a stone in the wild tide of the crowd. Signs were dropped and trampled underfoot. The line of red jackets marched toward us in perfect lockstep, like fascist caricatures sprung straight out of my father's pamphlets.

I watched them come with a sense of unreality, even irony; how funny it was, that I had betrayed my country and been given a medal, and now, when I was trying to serve it, I would be arrested.

The soldiers were so close now I could smell their aftershave. I would have stood there unmoving until the cuffs closed on my wrists, if it hadn't been for the hands that shoved me backward, up the steps.

"Up you get, son, by the wall, that's it." I wouldn't have believed it was my father's voice if I hadn't smelled the liquor on his breath.

I reached the wall and turned back just in time to see him fall. Maybe his bad hip failed; maybe he was pushed. All I saw was the look in his eyes as he went down: not surprise or fear, but grim relief. As if he knew one of us would suffer, and he was glad it was him.

I lost sight of him for a moment—there were too many bodies pressing between us, a wall of sour sweat and howling mouths. When I saw my father again, he wasn't moving.

He was draped over the steps, slack-spined, like a rug dragged out for airing. There were two soldiers standing above him. My own jacket had faded over the years, but theirs were still a gory Dominion red, collars stiff with starch. One of them raised the butt of his rifle above my father's body. The wood was already stained with something dark and wet.

Would I have done something—shouted, stepped between them, thrown my body over his? I never knew, because a hand closed on my shoulder and hauled me abruptly backward through a door I hadn't even noticed.

I stumbled into a cool, windowless hallway. The door clicked shut, and the sudden silence pressed like thumbs into my ears.

There was a discreet, well-dressed sort of person standing next to me, regarding me with such professional disinterest they must have taken special courses.

"Please, my father—he's still out there—" I was breathing hard, nearly panting, and my hands were shaking badly.

The disinterested person remained disinterested. I had an awful sense that I might burst into tears or scream or press my revolver between their eyes, and receive nothing but a politely devastating *Sir?*

"He's old, and probably drunk. He didn't mean anything by—"

But they had already executed a turn so neat it might have been plotted with a protractor. "If you would follow me, sir. She's waiting."

The hallway led to a series of staircases. With each floor we climbed the carpets grew thicker and the wood paneling more expensive. By the final floor there were paintings of historical monarchs lining the walls: a series of pale, lumpen men whose names everyone got confused, interrupted by much larger portraits of Yvanne the First, Tilda the Younger, Lysabet II. They seemed to glow from their frames, their hair electric yellow, their skin so white it shone nearly blue. Dominion has always loved its queens best.

We paused before a door guarded by a pair of extremely grim soldiers, who looked at me as if they would very much like to have me cuffed, searched, and interrogated. The strap of my holster felt suddenly very tight against my chest.

I was swept into the office before I could properly panic. "Corporal Owen Mallory, ma'am," said the discreet voice. The door clicked shut.

Velvet drapes. Waxed parquet. A heavy desk, and a woman sitting behind it. "Thank you for coming, Corporal Mallory."

"Oh my God. That is—ma'am—Minister Rolfe—"

"Zero for three, I'm afraid. It's Chancellor, now. The opposition are insisting on *Madam* Chancellor, but I think we both know that's just chauvinism with table manners."

A merciful pause followed this, during which I recalled the emptied streets and furtive whispers and wished very deeply that I'd bothered to buy a paper or turn on the wireless. Eventually I said, "Yes, Chancellor," in a voice that cracked only slightly.

The Chancellor of Dominion—the single most powerful person in the nation, perhaps the whole of the modern world—gave me a fond smile. "Call me Vivian. Sit down."

I sat.

"May I assume, from your expression of owlish astonishment, that you are unaware of recent events?"

"Yes, Chancellor."

"Ah, academics." She set a slim cigarette between her lips and leaned minutely forward. I found my hand already holding a match, as if I'd been waiting for this very moment. My vision doubled as I cradled the flame, so that my hands were trailed by their own twins. I blinked hard.

Vivian exhaled dense white smoke through her nose. She consulted the fine gold watch on her wrist. "Ten hours ago, Chancellor Gladwell was assassinated by anti-colonial radicals. Five hours ago, I took emergency control of our armed forces. Two hours ago, the other ministers voted me in as acting Chancellor." Her smile tilted. "It was still close. I won them a war and averted a crisis, and they nearly gave it to the Minister of Agriculture."

She unfolded a paper and slid it across the desk. The headline read GLADWELL ASSASSINATED; NATION IN SHOCK. The rest of the page rippled like dark water in my vision. Disquieting phrases floated to the surface: *anti-colonial extremists; act of treachery; emergency measures.* Most of the other ministers had declined to speak with the press, but Vivian Rolfe had given them their pull quote: *The most dangerous enemy is the one we trust enough to turn our backs on. Be warned: We will not turn our backs a second time.*

I said, weakly, "Oh." I thought of the grim-faced guards outside her door. The sound of boots on marble, and the butt of a rifle poised above my father. "So the protesters outside, as I arrived—"

"Are being interrogated as we speak."

"But surely they weren't responsible for the attack. They're certainly, ah, disruptive, but I know they're not *assassins.* Please, Chancellor, my fath—"

"It would not," she interrupted firmly, "be a wise moment to express sympathies with any radical groups or individuals, or to disclose any familial ties with the same."

I heard the clack of my teeth as I shut my jaw. I imagined my father—a drunk and a deserter, who would not be missed by anyone save the barkeep—interrogated by a government who badly wanted someone to blame. Even if he didn't confess, they would surely raid his house, and how long would it take them to crack his little cipher of misplaced punctuation and counted letters? I'd broken it when I was ten.

A voice in my mind said: *Every story needs a villain.* The voice was not mine.

Vivian was still watching me with the detached expression of a jeweler holding a gem up to the light, looking for flaws. I clenched my jaw so hard my molars hurt.

She nodded sharply, screwing her cigarette into an ashtray and squaring her shoulders in the manner of someone who has just mounted a podium. "Our country," she said, "is at a crossroads."

Then she told me that Dominion had lost its way. That glory was within our grasp, but that we had forgotten where we came from and what we fought for and needed to be reminded.

There were pauses spaced judiciously throughout this speech, as if for applause. Into one of them I said, perhaps less politely than I should have, "You have the book, don't you."

A flash of annoyance in her face, there and gone again. Her smile was indulgent as she set the book on the desk between us. "You have served your country well, Owen Mallory." Her voice lowered to a throaty near-whisper. "Are you the man who will save it?"

I felt then that I was standing outside my own body, watching the way her words worked on me. The shine of my eyes, the bob of my throat. The pitiful urge to please, to serve; the hunger of a useless boy to be used.

She told me they had chosen me particularly for this work, and I shivered all over, like a dog. She told me they needed me, and I went willingly to heel.

I watched myself and felt nothing but disgust, that I could so easily forget my father's face as he fell. The weight of a body in my arms—not my father's, after all—the wet heat of the blood that soaked my shirt, my knees, my hands—

I blinked down at my own hands. Perfectly clean. Perfectly dry.

"—time like the present. Get in touch when you finish your translation." Vivian spoke in casual dismissal, already rummaging through her desk drawers.

I stood unsteadily, reaching for the book with hands that were not covered in blood and never had been. I said, "Yes, Chancellor," but didn't leave. I ran the pads of my fingers over the cool wood of the cover, tracing the bent spine of the dragon. I found my mouth opening without my intention or permission. "Why?"

"Ah!" Vivian held a letter opener aloft in triumph. Then she said, coolly, "Pardon me?"

There was a craven, awestruck part of me that wanted to fall to the floor in apology. I locked my knees against it. "You don't really need *The Death of Una Everlasting* to gin up support for the occupation—"

"Reconstruction."

"—because the assassination will give you all the support you need. You're the Chancellor of Dominion, now. So why . . . bother?"

Why bother to slip a significant historical discovery onto the desk of a floundering scholar? Why flatter and entrance him, so that he was half ready to ride into battle in your honor? Why lock up an old, foolish man and his foolish friends?

Vivian didn't answer immediately. She regarded me with rueful good humor, as if I'd surprised her, not unpleasantly. "Well, you'd be no good to me if you were stupid," she murmured. Then, louder, "I meant everything I've said: We *are* at a crossroads, and we *have* forgotten ourselves. This story . . ." She nodded at the book, still flat on the desk. "It's who we are, how we make sense of the world. I've seen early drafts of tomorrow's papers. One of the cartoons shows a mob of radicals, and the caption reads *Sir Ancel's Heirs.*

There's also a rather striking drawing of me with a crown—do you think they could ever have conceived of a female chancellor, had it not been for Yvanne?"

A private smile, then, as if she were sharing a joke with someone who wasn't in the room. Then she tapped her knuckles briskly on the desk. "But you're right. I don't need the book to hold the Hinterlands, or to be Chancellor."

"Then why—"

"Honestly, it doesn't matter, because you aren't going to write it for *me*. You'll do it for her." An insufferable part of me wanted to push my glasses up my nose and correct her verbiage; surely she meant *translate,* not *write.*

But she was already reaching across the desk, sliding the book away from me and opening the cover.

My heart stuttered in my chest, then resumed at twice its usual pace. "The pages are—"

"Yes, yes." She took my hand in hers and pressed my palm to one of those awful, empty pages. "Now, hold still."

I didn't scream when she stabbed the letter opener through the back of my hand. I'm not even sure I felt it. I was already falling into the bright, sharp smell of pine and snow.

"She needs you, Owen."

Then came the yew, the branches bowed with frost, your sword resting sweetly at my throat. Then the dragon and the grail, the courtyard and the queen, the bier and the book.

God, please, don't ask me to write it all down again.

It's your turn to tell it, love.

11

I WAS ALONE, before you came.

The woods of my fathers had grown wild in my absence, the old paths choked with bitterthorn, the copses untended. Their home—our home—was not a house but only the remains of one, a corpse of wattle and thatch.

Of my fathers, there was nothing left at all. They had been shriven and buried in the manner of the woods then: their flesh taken by rooks and flies, their bones dragged down into burrow and den. I didn't think either of them would mind—Father Theo always said these woods were the only heaven he would see, and Father Foy was fond of animals—but still, I couldn't bring myself to sleep inside. I didn't mind the cold, and I liked the sound of Hen's snoring; it meant I was not quite alone.

As a girl I'd met pig herders and basket weavers in these woods, charcoal burners and wolf hunters. There had even been a boy who met me sometimes beneath the yew, though it was a half-day's walk to the nearest village. For years he was my shy, gamine shadow, watching me from under lashes as long and dark as a doe's.

I wondered sometimes if I'd seen his face again, unknowing, years later: If he had been one of those who knelt in the mud of some nameless village and cried mercy, or one of those who refused, and found none. I wondered if some part of me had been hoping, childishly, that I would find him still here, waiting beneath the yew.

But this was the Queen's Wood, now—where before it had belonged to everyone and no one—and any trespassers would be branded and pilloried.

I told myself I was glad of this because there would be no one to find my remains for years and years—yet, on the day I decided to die, I donned my armor. A lingering streak of vanity, I suppose: Even now, I wanted them to remember my name.

Or perhaps I only wanted Yvanne to get word, one day, and know I had abandoned her of my own free will.

I had loved her, once, as a child loves God. After the Black Bastion, I had hated her with that ardent, blazing hate that is merely love's other cheek—but lately even the hate had burned away, and left only a weary, ashen regret.

Now, walking toward the yew for the last time in my life, I felt nothing at all. Nostalgia, perhaps, for the woods where I had run free and feral as a lynx, barefoot and berry-stained, a beast among beasts. On summer evenings I would stay out past moonrise; in the winter I would curl like a cub in Father Theo's lap, and Father Foy would sing soft, silly songs by the firelight, replacing all the animals in the songs with my name.

I don't remember that name, now.

If I were any other child—if the sword had not come so easily to my hand, if I had not known, somehow, just where to slip the blade between a man's ribs, how to part one vertebra from the next—I would have died with them that day.

It was right, that my bones would finally join theirs, twenty years too late.

I reached the yew. High as a hill and old as a dragon, with some of a dragon's secret, wild otherness. Sometimes I thought I saw a stranger's face in the bark, and sometimes I saw my own.

I drew Valiance from my hip. It shone unblemished, still as perfect as the day I pulled it from the tree.

It was only I who had aged, and cracked, and finally broken. Only I who could no longer serve my purpose.

I would be sorry to die. I would miss the simple, animal joy of being alive in the world: food and sex and sleep, the scour of wind on bare skin, the sting of sweat, the smell of dragonscale flowers in full bloom. I would miss Hen. I would miss Bodrow and Gladwyn and even Ancel. I would miss Yvanne, or at least the way she sometimes looked at me, with a pride so ferocious it burned all my doubts away.

But I could no longer be what they needed me to be. I could not end the story as I should—fêted, beloved, remembered—and so I would end it here, alone.

But then, suddenly, I was not alone anymore.

I found you on the other side of the yew. You were standing very still, as if you were waiting for me, as if we'd agreed to meet here long ago and I'd somehow forgotten.

Your back was turned. All I could see of you was the black of your curls and the bowed line of your shoulders beneath that strangely cut coat. Yet I thought, with joy but not surprise: *You came back for me.*

Then I saw the little knife in your hand, slicked red, and before either of us drew another breath I had Valiance braced at the nape of your neck.

It took you far too long to turn around. My God, Owen, even a field mouse knows when a hawk is watching it! But you only stood, quivering and panting, until Valiance skimmed the fine hairs of your neck.

You turned slowly.

Your face was long and thin and sad. I thought you might have been beautiful once—fragile things are always a little beautiful—but somewhere along the way you'd been broken badly and poorly mended. Now your skin hung like old laundry from the sharp bones of your cheeks, and your jaw was roughly stubbled.

It was the face of an ascetic or a madman—who else would wear tiny panes of glass beneath their brows, like the windows of a fairy's church?—but your eyes were black and lucid.

I waited for those eyes to fill with terror, but they didn't. (They never did.)

Instead, you looked up at me like a condemned man who had been granted his last request. Like you would climb the gallows tomorrow with a smile on your face. Your lips parted, and I saw that you were still quite beautiful after all.

For a moment I couldn't speak. When my voice returned it was roughened, as if it had traveled far over hard ground. I told you to drop the knife.

Instead, you fainted.

I caught you before your head hit the earth. It seemed a shame to damage those tiny panes of glass.

I tried to be gentle with you, but I was not made for it. My hands felt awkward, overlarge, the gauntlets catching and pinching your coat. Your head knocked against the plate of my cuirass, and your legs—great gangling things, much longer than I expected—thudded sometimes into trees and low branches.

On the threshold of my fathers' house, I hesitated. But night was falling, and a bitter wind was rising, and your body was cold in my arms. Blood dripped gently from your sinister hand and left dark holes in the frost.

I ducked below the lintel. I hadn't needed to duck, the last time I walked through this door.

I kicked the leaf litter and mouse nests from my old pallet and laid hides over you while I fixed a fire. I made myself think only of flint and tinder, rather than the flames themselves.

Your injury I tended less gently than I might have. By then I'd seen the book you carried, and the symbol carved into the cover, and knew these were the hands of a bard or a scribe: finely wrought, fragile, uncallused but for the slight dent where the quill rested. The sight of those hands sent a bitter heat through me, a kind of resentment that anything so soft, so unspoiled, should have been left in my care. I wiped the blood away and wrapped the wound as quickly as I could, then moved across the fire, away from you.

You roused a little while later. You ought to have quaked when you saw me, but you smiled instead. A lover's smile, slow and hazy, which caused my mouth to bend in answer.

I tamped it flat. "Something amuses you?"

You said, "No. My apologies." I knew as soon as you spoke that you were no bard: Your voice might have been stolen from a jackdaw, high and rough and unlovely.

Yet it was familiar to me. As was everything about you: the angle of your chin, the black of your eyes; the way you slid those glass panes back up the long arch of your nose.

I had seen you before, though I couldn't say where.

One of the geweth, then, chasing stories, or a court scribe sent by Yvanne. It wasn't enough that I return to Cavallon with a miracle; I must also bring another legend in my wake, another tale of Dominion's hero.

I had liked being a hero when I was younger. I liked the songs they sang about me; I liked falling on my enemies, fast and fey. And if sometimes those enemies seemed too young or too old—if they fought with stones and scythes more often than steel—it was surely worth it. In Dominion, there would be no more good men slaughtered in their homes, no more monsters with black hearts and bloody hands.

But then had come the Black Bastion. Afterward, I had seen myself reflected in the eyes of a young girl—a giant in ash-stained armor, black-hearted, bloody handed—and understood there would always be at least one monster left, while I lived.

I could not abide the songs, after that.

I asked how you found me. You prevaricated. I may have raised my voice.

Then, of course, you told me you'd been sent from the far future to save Dominion, and I was ashamed for berating a madman.

You talked and talked that night, and I let you; I have always liked the sound of your voice.

I left the cottage before dawn. I wore no armor, this time, because this time I intended to return. I couldn't say why, except that your face was hollowed in the way of a man who has missed too many meals, and it seemed uncivil to disappear without at least feeding you first.

When I returned, Hen was canted toward the cottage, lips peeled up in the way that meant he'd met a new person and was hoping to kill them soon. "Be easy," I told him, firmly. "He's harmless."

You said, "I'm sure," and stood blinking stupidly in the doorway, unaware that your life had been spared.

I slung my kill—a tierce of hares—over a downed log to skin and dress them. You began talking again almost immediately.

Words had never come easily to me, but you seemed to have twice the usual supply. You argued and joked, muttered and questioned, observed and wheedled. You moved constantly as you spoke, a ceaseless fidgeting, as if your skin had difficulty containing all the sentences you hadn't yet said. It was strangely mesmerizing, like the swooping and twittering of a swallow, so that I found it difficult to focus on my work.

Until you asked, with the first stirrings of doubt in your voice, "What are you doing *here*?" Then suddenly it became difficult to look up.

I wanted to make you understand. But how could I explain the things I'd done to a man who'd never had anything worse than ink on his hands? How could I tell you—you, who looked on me with the hungry awe of a child in search of a hero—what I was?

I bowed my head, instead, and did not answer. You understood then that I was not seeking the grail because I no longer wanted to find it.

You were angry with me, and a little repulsed. I listened in silence until you mentioned Yvanne.

I stood and stalked toward you, my muscles quivering with the promise of violence, my vision shifting so that I saw you not as a man but as a list of ways you could die: belly, spine, throat, skull. I wouldn't even have drawn steel. I know what they say about Valiance, and God knows it's an uncanny blade, but my body has always been my first and best weapon. It is a goshawk kept tightly tethered, a mad horse on a short lead. I didn't need a sword to kill you, or even a reason; all I needed was a little slack in the reins.

You knew it, I think. Your eyes were wholly black behind your glasses and your pulse ran quick and wild as a rabbit in the hollow of your throat—yet you stood your ground. Whole armies had fled before me, and yet you—with your delicate hands and your doe's eyes—did not move.

The sight sent a prickling, reckless heat through me. I wanted to teach you better. To shake you by the shoulders. To take your chin in my hand and cover your mouth with mine, hard enough to bruise. You would learn then, too late, to be afraid of me.

Shame saved you. I stepped away, sick with myself. "Forgive me," I said. I tried, clumsily, to explain why I had come here, and why I had stayed. I thought disgust or pity would drive you away, where fear failed.

Instead, you crouched beside me. You unfastened your collar and bared your scars to me, and for the first time I thought you might have been telling the truth when you said you were a soldier. Only war could chew a man's flesh like that, down to the bone.

There was a brazen look in your eyes as you held your collar open, as if you expected me to flinch from the sight of your scars. I didn't, and you looked nearly faint with gratitude. I wondered idly who had flinched from you before, and if you would prefer their thumbs or their ears in recompense.

You were talking again, about honor and courage and the cost of loyalty. You told me I would be a legend. You told me it was worth it, and your voice was so sweetly broken that I nearly believed you. "Please," you said, "I—we need you."

Then you took my hand, and I lost hold of the reins.

Once I had touched and been touched easily, without thought. Soldiers would clap me on the back as I passed. Servants would rub salve into my bruises. A woman would slide my hand up her skirt, where the hair turns thick and damp as fresh-mown hay, or a man would put his open mouth beneath my ear. I was good at sex, as I was good at war; mine was a body born to be used.

But I had learned to mistrust myself, after the Bastion. I didn't touch anyone, now, unless I knew they could defend themselves.

You were sitting beside me, touching my hand, and then you were beneath me, flat on your back, wrists pinned.

For the first time since you'd woken, you stopped talking. You looked up at me with the color rising fast in your face. You swallowed. Said, softly, "Let go." You did not sound as if you meant it.

I released you hastily and stood. I was not—quite—so dissolute that I would take advantage of a madman, no matter how good he felt beneath me.

"You may stay if you like," I said, and offered guest-right, as my fathers would have. "But do not touch me unawares, and do not go unarmed in my presence."

Then I drew that useless little knife of yours from my boot and knelt to fold your long, fine fingers around the hilt. It wouldn't save you, but if I ever forgot myself again, I hoped at least you would make me bleed for it.

"And tend to that," I added, touching your bandaged hand. "The blood will draw beasts."

I left you there, laid flat, flushed. It was not easy.

As I walked away, you told me God would come to me in a dream. He didn't, of course. But you did.

I did not fear God. My fathers hadn't raised me to believe in anything higher than the sky or lower than the earth, and Yvanne's efforts to teach me piety had not survived my first battle.

Yet still: I did not sleep that night, or the next.

I slept only during the daylight hours, in fistfuls of minutes, waking at the first whisper of dreaming. I was in hiding, not from God, but from the truth: that these gentle, quiet days were stolen, and could not last.

But oh, they were sweet. I liked the honest work of the hunt—harder now, with only one good eye—and the clean smell of frost. I liked to watch your face as you scribbled in your book, your eyebrows arching and furrowing like a man performing a silent play. I even liked the fire, or at least the way it glittered in the glass of your spectacles.

You knew what I was doing, of course. You were quite clever, for a madman.

Eventually you said, "Let me tend the fire tonight."

I let you take the stick from my hand, and then—forgive me, I was so tired, and you did not pull away—I let my head fall to your shoulder. You went very still, and then you tucked your jaw against the crown of my head. I let myself sleep.

When I woke, I knew where to find the last dragon.

Your voice had spoken in my dream as clear and harsh as a rook, and even in the dream I had felt a great, wistful sadness. I would have stayed with you in those woods forever if I could.

I roused you roughly. You answered my questions with your usual excess—save the last one. I asked you if this was truly my last quest.

You looked me dead in the eye and said, "Yes," though your voice cracked on the word. "This is your last quest."

And for the first time since the queen's messengers had dragged me from my cups and slung me at her feet, I allowed myself to believe it, or at least to imagine that I believed it. That I would return in triumph with the grail and my kingdom would prosper forevermore. That my queen would be healed, and in her grace and gratitude, she would release me from her service.

I could go anywhere, then—even return here. I could spend a whole spring sleeping in those little white flowers, and a whole summer drying wheat for my fathers' roof. I could still disappear, but gently, in my own time, with my name untarnished. I could go to my grave knowing that all of it—the blood and the bad dreams, the endless carnage—had been worth it, in the end.

Still, I think I would have refused—except you were watching me, and God, the way you watched me: with a pure and piercing beseechment, as if you needed me more than you had ever needed anything else.

Yvanne had looked at me like that, the first time she saw me. She had needed me, and I had spent the last two decades becoming whatever she needed: her sword and her shield; her sinner, her servant, her saint; her butcher and her best beloved.

I couldn't do it any longer, not for her. But for you—I would be a hero. One last time.

12

THE NIGHTMARES FOUND me the first night after we left the wood.

It was the smoke that did it, I think; I'd built a fire rather than listen to your teeth clack, and the wood was green and sullen. The fire had smoldered in the night, and the smoke had fallen thickly into my mouth and nose. I can tolerate the smell during the day, but at night it brings the worst kind of dreams: memories.

I woke panting, half mad, with your face hovering above mine. You were very still, your eyes dark and yielding. I stared into them until I returned to myself, piece by piece. The cold. The faltering fire.

My fist around your throat.

I unclenched my fingers, swearing, but kept my hand at your neck in warning. "I told you not to come near to me, boy," I spat, ashamed and aggrieved by the shame. "I could have killed you."

You swallowed, and I felt the movement against my palm, the slight scrape of stubble, the slickness where the scar began. "You've called out twice in your sleep already tonight." You shrugged, demonstrating an upsetting disregard for your own survival. "You haven't killed me yet."

"I still might." I pushed my thumb back into the vein of your throat, shaking you a little.

But your pulse beat evenly beneath my touch, and the corner of your mouth lifted in that wry twist. "You won't," you said, and a hot surge of something—let us call it annoyance—made it briefly impossible to speak.

I looked at you—at the single curl hanging loose over your brow, at the fine, high bones of your cheeks and the red marks your spectacles left on either side of your nose—until I felt your skin warming beneath my hand. I released you suddenly, as if burnt.

It was bad enough, the way I'd touched you earlier. You'd been seized by terror, shaking and stuttering, as some soldiers do, and I'd held you until it passed. But then the bone of your hip had felt so good against my palm that

I'd kept it there, and entertained thoughts of such astonishing lechery that I'd had to dismount and walk to clear my head.

Now you returned to your own side of the fire in silence. Eventually I offered, with ill grace, "Forgive me. I dream often of things I would rather forget. Old battles. Old wounds."

It was not untrue; sometimes I even dreamed of battles I'd never fought, or hadn't yet fought, so that when I met my enemies on the field their faces were familiar to me. (I'd confessed this to Yvanne once. She'd told me they were visions from God, and stroked my cheek softly, over and over, until I quieted.)

But it wasn't battle I'd been dreaming of, this time, or even the Bastion. It was you. Your face, looking down at me with awful, endless grief, as if you were watching the world end, and as if you'd seen it before. There had been fine flecks of blood on your spectacles.

God knew what I'd been saying in my sleep. I tightened the cloak around my shoulders. "Many soldiers suffer so."

"So I've heard," you said, very dryly, and I was chastened, remembering your shaking, and your scars.

You lay back beneath the furs with that damn book as your pillow. The sight of it soured me, a reminder that you were here with me not as a companion but as a chronicler.

I asked, nastily, "Will you write that the great Sir Una cries out in her sleep, like a babe?"

You blinked at me. "No," you answered. "I will write that she gave everything—her sight, her youth, even her sleep—for her country." You paused. "And that she is a lout and a wretch who doesn't know how to say thank you."

A long pause before I said, "Thank you." Your teeth flashed, crookedly, and I added, "Keep to your own side of the fire."

But you disobeyed me.

When I called out again—that night and on the nights that followed—you were always there, near enough to touch. You spoke to me sometimes, your voice so thin and splintered I was never sure if I heard the words or merely imagined them: *Always,* you whispered, *I swear.*

When I traveled alone, I kept to the wild edges of the country, where the wind rushed unhindered through the grass and the only people I met were as wary and lonesome as I: vagabonds and brigands, thieves and poachers, the oathless and homeless. They neither loved me nor hated me, but only watched me carefully as I passed, like pine martens watching a hawk.

But you sat on a horse like a sack of swedes with legs, and I loved Hen too well to make him suffer your bouncing over rough country. The queen's roads were smooth and fine, so we would ride straight through the heartland of Dominion, and I would bear the glares and whispers.

I would have passed through every croft as quickly as possible, but we hadn't even made it through Farnvall before you'd charmed a pretty little baker's daughter out of half her griddle cakes and directions to the nearest bathhouse.

I preferred to bathe in springs and streams—I did not care to be gawked at—but your face tipped up to mine, wistful and wind tousled, and very soon I found myself stepping into the warmish, sour water of a Farnvall tub.

It felt—good. Gooseflesh chased up my arms. The fist I made of my body unclenched, just slightly. I sighed a little, and heard you make a small, pained sound behind me.

I asked, without turning, "Did you seek a bath only for my sake? Was I so rank?"

There was a long pause, during which I recalled how carefully and ineffectively you held your body away from mine in the saddle, how far away you walked to piss. Modesty, perhaps, or distaste; the first time I'd gone to bed with Ancel he'd touched my shoulders, gingerly, and told me I was lucky he liked men, too. Maybe you preferred your women small and soft-bodied, like that pretty baker's daughter.

I tilted my head against the wooden ledge and closed my eyes, firmly. I waited for the sound of the door closing behind you, the sting of it so clear in my mind it felt prophetic, preordained.

But instead I heard clothes hitting the floorboards, a faint splash. I slitted my eyes and caught the quick bronze flash of your limbs. You hunched yourself down into the water so that only your collarbones were visible. You ought to have hidden them, too, I thought; there was a pair of hollows right where the bones met the muscle of your shoulders, where my thumbs might fit perfectly.

You began to babble, of course, eyes bouncing comically from my breasts to my hair to the ceiling and back to my breasts. "Do—do men and women not bathe separately?" you asked, hoarsely. "I thought—"

I turned around to wash and your sentence ended on a sharp gasp. I felt your eyes on my bare back like a pair of live coals, hot and hungry; I did not think you liked soft-bodied women, after all, though it shouldn't have mattered to me. I stretched, purposefully, just to hear your breath catch.

But you did not reach for me. Instead, you washed yourself with frantic urgency and fled the room. I lingered for a while in the tepid gray water and let one hand slip between my legs, thinking of your collarbones and your long limbs and your quick, helpless gasp. I hardly lasted a minute; it was not easy, riding day after day with you in my lap.

By the time I emerged, damp and sated, you'd charmed all the laundresses into telling you stories about me, and your eyes met mine firmly, without wandering.

The same thing happened in the next town, and the one after. You were forever lingering and talking, charming the fishwives and gossiping with the stone masons' sons. You had a way of lifting one shoulder and ducking your head that made you look younger than you were, though your face was canny as a crow's.

"The Duel of the Stone Keep?" you would say, blinking those black doe's lashes. "You say your cousin's husband saw it all?"

And they would tell you everything they knew about me: rumors and slander; ballads they'd never heard properly and only half recalled; tales of heroes from far away and far before my time, which had been given to me like hand-me-down clothes; even the truth, or pieces of it. As we left each village you would badger me for my own account, and I would growl and glare, but in the end, I could resist you no better than the fishwives. I told you everything about everything—save the Black Bastion. I only rubbed the scar over my right eye when you asked, hard enough to hurt, and stared into the fire.

Later you would sit cross-legged by the coals, your hand moving back and forth across the book in your lap, and I would watch you with a jealous ache in my breast. I could tell from the look on your face you were half in love with her, this woman you were inventing. Sometimes when you looked at me your eyes would go hazed and warm, and I would wonder which of us you saw.

I did not take advantage of your confusion—I made my bed across the fire from yours and did not touch you except when I pulled you into the saddle each morning, or when you were taken by one of your shaking spells. Then I would wrap my arms around you and press your spine to my chest, holding fast until your breathing eased and your body slackened against mine.

I did not always let you go as quickly as I should have, afterward. Forgive me—a monster so rarely feels wanted.

We made it farther than I thought we would—to the very edge of the Northern Fallows—before you saw the truth of me.

We were passing through a gathering of hovels too mean even to be called a village, watched by thin, hateful faces. The last time I'd come north, I'd brought an army with me and left nothing behind but pyres and widows, and they had not forgotten it.

I didn't blame them. Theirs was a just and pure hatred, which burned straight through the shine of my armor and found the butcher inside it. It was nearly a relief, to be cursed and spat at, after days of your hazy, stupid looks.

We would have passed through that place without incident, if only they'd contented themselves with insults and thrown swedes.

But then that fucking fool grabbed me by the hair.

I want you to understand that I intended to kill him. That I would have, or already had. In that moment I could feel the memory of his death in my nerves: the gristling *crack* of his vertebrae separating; the wet, hollow sound of his head—no, it was his hand, only his hand—striking the mud—

I blinked. My fist was around my hilt, but the sword was not fully drawn. The villager was not dead, or even injured.

You were standing between us, looking up at me through the fine glass windows of your spectacles. Your fingers were tight around my wrist, as if you thought you could stop me. As if it had never crossed your mind that I might cut you down to reach him.

I was tempted, for a long red moment, to teach you better.

Then I felt something trickle warmly down my wrist, slipping between my knuckles, and I realized you were holding me hard enough that your wound had opened afresh.

I sheathed the sword with a quick metal slither and let go the hilt. I have never liked to see you bleed.

I looked up at the villager, now swaying with a strange, sick expression on his face, as if he knew how close his own death had flown by him and was not wholly relieved that it had missed. Half his hair had been burned away, replaced by slick pink scars.

"Run," I told him. He ran, and the others—his daughters or sisters, grim-faced Hyll women who could not afford the indulgence of dying—ran after him.

At the edge of the village, I knelt and linked my fingers together. After a pause, you stepped carefully in my cupped hands and let me lift you into the saddle. I walked; you surely would not want to touch me, now that you knew what I was.

We traveled miles before we made camp that night, and for once you had nothing to say. The silence was less welcome than I thought it would be, after so many days of your jackdaw chattering.

Eventually you said, "Bastard."

I shrugged. I had been called worse that day.

Then you said, "He shouldn't have touched you. None of them should have dared," and I realized that it was not me you were angry with. I watched a faint flush spread across the bridge of your nose as you paced and ranted. You gestured violently with your injured hand; a fleck of blood hissed in the fire.

"Come here," I said, and you did.

The wound was deep, still oozing, the bandages crusted yellow and pink. I ought to have tended to it sooner, but I had been reluctant to hold your hands in mine. It was sinful enough, the way I looked at them.

I spoke while I worked, to distract myself. I tried to make you understand why they hated and feared me, and why they were wise to do so. You argued with me until I snapped—no one else provokes me so—"They *should* fear me, boy. And so should you."

I tied the bandage and drew away, but you caught my hand in yours. "Well," you said, your voice high and hoarse, "I don't."

And this time when you looked at me, I knew you did not see the Una Everlasting you wrote about in your book, pure and true and beautiful. You saw me as I was: old and scarred and brutal, a monster that would turn on even a harmless villager.

You had seen the truth of me and yet you were still here, holding my hand, and I couldn't seem to pull away.

I watched, feeling both drunk and dead sober, as you turned my hand gently in yours. You studied it for a moment, running your thumb over the hard planes of callus, then bent and touched your lips to my open palm.

A shudder wracked me from skull to spine, and I knew suddenly how it would be with you. Most of my lovers—camp followers and soldiers, crofters' daughters and the idle sons of lords—had wanted only to take or be taken; they came to me warily or arrogantly, shy or swaggering, as to a caged wolf. But you—oh, you would come to me on your knees, as to a king, and you would give and give.

I was leaning down to you, ready to let you, when you looked up from my palm. You met my eyes—and flinched.

So you were afraid, after all. Good.

I pulled my hand sharply from yours and strode back to my side of the fire. I felt your eyes follow me, huge and dark. "Una, I—"

"Don't." The word was harshly hewn. "Don't." For once, you listened; for once, I wished you hadn't.

I fell asleep with my fist clenched around my own palm, as if your kiss were a dove or a lark, which would fly from me unless I held it fast.

Six days later, we climbed Cloven Hill.

You were nervy and overtalkative the whole way up. You dressed me well for battle—had you squired in your youth? had armor changed so little, in nine hundred years?—but your hands shook badly. I should have told you how many dragons I had slain, but I didn't; it was such a novelty, to be fussed over.

It had been one of Yvanne's very first decrees as queen, that Dominion should be rid of dragons. They were the devil's own creatures, she said, for they lived on and on, undying, and only the Savior was deathless.

There was some opposition at first, especially in the north, where dragons were still carved into lintels and coffin lids for luck. And there were the stories told by the Roving Folk: that a drop of dragon's blood could heal any wound or cure any sickness; that a dragon's heart might be planted, like a seed, and the tree that grew from it would live forever.

But these, the queen said, were pagan superstitions, which would not be tolerated in Dominion. If a person was pious and loyal, he would report all dragon sightings to the crown, and after the dragon was slain, he would burn the carcass three times over, and scatter the ashes.

I had slain nearly a score myself, and hated it every time.

I told you Hen's name before I left—he didn't usually kill people who called him by name—and you said, woundedly, "You're leaving me here?"

"Yes," I said.

Dragons were not especially vicious; in truth, I was not even sure they breathed fire. They reminded me more than anything of the whales I'd once seen in the coves of the Slant Sea: vast and placid, wholly alien.

But there was always the chance this dragon had learned to be vicious, over the years, and the idea of you standing nearby, unarmored—no.

Yet you argued with me! You told me I couldn't slay a dragon alone; I assured you that I could. You begged to come with me, although you looked nearly sick with fright as you said it.

I had never minded a coward at my side, in battle. A coward is reliable, in his way—every choice he makes is the one that serves him best. I didn't know what to do with whatever you were.

In the end I said, roughly, "Stay," and you did, though I felt your eyes follow me until I disappeared into the low, shifting clouds.

It was not hard to track, even in the mist. There were scuff marks on the stones where a long, scaled belly had scraped past, and furrows in the earth where something huge had launched itself into the sky.

The marks led me to a cleft in the mountaintop too shallow to be called a cave, too huge to be the den of a bear or lynx. The air around the entrance smelt of snake piss.

I did not slow down or even soften my steps; dragons were torpid in winter, like adders. I simply ducked beneath the granite ledge and there it was, coiled over itself like an enormous serpent. The last dragon in all of Dominion.

It was not the largest I'd seen—there had been one on the Isle of the Penitent with wings like a pair of ship's sails—but I thought it might be the oldest. Its claws were cracked, the points worn and blunted. Its scales, once lightning-white, had turned translucent, like old teeth. That must be how it had survived the dragon hunts—in the mist, it would disappear entirely.

It was sleeping. I was so close now that its breath fogged my armor, obscuring its own reflection. I drew my sword with only the meanest whisper of steel on leather, wrapped both hands around the hilt—and hesitated.

I had sworn once, in the ashes of the Black Bastion, with the warm fluids of my own eye oozing down my cheek, that I would never again take a life in the queen's name. But it was not for the queen that I lifted my blade, nor even for Dominion. It was for you, with your rook's voice and your doe's eyes and your long, fine fingers. You, who waited down the mountainside, a pen held in shaking hands, for the hero of his story to return.

The dragon opened one eye. Its iris was a shadeless gold, like all dragons' eyes, like mine. My reflection was distorted on its surface, so that all I could see was my own gauntleted hands.

I aimed carefully—there was no need to hurry—and drove my sword deep into its pupil.

There was a turgid pop as the sword broke the jellied surface of the eye, then the gristle of tendons snapping and the long slide into the soft tissue of the brain. A great shudder moved down its body. Its limbs and tail thrashed, and something whipped hotly across my brow.

It screamed. They always scream, at the end: a long, unearthly wailing that goes on and on. It was a sound that brought men to tears, or to their knees. Once I had seen a grown soldier drop his spear and shield and walk west. He had not returned.

I stood and listened with my head bowed, letting the sound burrow deep, letting it hurt, because when it was done there would be no more dragons in Dominion.

Quiet fell. I slid my blade from the eye and wiped it clean against the scales. Then I shoved at the cooling meat of its body, heaving the coils aside, boots slipping in clear ichor and strange-smelling blood. It took days and days to burn a dragon properly, but Yvanne insisted.

I'd never found any gold or treasure in a dragon's den—I had always suspected those tales were invented, to spur the hunt—but there, wedged in the very back of the den, was a small, fine casket. And inside the casket, there was a cup.

What an absurd, gaudy thing, to hold the hope of a nation. And yet this was the reason you had come back, the reason Yvanne would live and Dominion would prosper.

I wanted, suddenly and violently, to cast it off the mountaintop and let it rust at the bottom of some nameless ravine, forgotten.

Then I heard you crashing through the trees, breathing hard. Why can you never do as you're told?

You smashed into me before I could catch you. When you staggered back, I saw your eyes were white-rimmed, your cheeks bloodless.

"Una! Are you alright?"

"Of course." Had you really thought I wouldn't be?

I waited for you to ask after the cup or the dragon, but you didn't. You frowned and licked your thumb. Your fingers splayed carefully over my cheek while you rubbed at my forehead. It stung.

Eventually I said, "The grail. I have the grail."

I held up the cup and you cast it a brief, baffled glance, as if you'd forgotten all about it. "Oh," you said. "Good. Now sit down and let me see to that cut."

Later, as we rode away from Cloven Hill, you asked me if the dragon had been terrible, and I told you it had been beautiful.

"But we ride now to the Keep," I said. "And there the story ends."

There was a pause before you answered, and in that pause I understood—with piercing certainty, as if it were something I had known before and only forgotten—that I would never again see the woods where I was born, or the home of my fathers.

Whatever waited for me at Cavallon, I would not survive it. And you knew it.

But you said, in a voice like an early grave, "Yes. The story ends there."

It is a strange thing, to ride toward your own death, like running toward a cliff with both eyes open.

I daydreamed sometimes about turning away. I could have thrown you from the horse and run back to the woods. I could have tossed the grail into the fire. I could have simply slipped away in the night, and let you carry the grail alone.

But these fantasies seemed to belong to someone else, someone braver and freer than myself. I could only trot obediently onward, like a hog to slaughter.

I would have preferred silence—even condemned men are allowed a vigil—but you chattered and nagged and pestered and wheedled at me. I answered, if only to pass the miles. You asked about my armor, so light and strong, and I told you the queen kept the maker a secret, so that no one else might have anything so fine. You asked about Hen, and I told you about the mean red colt who had crippled the farrier and maimed several grooms, but who had eaten from my palm like a lamb, as if we were old friends.

You asked about Yvanne, and I told you the truth: that she was brave and brilliant. Not a woman so much as a force that swept over the world.

You said, relieved, "You do love her."

I didn't answer; it would only upset you.

At night I watched your face across the fire, searching for malice or subterfuge, and found only an awful, writhing guilt, which you tried and failed to hide. But if you did not hate me, how could you lead me hooded and fettered to my death?

I suppose you'd answered that question on the first day I spoke with you: *I swear to you, it was worth it,* you had said. At the time I'd thought you meant the dragon's death, or all the deaths that came before it—but really, you'd meant mine.

I would die so that Yvanne would live, and in this way even my death would serve Dominion. The thought settled over me like snow, beautiful and numbing. I had always wanted to be of use.

The weather turned as we left the hills. The wind blew hard and mercilessly, so that our fires snapped and leapt in the night, the heat whipped away before it reached us.

I listened to your teeth chattering with something glittering and sharp in my throat, like chewed glass. It galled me that you would cross to my side of the fire only for my sake, after a bad dream, but never your own.

Perhaps it was only ever pity that brought you to me. Perhaps you were simply a coward, as you had so often told me. Or perhaps you didn't want to share a bed with the woman you were leading to the gallows.

A sudden surge of bitterness made me say, one night, "It'll get colder, before dawn. Might even snow."

You were shaking so hard by then you could barely nod.

"We fought the Hyllmen in winter, did you know? At night we stripped bare and slept pressed together." It had only been Ancel and his squire, and they were occupied more with each other than me, but I wanted to make you blush.

You did. You looked at me and then away, your expression churning, almost panicked. You opened your mouth to make some excuse or apology, and I found I did not want to hear it. I wrapped my cloak tight around myself and lay down with my back turned to you.

I knew you would not come to me. Knew I would spend the night alone, hating both of us in turns—myself for inviting you, and you for refusing me.

But later—much later, when the fire was black and the stars were a clear, cruel white—I felt my cloak tugged away from my stiffened fingers.

I had your throat in my hand again before I even opened my eyes.

You gave a faint, polite cough, and I released you, swearing. "What are you *doing,* boy?"

"Trying not to lose any limbs to frostbite," you answered, somewhat testily. Then, less certainly, "I thought you'd offered to—but if you've changed your mind, you need o-only say so."

I was planning to refuse you, until you stuttered over that word. Your lips must have been numb with cold.

I held up the edge of my cloak. You burrowed awkwardly beneath it, in a chivalrous and absurd effort to sleep next to me without actually touching me. I let you wriggle unhappily for a moment before I hauled you firmly against my chest. I held you, my arm across your ribs, my cheek in your curls, until the shivering eased.

Then—you were very warm and pliant in my arms but not asleep, and my lips were very near the bare back of your neck. I exhaled, and a different kind of shiver passed through you, and I knew in a sudden flush of heat that I could have you, if I wanted.

And, Savior save me, I wanted. Not with tenderness, but with a kind of fury: When you dressed for my funeral, I wanted you to see the marks I'd left on your skin; when you raised your cup in my name, I wanted the wine to sting your lips.

And why not? Why should I go to my grave without a little pleasure, first? Why should you send me there without a little suffering, after?

I opened my mouth, just a little, as if by accident, so that my lip brushed the hollow behind your ear. You went very still, but I felt your pulse rise against my mouth.

I opened my palm across your stomach and your muscles tensed under my hand. Your coat had ridden up, so that two of my fingers found skin, and the coarse line of hair beneath your navel. You shuddered again, more violently, and I knew if I slid my hand farther down, I would find you hard and eager.

We lay like that, balanced together on the precipice: my breath ragged against your pulse, the tips of my breasts tight against your back. If you had said a single word—if you had moved at all—

But you didn't.

You might have wanted me, but not as much as you wanted my corpse. You had come to me tonight because you were cold, and I was of use to you. Let me be used, then.

I set my jaw and did not move until dawn.

In the morning I rode toward Cavallon, praying that you were right, and that it was worth it.

13

YOU TOLD ME I should wear my armor, before I rode through the gates of Cavallon, because "It's how it looks in all the paintings." You must have thought I was a fool.

Perhaps I was, because I did not run, or demand to know what waited for me beyond those gates, but only stood like a doll and let you dress me for battle.

You took your time with it, fastening and refastening each tie and buckle, adjusting what did not need to be adjusted. There was such grief in your face when you looked at me, as if you were already picking flowers for my grave, that I felt a certain degree of insult. You might have seen my future, but you hadn't yet seen me go to war.

You combed my hair. I shouldn't have let you—the expression you wore when you touched my hair was indecent, nearly heretical—but my time was running short, and I was greedy.

As you worked you asked, innocently, why I had worn armor on the day I met you.

I told you the truth, which made your lips go very thin and white. I found your anger a little tedious—why were you allowed to decide the time and place of my death, and not me?—but then you unbuttoned your collar again. You told me that you, too, were a deserter, and my heart broke for the boy you had been.

You picked up my hand and set it on the slick, gnarled surface of your scars. "When you ride through those gates, bearing the grail you won from the last dragon—it will all be wiped clean. Our doubts, our mistakes, will be forgotten."

Oh, how badly I wanted to believe you. "And what of our sins?"

"Those, too," you said, and I could see how badly you wanted to believe yourself.

An urge rose in me, ugly and irresistible, to wrest that belief away from you. "You don't know the whole of it. You don't know what I've done."

You didn't want to know. I could tell by the bob of your throat under my palm, the tacky sheen of sweat. You were clinging by the barest tips of your fingers to your idea of me—to Una the hero, Una the good and golden—and you knew whatever I had to say would sully her beyond saving.

But you said, in your gallows-bird voice, "Tell it to me," so I did.

"The Black Bastion was not always black. Did you know that? The walls were pure limestone, white as gulls." It had been winter when we reached the Bastion, after a long autumn spent chewing our way across the Fallows, and some of the men had mistaken the walls for the snowy cap of a mountain.

"We laid siege. Dull work, but we had all the grain and cattle the Hyllmen had left behind them as they fled. It was only a matter of time. Another fortnight, another month, and they would have opened the gates themselves, I swear they would—"

It was only when I felt your thumb rubbing soothingly over my knuckles that I realized I'd made a fist against your collar. I opened my hand, pressing the palm flat against the hot glass of your scar. "But Yvanne was impatient. She said a swift victory would serve Dominion best. I said there were too many innocents behind those walls, and she said if they were innocent, they would have no need of walls. I said it would cost us too many men, and she said *No, it won't.* And she was right." I felt my mouth wracking itself into an awful smile. "Fire is fast."

I should've stopped there—I could tell by your sudden stillness that you knew what I'd done next—but I couldn't. I wondered if this was how confession felt, like bad humors leaving a wound. "I don't know how long she'd been planning it. She had these silver casks of golden oil, so foul smelling they made your eyes run. We wrapped hemp and linen around our arrows and painted them with that oil, and they burned like nothing I've seen before or since." The flames had been an uncanny blue, shining coldly in the wets of our eyes.

"The only soldier we lost was a boy who spilled a cask down his front. I killed him before his screaming could give us away. And there were those few—those brave few, like you"—a slight hitch in your breathing, there—"who threw down their weapons. They were dead before their bows hit the ground. Fire is fast, but Ancel is faster."

The wind rose around us, tangling my hair before my face so that I looked at you through a shroud of white. "You wanted the tale of my greatest victory? Take it, then. Drink it down. I stood on a hill in the dark and watched a castle burn. I put wax in the ears of my men, so the sound of it would not torment them. I drank a cup of wine and cast it up again, but quietly, so the queen wouldn't hear." My throat had grown thorns, and the words came out ragged. "By dawn, we had won the Crusade, and the walls of the Bastion were not white any longer."

The wind blew harder, whipping hair across my cheeks. You tucked it carefully back behind my ear, one knuckle grazing lightly across my scarred brow. "And this?" you asked, softly. "If there was no battle, then—"

"After. A girl, hiding in the ruins." I'd gone half mad by then, or half sane. It was the smell that had undone me—not the battlefield reek of offal and spoiled flesh, but the disquieting, homey smell of charred wood and cooked meat. "She came for me with nothing but a piece of sharp stone in one hand, and I . . . let her." I had knelt in the street so she could better reach my throat. It should have been easy; Yvanne had never let me wear a helm or gorget. "But Ancel was with me. He cut her down before she could get more than my eye."

I had thanked him later, after I'd stopped swearing and weeping, and he'd said, lightly, *I could hardly let a peasant best the knight who bested me. Think of my reputation.* But his smile had been thin, and he had not liked to leave me alone for a long time after.

A little silence fell between us, broken by the dry click of your throat as you swallowed. "Th-there are always casualties, in war." The words had an echoing quality, as if you were quoting someone else. "But, for Dominion, it's worth—"

"The queen stitched the wound herself." My voice was a blade scraping from a scabbard. "She spoke as she worked. She told me—everything I wanted to hear. How proud she was. How well she loved me." Colder now, and sharper, a flash of naked steel: "How glad she was that it would be spring when we returned to Cavallon, so there would be fresh flower petals for the court to strew before us." Now, the killing blow: "And I knew then why she'd been so impatient for the Bastion to fall. So there would be flowers for our victory march."

I had looked up into the queen's face—the face I had loved since the day she found me in the woods—and felt the tipping of a scale in my chest. The next morning I went to the smith's tent and shattered my sword on his anvil.

Your voice, nearly frantic now: "It doesn't matter. I won't *let* it matter.

Una, please—don't cry—" I hadn't known I was crying, but I could feel my shoulders heaving, my spine rounding. It was only your hands holding me upright. Your palm found the nape of my neck, fingers cupping the curve of my skull. "In a thousand years, they will sing your name in the streets. They will raise their children on stories of brave Sir Una Everlasting, the Red Knight, who fought for crown and country. You may not have lived as a hero, but I swear: You will die as one. Just—" Your voice split. "Just do this last thing."

It had the cadence of a myth or a prayer, mesmerizing in its simplicity. Die, and be redeemed. Die, and be remembered. Die, and live forever. My destiny, and the last request of my queen.

I looked up into your face, made fractal by tears but still so familiar, too familiar. I knew those glasses, perched lopsidedly on the arch of your nose. The fine angle of your jaw, scruffed now with the beginning of a beard. The wide black pools of your eyes, full of guilt and want.

I could deny my destiny, and even my queen. I could never deny you.

I closed my eyes. "As you will." You made a small, strange sound, as if the words wounded you in some way, but your hand left my nape.

I did not look at you as I swung into the saddle and rode toward the gates. You walked beside me, unspeaking, even when Hen nipped you affectionately on the arm.

The shadow of the wall came over us. This was where you ought to fall back and send me on alone—I was always alone, at the end—but you didn't. You clutched at my stirrup instead, breath heaving in and out of your lungs. Another of your fits, I thought, and wished keenly that I could hold you one last time.

But you said, wonderingly, in a voice that did not shake at all, "I can't. I can't do it." And then, "*Fuck.*"

Your head tilted up, and I knew that face. It was the face of someone whose scale had tipped, who was about to break every oath and bond. "You have to run, now. There are twelve Hinterlander traitors waiting for you. They've taken Cavallon." You wet your lips. "If you ride through those gates, you die. Your story, Una—it's a tragedy."

I think you kept talking—you so rarely stopped—but I wasn't listening. A heady warmth was spreading through my limbs, settling in my stomach, like strong wine. You were trading away everything you cared about—your book, your future, your country's future—for my sake. Because you wanted *me,* more than you wanted the legend I would leave behind.

My fathers had loved me like that, just for being alive. Later, Yvanne had taught me that love was a thing received in trade, for the purpose I served. My survival did not serve your purposes at all—and yet there you stood, begging me to run.

I could not help it. I bent low over the bow of my saddle, took your face in my hands, and covered your mouth with mine.

The first kiss is like the first blow in a fight—a test, an invitation, a wordless question. But it seemed to me we already knew all the answers.

I already knew the way your lips would part for me, instantly, without hesitation, and the way your breath would catch. I knew how it would feel to kiss you in hunger or in comfort, sweetly or sorrowfully, early in the morning or long after moonrise, quietly, so we wouldn't wake the—

I pulled away, panting a little. I had to.

I loved you by then, or would soon, or always had. It was inevitable, foretold: When I look up, I will see the sky; when I fight, I will win; when I meet Owen Mallory, I will love him.

And you must have loved me, too, at least a little—but it wasn't me that you needed. It was Una the Everlasting, the Drawn Blade of Dominion, the hero, the saint, the story. For you, I would become her, just once more.

I unbent your fingers carefully from the reins.

"Una, did you hear me? There are *a dozen men* waiting for you. It's a trap."

I shifted my weight in the saddle and Hen took two high, prancing steps. He was old, but not so old that he had forgotten what it meant when I rode in full armor.

"What are you doing?"

Hen tossed his head as he broke into an eager trot. I was eager, too—how sweet it was to die, knowing someone wanted you to live.

"They have *archers*—God damn it."

Do not ask me to recount the battle. Every battle is the same, anyway: There is a beginning, and there is an end, and between them there's nothing but butchery.

There were arrows flying down from the ramparts, then there were three strange *booms*, and then there were no more arrows. There were enemies, then there was blood, and then there were no more enemies. There was screaming, then there was begging, and then there was quiet.

In the quiet I stood, breathing hard, returning reluctantly to my body.

I felt very little during battle beyond a vague, muscular satisfaction at my own skill, but coming back always hurt like the devil. That was when I felt, all at once, the arrows that had not missed, the bruises that bloomed beneath my armor. That was when I saw the bodies around me, their faces frozen in pain or terror or childish confusion, and remembered what I was and always had been.

I looked for Hen before I looked for you. Forgive me—I had learned over the years not to look for people, after battle, because they were not always there. But Hen was. Ancel liked to say that Hen would live forever because Heaven didn't want him, and Hell didn't want him back. Everyone always laughed no matter how many times they'd heard it before.

Hen was bleeding now, and favoring his foreleg, but still standing. He was nosing at a body huddled against the well. The body was wearing a red jacket.

He whuffed at you, impatiently, and you lifted your head. You saw me, and the relief in your face was so obvious, so unguarded, that I looked away.

You rested your head against Hen's jaw, and he nuzzled your hair. You said something to him too soft to hear but—I swear—there were tears in your eyes. I knew you loved him, despite all your complaining.

I lurched across the courtyard toward you, wading through carnage. I reached my hand down to you before it occurred to me that you might not want to touch me—my hair was clotted to my armor, and I smelled like a slaughterhouse. But you took my hand and kept it even after I'd pulled you to your feet.

Your spectacles were spattered with gore. Your skin had the patchy, greenish cast of bad fruit, and you were scowling up at me with perfect, angelic fury. "I told you to run, woman!"

I shrugged, and you made a frustrated gesture with that strange silver-and-black relic you carried. I recalled the odd booming sounds, and the archers falling from the ramparts. It seemed you were not so fragile as I had feared; the thought warmed me strangely.

You were still upset. "You knew. You *knew* what was waiting for you, but you didn't run. Why?"

I shrugged again. "I just . . . could not." I found it easier to answer if I looked away from your accusing, red-flecked gaze. "It was the whole reason you were sent here in the first place. You wanted a grand story, a fitting end to your book. And I wanted . . . to be what you wanted." Was that not how you loved someone? By hammering your body into whatever shape they liked best, and handing yourself to them like a hilt?

Apparently it was not, for you whipped your glasses from your face and began to scrub them roughly against your coat. Your hands were shaking so badly that I took them away and cleaned them for you.

As I settled the lenses back over your eyes, you said, tiredly, "To charge into battle, against terrible odds—to know the odds, and charge anyway—there is a word for someone like that, and it is not 'grand.'"

"Hero?" I suggested, not entirely in jest.

"Dead," you answered, and your voice wobbled a little on the word.

I took your hands carefully in mine. They trembled like a pair of caged doves. "Owen," I said, "I am not dead."

You exhaled harshly, only half soothed. "You aren't dead *yet*. It's the Betrayer who kills you in most versions, although some of the older iterations have you shot full of arrows." You cast an edgy, shadowed look up at the ramparts. "Let's get inside."

I tended to Hen first, which you didn't like, and then I might have stumbled a little, which you liked even less. You swore and fussed and hauled my arm across your shoulders. I grunted a little as the arrowheads shifted in my flesh.

It was slow going. Perhaps I'd lost more blood than I'd thought. I was dizzy and sluggish, and my vision kept doubling or tripling, so that I saw the same courtyard repeated over and over with minor variations. The corpses arranged differently. The sun higher or lower. I leaned too heavily on you, but you bore it well. You even spoke to me, softly coaxing, as if I were a lover, or a mule.

We passed into the shadow of the Keep. Through the great doors. Through the gawping, chittering court. I tilted my head toward the throne room. "There. She'll be waiting."

Yvanne was always wherever she would look the most holy and beautiful, as if she weren't a woman but only a series of staged portraits. And yet I could feel my heart hitting the back of my ribs as we approached, my breath catching in my throat.

There was the throne. There was the veiled woman in the dragonscale mantle, and there was the crown I had set on her brow with my own hands, when I was still young enough to believe she deserved it.

And there was that weary, hateful hunger rising in me again, as predictably as the sun. I had stopped loving her a long time ago, but I had never stopped wanting her love.

You hissed something in my ear. I didn't hear it. You asked again, urgently, "Where's Ancel?"

"Why?" I couldn't help the slight sullenness in my tone; it had never seemed fair, that I won every battle and Ancel won every heart. "You know his hair isn't even naturally yellow. He dyes it."

You looked at me blankly. Blinked twice. "Of course, you don't know. It's him. Ancel is the Betrayer."

"No, he isn't." The answer came easily, with certainty.

"Remind me which of us has seen the future?"

But it wasn't a matter of knowing the future. It was a matter of knowing Ancel of Ulwin. Ancel had been my brother, my comrade, my rival—even my lover, sometimes. After the Crusade he had been the only man I thought could stop me, or at least slow me down, if I tried to kill him. He had listened to my reasoning in silence, shaken his head, and said, "Oh, Una, you flatter me." He had not visited my chambers again.

I did not like him very much, but I loved him, and I knew him. He was spiteful and vain and viciously jealous; he was charming and brave and he would pluck his own eyes from his face before he betrayed Yvanne.

I opened my mouth to explain, but another voice called out—a thin, plangent voice that closed like fingers around my jaw and turned my head back to the throne. "Sir Una," said the queen, and the crowd parted like skin beneath the knife.

I flinched upright, away from you. Yvanne had never liked me to look weak.

You pressed the grail into my palm and whispered, "Take care."

I had a wild urge to turn away, to take your hand and flee, but a sense of inevitability had fallen over the scene, as if every step and breath had already been decided.

I walked to Yvanne without looking back.

There was a gap at her right hand, where Sir Ancel should have stood. He was never far from Yvanne's side, especially when I was away—for her protection, he said, but then he would let his collar fall open so that I could see the marks she left on his throat.

Yet still: I did not believe you. I knelt before the throne and bowed my head.

"And so, you have returned to me at last."

"Yes, my queen."

"And you have slain the last dragon of Dominion."

"Yes, my queen."

"And you have brought me the lost grail, which they say restores all that time takes from us."

"Yes, my queen," I said again, and lifted the grail between us. I heard the court inhale all together, like a many-headed animal. They had heard enough ballads to know when they were witnessing one.

Yvanne stroked my face once, gently, and I closed my eyes against a rush of shame and devotion.

I heard her call softly for wine. Then scurrying steps, the glottal splash of wine into wood. A single, delicate swallow, then silence.

The queen of Dominion stood and addressed her court. "So long I have prayed for one thing and one thing only," she said, and her voice was not the frail, cancerous whisper I recalled. "And now, by the grace of God and Sir Una, I am given it: *time.*"

I opened my eyes just as Yvanne pulled back her veil. The last time I'd seen her face it had been fatless and gray, the skin stretched like cobwebs between the sharp bones of her skull. Her hair had been so thin I could see the blue veins of her scalp, and her eyes had been a pair of candles at the bottom of a well.

But the face beneath the veil was smooth and young, her eyes blazing once more with vital purpose. She smiled down at me, and all the years between us seemed to slough away. I was a girl again, lost and desperate, struck dumb by the sight of her.

From outside came the high, wild scream of a horse. The queen's beautiful face creased in irritation. She hissed something in a language I didn't understand. The horse screamed again, and this time I recognized it as the warning Hen gave in battle, when enemies were approaching unseen. I heard the mad *crack* of hooves against the Keep door—and then sudden, sickening silence.

Oh, Hen.

Only then, too late, did I look away from the queen.

He came at my blind side—no fool, was Ancel—and by the time I turned my head he had already cut through the crowd and thrown back his hood. There was his dyed golden hair, there was his proud and perfect face, there was his blade falling through the air. I watched its descent with a strange, detached lassitude, almost like boredom. It would land above my collar, right where my neck met my shoulder.

But then—*you* were there, between us. You took the blow awkwardly across the middle, your body bowing around it. Ancel flinched. You staggered.

I was on my feet before you hit the floor. Ancel met my eyes. He smiled, and it was not his glittering court smile, nor even the caustic snarl he wore in private. It was sad and tired, and strangely gentle.

"Sorry, love." The tiniest lift of his shoulders. "Make it quick."

I would like to say I hesitated, before I killed the only brother I ever had, but I didn't. Valiance was drawn and the blow was struck before either of us took another breath. His head smacked heavily on the stones, still wearing that weary, sorry smile.

Then I was crouched at your side, rolling you onto your back, and you were—not dead, after all.

You were speaking, a near-whisper that was difficult to hear over the desperate rush of blood in my ears. "It's alright, I'm alright, it's really quite shallow—I think he pulled the blow, to be honest—"

"You . . ." I paused to swallow something; I decided it was fury. "You *bastard*—what were you thinking? Why would you—"

I stopped speaking then, because there was a knife in my left lung.

The blade had entered my back between the fourth and fifth ribs, right below the wing of my shoulder. A second knife entered closer to my spine, angled upward, and I found myself admiring the precision of it. Someone, at least, knew where to find the heart. Ancel had chosen his fellow traitors well.

"Una? What's—"

I coughed. Blood splattered across the glass panes of your spectacles. I wanted to apologize, but I couldn't seem to draw enough air, and there was something wrong with my vision. I closed my eyes, briefly.

When I opened them, our positions had reversed, so that I was lying across your lap and your face was hovering above mine, full of grief. Feet were running around us. The queen was wailing, "The crown! The grail! They've taken them!"

You were saying my name, over and over, and you were crying. You always cried, at the end.

I babbled and writhed, trapped inside a body that no longer obeyed me. "Come back for me, you have to come back—please—"

"Always," you answered, and I knew suddenly that it was true, and that you had said it many times before. I remembered, and in remembering came a great peace.

I was dying, but I had died before, and would die again. We had told this story so many times, you and I, and we would tell it so many more, and it would always end here, like this: with my blood on your hands and your tears on my face.

Call it God or fate, bad luck or good—all I knew is that I would see you again, and it was enough.

I lifted my arm, feeling the muscles of my back rip like poorly sewn seams. I touched your face, knuckles scraping the stubble of your jaw, thumb resting on the bow of your lips.

"Wait for me," I told you, with the very last of my breath, "beneath the yew tree."

You went entirely still. You met my eyes, and I knew by the sudden weight of years in your gaze that you, too, had remembered, at least a little.

That time, I died smiling.

You'll have to tell the rest of it.

14

THIS TIME, WHEN you died in my arms, I did not go mad. This time, when they pulled your corpse from my lap, I let them take you.

I hadn't remembered everything—it was like remembering someone else's dream, or a play you'd heard described but never seen yourself—but I had remembered enough to know this was not truly the end, but only the turning of a great wheel. I knew one day I would stand again beneath the yew, and one day you would find me there.

They led me up to that high, cold room. I went placidly. I sat without speaking while the blood clotted and congealed, itchily, on my chest. The cut truly wasn't deep; the bruise around it, already blackening, would take longer to heal. Odd, that a traitor would hesitate to kill a bystander.

Had I been hurt, the last time? No—I'd been too slow, and Ancel's sword had run you through. He had been alone, before, but this time there had been a shadowy swarm of cloaks and daggers. My memories were hazy and out-of-focus, but I felt the truth of them in my skin, as if my body remembered what my brain could not.

Eventually the queen arrived. I did not bow or kneel. I only said, evenly, "I'd like to see her."

She—who was the queen, who was Vivian Rolfe—opened her mouth, then closed it. She nodded once.

I let her lead me down into the catacombs, though my feet knew the way. The air grew stale and greasy, the scent so familiar that I hardly flinched when I saw you laid out on your bier. I remembered the ulla flowers gathered around your corpse, the perfect white fall of your hair, the mesmeric gold light of the candles. In another life, Vivian Rolfe might have made a very fine photographer, or perhaps a stage director.

My hands were steady as I lit a cigarette. I did not offer one to Vivian.

Eventually she said, "I know none of this is easy, Mallory, but I need you to understand why we're here, why *you're* here, particularly."

This was the opening line of what proved to be a long and fairly compelling speech. She spoke of fate and God, of Dominion and Una Everlasting, of a woman who had broken time itself to serve her country. There were little pauses after certain lines, as if she anticipated questions or objections, but I said nothing at all.

"In order to have a future worth fighting for," she said, "you must have a past worth remembering."

A more significant pause followed, and I realized this was her closing argument. I took a long drag from the cigarette and asked, "How many times?"

"Pardon?"

"How many times has this happened before? How many times has she died?" My calmness was a porcelain shell over my skin, encasing me. I might have been asking if she had any plans for the holiday weekend.

Vivian's expression underwent several rapid changes, the muscles of her face twitching too quickly to seem quite sane. She settled on a look of mild chagrin, as if she'd been caught in an accounting error. "Do you know, I've lost track," she said, and I punched her as hard as I could, full in the face.

The knuckle of my index finger split. Vivian fell back against the stone wall and slid down it, landing cross-legged on the floor. She rolled her jaw several times, said "shit," and spat a sticky stream of blood to the floor. Something wet and white shone in the blood: the point of a canine.

She tongued the blood from her teeth, thoughtfully. "Answer me this, Mallory—does it matter? No, no, *think*"—she held up both hands, palm out—"I've told you what this story means, how much depends on it. Does it truly matter how many times it takes to get it right?" Her lips were swelling fast, so that the edges of the words were slightly slurred.

I was looking down at my own hand, pinching the skin of the knuckle back together, experimentally. "I don't understand why you would need to repeat it at all—ah." I shook my head. "You're not repeating it, are you? You're altering it, changing the story to suit. That's why I remember—different versions of events."

There had been a time when I had kissed your hand and a time when I hadn't; a time when I shivered alone all night, tormented by your absence, and a time I had slept beside you, tormented by your presence. A time when I had felt your mouth on mine, a second's stolen joy, and a time when I had only dreamed it. The two of us were like a pair of merlins circling overhead, or two dancers in a line; with each pass, we drew a little nearer.

Unless we were actually paper kites on a string, flying only where we were led. Had she somehow manufactured each look we exchanged, each passing touch? "No," I said, a little too loudly. "I don't see how you could have—you weren't even there. You can't control every tiny choice, every variation—"

"No," Vivian said comfortably, "but I can control everything that counts. The details don't concern me."

I felt selfish relief that, at least those little details—which didn't count, which didn't matter at all in the course of history—still belonged to us. "I see. So all the conflicting historical narratives are actually leftovers, relics of each iteration. I bet Ancel really was a hero, once. God, Professor Sawbridge had it right."

Vivian pulled a face. "Remind me to have that woman arrested."

"But why make him into a traitor?"

"Because you got too soft, and she got too damn good." Vivian, still sitting, nodded at your body. Her expression was proud and a little exasperated, like a mother despairing of her precocious child. "She started making it past the Hinterlanders—twelve seasoned soldiers, and she barely broke a sweat. I even gave them archers, but by then you'd decided you loved her more than you loved your country. It's a shame you're such a crack shot, but I suppose anyone will pick up a few tricks if they're sent to war enough times. Even you."

This last sentence gave me a severe and instantaneous headache. If I had been to war more than once, then when did this story start? How far back did the circle go? I felt like a man holding a snarl of thread, unable to find either the beginning or the end of it.

Vivian continued, casually, "I had a devil of a time getting Ancel to do it. I told him I loved Una best. I petted and kissed her and made him watch. I told him Una was the traitor, planning to kill me—he laughed in my face. In the end I told him the truth: that Una must die, so that Dominion would live. He argued, he raged, he drank—but he did it. Ironic, isn't it? That my most loyal knight would make the best traitor? But!" She sniffed. "Ancel the Betrayer has proved much more useful than Ancel the Good."

I didn't see how Sir Ancel's character could affect the political ambitions of a woman born nine hundred years after his death, but then I remembered the cartoon in the paper with the radicals labeled *Sir Ancel's Heirs.* My father's body slumped over the capitol steps. *Every story needs a villain,* I thought, and we had all heard this story before.

After a moment I asked, dispassionately, "Did you have the Chancellor killed, or did you do it yourself?"

Vivian *tsk*ed, then winced and touched her lip with her tongue. "Don't be unsubtle, Mallory—on any given day, *plenty* of people want to kill the Chancellor. The chain of causation is really such a delicate thing. You change a few tiny details—a custodian has a date and forgets to lock a door, a guard has a stomachache and leaves his post three minutes early—and you change the entire flow of history. Give me a lonely secretary and a laxative and I can move the world, to coin a phrase."

I remembered, patchily, the speech she'd given me the last time around. *Do you honestly think it was* chance*?* she'd asked, and it wasn't. It was always and only her. Which meant—"There was never a woman named Yvanne, then." How had I swallowed that story? "You didn't conveniently replace her on her deathbed. You *are* her."

Vivian blinked. "I knew the body-double thing was a little much." She got to her feet, laboriously, and went to your bier. One hand toyed with your hair, idly possessive. "Very well. Yes. I came back much, much earlier in the tale. In the middle of nowhere, in the dead of winter. I was taken captive—I do not recommend traveling alone as a young woman in this or any other era—and Una rescued me." Her fingers were combing through your hair now, tracing the shell of your ear. "I saw her potential at once. Even that first time, I could tell she was something special. And I knew I could make her something extraordinary."

Anger rippled somewhere beneath my porcelain shell. You weren't *made.* You simply *were,* a giant who strode through the world scarred and shining, strewing legends in her wake.

But: "I invented a lineage for myself. Gave myself a name, a title, a birthright—oh, don't give me that look, how do you think any king gets his crown?—and made her my champion. She was very good, but I made her better. Each time I sent her back, she was a little faster, a little stronger. Her blows were more precise, her deflections more perfect. The body remembers, you see, even when the mind forgets. The first time Ancel challenged her in the name of the False King, I had to send her back through the book in *pieces.* By the tenth time, she could disarm Ancel in forty seconds."

I pictured it: you as a young woman, untried, desperate to prove yourself, falling in your very first duel. But you were not buried and mourned. You were dragged back to the beginning, sent out to die and die again. You were not a girl, but iron in the furnace, and Vivian was the hammer that fell over and over. She had not made you, but forged you, and whet you in your own blood.

I asked, thickly, "Why?"

"There is no Dominion without Una Everlasting."

"No, I meant—why does she have to die?"

"Ah, a much better question." Vivian looked genuinely pleased—a clockmaker, finally asked how clocks work. "I tried it other ways, of course, but the tragedy is absolutely critical. If there's something lost, there's something to restore. If there's sacrifice, there's something worth sacrificing for. There are only two kinds of stories worth telling: the ones that send children to sleep, and the ones that send men to war. I needed the second kind." She added, less grandly, "And it keeps us exceptional, she and I. Alive, Una would be an inspiration to every schoolgirl and housewife. Dead, she's a warning."

But I wasn't really listening. I was feeling my way back along the story of my own life, lingering on the little twists and flourishes that had altered the course of it: the storybook that found its way into the barkeep's basket when I was nine, the poster that sent me to war when I was twenty-three, the strange luck that kept me alive on the battlefield, that killed Colonel Drayton just before he killed me.

If my throat hadn't been cut, perhaps you would have heard my warning before Ancel struck; if your eye hadn't been gouged out, perhaps you would have seen him coming.

The work of fate, I'd thought, or maybe even God. But there was no God in Dominion; there was only Vivian Rolfe, telling a story.

And she wasn't finished. She was telling it again, tweaking the ending. I said, slowly, "You had the grail and the crown stolen, this time. Why?"

"Because of the prophecy, of course."

"What prophecy?"

"The one you'll put in the book. Something like, 'When the cup and crown return, so, too, will the rightwise queen of Dominion.' Or perhaps it ought to rhyme—I defer to your judgment."

A little silence fell. I could see, reluctantly, how it would go: Chancellor Gladwell assassinated, Vivian sworn in on a wave of patriotic verve, the crown and grail discovered, the prophecy fulfilled—the monarchy reinstated. Vivian would win the Last Crusade as she had won the first one:

wearing a crown. There was a madness to it, a labyrinthine complexity that suggested a somewhat warped mind, but I thought it would likely succeed. Dominion has always loved its queens best.

And so all of this—my life and your death, and the lives and deaths of every soldier in every crusade—was to put the same woman on the same throne, twice.

I flicked my Lucky Star to the floor and ground it out beneath my boot. Then I said to Vivian Rolfe what I should have said to her the last time, and the time before that: "Go to hell."

"Probably," Vivian answered, unoffended, "but may I ask why?"

"Because it isn't worth it. None of this is worth it."

She was still stroking your hair. "A whole nation—a safe nation, a peaceful, proud nation—is not worth the life and death of one woman? Are you quite sure of your math, Corporal?"

I wasn't. I'd been a soldier. I'd gone to war—more than once, apparently—and the whole calculus of war depends on the belief that the nation is more valuable than any one life or death. But I looked at you laid out on your bier, your face stern and harsh even beneath the powder and pink rouge, and found I no longer believed it.

Perhaps this is what happened to my father. Perhaps he went to war and met a Hinterlander girl—my mother—and lost his faith, or found a new one. Perhaps he and I were the same and hating him had been like spitting in a mirror over and over.

I said, again, mulishly, "It's not worth it."

An impatient *tsk* of her tongue. "You are not the only one in this room who loves her, Mallory."

I looked very deliberately at the place where Vivian's hand still rested on your head. Her fingers had curled into claws, knotting in your hair. "I disagree."

Vivian's mouth twisted, the swelling stretching her lips ghoulishly. "If it weren't for me, she would have died in those woods, alone and forgotten. I'm the reason you even know her name, boy."

The porcelain shattered. "You're the reason she's *dead*!" Why had I stopped hitting her, once I'd started?

"Nothing that lives lasts forever," she said, softly. "But her name—that will never die, I swear." Vivian's face was ardent, full of conviction. She fumbled something from her skirts and thrust it toward me: an ancient book, bound in wood. "If you loved her at all, Owen—"

"Don't—"

"You would make them remember her."

I stood breathing hard, staring at the book. I could not imagine, in that moment, ever touching it again. "I won't do it." My voice was so low it caught, like the belly of a truck scraping over gravel.

The urgency went out of her face. It was replaced by the same chilly, pragmatic expression she'd worn just before she plunged the knife into my hand. "You will, actually."

"Like hell I—"

"Because it's the only way you'll get another chance to save her." Vivian gave a little shrug which suggested she was sorry for my troubles, but that her hands were tied. Then she called two names in Middle Mothertongue and tucked the book back inside her skirts.

I lunged for her, but before my fingers found her throat, there were guardsmen pouring through the door, prying me away. A boot slammed into the back of my leg with a sound like an oyster popping. My knees hit the floor.

Vivian straightened the crumpled collar of her gown. She said, "I'll give you a little time to reflect, I think," and swept out.

I struggled—not toward the door, but toward the bier, fighting with a mindless, animal desperation—until one of the men cracked my head, quite hard, against the stone wall. I kept struggling, but my limbs grew weak and disobedient, and one of my eyes refused to focus.

They dragged me up flight after flight of stairs, and I knew by the sudden chill that we were back in that miserable tower room. This time they tore the curtains from the windows and the blankets from the bed. They stripped my service jacket from my limbs and left me shivering in my torn, blood-stained shirtsleeves.

They locked the door behind them. This, I thought distantly, must be why I had never liked locked doors, or the cold; the body remembers.

When they returned, three days later, the bottoms of my feet and the tops of my ears had turned the mottled black of old fruit, and there were blisters in the creases of my fingers. They asked me questions, but my tongue was too swollen to speak.

They went away again. A little while later the queen arrived.

Vivian studied me dispassionately. I closed one eye so that her features came into focus and saw her shake her head. "I told them no head wounds, but these peasants have no respect for the frontal lobe."

She bade a serving girl to fetch bread and water and light the fire. I stared at the flames in an agony of longing, knowing how badly the heat would hurt and desiring it anyway. It was birchwood, and the flames were the same driven white as your hair.

The serving girl set a stack of vellum and a fresh-cut pen at my elbow, along with my battered spectacles. I slid them carefully over my nose and saw Vivian's smile splintered and multiplied by the cracked lenses.

She turned away. Over her shoulder, she said, "Make sure you work that prophecy in."

I did what I was told. I always did, in the end.

It was harder, this time. My blisters kept bursting and oozing, and my head hurt badly. At least two pages were blotched by tears, which ran down my face in a continual seep, like a spring from a mountainside.

But I finished your story, as I had before, and would again. I changed only the final few paragraphs. Ancel betrays you, and while the two of you duel—I could not bring myself to cheat future generations of a good fight scene—his wicked accomplices make off with the crown and grail. It struck me as a clumsy addition, inserted without foreshadowing or gravity, but perhaps Ancel's treachery once felt similarly abrupt. Perhaps there's no story we won't swallow, so long as we've heard it before.

I crammed the prophecy into the last lines:

> **But the queen cared not for her stolen treasure. She knelt on the floor, humble as a peasant, and took Una's head into her lap. Gently she touched her face and wept with love for the first and best of her knights.**
>
> **But Sir Una did not weep. She spoke, and though her voice was weak, it rang out so that every corner of the court heard the words and remembered them after. She said, "Whoso finds the crown and cup once more is rightwise queen born of all Dominion."**
>
> **And as the last of her heart's blood stained the stones of Cavallon, she smiled up at the queen, for she knew one day, in Dominion's darkest hour, the cup and crown would return.**
>
> **Two words left her lips before she died: *Erxa Dominus.***

I stared for a long time at those two final words, the last, tiny lie in a whole book of them. Then I flipped back through the pages and added twenty-six grammatically incorrect punctuation marks, spaced very deliberately throughout the text. It didn't take me long; I learned this trick when I was ten.

I slept for a little time after that, and dreamed of ███, the girl I used to visit beneath the yew, who never existed. It's summer in the dream, when the shadows are deep blue, and the shafts of sun are so bright they seem almost solid, like poured gold. ███ is sprawled like a great cat beneath one of these, her face tipped up to the light. Her hair is so bright it's difficult to look at her, but I do.

I have always liked to look at you.

When I woke, Vivian was standing over the desk with *The Death of Una Everlasting* in her hands. My new pages had been sewn hastily into the back, the edges sticking out from the binding like wagging tongues.

Vivian was smiling down at the book, shaking her head in admiration. "I know I've said it before, but truly: Well done, Owen. I choked up at the end, and I love what you did with the prophecy. There are perhaps more grammatical errors than I'm used to seeing from you"—they were not errors—"but I think we can chalk that up to frostbite and a mild concussion."

She set the book on the desk, and beside the book she set a slim silver knife. "Thought you might like to do the honors yourself, this time."

I picked up the knife, turning it clumsily in my crusted, numbed hands. It was small, but sharp; I might have slit her throat quite neatly, if my fingers could've closed properly around the hilt, if my feet could've borne my weight, if both my eyes could focus properly. I wondered if this, too, had been accounted for, arranged just so.

I asked, "Why do I forget? When I go back."

I expected obfuscation or reprimand, but she answered promptly, "Because you're going back to your native lifespan."

I considered this. I didn't think it would've made sense even without the concussion. "Pardon?"

"There's only ever one of you, in the course of time. You cannot travel back and have tea with your younger self—if I sent you to your childhood, you would be a child again, and know only what you knew in that moment. You cannot remember what hasn't happened to you yet."

I considered this, too. Then I said, "But I do, or at least I've begun to. How?"

"How do birds know where to migrate?" A dismissive flick of her chin. "Sheer repetition, I imagine."

I slid the tip of the knife into the barely healed wound in the center of my left palm. The pain was familiar to me, almost intimate, as if my flesh recalled every time this blade had cut me before. *The body remembers,* she'd said.

But if the body remembered pain, it surely remembered pleasure, too. Perhaps your lips remembered mine, and my hands recalled the shape of yours; perhaps each time you touched me it left a subtle mark, so that my skin had become a map drawn in invisible ink, which might lead me back to you.

Perhaps those little details mattered more than Vivian thought.

I dug the knife in deeper, making it hurt, thinking of the red *X* on a child's treasure map.

As I laid my hand on the book, I met Vivian's eyes. "Next time, I'll remember more. Next time, I'll save her."

She nodded. "I agree," she answered, as the world fell away. "That's why there won't be a next time."

15

SEVERAL YEARS AFTER the war, during the mid-afternoon hour I generally put aside to fantasize about setting fire to my manuscript and disappearing into the countryside to raise goats, I received a book in the post.

I was aware, as I unwrapped it, that I ought to be filled with awe or terror, or at least the simple thrill of discovery. But all I felt was an odd ache in my chest, and a sudden, sharp pain in my left hand. I flexed it twice, but the ache remained.

I tucked the book under my arm and left my office immediately. I knocked hard into Harrison as I rounded the corner, not even pausing to apologize.

I was halfway home before it occurred to me that I might be suffering from another of my delusions. As a boy they'd been dismissed as flights of fancy—I would wake screaming that my feet had turned black or come home full of stories about a girl I met in the grove—but they worsened during the war. For the week after the battle at the dunes I'd refused to speak or swallow, to the bafflement of every field nurse and doctor. They'd had to tie socks over my hands so that I wouldn't claw my own throat bloody, searching for a wound that wasn't there.

In the end they'd decided I had suffered some mysterious head injury—I'd been found crouched over Colonel Drayton's corpse—and sent me home with prescriptions that didn't work and a medal I didn't deserve.

There was a boy seated beside me on the train. He had very long, reddish lashes.

I found myself opening the book, asking in my smooth and edgeless voice, "Can you read this?"

He couldn't, of course, but he liked your device on the front. He expounded on this subject for a while, and I listened with that strange panic rising in my throat. I felt wildly, inexplicably fond of him: I liked the high pitch of his voice, which he tried and failed to lower; I liked the stubby shape of his fingers; I liked his mismatched front teeth—one full-size, one still a baby tooth.

I forced myself to stand at my stop. The boy nodded at the book. "What's it called?"

I pictured him reading it one day. Pictured him enlisting, shipping out, fighting, killing, dying, another hero of Dominion.

Something swelled painfully in my chest—fury, I thought. I didn't answer him, but fumbled for my wallet and shoved the entire thing into his small, scarred hands.

It took me three days to translate the first page.

I don't know why. Perhaps I was ill—my head hurt badly whenever I read more than a few sentences, and I couldn't keep warm, though the air in my flat was hot and sour as boiled milk. The pain in my left hand had settled into a dull ache between the bones of my middle and ring fingers, which persisted no matter how I wrapped or bound it. The bandaging provoked another one of my little delusions—I could feel the ghosts of other hands around mine, the rasp of calluses that didn't exist—so I threw it away.

I was plagued, too, by a strange, listless futility. I would find myself crawling back into bed before the sun had set, or chain-smoking at my desk, watching the clock as if I were waiting for something.

On the sixth day I cabled Professor Sawbridge. She never wrote me back. I wish to God I'd wondered why, or made inquiries, or gone looking for her—but I didn't.

On the seventh day I went out for cigarettes and milk. A man spat on my boots and I smashed the milk bottle across his face. It occurred to me, as I watched him sputter bloodily at my feet, that I was hugely, incandescently angry, and had been since the moment I unwrapped the book, since before that, since always.

I returned to my flat at a near run. I burst back through the door, breath whistling in my chest, filled with a wild urge to rip the pages from the spine—but the book was gone.

In its place there was a crisp white card, bearing no name, but only an address.

I held the card and thought, grimly: *Finally.*

The streets surrounding the capitol were empty, oppressively quiet. The white marble steps were littered with odd trash: trampled pamphlets, snapped poster boards, a single shoe. Near the top there was a pool of something reddish and gelid, which I stepped carefully around. I thought, for no reason, of my father.

An unmemorable, polished sort of person was waiting for me at a side door. I followed them through a series of unmemorable, polished hallways, until we reached an office with four guards posted at the door.

The woman inside—handsome, ageless, with metal-yellow hair and very blue eyes—greeted me warmly. "Thank you for coming, Corporal Mallory."

"Vivian?" I said, as if the Minister of War was the mother of an old school friend. Her smile didn't waver, but she blinked once, and I went dizzy with shame. "That is, ma'am—Minister Rolfe—"

"Vivian is fine. Sit down."

I sat.

"Our country," she said, "is at a crossroads." Then she talked for a while about the war and the nation and the glory that was within our grasp. I had the sense that it had once been a very good speech, but that it had been delivered too many times, and gone stale.

I found myself watching Vivian's mouth. Every so often her lips would move in a way that allowed me to see her left canine, which was badly chipped, the tip jagged, the bone gone grayish and dead. I stared at it until my knuckles began to throb, fiercely.

I became aware that she had stopped talking some time ago. I jerked my eyes back to hers and found her watching me with the tolerance of a teacher for a bright but wayward pupil. "Why don't we cut right to it," she said, gently, and drew a square wooden object from her desk. The book landed between us with a hollow wooden *thock,* and my pulse leapt urgently in my throat. Whatever I had been waiting for was very near now.

Vivian tapped the cover. "A discovery like this is too important to leave to the ivory tower types. Sir Una belongs to the people. To that end, we intend to commission a translation, to be published in the spring by Satford & Gills. We arranged for you to receive the book as a sort of audition, which you passed."

I blinked, stupidly.

"*The Death of Una Everlasting,*" she said, in a voice like a radio announcer, "translated by Owen Mallory, by order of the Chancellor of Dominion. How does that sound?"

It sounded like the sort of fevered daydream an undergraduate would invent to get himself through his exams, involving a level of wealth and prestige that simply did not exist for medieval historians. A small, slimy part of me went slack-jawed with ambition; the rest of me watched coldly, from a great height. "What an honor," I said, because I was supposed to. "And Chancellor Gladwell—"

"Was murdered by radicals twelve hours ago. You are speaking now with Chancellor Rolfe, but let's not get bogged down in the details."

I waited for shock to arrive; it never did. I said, faintly, "I see."

The Chancellor of Dominion crossed her arms on the desk and leaned toward me. Her expression became almost comically severe, like the queen of hearts in a deck of cards. "You have served your country well, Owen Mallory." Even her voice changed, the accent turning oddly archaic. "Are you the man who will save it?"

This was the moment, I thought, for a show of emotion. I made myself swallow, as if overcome. I nodded.

Vivian's face relaxed again. There was something unsettling about the way her expressions shifted, a fractional delay. "Excellent! Let's go ahead then—no time like the present, is there?" She clapped her hands twice, very loudly. The door opened, and the unmemorable person said, "Chancellor?"

Vivian issued a series of instructions, but I barely heard them. I was reaching for the book, sliding it across the desktop. My left hand was hurting so badly now it was difficult to make my fingers close around the cover.

I opened the book. For the first time since it had arrived in the post—for perhaps the first time in my life—I experienced true surprise. "The pages," I said. "The pages are—" I swallowed, this time in genuine and wholly inexplicable distress. "Not blank."

Vivian gave me a quizzical smile. "Well, I should certainly hope not! Did you think I gave you a fake?"

I swayed a little. I could smell the clean, wild scent of frost, the green bite of pine.

Behind me, the door opened again, this time admitting a pair of men who both looked like they knew the difference between stocks and bonds. "Ah, Mr. Satford, Mr. Gills. Make yourselves comfortable. This is Corporal Mallory, the young man we discussed."

The men introduced themselves and expressed their extreme joy to be working with me on a project of such national import. They produced glossy leather folios and began to turn the pages, describing the terms of their offer in a language that seemed to bear very little resemblance to modern Mothertongue. What, I wondered, was an *advance against royalties*? My hand was screaming now, the pain traveling in hot waves from my wrist to my jaw.

Vivian cut in sometimes with questions and clarifications. The men nodded and made tiny amendments to their papers. I sat in dazed silence, thinking, over and over, for no logical reason: *This isn't how it goes.*

But apparently it was. Someone handed me a pen. I signed my name twice and shook three hands. Mr. Satford assured me that a check would be delivered by special courier the following morning. Then everyone stood, so I stood, too.

I reached for the book, but Vivian pinned it to the desk with one finger. "Property of the state, I'm afraid. We'll get you an office here, and a couple of assistants."

I nodded because I didn't know what else to do. Turning away from the book felt like missing a step on the stairs, a sick swoop.

Vivian gave me a bracing slap on the shoulder at the door. Her eyes flicked to my forehead, slicked with sweat, and she shook her head, fondly. "Poor thing. You must be absolutely stifling in that coat. You'd think you were expecting snow."

Everyone laughed, and so I laughed, too.

I finished the translation well before winter.

It wasn't hard. The Chancellor gave me a very nice office in the capitol building, two security guards, and crisp, glossy photographs of each page of *The Death of Una Everlasting.* (The original text was packed carefully away; the college archivist would have approved.)

I was also provided with a pair of painfully deferential graduate students who insisted on addressing me as Professor Mallory. When I corrected them—I was only a lecturer—they said, instantly and simultaneously, "Yes, Professor Mallory."

One of them, an anxious young woman named something like Daphne or Shelly, scrambled to explain. "It's just, that's what the Chancellor called you. And Professor Sawbridge talked about you so much when we took her Material Cultures of Middle Dominion course. She said you were—"

"A feckless sycophant?"

"—worth ten of us."

I was shocked to feel a sudden surge of affection; I hadn't felt much of anything since I walked out of Vivian's office. "Oh."

The other one, a rowing-clubbish boy named Georgie or Frankie, said, glumly, "And twenty of me."

I sent Professor Sawbridge another telegram that evening but received no reply. The term had started the previous week, but her office on campus remained locked, and her usual courses had been assigned to harassed-looking junior faculty.

I made an effort to be nicer to the graduate students after that. Partly because anyone who had survived Material Cultures of Middle Dominion deserved reparations, and partly because I needed them rather badly. Their Middle Mothertongue was quite poor—why did everyone struggle so much with strong and weak noun classes—but I kept forgetting to eat or drink, and my hand often hurt too badly to type.

I would translate aloud, instead, while they took turns transcribing. Once I caught Georgie (Frankie?) staring glazedly at me rather than typing. "What?" I asked him.

"Sorry, Professor! It's just"—some revelatory throat-clearing and blushing here—"you have a lovely voice."

I did. I always had. There was no reason it should startle me so. "Thank you, Frankie. Did you put that second comma in the last sentence?" He nodded, still blushing. "Well, strike it out. Whoever wrote this had a very loose grasp of punctuation."

The day we finished the first draft, the Chancellor herself arrived with a bottle of expensive-looking brandy, the color of which reminded me of someone's eyes, though I couldn't recall whose. We raised our glasses to Dominion, and to the First Queen, and to you. My voice caught and snapped on your name, like a loose thread around a nail.

Before she left, Vivian took me aside. "Well done, Owen. You've done everything I asked, beautifully. You've kept the faith. It hasn't been easy, I know, but"—here she actually winked—"God rewards the faithful."

I tried to believe her. But when I thought of God, all that came to mind was a wide smile with a chipped, graying tooth.

The first edition of my translation was published in a matter of months, with a level of fanfare even I found vaguely disquieting. Surely it wasn't usual for every academic review and newspaper column to adopt the same awed, idolatrous tone; surely someone had doubts about the provenance of the original book or the quality of the translation. But if anyone asked questions, they asked them quietly, from the corners of their mouths.

Chancellor Rolfe had, after all, declared the book a national treasure. She read long passages aloud on the radio, drawing lessons and parallels from them as priests did from scripture. She had cheap pocket editions printed for the troops, and there were rumors that she slept with the original text on her bedside table.

Satford & Gills shipped me off on an extensive lecture tour following the publication. This, I thought, they would soon regret; I had a fine, strong speaking voice, but I was uneasy on the stage, inclined to fidget and stutter. I doubted whether anyone would come.

But they did. At first in the twenties, then the hundreds, packing every hall and forum. Each event might have been plucked from my most ambitious, unlikely fantasies: shaking hands with leading scholars and critics, fielding invitations to clubs and societies I'd never even known existed, standing behind tall oaken lecterns, looking down upon a sea of eager pink faces.

I supposed in my fantasies Professor Sawbridge might have been among the crowd, or even my father. But Sawbridge was still busy with her tomb, apparently, and my father must have still been angry with me. Admittedly, I'd called him a liar and a traitor when last we spoke, and expressed the hope that he would never again darken my doorstep, but it struck me as rather shabby of him to respect my wishes after thirty years of ignoring them.

But what did I care? I had the adulation of thousands, now. I was a respected scholar, a war hero—a knight of the nation, even. The Chancellor had taken my oath in a somewhat hurried ceremony just before the first edition went to print; Satford & Gills had been very eager to put *Sir* on the cover.

The people of Dominion—who had laughed and spat at me, who had scorned and doubted and reviled me—now loved me as one of their own. I had been born outside of Dominion, which I imagined as a grand house with shuttered windows and locked doors. *The Death of Una Everlasting,* it appeared, was the key.

But then a woman had lingered after one of my lectures to pat my hand and tell me she only wished the rest of "my type" would devote themselves to their new country. Later, a photographer had asked if I would be willing to pose in my "native costume." Then I'd overheard a pair of scholars who'd invited me to join their society: *Oh, come now,* one of them said, laughing, *you're always saying we need a mascot.*

And I understood finally that a nation is a house with no windows or doors at all. That no matter what I did—no matter how much blood I spilled in its defense or ink I spent in its praise—it would never, ever be my home.

But if Dominion was not my home, where was it? Not the fetid flat above the butcher shop. Not my father's narrow gray row house in Queenswald, and surely not my mother's country, which I had known only as an infant and, later, as an invader. I would only be a different kind of stranger there, anyway: Instead of being surprised when I spoke their language, people would be surprised when I didn't.

No. The word *home* evoked only the sweet green smell of the woods, long gone, and sometimes another word: *Yew,* I thought, or perhaps *you.*

16

WHEN I RETURNED to campus the following summer, I found my office had reverted to its natural state as a storage closet. I wandered, adrift, until a smiling secretary guided me to a palatial room on the fourth floor. In the middle of the room there was a desk that must have taken ten men and a crane to move, and on top of the desk there was a brass nameplate: *Sir Owen Mallory.*

I had settled behind the desk, feeling like a child trying on grown-up clothes, when Harrison finally found me.

I hadn't seen him since the day the book arrived in the post, and the past year hadn't been kind to him. There was a pouchy, droopy quality to his features, as if the air had been let out of his face, and his skin had gone the color of chewed nails.

He made a circuit of the office, wearing an arch expression that suggested he found it all rather gauche. "My, haven't you done well for yourself," he drawled.

I had. In the past month, I had received two honorary degrees, a handful of prestigious job offers, and a prize which I suspected the Cantford Board of Fellows had invented and bestowed purely to get me to stay. I had the fawning, if somewhat false, admiration of my colleagues; I had an embarrassingly large office with mullioned windows and thick carpeting; I had more money than I knew how to spend, a knighthood, and the endowed faculty position in Middle Dominion Studies.

I stared at Harrison, willing myself to feel even a flicker of pride or accomplishment, or at least petty delight at having won our inane little war. But all I felt was the impotent regret that follows a bad trade. I knew I had lost something in exchange for all of this, and I knew it had been precious to me, though I could no longer quite recall what it was.

"Thank you," I said, in that steady, smooth voice that never sounded like it belonged to me. And then, surprising myself: "I'm not sure it was worth it."

Harrison wheeled on me. "Of course it's—any of us would—" I watched as the last tatters of his composure slipped from his hands. He stepped forward and leaned over the desk until his face was so close, I could see the cobwebs of blood in his eyes and the tremor in his jaw. I wondered if he'd had trouble sleeping, too, and if the doctors had prescribed him the same chalky white pills.

"It should have been me." The hate in his voice was bare now, unadorned by false manners or good breeding. "It was *supposed* to be me. I remember—I can remember—" He broke off abruptly. He was looking down at his own hands with an expression I knew well: a weary, mad dread, as if he knew there was nothing there, but still expected to see a knife between his knuckles.

Our eyes met, very briefly. I wondered, with an irrational rush of jealousy, if Harrison had read your stories when he was a boy, as I had. If he, too, knew your eyes were not blue, and did not know how he knew it.

He left without saying anything more.

At my appointment later that day, my hands shook too badly to sign the receipt. The doctor prescribed a long visit to the seaside. The sunlight and the sound of the waves would calm my nerves, he said.

So I was looking out at the Slant Sea, quietly despising the sunlight and the sound of the waves, when I first heard the news. Someone had a wireless playing in the back of the café, and the Sunday sermon had just been interrupted by a breathless announcer.

"The cup and crown," he panted, and even through the static I could hear the awe running under his voice, as if he knew already that people would tell each other, years later, where they'd been when they first heard the news, "they've been—well, they've been found."

By noon the following day I was back on campus, sweating outside Professor Sawbridge's office door. It was slightly ajar, as it hadn't been in months, and light shone around the frame. I could hear someone moving on the other side.

I walked in without knocking, the way I used to.

"It was you, wasn't it." My lips felt strange, and I realized I was smiling. "That's what you've been up to all year."

Professor Sawbridge—who did not flinch from anything, who teased the college archivist and kept uncensored versions of dirty novels on her shelves, where anyone could see them—flinched from the sound of my voice.

When she recognized me, she closed her eyes in relief. "Saints, Mallory."

"Sorry, Professor, I—"

"What are you doing here?" Her eyes snapped open, blue and querulous as they always had been. "Shouldn't you be cutting a ribbon or kissing a ring?"

Cutting remarks were Sawbridge's standard greeting, but there was a new jaggedness to her voice, as if it had been snapped off and poorly sharpened. Her cheeks, once broad and well-freckled, were now sallow, and her hair was thin and brittle.

My smile faltered. "I came straight here, as soon as I heard. It was you, wasn't it, who found them?"

"Yes. It was me." Her eyes were on her work, which seemed to be sorting books into piles of varying height and stability. The air in the office was stale and swampish, like the inside of a closed mouth, but she hadn't opened a window. "Well, me, Sylvie, and a couple of interns."

"Sylvie?"

"Mistress Sylvia Shaw? The archivist."

I tried and failed to imagine anyone addressing the college archivist—a woman with the stature and temperament of a starved heron—by a nickname. I wasn't even sure I could imagine her outside the archives; I had assumed until now that she spent the night in one of her own glass cases, arms folded across her chest. Eventually I offered, "Congratulations."

Professor Sawbridge ignored this, as if the greatest—well, perhaps second-greatest—discovery of the century was not worth mentioning. She hauled another armload of books off her shelves and began sorting it according to her own inscrutable system. Some of them—mostly dirty novels, a few dictionaries—she piled in a musty traveling trunk.

My smile returned, somewhat battered. I would miss her terribly. "Let me guess. Head of Curation at the Royal Museum? Vice-Provost of Cantford?"

This earned me a harassed look. "What?"

"I was trying to guess which position you've accepted. You wouldn't pack your favorite books unless you were switching offices."

She paused, finally, and looked at me with her customary mix of pity and love, as if I were a very stupid pet that she was inexplicably fond of. Gently, she said, "I was fired, Owen. I have until Friday to clear out my things, or what remains of them."

It was only then that I registered the state of her office. Sawbridge was not a naturally neat person, but she did not typically rip all the drawers from her desk or smash her potted plants against the wall. There were loose papers covering the floor in drifts, and the shelves were half emptied, the remaining books slumped over one another like witnesses to some awful disaster.

Sawbridge nodded at the shelves. "They took all the really filthy stuff, of course. I hope they get an eyeful. Even plundering goons deserve an education."

"I—I don't—*Fired?*"

Professor Sawbridge had been the second woman ever to receive an advanced degree from Cantford College. She had spent the next decade traipsing across the countryside, digging up the most astonishing artifacts and publishing monographs under the name G. Sawbridge. She didn't reveal her gender until the Board of Fellows had begged her on bended knee to accept a faculty appointment. And—despite decades of inflammatory statements, seditious lectures, and illicit book collecting—they hadn't fired her. She was a genius, a real one, and geniuses are permitted their eccentricities.

"Why?" My voice was hoarse.

"Attempted destruction of objects significant to our national heritage." When I blinked at her, she clarified, "I tried to smash the grail with a big rock."

I blinked some more. I was aware that I ought to be worried about the destruction of a priceless historical artifact, but I found myself saying, almost in awe, "Mistress Shaw must've tried to skin you alive."

"Sylvie was the one holding the flashlight, love." There was a nearly imperceptible softening around her mouth. "I know she likes to frighten the undergraduates, but who doesn't? She's really quite . . . decent." This constituted the highest praise I'd ever heard Professor Sawbridge offer a living person and caused me to blink several more times.

She returned, somewhat showily, to her book sorting. "We would have managed it, but one of the interns turned out to be on the Chancellor's payroll. Sylvie and I were marched off the dig site with rifles to our backs."

"But—but—" I said, inanely, as if I could offer some counter or defense, as if this were an argument I could win if I only cited the correct source. "Where have you been? Why didn't you write?" I sounded peevish and young, even to myself.

Sawbridge's eyes narrowed. "Mallory, I have spent the last five weeks detained without trial while my home and office were searched for evidence of conspiracy, answering very boring and repetitive questions about my loyalty to crown and country. Forgive me if I didn't mail a letter." The corner of Sawbridge's mouth curled sourly. "They might be good with trains, these fascists, but they're quite stingy with postage."

Her voice was perfectly dry, as if she were reviewing a second-rate hotel, but I saw her teeth worrying her lower lip, a nervous habit she hadn't had before. The flesh between her teeth was raw and red.

"Professor, I'm so—"

"Your father sends his love, by the way," she said, in the slightly disgusted tone she used to deliver the killing blow in a debate, as if she knew there was about to be a great deal of blood and only hoped it didn't stain her good coat.

"My father," I echoed, faintly. "My father is—detained? And he said—"

"Well, no, actually he said something like 'The boy—tell him I—never mind.' Eloquence must run in the family. I chose to communicate the spirit of his remarks."

I thought of all the headlines I'd ignored for the last year, the raids and protests and mass arrests. I thought of my father as I'd last seen him, furious and sorry and old. I thought of the blood I'd seen congealing on the capitol steps—his, I was sure of it, though I couldn't say why.

Had I been lecturing on my stupid little tour, while the only two people I cared about were imprisoned? Had Vivian known, when she clinked her glass against mine, that my father was shackled in some windowless basement?

I looked at my own hands, and found they were shaking badly. I couldn't tell if it was another of my fits, or simple rage. "I'm sorry. I should have looked for you." I swallowed, hard. "If you are in need of legal or financial assistance, I am in a position to help."

Sawbridge was attempting to close her traveling trunk, apparently under the impression that books might shrink themselves if glared at with sufficient force. "Thank you, dear," she said, "but Sylvie and I have decided not to wait around for the next arrest. We're going abroad—tonight, if I can get this *damn* thing—to shut—"

I crossed to the desk and added my weight to the trunk lid. There were several worrying pops from the hinges. "You're fleeing the country? That doesn't strike you as a little . . . premature?"

"Speaking as a recent guest of the government: It strikes me as post-mature, flirting with postmortem."

The latch clicked. Sawbridge hauled the trunk around her desk, marching for the door with her chin high, as if it didn't bother her in the least to leave behind her research and notes, the desk where she had worked for so many years, the place she had carved for herself in a college where nine-tenths of her students still assumed she was a secretary on the first day of class.

I touched her arm, lightly, as she passed. "Why did you do it? Why would you destroy the grail?"

She made an amused sound in her throat. "I would set fire to the national archives myself if I thought Vivian Rolfe wanted them." She sobered, looking up at me with an expression I didn't recognize on her face. I'd never seen her uncertain. "There's something wrong with it, Owen, with the structure of it all. I've spent my whole life chasing it and have nothing to show except bad eyes and back problems. But it's not right, I *know* it's not."

"What's not right?" I was careful to keep my voice neutral.

Her lips thinned anyway. "You are a great historian, Mallory, or you could have been. You know that history is mostly happenstance. Accidents piled on top of mistakes, a series of dice rolled in dim rooms by careless hands. It is not a lesson, until we learn it. It is not a story, until we tell it. And every story serves someone." This was an abbreviated version of the lecture she gave in every class she ever taught. I nodded, somewhat warily. "It's why I listen more to material evidence than the written word. Words lie, but—"

"Bones don't," I finished for her.

She very nearly smiled at me. "But this—it's all so neat. The book, suddenly resurfacing. The cup and crown discovered. The prophecy fulfilled after a thousand years. I'm surprised Sir Una herself hasn't popped out of her grave, Valiance in one hand and the flag in the other."

A chill crawled down my spine, settling like swallowed ice in my stomach. "What are you suggesting?"

"I am suggesting that someone is *telling* this story because it serves them. I was given my little part to play and—Savior save me—I played it." That jagged bitterness had returned to her voice. "Just as you played yours."

"If you are referring to my translation of *The Death of Una Everlasting*, a perfectly legitimate contribution to—"

"You know I'm not. Or do you?" Her eyes moved over my face, and I had the old sense of being professionally vivisected. More quietly, she said, "You haven't asked me where I found them. The cup and crown."

"Where did you find them?"

"In the tomb of Una Everlasting," Sawbridge said, and I wasn't surprised, not at all. For a moment I could picture it so clearly that the cluttered office fell away, replaced by cold limestone and the fresh green smell of ulla flowers. In my ears I heard the snap and pop of tallow candles.

Sawbridge's voice turned musing. "If anyone had asked me, I would have told them the Everlasting was just a myth, an amalgamation of heroic traditions stuffed into a single character." She had, in fact, said this often, to anyone nearby, without provocation. "But then we unsealed the chamber, and there she was. There was her armor, and there was her sword—though if that damn thing was forged in the ancient age, I'll eat my left boot—and there were her bones."

The tremor in my hands was worsening. My head hurt, suddenly and badly, and my lungs no longer seemed to be the correct size. I took sharp, shallow breaths.

"And beside her—placed there long after her death, judging by the sediment deposits—were the grail and the crown. Don't ask me how they got there. The Chancellor's pet priest has produced a letter from the Church archives claiming that Sir Ancel repented on his deathbed and had the items secretly returned, but I'd swear it's a fake. Anyway, the grail and crown were only the second- and third-biggest mysteries in that tomb." Sawbridge fished a twist of grubby paper from her pocket and handed it to me. "*This* was the first."

I unfolded the paper clumsily, and a single cigarette butt rolled into my palm. It had been smoked down to the last pinch of paper and tobacco, then ground flat beneath a boot heel, but I could still make out the crumpled edge of a tiny silver star.

I stared and stared at it, remembering the taste of cheap tobacco in my mouth.

Sawbridge said, softly, "I don't know anyone else who smokes those damn things. And I'm telling you, that tomb had been bricked up for hundreds of years. I don't . . ." She shook her head once, sharply. "I don't know how or why any of this is happening, but I sure as hell know who it serves."

I couldn't seem to reply. My blood was rushing in my ears, and the walls around me felt tenuous and unconvincing, like cheap stage props.

I heard Sawbridge say, dryly, "Enjoy the coronation." Then, softer, "And take care, Mallory."

Then she was gone, leaving me with nothing but a faint heat against my cheek, as if she had kissed it before she left, and a cigarette I'd smoked a thousand years ago.

I didn't remember everything, not then.

But I knew, finally, for certain, that there was something I could not remember—and once I knew that, it was only a matter of time. Sawbridge used to say that a good historian tells us what's in the records, and a great historian tells us what isn't. And I had been a great historian, once.

I tucked the cigarette butt in my coat pocket, gathered up the remains of Sawbridge's papers, and went to work.

I barely left my office for the rest of the summer. It was restful, in a way; I declined every invitation and engagement. I asked—loudly, in several crowded faculty meetings—to be excused from teaching duties, as I was busy working on my new monograph. A history of the First Crusade, I said, intended for a popular audience. My colleagues recoiled—if I would stoop to popular history, what depravity might be next? fiction?—but I had the somewhat paranoid idea that one of them might send a discreet telegram to the Chancellor, and that the Chancellor might decide she had nothing to worry about from me.

I worked methodically, without rushing; it seemed to me I had all the time in the world.

I began with the earlier fragments of the Everlasting Cycle, moving steadily up through Lazamon and Montmer, guided by Sawbridge's private notes. I'd read it all before, of course, but this time I tried to see it as a story told over and over, rather than historical fact, and to wonder who it served.

A pattern emerged, hazily, like one of those pictures that doesn't come clear until you unfocus your eyes. I don't want to bore you, but consider:

In Lazamon's compilation of legends—the earliest complete version of your story—it isn't the Hinterlanders who betray Yvanne, but the Norns. This legend was recorded just before the Nornish Plot, which resulted in the death of a king of Dominion and all his heirs. The only survivor was the wife of his youngest son: Tilda the Younger.

Several centuries later, de Meulan composed her Everlasting Psalms—based, she claimed, on *The Death of Una Everlasting,* which had been given to her by an angel. Lazamon had mentioned God only in passing, but de Meulan spent long verses on your piety and chastity. It was the first time you were referred to as a saint.

The psalms were written during the reign of Lysabet I. She was under pressure from her archbishop to marry and give the throne to her husband or son, but she refused—in the name of Saint Una the Virgin. The archbishop was found to be a heretic and burned, as part of the spiritual cleansing of the country. It was during Lysabet's reign that the last of the Gallish temples were destroyed, and the Roving Folk were driven south.

It was Montmer's *Dominion Historica,* in the early modern period, which first named the Hinterlanders as your killers. When a Dominion ship was sunk, shortly after, everyone knew it must have been the Hinterlanders: They were, after all, Dominion's oldest enemies. Our first war with the Hinterlands began shortly thereafter.

Do you see, now, what Sawbridge did? That's not *history*—that's a story, designed to teach us who to hate and who to obey, what god to worship and what flag to fight for and what color eyes are the most beautiful. It's a story that made a continent into a kingdom into an empire, that put a woman on the throne—more than once, I suspected—and was about to do so again.

Shortly after Professor Sawbridge fled the country, the ministers had voted to restore the monarchy. Vivian Rolfe would be crowned before winter. She would take the name Yvanne the Second, she said, reverting to the Middle Mothertongue version of her name. Dominion would have a queen once more.

I looked at her face in the paper and imagined a crown on her brow. It was very, very easy to imagine.

I decided abruptly to copy all my notes into code, in case she had spies going through my office. It was a quick and simple cipher—one simply made a great number of punctuation errors in a given text. If there were an even number of errors, you wrote down the first letter following the mistake; if there were an odd number, you wrote the second. I hadn't used it since I was a child.

But, as I made the first false comma on the page, I thought: *Yes, I have.*

I considered this thought carefully, turning it like a stone in my hands. I considered the Lucky Star cigarette in your tomb. I considered my dreams, which were still, always, of you.

Then I unlocked the bottom drawer of my desk and withdrew the thick folder where I kept the photographed pages of *The Death of Una Everlasting*. They were the property of the state, technically, but I hadn't been able to bear leaving them behind.

It didn't take me long, now that I knew what I was looking for. I counted twenty-six false punctuation marks. An even number. I copied out the first letter past each mark.

W a i t

F o r

m E

My hands were not shaking at all. I wrote the rest of it quickly, easily, barely even pausing to look up each letter, and when it was finished, I said the whole of it aloud.

"Wait for me, beneath the yew tree."

I remembered hearing those words, over and over, in your voice. I remembered holding your face with my bloody hands.

And then I remembered everything.

I became aware, after some little while, that I was on the floor, with my cheek resting on the thick carpeting and the contents of the folder scattered around me. My head hurt, as if my skull was too small for all the memories inside it.

I stood, somewhat unsteadily. "I'm coming," I said, and my voice was smooth and sweet because—this time—my throat had never been cut. Because, this time, it hadn't needed to be. "Oh, Una. I'm coming."

Following my conversation with Professor Sawbridge, I'd sent letters and telegrams to every government office I could think of. In response I had received a truly masterful range of administrative stonewalling, including outright denial, waffling, misdirection, subtle threats, unsubtle threats, lies, and envelopes marked RETURN TO SENDER. No one would tell me the whereabouts or health of my father, or even admit to his existence.

It took me far too long to realize I could not only afford a solicitor, but a good solicitor. I had immediately engaged the services of an openly unethical young man who did not seem to blink with normal human frequency, and who had produced, just the previous day, an obsequious letter from the Ministry of War, apologizing for the confusion and inviting me to visit my father and ascertain for myself his physical health.

Now I went straight from campus to the address listed in the letter. It was several hours before dawn, but the wait no longer struck me as significant.

I tried to lean unobtrusively against the wall, but passersby still cast me concerned looks and made wide arcs as they passed. It was the twitching of my hands and face, I imagined; a person wasn't meant to remember several different lifetimes, all at once.

At half past eight I walked into the building—a blandly carceral structure, like a sanitarium or a school—and presented my solicitor's letter to the clerk. The clerk called her supervisor, who called his chief, who escorted me to a small room the color of soap scum.

I waited. Eventually the door opened, and my father walked through it.

He wasn't wearing chains. For a moment I was relieved—but the skin around his wrists was chafed and pale. His limp had worsened, so that his top half had canted sideways, like a building with a crumbling foundation, and the whites of his eyes had turned the faint, malarial color of old lemons.

He looked—to my profound shame—genuinely surprised to see me. The corners of his eyes folded up. "Hello, son. How's the autocracy faring, these days? I have to bribe these boys"—he gestured here to the guard behind him—"for newspapers, and I'm out of booze." He sat, legs wide, expression determinedly jovial, because he was the kind of man who would wink at the executioner as he walked up the scaffold. It had embarrassed me once, his flippancy, his refusal to worry, but now I wondered if it was a species of bravery.

I gave the guard an imperious nod, praying that my solicitor had put the fear of God, or at least civil damages, into them all. The guard left.

I wet my lips. "Hello," I said, and didn't know what to say next.

When I'd received the letter from the Ministry of War, I had indulged in a little fantasy of sweeping heroically into my father's cell and rescuing him—somewhat belatedly—from his imprisonment. Perhaps he would forgive me. Perhaps he would even be proud of me.

In the fantasy, I had come to save him, rather than to ask a very specific and highly criminal question.

My father had never suffered silence well. "How'd you rig this, then? Did Her Majesty grant you a boon?"

"No, I paid a bad man a lot of money. But, speaking of Her Majesty, I was wondering if . . ." I laughed, extremely awkwardly. "If you could tell me how a person might break into the personal quarters of the Chancellor of Dominion. If they needed to."

For the first time, my father's smile faded. "Now, why would I know a thing like that?" His voice had acquired a hard, hollow ring, like knuckles on a shut door.

"Well, *someone* certainly broke into Chancellor Gladwell's room and painted the names of dead boys on his walls. If it wasn't you, at least tell me who it was, so I can go ask them."

My father had looked at me with variations of disappointment for most of my life. But the expression on his face now was far worse: a bewildered betrayal, which soured quickly into something meaner. He said, with dignity, "I know I wasn't much of a father to you. I know we've never seen eye to eye on—well, most things. But there's no call for this." He shook his head. His scalp shone pinkly through his thinning hair. There was a livid scar on the left side of his skull that hadn't been there before. "I already told them everything, anyway."

Mortification arrived, thick and sour in my mouth, but I managed another awful laugh. "Like hell you did. You always said the worst circle of hell was for sympathizers and squealers."

"And centrists."

I swallowed, dry mouthed. "I'm not—this isn't a trick." That my own father would suspect me of informing against him—that it would not be the first time I'd led someone I loved to their death—the scum-colored tiles swam, sickly, around me. "I'm not trying to get a confession out of you. I swear."

Bewilderment returned to his face. "Then what exactly are you trying to do?"

"I am trying," I said, tiredly, "to break into the personal quarters of the Chancellor of Dominion."

He looked at me, closely and for a long time, as he rarely had. His eyes had always tended to slip over me, as if it pained him to linger.

The silence thinned like stretched putty between us. I broke it in a guilty rush. "I understand how you must feel about me. But I didn't know you were in here until a few weeks ago, and then for a long time no one would admit they had you, and—" I broke off, swallowed again. My memories were piled atop each other now in unwieldy stacks, so that every scene was haunted by its own variations. But I remembered our last argument clearly enough; it always went the same. "I said some—very cruel things, the last time we spoke. I'm sorry."

"Don't you dare apologize. Not to me." My father was breathing hard, and the color had left his face, so that the burst veins stood out like wet fireworks. "You don't owe me anything—not a damn thing."

"Yes I—"

"You don't understand!" A shrill, almost petulant note entered his voice. He passed a hand over his face, scrubbing hard, and then he said, "I thought I was doing the right thing. Just one good and proper thing, after so many wrong ones. Or maybe I just took a shine to you—I was half cracked, by then."

I knew then that he was speaking of his time during the last war, which he hadn't done in any of the dozens of lives I could remember. I willed myself into total stillness.

"We'd made it to the Marro River, far in the south. We were hungry and frightened, just beginning to understand that we were losing. That a backward little island could outlast and out-fight and out-hate the most powerful country in the world. And then we heard movement in the rushes, and we . . ."

He trailed away, unable to say what they had done. But I, too, had once been a frightened young man surrounded by other frightened young men, far from home; I already knew. I could almost hear the *whizz* and *thock* of bullets into muddy ground.

He continued, eventually, "When . . . when it was over, and nothing was moving anymore, we went to look. We found ten or twelve people on the bank. Roving Folk, probably—they had the finest little ponies, and hundreds of scrolls rolled up in their packs . . . not that it mattered. We wrote them down as hostiles, in our report."

His right foot had begun tapping, arrhythmically. "Anyway. There was a girl—a woman, I suppose, but God she looked young. She hadn't tried to run when the shooting started. She'd just knelt down, curled around something, like it was the most precious thing in the world." His eyes, rheumy and yellow, met mine. "Which it was, of course."

A tide, cold and prickling, seemed to be tugging at my limbs, pulling me under. I had wondered, in an idle, morose sort of way, who my mother was: a desperate camp follower, or a reckless village girl, or one of the Hinterlander guides that sold maps to the soldiers.

I had never, not once, wondered who my father was.

He had not looked away from me. I had the idea he was refusing to spare himself.

I said, like a child, "So you didn't—you weren't in love with her, or anything. My mother."

"I never even met her. She was dead before we found her." His voice matched his expression, hard and unflinching. "Just the one bullet, straight through the spine. It might have been any of ours, but I was always a dead shot."

I thought: *I must have gotten it from him,* out of habit, before I realized I hadn't gotten anything from him at all. The two of us had lived in that narrow gray row house not as father and son, but as two strangers, tied by nothing but bad luck and clumsy, unsober love.

He coughed, twice, phlegmily. "You were crying. I picked you up, patted you like I used to pat my baby brother, before he died, and you quieted right down. And it felt—it was like a miracle to me. That anything or anyone would still trust me, after what I—" He rubbed the back of his fingers beneath his nose. "I don't think I set you down once over the next hundred miles of marching. When we reconnected with the main force, I told them I was through. I'd known it was wrong all along, begun to see that I was a tool of empire—one of the other boys had a copy of *The Sin of Statehood*—but I'd been too much a coward to do anything about it. Until you."

"But you weren't charged with desertion. I looked it up." It was the second or third thing I'd done when I arrived at Cantford. It had been a small, secret comfort to me that he hadn't been a true deserter, despite what people said. "You were relieved of duty and stripped of rank and benefits, following an injury."

The man who was not my father made a small grimace of embarrassment. "They, ah, didn't accept my resignation. Tried to keep me marching at gunpoint, so I shot myself right through the hip." He rubbed his thigh, in a gesture so familiar it made my throat suddenly tight. "I was half cracked by then, like I said. But they couldn't make me march on one leg."

His eyes finally left mine, moving mistily around the little room. "All these years, I told myself I was sparing you. Giving you a good Dominion name, pretending you were my own flesh and blood. But really, I was just selfish. I wanted you to love me, or to forgive me, though I didn't deserve either. I wanted to be—to you, if no one else—a good man. And I thought, if I made Dominion a better place—more just—less hateful . . ." He gestured, not without humor, at the red marks around his wrists. "Hell of a job I've done, eh?"

He sobered. He looked at me, his eyes damp and pink-rimmed and full of regret. "Should've told you the truth. I owed you that much. I owed you . . . everything."

"Was it guilt, then?" My own voice sounded clinical, incurious. "Is that why you drank?"

"I drank because I was a shit father and my leg hurt like a bastard." I watched him chewing the inside of his own cheek, jaw flexing hard enough to hurt. "And because I loved you, but before I loved you—before I even knew you existed—I'd hurt you badly. And there was no fixing it. No going back."

Both of us let the silence stretch, after that.

I was sifting through the heaps and drifts of my memories, holding them up like flawed gems to the light of the truth: I was not my father's true son, nor a true son of Dominion. I had no grand destiny or secret purpose. I was a mere byproduct of war, one of tens of thousands of orphans left by centuries of wars and crusades, and I had never been destined for anything except a shallow grave on the banks of the Crown River, which was once called the Marro.

But I had lived, because my mother loved me enough to take a bullet to the spine, and my father—yes, he was my father, though perhaps not my only one—had loved me enough to put a bullet in his own leg.

With this thought came a great clarity. Everything I had believed in and fought for—crown and country, the flag and the church, even the past itself—had proved false. What remained were those trivial, nameless moments which would be swallowed up by the tide of history and forgotten: my father's hand on my hair when I was a boy, ruffling it awkwardly; the brusque press of Sawbridge's lips on my cheek; your eyes on mine at the very end, full of faith, so certain I would come back for you.

If I serve anything, let it be that. If I die for anything, let it be you.

A tear splashed on the back of my hand, and I realized I had been crying, steadily and quietly, for some time. My father was watching me with the stoic heartache of a man who had just broken something which he had always known he would break. I opened my mouth but couldn't decide whether to say *thank you* or *I'm sorry* or *I forgive you,* so I covered his hands with mine. The knots of his knuckles trembled beneath my palms.

Eventually I said, "I hurt someone I love, too." I had killed you, actually, over and over again, for all it hadn't been my hand on the hilt. "But I *can* change it, Dad. I can go back." I wondered for the first time what else I might change. If I saved you, would Dominion still invade the Hinterlands? Would my mother live, and my father walk without a limp? The chains of causation seemed to crack and reform, fractal, ineffable.

My father asked, "How?"

I felt myself smiling, lopsidedly. "By breaking into the personal quarters of the Chancellor of Dominion."

My father looked at my face for a full minute. Then he leaned forward across the table and whispered a name in my ear.

I had anticipated a certain amount of difficulty. I had imagined unclimbable fences and unpickable locks, and perhaps an exchange of fire with twenty men in red coats shouting, *Seize him!*

But my father's friend—an unamused woman who had worked in the capitol laundry room for ten years—had suggested dryly that I simply walk in the front door and ask to check something in the archives. Then, when everyone forgot about me, which they would do almost instantly, I could hide in a linen closet until nightfall and take the service elevator to the Chancellor's bedroom. She added that my father was a good man and that, if I ever so much as thought her name in the presence of the authorities, she would put me through the mangle and dissolve my remains with lye.

Which is how I came to be sitting in the humid dark of the Chancellor's bedroom, two hours after midnight. The air was thick and floral, sweetly familiar.

I rapped my knuckles smartly on her bedside table.

Vivian shot up, displaying the reflexes of a woman who had been surviving assassination attempts for a thousand years, and might continue for another thousand. One arm was already fumbling behind the headboard, reaching for whatever bell or button would summon help.

In the muffled bedroom, the doubled click of the hammer was loud. It was difficult to see anything but the spectral white of the Chancellor's nightgown among the rich drapes and shadows of her bed, but I could tell she had gone very still.

I propped my service revolver casually on one knee and said, mildly, "I will not miss. As I think you know."

I saw the nightgown sag petulantly back into the pillows. "Corporal Mallory." Her voice was not as surprised as I would have liked it to be, but it had a pleasingly tense undercurrent. "I feel bound to inform you that you will not get away with this, whatever it is."

I had an inappropriate urge to laugh. I was filled with a reckless, fey delight, born from the knowledge that I had, for the first time in any of my lives, stepped off the path that had been laid out for me.

I cleared my throat. "Where is it?"

"Where is what?" From a woman who had lied to me more or less continuously since the day we met, it was a weak effort. I waited, not particularly patiently, until she clucked her tongue. "It's under my pillow. Don't you read the papers?"

"Remove it, please, and place it on the floor between us."

She did so, moving with an exaggerated show of caution. She perched on the edge of her bed with hands raised mockingly high.

I kept the revolver dead level as I retrieved the book and opened it across my lap. The smell of woodsmoke and winter rose from the pages like cold hands, beckoning.

I brought my left knuckles to my teeth and bit down hard, stopping only when I tasted blood. Then I held my hand over the page, palm hovering just above the paper.

I could make out the wet shine of Vivian's eyes as she watched the blood well, not quite dripping. "Ah," she said, without any emotion at all. "You've remembered."

"I have." It was unexpectedly difficult to keep my hand still. The centuries between you and I had been reduced to a bare inch, a single gesture, and my arm shook slightly with the effort of restraint. "And yet, I neither intend nor desire to kill you." I hoped, fervently and with all my heart, that I would never again wipe anyone else's blood from my hands. "However, if you lie to me, or attack me, or scream for help, I will instantly overcome my personal preferences and pull the trigger. I have three shots, but I assure you I will only need one."

Her hands returned to her sides. She inclined her head, very slightly, and I saw the dull gleam of gray hairs among the brass. I wonder if she ever let it go wholly white, or if she constantly traveled back to her own youth, making herself whatever age she pleased.

"Now. The queens that came after Yvanne—Tilda the Younger, Lysabet I and II, et cetera—they were all you, weren't they? At different ages, perhaps?"

She tilted her chin, considering me. The gas lamps on the street below cast a ghoulish green-gold light across her face. "The queen is dead," she said, and spread her hands. "Long live the queen."

"Answer the—"

"*Yes,* they were me." Her lips twisted. "I knew I should have burned the archives somewhere along the way, but it's a delicate balance. You want a robust national history, but you also want to cover your tracks."

"And Lazamon and de Meulan, and the others. You gave them this book, the book I wrote, in different iterations?"

"Yes."

"And then you spirited it away until you needed a new version. At which time you returned to the present, mailed the book to me again, and sent me back to her."

"Yes." Vivian was perfectly calm, even a little proud. "You could never refuse me, and Una could never refuse you."

"Do not," I advised her, with a little flick of the barrel, "ever speak her name again." My temper—which had been absent since the day Professor Sawbridge put the cigarette butt in my hand, lost in a tide of urgent hope—was simmering once more in my chest, licking up my throat. "What I don't understand is why you had to make it real. Why not just rewrite the book yourself, however you wanted? Why make me—why make us—"

"I tried that, obviously." Vivian shook her head, much in the manner of a master craftsman reflecting on the quality of his early-career work. "But—to my lasting dismay—the truth matters. It matters what the court of Cavallon sees on the day she dies. It matters what the villagers of Dominion whisper to one another, and what stories they tell their children and grandchildren about the time the Red Knight rode past. Without them, without that germ of actual memory, her story is just a story, and your book is just a book. Also," she added, wryly, "I could never quite capture the tone. You bring a real pathos to the project, Corporal."

I found my finger had tightened on the trigger. I loosened it, fractionally. "But I wasn't the first person you sent back, was I?"

"You were not." For the first time, I detected a note of genuine surprise in her voice. "It was a bit like holding auditions, for a while. I needed someone who was clever enough to play the part, but not so clever that he would realize he was reading from a script. Someone who loved her legend enough to let her die but loved *her* enough to write a hell of a eulogy. It's a—"

"Delicate balance." My lips felt numb, separate from myself.

"But of course, what I needed most was the person she was willing to die *for.* I was that person, once, at the beginning." A look of such longing crossed her face that I understood, against my will, that she really had loved you, and perhaps still did. But the look passed, and I understood, too, that it did not matter. She had killed what she loved, over and over, and would do it again, and would not lose a single moment's sleep. "None of my other candidates even came close. The Harrison boy—what a disaster. That fucking horse killed him, the first time around. Make a note—if you're trying to engineer the perfect warhorse, you can only send them back in time about twenty times before they get absolutely *demented*." Oh, Hen, you poor bastard. "Anyway, I tried Harrison a few more times. He never even got her to the dragon. But you . . ." Another shake of her head, indulgent this time. "It was like you already knew each other, even that first time."

The scent of flowers seemed to thicken the air, pooling at the back of my tongue like bile. It was a moment or two before I could ask my final question. "Why?"

"Why does anyone fall in love? Brain chemistry and proximity. Although I always wonder how it works between you two. Do you take turns giving the orders? I hope you listen to her better than you did to poor Colonel Drayton—"

"*Stop.*" I caught the shine of a jagged gray tooth, the curve of a pleased smile. I thought a little nauseously of that night when you'd wrapped me in your cloak. If you had moved your hand half an inch farther down—if you had begged or demanded, shouted or whispered—

But you hadn't. Perhaps some wary, battle-tried part of you knew bait when you saw it. You'd wanted me—I'd felt it, smelled it—but perhaps you wanted your free will more.

It was a moment before I could retrieve my line of questioning. "I meant—why did you do it? What could possibly be worth it?" My voice was fraying. My shoulders ached from holding my arms so still. "Did you want to be on the radio that badly?"

Vivian's smile vanished. "Mallory, look around you. We are standing in the capitol of the most powerful nation on earth. A prosperous, united, peaceful nation, which I have spent a millennium building with my own two hands, my own sweat and blood—"

"Not yours." My voice dragged across hers, a serrated whisper.

She exhaled, annoyed, then stood. I kept the barrel of the revolver pointed just to the right of her sternum, hardly breathing, but she came no closer. She edged around the bed and leaned on the nearest windowsill, slope shouldered, infinitely weary. She looked like a woman badly in need of a cigarette.

"I was nothing, once," she said to the window. Her face was so close to the glass that her breath misted over it. "I mean that literally: I came into this world lower than the meanest pig farmer, lower even than his scrawniest sow. But I was smart, and I was hungry, and I would not remain nothing."

I tried to picture her as a girl, spindly and square jawed, perhaps begging on street corners or scrounging scraps from alleys. But it was like imagining an asp as an egg; it may have been true, but I couldn't see how it mattered.

"I found my way, eventually, beneath the wing of a great man. A powerful man. One night I told my—teacher, we'll call him—that I would be great, too, someday. He laughed. He asked me to name a great woman of history. Just one. And then, in the silence, he kissed me on the forehead." One of her hands drifted upward to rub, hard, at her brow.

When she turned back toward me, the light from the street fell full on her face, and I could see the black gash of her lips, the beaten steel of her jaw. In her eyes I could see what she kept so carefully hidden behind rueful smiles and ugly jokes: a bottomless, terrifying resolve, of the kind that could bend the whole history of the world to its will.

"There were no *precedents* for what I wanted to become, you see. No stories. So I made my own precedents." A small, proud smile, here. "I built my own ladder, rung by rung, and climbed it all the way to the top. And now every child on the street could tell you their names, and *every name is mine.*" The smile widened, became beatific, so that she looked younger and more alive than I had ever seen her. "Of course it was worth it."

This part of the speech was, I understood, intended to make her cause more sympathetic to me. To recast the last few centuries of bloodshed as a noble struggle toward justice. But all I could see was your face as you died, over and over. Was it a ladder she had climbed, or a pile of bodies? Was it justice, if it only served one person?

I thought then of the queen's other guards, who had not looked as I expected them to look. Who had been altered, erased, unsubtly remade in the image of one woman. "What color was Ancel's hair, before you made him change it to match yours?"

Vivian blinked. "Red." Her nose wrinkled. "A Gallish grandmother, I believe."

"How trying," I said, dryly. "Last question. Once you had your crown—crowns—why did you rule Dominion so . . ."

"Competently?"

"Ruthlessly. Violently. Every one of your reigns is marked by wars, executions, arrests. The First Crusade, the burning of the heretics, the conquest of the Hinterlands and the occupation after. The indecency laws—my father—" I choked on the word.

"Oh, I see." Vivian widened her eyes and flapped her lashes with showy, false innocence. "Why didn't I hold bake sales for the schools? Why didn't I tax the rich and tie a suffragette sash around my waist? Perhaps at my coronation I could have called for world peace and released a flock of fucking doves." She stopped flapping her lashes. "I wouldn't last a month, you sweet, stupid child. Even now, after all my *precedents,* there are jackals at my heels. Wealthy men waiting for the slightest sign of weakness, the smallest dip in the polls. I've given them contracts, factories, new markets—prestigious appointments for their shitty sons, quick divorces for their inconvenient wives—I've given them an *empire*—and still, *still,* I am not safe. I cannot be too young or too old, too beautiful or too ugly. I cannot weep or rage. I cannot refuse a man nor fuck him nor marry him—a queen is only powerful if there are no kings or princes nearby."

In the electric glow of the streetlight, her shoulders rose and fell. Her voice was hoarse and honest, and very tired. "I will not apologize for being powerful, but . . . it can be a prison, too."

I thought of the red marks around my father's wrists. "Spoken like someone who's never been to prison."

"I rule as I *must,* Mallory," she snapped. "Because if I don't—if I falter—they will eat me alive."

I said, sincerely, "God, I hope so," and watched her eyes calcify into a pair of small and nasty rocks. I rolled a crick from my neck. "When I take this book back and unwrite it, and unmake your whole house of cards, I hope they forget you so quickly they don't even know what name to write on your fucking tombstone."

Her jaw worked briefly. When she spoke, it was not with her radio voice or her sincere appeal voice, but with the flat, disinterested certainty of an oracle. "I will find you. There is no period in history where I am not. If I am not on the throne, I am very near to it, and there is no corner of Dominion, no cave nor hollow nor dreary little village, that is not marked on the maps of Cavallon. I will know what you have done as soon as you do it, and then the hunt will begin."

She wasn't looking at me as she spoke. She had turned to a bookshelf and was running the flats of her hands beneath the shelves. "You might hide, for a time—perhaps even a long time. You might begin to convince each other that you are safe, that I have given up the chase. When you have stopped waiting for me, when the hairs on your neck no longer prickle—then will I find you, and then will you suffer. You will lament, and there will be no end to your lamentation. You will weep, and there will be no end to your weeping." She had slipped into Middle Mothertongue as she spoke, as easily and naturally as if she had learned it in the womb. "You will wish, with all your shattered heart, that you could return to this moment and walk away. You will beg me for it, before the end. And I will laugh."

There was a brief moment here, which hung suspended between us, swollen with the weight of unmade choices. And then the moment ended, and all the choices were made, as neatly as dominoes clacking one against the other.

I dropped my left palm to the page.

Vivian Rolfe made a small, satisfied sound, as when a person finds their lost hair pin, and turned back to face me. In her hands was a sword I'd last seen laid atop your bier. She held it awkwardly across her breast, but it was already half drawn.

I didn't hesitate. I tightened my right index finger that last, fatal centimeter. For you, for us, I would bloody my hands a hundred times over.

There was the familiar *boom* of the revolver, the kick of the grip in my hand—then a weird, metallic *slap*, like a hammer on a nail.

Vivian had been thrown back against the bookcase, but she did not look distraught to have been shot. Valiance was still in her hands, but she had moved it four inches to the left, directly over her heart. There was a small, round pock in the blade, just below the hilt, and I realized she had not intended to kill me, after all.

The room was falling away from me. The scent of summer flowers was replaced by the cold, wild smell of winter.

The last thing I saw before I left was Vivian, smiling patiently, as if she had known exactly where my bullet would fly, as if it had all happened just this way, many times.

I was alone, before you came. (You'll forgive me for telling this part, but it always makes you cry, Owen.)

The woods of my fathers had grown wild in my absence, the old paths choked with bitterthorn, the old cottage covered over with bracken. It occurred to me that they would not find my remains for years and years, if they ever did, and the thought did not distress me as much as it once would have.

I did not even wear my armor, on the day I went to the yew. Let them think me a lost herdswoman, an unwise traveler, and let them bury me with only a plain stone for a marker, if indeed there is anything left to bury.

Yet, as I approached the yew, there was no peace in my chest, no resignation. I felt instead a sudden, sharp joy, like the snap of a harrier's wings at the very bottom of the dive. I walked faster, and still faster, till the bare branches struck my cheeks.

There was a man waiting for me beneath the yew. His back was turned, so that I saw only the battered red of his coat, the careless profligacy of his hair.

One hand was pressed hard to the bark of the yew, and the other was holding a lumpen iron ornament. (*A gun,* I thought, and did not know where the thought had come from.)

I drew my sword. The blade whispered against the sheath.

He turned, and it was—you. Of course it was you.

You smiled at me, and I remembered that smile. A little crooked, a little wry, as if you were trying to make up for the ardency of your eyes.

You said my name, and I remembered your voice, though I remembered it lower, harsher, like a frayed rope.

You stumbled over the roots until you were near enough to reach out—foolishly! trustingly!—and touch two long fingers to the back of my hand.

I did not pull away. I looked down, saw the ink that stained the beds of your nails, admired the delicate callus where your pen rested. I have always liked your hands.

I turned my palm slowly, wonderingly, until it met yours, until we stood hand in hand beneath the yew.

And then I remembered everything.

It came on me suddenly, the remembering, like a spring storm, and took me to the ground. You were there with me, kneeling in the snow. Your hands were cradling my jaw, and you were saying my name over and over, in a kind of terror.

I felt myself smile, wide and loose, the way I hadn't smiled since I was a girl. "You came back for me."

I watched you choke with relief, eyes closing as if you could hardly bear the sight of me. "Always," you said, and your voice sounded more like the voice I remembered: fractured, scarred over.

I lifted my arms, hesitating still, just a little. But in all the lives that I could remember—and Lord, there were so many—I had never once hurt you.

I buried my hands in your hair, wrapped them in the boyish extravagance of your curls, as I never had, as I had done many times, as I would do many more. I felt time unweaving between us, the beginnings and endings lost in a reckless tangle, and I tightened my fists in your hair, holding fast to this one moment. You made a small and lovely sound, deep in your throat, and pressed your brow hard to mine.

We remained like that for a time, clinging to one another like children, our breath mingling and rising, riming our lashes with silvery frost.

You spoke first. "She's coming. She knew I would run, I think, and she knows where we are—or at least, *when* we are—"

I pulled my face back from yours, just a little, so that I could see the lovely loam-black of your eyes. "Who is coming?"

You didn't want to tell me. You stretched the moment out like a gift, letting me linger a little longer in a world where I didn't know what you knew.

There was only one name you could say that would hurt me. I felt my fingers sag and fall from your hair. I closed my eyes and said, without any real conviction, "No."

Your hands caught mine, thumbs circling soft as moth wings over the cracked stone of my palms. "I'm sorry," you said. "She's not who she says she is. She's—her name isn't even Yvanne."

I did not answer. I did not open my eyes. I only listened, while you told me the story of the queen-who-was-not-the-queen, who was every queen. You told it well, of course; you had been telling stories for more lifetimes than either of us could remember.

Once, there was a woman who wanted more than she was given. She wanted it so badly that she shattered time itself beneath her heel and pieced it back together in the way that suited her best. History no longer simply happened, like an accident; it was told, like a story. And the queen told it many times.

The story of Dominion had many villains over the years, shifting along with the borders of her empire, and many storytellers. But it only ever had one hero, and her name was Una Everlasting.

Una the dragon-slayer, Una the queen-maker, Una the tragedy. Una, who died and was resurrected a hundred times, until she fought as no mortal could fight, with the memory of every battle burned into her very bones.

(There was awe in your voice, even now—but surely a dog might learn any trick, given a thousand years of practice.)

I was not alone, in your story. I was trailed always by a cowardly historian, a man chosen by the queen to lead me to my death, like a farmer driving a balking animal to the butcher. And so—here your voice turned bitter as burnt hair—the historian buried the hero, over and over, and wrote her tale in the queen's book.

Until at last they began to remember themselves, or at least each other. This the queen could not permit. So she told one final story—a story so perfect it gave her an empire and a crown, a thousand years from now—and hid the book away. But the historian stole it and ran back to his hero.

And now, finally, we might write our own ending.

I let myself go slack, sagging against you, so that your voice hummed and buzzed in my skull, lingering even after you fell quiet.

I was sorry, I supposed, to lose whatever stubborn pride still remained to me. To learn that all my great deeds and noble battles had been carefully staged performances, my victories assured, my death predetermined.

I was even sorrier to lose the last scraps of my selfhood, to know that I had not lived a life but merely played a part. That I was not a woman but only a painted icon, with lacquer for skin and oil paint for eyes.

But I was sorriest of all to lose Yvanne, finally and forever.

The woman who gave birth to me, whoever she was, had abandoned me beneath the yew soon after. I had neither missed nor resented her as a child; I had a full belly and two parents who loved me, and I'd seen enough of the world beyond the woods to know myself lucky indeed. I hoped she was well, but it was a polite, impersonal emotion, as you might hold for a stranger.

Then I lost my fathers, and learned what it was to be hungry, to be alone, to be no one at all. When I first saw Yvanne that day in the woods, gazing down at me with such endless needing—when she whispered my new name in my ear—it was like being born anew. In this new life, she was my god and my religion, my savior, my queen—my mother.

I knew now I had never been her daughter. I was just a tool well suited to her work, a lost girl she had stumbled across by chance in the woods one day.

But—my heart went suddenly cold—was there any such thing as chance, in Dominion? If my fathers had not died, would I ever have drawn the sword from the yew? Would I have slain the Brigand Prince? Would I have so eagerly abandoned my old name, and taken the one she gave me?

I felt all the muscles of my back drawing tight, pulling away from you. I remembered my fathers the way I'd found them so many times: side by side, hand in hand, as if, with the very last of their strength, they had reached for one another.

The cruelty of it had sunk into me like the iron point of an arrow, and never fully worked loose. Father Foy and Father Theo were not weak or fearful men, but neither of them would have risked the other's life for the sake of a few pigs; they would not have fought the Brigand Prince and his men. Their deaths had been senseless, serving no purpose.

Save, perhaps, the queen's.

I wondered how many tries it had taken her, before she found the thing that would send me to the yew, and then to war, the single moment that would turn me from a child to a blade. I wondered how many times my fathers had been killed, how many times they had clasped hands as they died.

And suddenly I didn't want to run away at all. I wanted to ride back through the gates of Cavallon, sword drawn, and scream the queen's name until she met me in the yard.

If it was a tragedy Yvanne wanted, I would make her weep; if it was blood she wanted, I would drown her in it.

Your voice came to me in pieces, between the pounding of my own pulse in my ears. "Please, Una," you were saying. "Please, let her go. It doesn't matter. None of it matters."

I felt your fingertips on the back of my hand and discovered that I had clenched my fist hard around my hilt.

I had climbed halfway to my feet. You were still on your knees, a supplicant to some vengeful god. Your head was tilted back so that I could see the long, clean line of your throat, unmarked by war.

"Please," you said again. "Come with me. Leave her, leave all of it."

The hinge of my jaw creaked when I opened my mouth, stiff and reluctant. "The things she has done—the things *I* have done, in her name—"

"We can't go back anywhere within our own true lifetimes. We could forget again, and she could find us too easily. She'll be looking for us." You tilted closer, urgent now. "But I have the book, which means we can go further and faster than she can follow. I know how it works, more or less—"

I looked away from you, at the bare bones of the trees. "You want to run."

"I told you I was a coward." I heard the flinch in your voice.

"You want to run, and leave her alive."

"I want to run and leave *you* alive, you *ass*." You ran your hands over your face, so that your spectacles lay crookedly over the too-sharp bridge of your nose. "If we run now, we leave her story without its proper ending, and we take away her chance of ever fixing it. I don't know if it will be enough to take away her throne, but it will weaken her badly."

I said, stubbornly, knowing I was a fool and not caring, "There is no honor in running."

And you answered, with infinite exhaustion, "Fuck your honor, Una Everlasting."

I was struck silent.

You reached for my sword, and I let you ease my fingers from it, joint by joint. I even let you draw it, clumsily, and cut away the fine leather cording of the hilt. Beneath the leather there was a sign stamped in the steel: the letter *S,* repeated twice.

Then you set your gun beside my hilt, turned so that I could see the same mark pressed into the grip. I looked up at you, bewildered.

You tapped the mark on Valiance. "Saint Sinclair. The finest weapons maker of the modern age. Vivian must have had fifty swords made, a hundred. Each time it broke or chipped, she simply replaced it with a new one. Manufactured magic." More quietly: "It's a prop, Una. A fake. All of it is."

I remembered shattering that sword and finding it whole again in the morning. I remembered the strange comfort of it; if I was cruel or violent, if I cut like a knife through the world and left a bloody wake behind me—perhaps I had no choice. Perhaps it was my fate.

You went on: "You and I both swore to serve crown and country when we were too young to know better. But we served a lie. We have no honor. We have no duty. We are sworn to nothing and no one, now—save each other."

You lifted your hands and laid your palms along the planes of my thighs. You were not a supplicant now, but something much more dangerous, and a shudder moved through me at the sight of you.

You said, low and ragged, "I have loved you since before I was born, I think. I have studied you, worshipped you, lost you, mourned you. I have wept at your bier and fought beneath your flag. I have *killed* you, Una, over and over." Your voice dragged now like a dull blade, whetting itself against me. The tips of your thumbs pressed into my flesh. "This once, please—let me save you."

I sagged back to the earth. I nodded my head once, very slightly.

It felt awful, that letting go. Like falling on the field, like losing a limb.

Like killing the girl who'd been born that day in the woods, bathed in the blood of her enemies, and not knowing who was left.

You asked for my hand. I gave it to you. You took Valiance in your other hand and drew my thumb carefully, so carefully, along the blade. You hissed as the skin parted, as if my flesh were yours.

You pressed our hands to the open book, and our blood swam together on the empty page. I did not ask where or when we were going; it did not matter where we ran, so long as you ran beside me.

Very soon we were gone, and there was nothing beneath the yew save a gun, misplaced in time, and a sword beside it.

THE THIRD DEATH OF UNA EVERLASTING

17

IT IS DIFFICULT to keep track of time when you are traveling through it. We dove and rose through the years like a needle through cloth, and the needle does not count the stitches.

But you began to mark the days, after a while—even in rags, on the run, you were a scholar—and you tell me it was nine years, all told.

Nine years, we ran. Nine years we stole, hour by hour and page by page, from the miser of history. Nine cowardly years; nine perfect years.

I know you want to write the whole of it, every detail, so that we'll never forget again, but Owen, have mercy: Don't make me remember too well. Don't make me lose them again.

If you must write it, write it as a story or a song. A tale overheard, about other people. Write it without *you* or *I,* but only *they.*

Say: *They ran and ran.*

Say: *They ran until they found heaven.*

Say: *They ran until the devil caught them.*

Alright, love. Like a story, then:

Once upon a time, there were a knight and a scholar who both served the same wicked queen.

(We've been so many things—a legend, a history lesson, a lie—why not a fairy tale?)

The knight and the scholar did not want to serve the wicked queen any longer, and so they ran away. But they did not run in the ordinary way, over land or sea. Instead, they ran through time.

The scholar had stolen the queen's enchanted book, you see, which could send them into the distant past or the far-off future. They had only to set their hands on the pages, close their eyes, and bleed. Both of them had spent more blood, for worse causes; they did not mind a little more.

The first time they opened their eyes, they found themselves precisely where they had been before: beneath the yew, in the heart of the dark and wild wood.

Except now their palms were pressed to the bark, instead of the book, and it was spring. The air was raw and quick and full of birdsong, and the sap hummed greenly beneath their hands.

The knight said, 'But,' and then, 'how.'

The scholar, who did not always understand when questions were rhetorical, answered, 'Honestly, I'm not sure. Vivian told me it was God's will that the book sent us where and when it did but given that she lied almost constantly about everything else . . .' He shrugged. 'It was never God's will. It was *hers*. So why couldn't it be mine?'

The knight looked out at the wood, which she knew in all its seasons, as she would know the face of a dear friend. But the wood had changed, as though her friend had grown suddenly much older. The great yew still stood at the center, with its gnarling, deep-furrowed bark, its vast roots, its dense green crown—but the forest around it was subtly incorrect. There was shade where there ought to have been shafts of sun, giants where there ought to have been saplings. At her feet, something rusted between the roots: a scrap of metal, long since swallowed up by the earth.

'So,' said the knight, 'when did you send us, boy?'

The scholar blew out his breath. 'Sometime in the first regency? About a hundred and thirty years after you died, and eight hundred or so before I'm born.' He shrugged. 'I figure we're safest in times without a queen on the throne.'

The knight, who was very brave, had no talent for running away. She asked, uncertainly, 'And where will we go now?'

The scholar, who was a coward, answered grimly, 'As far and fast as we can.'

And they did.

They ran and left everything behind them: the yew and the wood, the dragon and the grail, the legend of their lives and the queen who told it.

They left their names, too, inventing new ones for each curious shepherd or bored tavern-keeper. In a Nornish village they left most of the knight's long flaxen hair, sheared away and buried in the churchyard. What remained they soaked in madder and vinegar, so that it curled muddily around her ears.

The scholar left his red coat, and the knight left her shining armor, bundled together and tossed overboard as they crossed the Slant Sea. The knight missed her armor sometimes—the certainty of it, the punishing weight—but not half so much as she missed her horse, who they had left wandering alone in the woods more than a century ago.

They left even their sexes behind, dressing sometimes as two men or two women, binding or stuffing their chests, lengthening or shortening their stride. This, at least, came easily to them, for neither of them had ever quite been what they were supposed to be, or acted how they ought to act. They were too manly or too womanish, too loud or too soft-spoken, too tall or too slim, too strong or too weak. It was no hardship to trade one disguise for another.

They left so much behind them that they were not always sure what, if anything, remained to them.

It was especially hard in the beginning, in those lean and hunted months when they were still learning how to run. The scholar was lost and often afraid and strangely ashamed, a more thorough deserter than his father ever was. The knight was bewildered, uncertain of herself, adrift, reaching always for the sword she no longer carried. She found herself reaching instead for the scholar, canting toward him—but he held himself carefully away from her.

If he touched her, it was only impersonally, accidentally. If he slept beside her, it was only for warmth. The knight lay next to him, baffled and aggrieved. His pulse had raced when she touched him; his breath had caught when he looked at her. But perhaps it had been a passing attraction, hot and brief as a fever. He'd said he loved her—but perhaps it was the chaste, courtly love of which bards so often sang.

Or perhaps it was her legend that he loved, a woman who no longer existed, or never truly had. In her place there was only the nameless knight, without oath or honor. Who, loving a painting, would want the raw canvas beneath it?

But then one morning the knight woke to the feel of the scholar's arms around her, his breath panting in her ear, his cock stiff and urgent against her hip. He woke abruptly, on a gasp, and rolled away from her. 'I'm sorry.'

She remained still, curled away from him, feeling the prick of horsehair through the mattress. Perhaps he had been dreaming of someone else. 'There is no call for apology.'

He swore, softly. 'The hell there isn't.' The mattress shifted as he climbed from the bed. He kept his head ducked as he fumbled for shirt and spectacles. They were in the drafty attic of a boardinghouse, and the beams were low. He said, stiffly, 'I don't—I wouldn't want to presume any intimacy, between us.'

He was blushing hard as he said it, and the knight found that some unkind, desirous part of her wanted to make it worse. 'I've died in your arms more than once. Is sex so much more intimate than death?'

'No—of course not—it's just . . .' He raked his fingers through his curls. 'You were hers, before. Because you had to be.' He scowled at her, blush deepening. 'You don't *have* to be mine. You don't have to be anyone's, ever again.'

Was this why he had not touched or kissed her, all these weeks? The knight swung her legs over the edge of the bedstead, marveling at him. 'We all belong to someone,' she said, gently. The whole of her world was a system of allegiances, long chains of bent knees and bowed necks that ran from sinner to pulpit, from peasant to throne. It disoriented her even to imagine herself outside of it; no link could be removed from the chain unbroken. 'We all serve someone. We all command someone. But *who* . . .' She caught his eyes with hers. 'That choice, at least, is now ours.'

She shrugged, and the loose collar of her shirt fell down over one shoulder. The scholar's eyes fixed on her skin, helpless and avid and black as fresh ink, and she knew it was her he wanted, after all, and not chastely.

He said, a little desperately, 'But what if we didn't choose, not really? What if it was only—proximity?' His mouth twisted around the word, as if it tasted bad. 'What if it's not real?'

The knight let her eyes fall to his trousers and said, filthily, 'Looks real enough to me.'

The scholar choked a little. 'I—I want to be sure you choose freely, that's all. You deserve to be free.'

'Who is free, who loves another?' the knight asked lightly, but she could see the question troubled her scholar. His thoughts drew his brows down and pressed his fine lips together, and she decided he ought to have fewer of them.

The fashion in this era was for flowing, silly shirts that laced up the front. She pulled the laces free and slipped her arms from the sleeves, so that the cloth slid and pooled at her waist.

The scholar tried not to move. He tried, as he had tried for weeks now, to take nothing he wasn't expressly offered: The knight had spent the whole of her life serving at the pleasure of others, and he was determined that she would not serve his.

But then the knight stretched her arms upward, lazily, purposefully, so that the muscles of her stomach and shoulders rolled, and the scholar found himself stepping forward. He stopped only when he stood, hazed and overwarm, between her spread knees.

His hands found her hair—still long, then—and pulled it around her shoulders so that the ends dragged softly over the tips of her breasts. 'God, Una,' he said, reverent. 'I would command you, if you would let me.' Then, hands tightening in her hair, voice roughening so that it reminded her of his old jackdaw's scrape, 'I would serve you, if you would have me.'

The knight leaned forward and pressed her mouth to the arch of his stomach, just where the wings of his ribs came together. She felt his flesh tremble beneath her lips and was struck suddenly by an awful terror. He was so vulnerable like this, so fragile. His head was thrown back, and even the skin of his throat was whole and unmarked, though she remembered the slick twist of scars.

She pulled away. 'Perhaps we should not.'

'What?' He blinked down at her, flushed and unsteady. Then his eyes went to her hands, and the knight realized she had curled them into fists, rather than reach for him. He touched the white points of her knuckles, smiling a little. 'Do you truly think you would hurt me, still? I am not afraid, Una.'

Darkly, she answered, 'You would be, did you know my thoughts.' She wet her lips. 'It is not—gentle, the way I want you.'

'Ah,' the scholar said, '*you're* the one who's afraid.'

'I'm not—'

'Shall I tell you what *I* want? Shall I make an order of it?' The knight drew a sudden, sharp breath and the scholar knew he was correct. There was a certain pleasure, God knew, in following orders, in placing the heavy reins of your life in someone else's hands. All your sins were not truly yours, then; all your unruly desires were safely curbed. But now the knight held her own reins, and her hands shook with the weight of them.

The scholar leaned down so that the stubble of his cheek scraped along her jaw. 'Take me however you want. Use me cruelly or kindly, as you like. Command me, if you can.'

He smiled as he pulled away, a sly and arrogant smile that made the knight's fists loosen suddenly. It was a thrown gauntlet, a taunt from a challenger who stepped grinning into the ring. It made a battle between them, and oh—she liked to win.

'Though I warn you,' the scholar added, and stroked the back of his hand down his own throat, where his scars had once been, but were no longer, 'I have a history of mutiny.'

She said, shakily, 'Then kneel, boy,' without knowing if it was a plea or an order.

'Make me,' he answered, without knowing if he was begging or demanding.

The knight grabbed the hem of his shirt and pulled him to the floor. He went too easily, forgetting to resist. His face was very hot. He could feel his pulse in his skull, his stomach, his cock.

The knight lifted the long hem of her shirt and let her knees fall apart. He said, in some torment, 'You weren't—you weren't wearing anything under—God.'

He stared, trembling a little, until the knight made an impatient sound and reached for him. But she hesitated, hand hovering just before it reached him. Gently, the scholar covered her hand with his and brought it to the back of his head, curling her fingers into his hair.

Then she brought his mouth to her cunt and kept it there.

He came to her ravenously, almost roughly, and she had to pull his hair hard to slow him down, make it last. Still, the sight of him kneeling between her legs—his lips slick and swollen—

She pulled him away from her, panting, thighs shaking.

He groaned. 'Just let me—you were close—' Her scholar, always so articulate, was slurring slightly.

She stood, pulling him clumsily to his feet, bringing his mouth to hers. 'Shh,' she whispered into his mouth, and felt a tremor move through him.

Then she turned and shoved him down on the mattress. She stripped his trousers roughly from his legs—his fault, for coming fully dressed to her bed.

He protested. 'I won't last—you don't understand how long I've—'

The knight climbed astride him. He struggled beneath her, and oh, she liked that. She caught his wrists and pinned them above his head easily, one-handed. He stopped struggling, abruptly, and she liked that even more.

The knight lowered herself onto his cock in one fast, merciless push, and rode him until he lost their first battle. He came hard and helpless, on a hoarse shout.

When the scholar recovered (he did not think he would ever recover), he turned in bed to find the knight breathing very carefully, strangely still.

Almost resigned, as if she were accustomed to being used and left like this, flushed and hazy, unsated.

The scholar rolled her gently onto her back and slid his fingers between her legs.

'You don't have to—' the knight said, but she had thought of those long, clever fingers often, almost more often than his mouth.

He spoke into the shell of her ear—of course he did. Of course he would not stop talking, even now, with his hand working inside her and his cock pulsing thickly against her. He told her how good she was, how beautiful, how badly he needed her. He brought her to the very edge—and she hung there, tense and sweating, unable to let go.

It was a surrender, and a knight does not surrender until she's told to.

The scholar said, softly, 'It's alright. I have you. Come, Una,' and she did.

He held her afterward, her head on his chest, her leg pulled across his. He stroked her hair, wonderingly, and touched her scars, until the owner of the boardinghouse knocked politely on the attic door and asked them to please leave, as this was a decent establishment, and neither of them wore wedding rings.

Later, the scholar asked the knight if she would like a ring. 'Or, I don't know, a proper ceremony, with a priest. Or a certificate from the state, though not under our legal names—'

'No,' the knight said, in some alarm. The crown and the church were the reason they were running; why would they seek sanction from their enemies?

'Oh,' said the scholar, in a slightly crushed voice.

'But I hope you do not need a ring to keep you at my side,' the knight said. Her voice was lower and more serious than she meant it to be. 'I fear I am a jealous woman, and do not share what is mine.'

'Oh,' the scholar said again, in a much happier voice.

When, in the years that followed, the knight and the scholar felt their losses too keenly—if they missed the glory of war or the labor of study or the sounds of their own names—if they felt like cart horses cut loose from their traces, running in no direction save away from the lash—they reached for one another. The knight would put her mouth to the scholar's collarbone and his pulse would rise under her lips and they would think: *We have this.*

And it was enough, or would have been.

The knight, who had died many times, had no talent for survival. So the scholar was obliged to lay down certain rules.

The first rule was that they could make no home for themselves for very long, lest word spread of a tall, grim woman and a slim, nearsighted man, or of two strangers who spoke with old-fashioned accents.

The second rule was that they could not travel before the knight's death or after the scholar's birth, lest they forget themselves again, and become lost.

The third rule, which the knight resented most of all, and which the scholar was most adamant about, was that they could not interfere.

The wicked queen could not travel in time without her enchanted book, but there were so many versions of her already tangled into the history of Dominion that no era could be truly safe from her. Even if she wasn't wearing the crown, she was surely lurking nearby it—as a princess, perhaps, or a duke's wife, an angel or an abbess, a minister or a general—tending her terrible dream as carefully and ruthlessly as a vintner tended his fields.

And now that dream was shriveling like a grape in a drought.

Dominion didn't die outright. The knight had vanished only at the very end of the queen's plot, after all. The crown had already been won, the crusades already fought. But the grail had never been found, and the Queen's Champion had never returned from her grand quest.

There were many endings invented for her story, none of them satisfying. Some claimed they had seen the knight themselves decades later, still miraculously young, and so she must have stolen the grail for herself. Others said no, the dragon must have taken her, for she would never have abandoned her quest. (At this the knight would snort, meanly, and the scholar would contrive to step on her foot.)

But no one disputed what happened next: The first queen had died tragically young and named no heirs. For the next few decades, the throne was traded between squabbling usurpers, like a sweet among children, while the Hyllmen and Galls quietly slipped Dominion's leash, and the Hinterlands were lost once more.

If the wicked queen ever clawed her way back to the throne, it was not an empire she would rule, but only its remains. Wherever she was, whatever name she used: She was angry, and she was looking for them.

There could be no rumors of a white-haired woman who swung a blade as if it were a stalk of wheat. There could be no whispers of a dark-eyed man who knew too much about the future. There could be no change or break in the pattern of history, which the queen might follow, like a dropped stitch, back to them.

The scholar had explained all this to the knight many, *many* times, and still she argued with him.

If they found themselves lingering overlong after one of those paganish village festivals that had sprung up as the church lost its hold on the countryside—if they were dizzy with mead and sex and the playful taunt of the lyre in the distance—she might say, softly, 'There's a cottage out on the marsh, empty since their last peat cutter died.' Then, even more softly, 'She might never find us.'

And the scholar would shake his head and say, 'Rule one.'

Or, as they dragged a pair of mules over a craggy white mountaintop, she might burst out: 'What of Hen? He suffered as much as you or I. You said she sent him back like us, over and over. Let me go back before the crusade, when he was a colt—'

'Rule two,' the scholar would say, wearily.

'—and take him with us. You miss him, I know you do—'

'Rule three, and no I don't.' (He did.) (A little.)

Or, worse, when they came upon three soldiers in Dominion red, laughing as they beat a beggar in the streets of Old Cantford, the knight would lunge forward—she carried no sword, but she was weapon enough—and the scholar would catch her wrist.

'Please,' he would say.

Eventually she would answer, grinding the words through her teeth, 'As you will.'

Late on the night they left the beggar to his fate, she said, bitterly: 'Well done, boy.' She threw a branch onto the fire, and the sparks wavered in her vision, distorted by tears. 'You've killed Una Everlasting once and for all.'

'God knows I'm trying,' the scholar answered, too sharply. Then, with more patience: 'She has to die, for you to live. Or at least disappear so thoroughly that no one ever, ever finds her.'

'I know,' said the knight, and she did. 'It's only that I miss her, sometimes. I miss being . . .'

He said, gently, cruelly, 'You were never a hero, love.'

She flinched, as he knew she would, because it was not only the beggar she wanted to save; it was the cities she'd burned and the soldiers she'd slain, the villages she'd pillaged and the heretics she'd put to the sword. It was everyone who suffered still under the failing, grasping, lurching power of Dominion; it was her evil horse; it was her fathers, most of all, who were the first reason she held a sword, and the first people she hadn't saved.

The scholar rose to his knees at her back. 'You were only ever a weapon. A tool, fashioned for a purpose.' He set his lips beneath her ear, so that she shivered. 'But at least you are no longer hers.'

Then he lay back and pulled her astride him. She took him deeply and not gently, the way he liked best, his wrists pinned, his pulse beating frantic in his throat. She rode him until he arced beneath her and came, shouting her name so loudly against the dark that she knew she had not—not quite, not yet—disappeared.

18

IF YOU RUN far enough, for long enough, you will catch the rhythm of it. It's the same thing that drives the swifts south before the frost and rats uphill before the flood: a thrum in the blood, a second pulse that whispers *now, now, now.*

The knight and the scholar followed that pulse north and south, forward and backward in time. They went by foot, most often, but they went, too, by ferry and galley, by coach and carriage and even—once the knight could tolerate the stink and noise of them—by automobile. They traveled along ancient dirt tracks and roads so freshly paved the tar still stuck, hotly, to the soles of their shoes. They slept in lofts and fallow fields, in boardinghouses and shabby hotels and, once or twice, gaols.

They learned which elements of the world change most quickly and dramatically (hairstyles, fashion, medical advice) and which linger, stubbornly, no matter the decade (filthy words, trade routes, children's rhymes). They learned how to ask for work in half a dozen languages, which crossroads would always have inns no matter the century, which streams would never be dammed, and which borders would never be well guarded.

Most of all they learned one another, as few people ever have or will. In the churn and tumult of their lives—where summer did not always follow spring, where even their own names were tricksome and shifting—they were to one another what fixed stars are to sailors: the only way through the dark.

They knew each other's taste and smell, the sounds they made in the night and the old wounds that turned stiff in the rain. The scholar knew every scar on the knight's body and where it came from—save the small, silver circle between her breasts, which she must have gotten as a child, for she couldn't recall a time when it wasn't there.

Each knew the other's face by moonlight and rushlight, candle and gas, and even by the sharp-edged glare of streetlights—though they spent less time in the modern age than in others.

The knight found it overloud and overcrowded, and it found her wrong sized, roughly hewn, almost comical in scale. The scholar didn't miss his own time much, save for the cigarettes; the whole of modernity—with its bank accounts and receipts, its leases and cameras and pay stubs—seemed engineered to expose them.

And if they were exposed, she would find them. She came very close, sometimes. Once when they lingered too long in the same year and town and were heard to call one another by names other than they ones they'd given; once when the knight challenged their landlord to a duel, long after duels had fallen out of fashion; once when the scholar left his spectacles on the table of an inn, long before their invention.

Soon after such blunders they would wake to fists on the door or boots in the street, or perhaps the rumor of a cold-eyed stranger asking if anyone had seen a man and woman traveling together. Once there were even dogs, great black hounds that cornered them in a narrow alley; the scholar had never liked dogs.

But they were never truly cornered because they had the book.

They tried, though, to use it as little as possible. Partly because there was always an awkward few days while they adjusted their accents and outfits and overheard enough political gossip to determine whether there was a queen in Dominion, and if her hair was the color of beaten brass; partly because people talk when two strangers vanish from inside a locked room, or when two hungry travelers never return to finish their meal. Even their absence left footprints.

But mostly they avoided the book because there was, to their bafflement, a fourth rule: No matter where they were when they touched the book—no matter how carefully they willed themselves elsewhere—they always found themselves back beneath the yew.

The scholar had a dozen theories. Perhaps the book somehow sensed their secret desire to return to the place they'd both felt most at home. Perhaps the wicked queen had sent them back to those woods so many times that their souls had left grooves along the path, like penned animals wearing tracks in the grass. Perhaps the yew was so unspeakably ancient it made a sort of well in time itself, which they fell back into, over and over.

The knight did not care why. There was no place in the world she liked better than those woods, and the queen—who had found them in caves and foreign cities, in the swede fields of the north and the cold deserts of the far south—had never once found them there. She'd claimed the land for the crown and driven the small folk from it, and seemed to have forgotten it, as if what is conquered will remain so.

Slowly, even the scholar came to trust the woods. They began to loiter there, for days, then weeks, then whole greedy seasons, seeing no one but pig boys and berry pickers, runaway lovers with flushed faces and ragged peasants fleeing the queen's soldiers.

They began to bury caches there for their future selves to find: rolls of bandaging, tins of fish and beans, arrows, fresh socks, soap, clothes from twenty different decades, furtive cartons of Lucky Star cigarettes. They shored up the walls of the woodcutter's cottage with fresh daub and left firewood split and stacked beneath the eaves.

They began to miss it when they were away from it. They began to think of it—guiltily, secretly—as home.

And so they broke the first rule.

The first time the knight missed her menstrual cycle, she cursed, dressed in the dark, and went to visit the nearest brothel. After a short and practical conversation with a very pretty woman, the knight was given a sachet of sharp-smelling herbs. She thanked the woman, who blushed a little and encouraged her to return 'if she was tired of men.' The knight kissed her hand, gallantly, and apologized; she did not think she would tire of this man.

The tea she brewed with the herbs had a familiar, grassy taste—the queen had kept a supply for such occasions.

Later, when the knight explained to the scholar why she was ill, he turned very white. He stammered and apologized many times, as if she hadn't known the risk, as if she hadn't held him inside her while he thrashed, only because she liked the feel of it, and liked it even better when she took him again later, still slick with it.

But the scholar rubbed the muscles low in her back and boiled cloths for the blood. His fretting startled the knight—it was only one of those dull bodily tasks, like picking dirt from a wound, or pulling a bad tooth!—but that night she let him curl around her, like human armor, as if she needed protection.

The second time the knight missed her menstrual cycle, they were in the woods. The scholar kissed her sweetly on the brow, opened the book, and disappeared. He returned two minutes later with his arms full: fresh white cloths, paper sachets of tea, a hot water bottle, and a glass vial of pills.

She rolled the pill between her fingers, hesitating, though she couldn't say why. It was just that the light was dappling through the cottage door the same way it had when she was a girl. It was just that it was spring, when the whole world quickens, and the forest was littered with pollen and shed teeth and the fragile, speckled shells of hatched eggs.

It was just that she had always known precisely what purpose her body served—bloodshed—and she felt suddenly uncertain.

Ancel had fathered six or seven bastards, who he supported so handsomely that their mothers never made a fuss about their red hair. But Saint Una the Virgin could never be allowed to fall pregnant. Nor could Sir Una the Queen's Champion—how would her armor fit? Now, though, the knight had no armor to wear or name to uphold; she caught herself wondering what other names she might bear.

And then she wondered if *mother* was another of those names, like *saint* or *sir,* that built a cage around you. She was through with cages.

She swallowed the pill. It tasted like metal.

The third time the knight missed her cycle, they were still in the woods, and she noticed that the scholar's hands were shaking when he handed her the glass vial.

She said, stunned into bluntness, 'You *want* it, don't you?'

He flushed, guilty as a child caught with his nose pressed to a bakery window. 'No. I mean, yes, of course, if—but it's not safe. We couldn't.'

The knight said, slowly, surprising both of them, 'We could.' It felt like biting into a fruit long forbidden to her. The heady taste of it filled her mouth.

The scholar's eyes went very wide, filling with such obvious, reckless wonder that the knight coughed and looked away.

She said, roughly, 'Though I'm not—I don't know how—that is, I don't know that I'd be everything a mother should.'

The scholar tilted his head at her. 'I suppose I wouldn't know—I never had a mother, either. But . . . I'm not sure you've ever been what you *should* be, love.' She scowled at him; he smiled his crooked smile. 'You were a woman who carried a sword. A saint who slept with nuns—don't pretend you never visited Morvain in the convent! Now you're a knight without armor, and a wife without a ring. No matter what you are, you're always . . .'

'Bad at it?'

'*Yourself,*' said the scholar, stubbornly. 'And you'll remain so. Whatever you become next.'

The knight rolled the pill in her fingers, marveling a little at the certainty in the scholar's voice when he said the word *next.*

There had never been a next for her, no after. How had she never noticed it? The queen had showered her with praise songs and titles, but never land or tithes. Lovers had been tolerated, but never marriage or children. Men might follow her into battle, but never be sworn to her service. There had never been any provision for her future because she had never been intended to have one.

But now the future hung on the vine, hers for the taking, and she found she was ravenous for it.

She dropped the pill to the earth and ground it dispassionately beneath her heel.

The scholar gasped. 'But how—we couldn't raise a baby, the way we live.' His voice was miserable with want. 'Wherever we went, she would find us, eventually.'

'Unless we go where she never was.' It was an argument they'd had before. But—before—it hadn't seemed worth winning. 'Unless we went back further, before all of this.'

Now the scholar's hands were running frustratedly through his own hair. The knight liked the way his curls looked afterward, startled, harassed. 'And what if we forget everything again? What if the book doesn't even go back that far? What if she anticipated us, and she's waiting, somehow, before you were even born?'

The knight had learned that it was best, at these times, to let the scholar argue both sides against himself. He paced and gestured while she watched. 'Although . . . without the book, how would she ever travel to us, even if she suspected where we'd gone? Suppose I tested it, first, just in case—'

Eventually the knight caught his hands in midair and tugged him down into her lap. 'We could settle here in the woods, long before I was born. Before even my fathers were born, or Yvanne! I could build a fine home for us, you know I could.' This was true; there were few kinds of work they hadn't taken, in their years of travel, and even fewer she hadn't taken to. She looked up at the thatched roof of the cottage and added, musing, 'Father Theo said he found it standing empty when he first came to the woods. It might be this very house that I build for us. Perhaps I already have.'

Still the scholar hesitated, until the knight took pity on him and said, in the same voice she used to drive men into battle, to make them forget their fears and fight for victory rather than mere survival, 'Please.'

And he answered, in relief, 'As you will.'

And so they broke the second rule.

They ran again, further than ever before, to a time when the woods belonged to no one, when Dominion was not even a whisper of a dream, and the yew was so young the sun could fall cleanly through its canopy.

For a moment they stood wondering and disoriented, but then the scholar said, 'No.'

The knight turned and saw it buried in the bark of the yew: the hilt of a sword. The sword she would pull from the tree as a young girl, a century from now, which had been placed there like a stage prop by the wicked queen. The wood had already swelled around the metal, like an unlanced boil.

'But if it's *here,* this far back—then Yvanne must have been here before us. We're not safe, we'll never be—' the scholar broke off, swearing.

But the knight studied the hilt carefully. Then she drew a knife from her hip and cut the rotted leather wrapping away. 'Look,' she said. 'No mark.'

The scholar looked and saw that it was true; the tang of the sword was perfectly smooth. His brows arced and furrowed as he thought. 'If it's not a Saint Sinclair . . . then it's not one of hers. Perhaps there really was a sword in a tree—the stories about Valiance certainly predate yours—and she merely made copies, later. Perhaps she never came this far back.'

The scholar chewed at his lips, fretfully. The knight put her knuckle beneath his chin and tipped his face up. 'Even if she did, she cannot return here without the book, and she will not have any reason to try, because she will never hear of us.' The scholar swallowed, wanting badly to be convinced. The knight said, 'There is no crown and no country here. There are no legends about a lady knight. We are safe, the two of us—three, I suppose.'

At this, the scholar buried his face in the soft hollow of the knight's throat and wept.

The knight stroked his back, soothingly, and did not look at the sword.

Eventually the scholar took her hand and pulled her away from the yew, toward the clearing where they would build their home. She told him about the fen where she would dig the clay for their walls, the hazel copse where she would cut the wattle, the distant farmstead where she might find wheat for their thatch. They would be simple folk of the forest, and such people had no need of swords.

The cottage was finished well before the cold came, and they'd only cheated a little. If it rained, they traveled a few days later, when it was dry. If the wheat was too green, they took it with them a few months back, and left it to cure. The scholar made a single, furtive trip into the early modern age, returning to the yew with a bow saw and mallet, an ax, and a good sharp augur.

He also brought a cheap mirror, which he hung by the wash bucket for shaving. The knight found herself moving carefully around it, keeping her back turned, until one day her own reflection caught her unawares. She was still herself—big and rough, badly scarred—and yet different. Changed. The line of her jaw had softened with fat. Her hips had widened, and her belly and breasts pushed against the rough wool of her dress. She had always been a woman, she supposed—but she'd never looked like one.

She didn't mind it, really. She had found ordinary skirts much easier to manage than court dresses, and she and the scholar both liked to run their hands over her belly like cartographers surveying a brand-new country. And yet—she felt something like grief, that her child would never see her in full armor. He would only ever know her in hiding, half disguised.

The scholar came home then and found her looking at her reflection as if it were a stranger in their home. He took the mirror down without saying anything, and neither of them mentioned it in the months that followed.

It was midwinter when the knight felt the first ripple of labor. She looked out at the bare gray branches and decided that she wanted her child to meet the world when it was warm, and the sun was shining. So they traveled to spring, as other people might travel to the sea or the market, and their son was born, sudden and pink and slick, beneath the yew.

His hair was thick and curling, but so pale it could be mistaken for a caul. He had very fine fingers, long and delicate as willow branches, and a round birthmark, red as a yewberry, on his left foot.

The scholar looked down at his son and thought: Here, at last, is something worth dying for. The knight looked at the scholar, looking at his son, and thought: Here, at last, is something worth killing for.

They named him—but no. You asked for mercy. I will not make you remember his name.

19

THE KNIGHT, WHO had killed a thousand men a thousand times, had no talent for keeping anything alive.

Her calluses caught and pulled the threads of her son's soft blankets. The only songs she knew were either dirty or bloody or both; her hands, so natural with a blade, were clumsy with an infant. It seemed best to leave him in his father's care; surely the Red Knight ought never to be entrusted with anything so small, so desperately fragile.

When the baby fussed in the night, it was the scholar who went to him. When the larder grew low, it was the knight who went out hunting. When she returned, she often found her son sleeping on the scholar's chest, lashes lying soft and white as moonlight on his cheek.

But most of the time the scholar was only feigning sleep, because when he slept, he dreamed of his own father. He saw him marching across the Hinterlands with an infant tied to his chest, then crippled and drunk in Queenswald with a toddler to care for. He saw him fumbling, striving, often failing; he saw the townspeople shaking their heads, averting their eyes. They'd thought him a poor father, and the scholar had mostly agreed—but now he was unsure what a good one ought to look like.

In Dominion a good father was any man with a decent living who produced a child with his wife—a woman he had married in a church, who had been trained to be a mother from the time she was a child herself. He need not be sober, affectionate, or even present very often; he needn't know how to soothe his son to sleep, or how to tie his diapers so they didn't leak.

And yet: The scholar's father had learned those things. He must have. He must have sat sometimes in the night, just like this, worried and tired, feigning sleep. The scholar wished, suddenly, that he could speak with his father. Or at least ask him how to tie the damn diapers.

The knight saw her husband smile, wistfully, crookedly, and cup his hand around their son's head. She backed carefully away from the two of them, thinking of the yew, and of the hilt that waited still for her hand. Thinking: Nothing this precious could go undefended for long.

This is why, when a knock came at the cottage door some five or six months after their son's birth, the scholar was shocked and frightened, but the knight felt almost peaceful. Here was the danger, finally; here was her fate, caught up with her at last.

But it was only a young man, shaking from a long run in the near-dark, stinking of fear. He was the son of the crofter whose wheat had thatched their roof. The knight brought his family game, sometimes, or honey, in trade for butter and salt. She knew this boy to be a laughing, mischievous middle son.

He was not laughing now. 'Raiders,' he said, and what else was there to say?

This was Dominion before the wicked queen: A series of small kings and lords who took turns scribbling new lines across the map, dividing the land into what was theirs and what was theirs to take, until their thrones were stolen in turn, and the lines drawn anew. None of them lasted long; the scholar thought they should meet Vivian Rolfe and see how a real empire was made.

And so violence still swept sometimes across the land, like a swarm of locusts. It nibbled at the woods: ash was taken for the hafts of spears; cedar for arrows; oak for the hulls of boats. Exiles and hungry peasants hid among the trees, and their gaunt faces made the knight wonder if it was truly the queen who was wicked, or the crown itself. If a throne was a kind of weapon, by which the world was cut into two halves: the dead and the kneeling.

But the knight had not interfered. She and the scholar wanted no word of a light-haired woman who fought off soldiers and raiders, who protected the small folk and lived deep in the wood with her dark-eyed husband. What if the queen heard such tales, decades or centuries in the future? What if she somehow clawed her way back to them? They didn't know where the book had come from, after all; better by far to disappear.

But now one of those small folk had come to her door, and the knight felt the old battle tide rising in her, clean and righteous as a prayer.

The scholar, who had placed himself between the cradle and the door, said sharply, 'Why did you come running to us? What makes you think we could help you?'

The boy looked baffled. He glanced, speakingly, at the knight, who understood that her disguise was not so perfect as she had thought. It was the size of her, maybe, that gave her away, or simply the way she moved. What simple woodswoman sometimes forgot herself and swung her ax one-handed, as if it were a sword? What good wife or mother strode through the world so boldly, without smiling or ducking her head? She was still, as the scholar had promised, herself.

'Please,' the boy said. Then, trembling and trying not to, 'My brother. He—they—' He said no more; what else was there to say?

The scholar gestured gruffly to the floor by the fire. 'Sit. Eat something.'

The boy sat, cracking nuts and digging out the meat with the thoughtless, jerky motions of a clockwork toy. Over his head, the knight and the scholar spoke to one another in the way of old couples who had met very young: in silence, by look and gesture.

The knight met the scholar's eyes squarely: *Will we let them die, then? Will we send him home without aid, to whatever remains of his family?*

A muscle moved in the scholar's jaw: *Will you risk ours, for theirs?*

The knight looked away, and the scholar watched her face with a familiar, leaden guilt. He'd told her once that she was no hero—what a lie. The queen had tried for years to make a mere weapon of her, a blade that killed coldly, without hesitation; the scholar had tried for years to make a coward of her, a woman who lived selfishly, without risk. Both of them had tried to cut the honor out of her and leave only what served them best, and both of them had failed, for here she stood: so full of honor even a child could feel the heat of it and run to her for help.

The scholar was suddenly sick with himself, with the gory work of carving away what he loved best. He touched the knight's elbow with two fingers. 'We have already broken two rules,' he said. *What's one more?* said his eyes.

Her lips parted. She looked at him, and then at the crofter's son, and then at her own son, just beginning to frown in his sleep. Soon he would begin the mysterious squirming, flailing motions by which he escaped his swaddling. Already his left foot had worked free. In the dark, his birthmark looked like a wound.

The knight left the cottage without speaking, and the scholar watched her go without weeping. She walked in the dark to the yew. She did not stumble; she had walked this path many times.

Beneath the tree her hand found Valiance. Her fingers wrapped around the hilt, and it felt good. It had been too large for her hands when she was a girl, but now it fit her palm perfectly.

She imagined drawing it from the wood, stalking to the near edge of the woods, slaughtering the raiders, saving the farm, righting this one small wrong. She imagined washing the blood from her hands before she returned to her son. There would be some left in the beds of her nails or the crease of her elbow; there always was.

She imagined the queen discovering that the sword had been drawn too early from the yew and realizing, at last, where they'd hidden themselves.

Slowly, knuckle by knuckle, the knight took her hand from the hilt.

She returned to the cottage and knelt, empty-handed, before the crofter's son. 'I'm sorry,' she said, and the words were grave dirt in her mouth. 'We cannot help you.'

Later in the night, when the baby fussed, it was the knight who went to his cradle. She held him tenderly, uncertainly, with hands that would never again hold a sword. Already her calluses had changed, adjusting to the simple labor of living.

The scholar watched her, softened by moonlight, and knew Una Everlasting had died another death at his hands.

We are coming now to the end of their fairy tale, and every fairy tale ends the same way: happily ever after.

This was theirs, and Lord, it was sweet. I know you don't like to remember it, but try, for me.

Remember the book tucked away on a high shelf, nearly forgotten, gathering dust, because they were no longer on the run. Remember the seasons returning to their proper order, coming one after the other.

Winter. The yewberries are covered in frost, chiming softly, and their son is beginning to talk. *Ma ma ma,* he calls the knight, a pattern more than a word. She meant to choose a new name for herself, but never quite did. She answers now only to whatever her son and the scholar call her—mother, wife, beloved, mine—and when she dies it is only by those names she will be remembered. She decides it is enough.

Summer. The honey tastes of dog rose and their son's hair is long enough to make a slim white braid. His father tells him stories as he braids it, of dragons and crowns and swords. The boy says one day he will be a knight, and the scholar says, too sharply, '*No.*' He tells no more tales, after that, and eventually his son stops asking for them.

It occurs to the scholar that he has slowly become his own opposite. As a historian he chased stories—collected them, cherished them, pressed them tenderly between the pages of books so that the whole world could read them. Now he stamps them out, frantically, and buries the remains. He misses his work; he misses the university library even more.

But if the knight can put away her sword, then he can put away his pen. He no longer fears the cold, and the knight no longer flinches from the fire. Surely, it's enough.

Spring again. The thrushes are singing and their second child is born. Her hair is a wet black cap and her eyes are the lucent brown of acorns in the sun. Her brother, upon meeting her, comforts his parents. 'Maybe the next one will come with teeth,' he says, patting his mother's knee.

It's a funny story, and the scholar finds himself wishing, guiltily, that he had someone to tell it to. Professor Sawbridge, maybe—she didn't like children, as a genre, but she would like his. Or his father—he was forever pulling faces at babies in their prams, laughing his loose drunkard's laugh. Perhaps he would do a little better as a grandfather than he had as a father.

But no: Their children can have no grandparents or aunts, no uncles or cousins or teachers or scuff-kneed neighbor children. They have no lineage and no inheritance. No past, and an uncertain future. Will they leave the wood and go out into the wide, cruel world? Will their sweet son one day go to war? Will their loud daughter sit silent in the pew, head bowed?

All the children have is *now*, hidden away. It will have to be enough.

A year passes, and another, and another. It's summer again.

Their son is hiding from his sister in the woods, flashing from tree to tree like quicksilver, and she is chasing stubbornly after him on legs that are still bowed and dimpled with babyhood. She does not cry, when she falls; she reminds her father of the girl he used to meet beneath the yew.

The knight, who is no longer a knight, is lying on the warm earth beside the scholar, who is no longer a scholar. They are sharing a basket of berries so fat and ripe they catch the sun, like fine jewels, and there are tiny white flowers blooming all around them, between and beneath them.

The knight picks one of these and tucks it behind the scholar's ear. He hasn't cut his hair in a long time, and the fragile petals are nearly lost in his wild black curls.

'They're called dragonscales, in my time, or ulla flowers,' the scholar tells her, and the knight's eyes open very wide, as if she's just found something she thought was lost forever.

Then she is laughing, head thrown back, and there is berry juice running over her chin, down her throat. The scholar wipes it away with his thumb and puts his thumb to his own lips. He has had this dream before, he thinks, but no dream ever tasted this sweet.

Like home; like heaven.

He knows what it cost to get here. Sometimes in the night he sees their faces: the Hinterlanders he killed in the war and the Dominion boys who died beside him, their blood made invisible by the red of their coats; the soldiers who fell to the knight's sword in the First Crusade and the heretics who went to the flames; the crofter's son who still turns his face away when they visit, in memory of the brother they didn't save; everyone who will still suffer under the queen's faltering, grasping rule, and everyone they will turn away, lest they draw her eye.

He doesn't know if it was worth it. But he knows he would pay the same price all over again, if only he could find himself here, on this stolen summer evening, with the taste of berries in his mouth.

It's then—just then, when he has begun to believe in his own happily ever after—that he hears it: Branches snapping, boots approaching, and a voice he hasn't heard in nine years. Nine long, good, golden years.

The voice says, in a language that won't be spoken for another millennium: 'Hello, Corporal.'

He should have known, of course: Heaven is only a fairy tale.

The devil is real.

THE FOURTH DEATH OF UNA EVERLASTING

20

IT HAPPENED SO quickly: We were dreaming, and then we were awake. We were safe, and then we weren't. We were nameless, forgotten, hidden away in time, and then I was Corporal Owen Mallory again, and you were—

"Sir Una," said the voice. You flinched from the sound of your own name. The line between your brows returned, harshly drawn. The voice said, more softly, "It's been too long."

It sounded as if she meant it. As if she'd missed you, these nine years, and longed to look at you. You kept your eyes resolutely, almost desperately, on mine; it occurred to me that you'd run away from her without ever once facing her.

A sigh, from above us. "Up, now—carefully. I've told these boys you're witches, and heavily implied cannibalism. They're jumpy."

I got slowly to my feet, arms half raised. The ulla flower slipped out from behind my ear and fell to the earth.

Vivian Rolfe greeted us with the warm, delighted smile of someone who has run into old friends unexpectedly. She was in one of her more modern incarnations: short hair, crisp martial clothing. But the men behind her—six or seven of them—surely belonged to this era. They wore boiled leather armor and carried short, brutish blades.

I glanced sideways at you and found your gaze judging the reach of their arms, calculating the force of each blow. Your face was very remote, as if you were watching your body from a distance.

Your eyes skipped over Vivian—you still hadn't looked directly at her—and met mine, eerily flat: *Now?*

I lowered my lashes: *Not yet.*

"So," I said, in modern Mothertongue, loud enough that it might carry to the glassberry thicket where the children were playing. "You've found us." I'd taught them enough of my native language to recognize it if they heard it, and if they heard it, I'd taught them to hide. The rustling, scuffling sounds from the thicket fell suddenly still.

"I *did* warn you I would. Don't tell me you forgot my little monologue." Vivian looked very slightly put out. "It was a good one."

You will lament, she had said, *and there will be no end to your lamentation.*

"No." My throat was dry, the words rattling from it like dice from a cup. "I didn't forget." But I had. I'd stopped running, and she'd come for us, just as she'd said she would.

"Good, then we're all working from the same script. Now, what have you done with my book?"

"This way." I turned sharply and led them to the cottage, the only place in all of history that had ever felt like home.

I could hear your steps behind me, a steady pulse: *Now?*

I jerked my head: *Not yet.*

Say you killed her. Say you killed all of them. Say you survived it, even—would you? unarmed, nine years out of practice?—Vivian had found us once, somehow. What would prevent her from doing it again? I felt like a rat caught in a mill, watching the stone roll inexorably toward me.

The cottage was too small for a group of this size. Vivian's men pressed against the walls, trampling furs, overturning baskets. I wondered if any of them would notice the doll fashioned from sacking and twine, the too-small pairs of shoes, the crib our daughter had learned to escape before she could walk.

Vivian snapped her fingers. "The book, if you please."

It was too late in the year for a fire, but the children had wanted porridge for lunch, and the last log was still crackling in the pit. The air was close and warm as a gullet. It smelled, sickly, of flowers.

Beside me, you inhaled: *Now?*

I touched my shoulder to yours: *Not yet.*

But I felt the slab of your muscle through your shirt, tense as coiled wire, and knew I didn't have long. I should have kept my fucking revolver; you should have kept your sword. We should have known we couldn't hide forever.

I took the book from its high shelf. Unwrapped it, clumsily. My hands hadn't shaken like this since our son was born.

Vivian said, "Open it."

I opened it. The pages stared blankly up at me, still empty. I'd thought they might remain that way, but now it seemed our story would be written again and again, no matter how far we ran or how thoroughly we disappeared.

The log popped brightly. The coals were a fresh, hot yellow. I thought, distantly, that the only way the rat could escape the mill is if it burned to the ground.

There was no one standing between me and the firepit. Perhaps Vivian thought a Cantford-trained historian would balk at the burning of a book, lest the archivist somehow got wind of it. Or perhaps she thought I loved the book more than I loved you. She had convincing evidence; how many times had I let you die, so that your story would survive?

But not another. In a single, easy motion, without hesitating, I threw *The Death of Una Everlasting* to the flames. I didn't wait for it to catch, but spun, half crouched, ready to fend off Vivian's men. A few lifted their blades, uncertainly. At my side I felt you loosening, uncoiling, rising to meet them—

But Vivian raised her hand and said, in Middle Mothertongue, "Hold."

A tenuous silence fell, as smoke gathered thickly at the eaves, seeping through the thatch. It was bluish and sweet smelling, like burning pine.

Vivian observed the smoke with no particular expression. I wondered if she was truly unsurprised, or if the muscles of her face had simply forgotten how to form the necessary shapes.

"It's done." I said, willing it to be true. "We are finished." At my back, the pages caught with a faint rush of air.

The sudden flames cast garish shadows up the walls, dancing madly in Vivian's eyes. She closed them. "No," she corrected, "we are *annoyed*." Her eyes opened, and the mad light was gone. "I had forgotten how much you love a grand gesture, Corporal. Now if you'll both come with me—"

"Why?" My voice was pitched too high. "We are *stuck* here, all of us, a hundred years before your sick little play begins. You can't send us anywhere, ever again."

Vivian opened her mouth, but another voice interrupted her. It took me a moment to recognize it as yours. You had never sounded so young, so uncertain. "Even if you could, it would do you no good." You were looking Vivian dead in the eye, finally, but the tendons in your neck were tight with the strain of it. Some part of you still wanted to bow before her, to fall to your knees and beg her favor. "I am no longer what you made me. I will not fight for you again. I will not"—your voice shook, then steadied—"die for you."

Vivian smiled, not without sympathy. "You will, though. Do you want to know why?"

"There is no reason you could give that would—"

But Vivian held a finger to her lips, and you were so accustomed to obeying her that you fell quiet. Through the silence, which stank of sweat and pine and flowers and the bitter copper promise of violence, came the distant cry of children's voices. *Mama? Papa?*

Vivian took her finger from her lips, pointing over her shoulder, toward the woods, where our son and daughter were calling for us. "That's why."

You made no answer, but only turned your body very slowly so that you and I stood back-to-back, our shoulder blades brushing. *Now?*

I whispered, "Now."

It was like pulling the pin from a grenade. You didn't move so much as detonate. Your shoulders left mine, heaving forward, as if there weren't four naked blades facing you. It was how you'd always fought—unfeeling, heedless, as if even your death wouldn't stop you. It had been true, before. But I'd burned the book, and made you suddenly, horribly mortal.

From behind me came a yell, cut short. The muffled snap of a bone breaking. The wet slap of viscera on bare dirt.

The men facing me started forward and I kicked the fire at them, scattering coals, sending a rush of sparks between us. They blinked, blinded, and by the time they opened their eyes you were there.

For nine years, I'd tried to make you forget yourself. I'd taken away your sword, your story, your armor, your honor, your name. I'd wanted you to disappear, and for my sake, you'd tried.

I should have known: If you couldn't kill Una Everlasting, then what chance did those poor bastards have?

You went through them like a scythe through late-summer hay. You came bare-handed, unshielded, blood-slicked, and you left only bodies behind you. A sword arced downward; you caught the hilt and thrust it through another man's throat. A hand reached for your ankle; you stamped it with a sound like dropped porcelain.

The last man—a little older than the others, clever enough to know what his own death looked like when it came for him—did not even try to strike at you. Instead, he struck at me.

I watched his sword drive toward my chest, aimed just to the left of my sternum, where the blade wouldn't get caught in the bone. I minded less than I thought I would; I had sworn never to watch you die again, and now I wouldn't have to.

But the blade never arrived. You caught it, inches from my breast, in your bare hands.

I watched the blood well up from your fists and knew a moment of sick vanity. When you had fought for your queen, you had conquered Dominion; if you had fought for love, you might have conquered the world.

You ripped the sword away from the soldier, lips peeling back in an animal snarl. You turned the blade—still holding it by the naked edge—and drove it into his belly. The only mercy you had in you was that you killed quickly, but you had none for him: You twisted the sword, burrowing cruelly into his bowels, before you drew it out.

You stood watching him choke and whimper, your chest heaving like a great bellows. You held the blade one-handed now, the edge biting so deep into your palm that blood coursed down the blade and dripped from the point. The man fell to his knees, hands full of his own guts, and still you watched him.

I said, gently, "Una."

You didn't look at me, but your grip eased on the sword. You drew it cleanly across the man's throat—his eyes closed in awful gratitude—and let it fall.

I went to you then, stumbling over sprawled limbs. You turned to face me, and I reached for your hands—God, your *hands*—

I stopped myself just before I touched them, in case my shaking hurt you worse.

"I'm sorry," you said, earnestly. Your pupils were huge and black. "I know you wanted me to be other than I am, and I tried, I swear I tried. But . . ." You looked vaguely around at the scattered corpses. A shudder moved over you, and your voice went low and raw. "Have you learned to fear me yet, boy?"

I touched my palms very carefully to the backs of your hands. "Never."

You exhaled, shakily. "Madman."

"Yes, but I'm your madman." You snorted, then hissed as your hands jostled. You looked down at them as if surprised to find them still attached to your wrists.

"We've still got some iodine, let me—"

But when you lifted your face again, you were smiling. A summertime smile, sweet and easy, as if we were still eating berries in the woods, or would be soon.

You lifted both your mangled hands high, a pagan priest blessing his flock. Blood ran down your wrists and several of your fingers flopped obscenely. The blade had cut through tendon, straight to the bone. I'd spent enough time in field hospitals to know you would never hold a sword again.

You looked over my shoulder and said, still smiling, "I'm no good to you now."

I wondered, briefly, who you were speaking to; it simply didn't occur to me that you would have spared her.

But you had. Vivian answered easily, calmly, as if she wasn't standing among her butchered men, "But you're still mine."

You shook your head. "Not anymore. Not ever again," you said, and stepped around me. Our floor—packed earth, swept clean—had turned to black, brackish mud. Your feet sank slightly into it as you crossed the cottage to face Vivian Rolfe.

You placed your ruined hands carefully, almost respectfully, around her neck. She didn't flinch or blink. She tucked her own hands in her trouser pockets, showily indifferent. Well, perhaps she was right: You had refused her, and you had run from her, but you could barely meet her eyes.

She smiled fondly up at you. I imagined the scene as a painted portrait: two women standing face to face, both bright-haired, both tall, both unbending. You might have been sisters, if it weren't for the blood seeping from your palms to stain her collar.

"You'll always be mine, love," Vivian said. Then she stood on tiptoe and laid her cheek along yours. She whispered something in your ear.

And you—faltered. Your lips parted soundlessly. Your hands lifted away from her collarbones. They trembled slightly.

I like to imagine you would have recovered, given another second. You would have remembered everything she'd done to you and everything you'd done for her, and you would have killed her. We wouldn't have been free of her—if she'd found us once, then some iteration of her would find us again, and now we didn't even have the book to help us run—but we might have had another year. Another decade, even. It wouldn't have been enough—a lifetime with you wouldn't be enough, my love—but it would have been sweet.

In that second of hesitation, Vivian Rolfe drew a revolver from her pocket, put it to your breast, and pulled the trigger.

Of all the times I'd held you as you died, that was the worst.

That time you wore no cloak or armor, so I could feel the heat of your skin through your shirt. I could feel the weight and shape of your shoulders in my arms, which I'd held every night for nine years. I could feel, too, the soft pulp where the bullet left your body. I pressed my hand over it, knowing it wouldn't save you.

That time, too, I could hear the voices of our children, coming nearer. It seemed impossible that they hadn't reached the cottage yet, but it had only been a handful of minutes since we'd arrived. And perhaps the alien boom of the gun had startled them; perhaps they were hesitating at the edge of the clearing, wondering whether they should run.

That time it was a bullet that killed you, and it killed you too quickly. You had only moments. You touched my face once, clumsily, with torn and stiffening fingers, and spoke the names of our children.

I said, "I know, I will, I promise."

Then you said, "Wait for me," and that was all.

I had to finish it for you, pressing your face to my chest and whispering it into the curve of your ear, still warm against my lips: "Beneath the yew tree." My hands seized around you, fisting in the sodden fabric of your shirt, tangling redly in your hair. "Always."

But—that time, for the first time—I was lying. Because the book was nothing but ash and char, and I would never again meet you beneath the yew.

"Oh, get up." From above me came the metal ratchet of a hammer drawing back. "And stop making that noise."

I looked up to discover that Vivian Rolfe's good-humored mask had finally fallen away. There was no madness or passion beneath it, after all, but only the grim irritation of a woman doing the work no one else would do: whipping a horse, or a digging a grave. Her eyes and cheeks were reddened, as if she'd scrubbed them hard, but she held her revolver in perfect military form—two hands on the grip, feet spread, barrel pointed steadily at my skull.

The sight of it sent relief rushing over me, so sweet and fast I was nearly dizzy with it. She knew I wanted to kill her, and she knew I could—anyone will pick up a few tricks if they're sent to war enough times—but she also knew I was a coward. She thought a bullet would stop me because she thought I was afraid to die.

I almost laughed. The only thing I wanted more than my own death was hers; if I moved quickly enough, I might have both.

I gathered myself, loosing my fingers from your hair, setting your head gently on the churned earth. Your eyes were the dead, transparent yellow of old sap. They bored into mine, mutely accusing. Even in death, I understood you: *You promised.*

I closed my eyes in supplication. *I can't. Don't ask me to.*

But I felt your endless, unblinking stare pressing like thumbs into my eyelids. I imagined our children finding us dead together in the cottage, as you had found your fathers. I imagined them running barefoot and tear streaked through the woods, as you had. If there was no hell waiting for us in the afterlife, I imagined you would build one with your bare hands, just for me.

I thought: *As you will.*

I opened my eyes. Climbed slowly, drunkenly, to my feet, a condemned man granted mercy he didn't want.

Vivian sniffed. "Good man. Now out we go." She stepped carefully backward through the door. I followed her over the threshold, stunned by the soft light of summer. It ought to be cold, I thought. It was always cold, when you died. "And call the child out from wherever it's hiding."

I must have twitched or blinked, because Vivian laughed, a little of her unsettling cheer returning. "Don't tell me you had more than one? I turn my back for five minutes, and you turn my great hero into a housewife." She shook her head. "Call them both, then."

I shouted, in modern Mothertongue: "Come out, children! Right now!"

Not a single sound came from the woods, not a creak or a rustle or a drawn breath. Oh, Una, they were so clever, our children. Bright as comets, and just as fleeting.

I turned back to Vivian, smiling, helplessly proud, "They must have run off, I'm afrai—" I began, but she put a bullet through my left knee before I could finish. The knee folded under me like wet paper, and I went down hard. I stared up at her, alight with pain, lips sewn shut over a scream.

She gave me a look of extreme fatigue. She said, neutrally, "The problem with playing the hero is that someone will have to play the villain," and then she kicked my left knee, hard. I screamed.

Vivian lifted her voice, addressing the trees. "I've hurt your father very badly. Come out now, or I'll hurt him worse."

I yelled "*No!*" but it was too late. Our son burst out from behind a tree, his eyes black with terror, his knuckles white around his sister's fingers.

Vivian watched them come without surprise, or even much interest. I wondered if people were merely systems of levers and buttons to her, predictable and dull as engines: For you, I would keep living. For me, my children would come running.

For them, I would do anything at all.

I caught them both in my arms, half kneeling, and pressed their small and perfect heads to my chest. "It's alright, I'm alright," I lied. My knee snarled and gibbered with pain, a rabid animal more than a limb, and Vivian's revolver was pointed between my eyes. As I watched, the barrel wavered between our children, weighing their worth. It settled on our son's quicksilver hair. My arm around him tightened.

"Where's Mama?" That was our daughter, though I hardly recognized her voice. She had so rarely been afraid.

"She." My voice flailed to a full stop. I tried again. "She got away. She's well."

Our daughter's body untensed, but her brother turned his head slowly toward the cottage. There was blood seeping from under our door, thick and dark as motor oil. I turned his face back to my shirt. "Don't look." I said it sternly, without quarter, one soldier giving orders to another. I had never wanted my son to take orders from anyone.

Vivian said, patiently, "Up, please," and I stood, sweating hard, feeling the bullet move like a hot tooth in my leg. Then, less patiently, "Move out, Corporal."

"To where?"

"To the yew, of course." Vivian tipped her head, quizzical. "Where else? You first, then the children."

It wasn't far to the yew, but it seemed to take years and years, epochs, whole ages of the earth. There was time for the flesh to swell and weep around the shattered bone of my knee, until my leg dragged behind me, a sausage casing stuffed with glass. There was time to listen to the sweet patter of our children's feet and wish, as I had wished my whole life, that I were someone else, someone like you: strong and brave enough to save them.

There was time to think of the yew, and the girl I'd played with once beneath its branches, and the book that took us—always, over and over—back to it. A strange chance, I'd thought, that the pages of *The Death of Una Everlasting* had been milled from wood pulp, rather than the vellum or parchment that would have been more common, in this era.

But there was no such thing as chance, in Dominion.

Hope hit me like a second bullet, straight to the heart. I stumbled to a halt, breathing hard. The yew stood before me, a thousand years younger than I'd known it as a boy, and still older than the Savior Himself. It struck me suddenly as the only true miracle I'd ever seen, a slow and green magic that defied time itself. You'd told me once that you thought even dragons had no true sorcery in them, save their long, long lives.

But the yew hadn't lived forever. I had come home for the war—so many times, I'd come home from the war—and walked up the rise and found nothing but stumps and rotten roots where the grove had once stood. Of the yew, there had been nothing left at all.

I said, belatedly, "It was you."

"Most of the time, yes," Vivian answered, from behind me. "You'll need to be more specific."

"You had the tree taken down." I swallowed, remembering the sharp pine-needle smell of the book as it burned. "And you had the wood made into paper." How had I ever believed that she'd simply *found* a book like that? She was a woman who engineered all of history, who made her own fate. I could almost hear Professor Sawbridge: *Everything that is, was made, and everything that was made, was made for a reason.*

"Well, you can see how an entire tree is something of a logistical challenge, as an instrument of time travel." I had forgotten how eager she was to discuss her schemes; it must be lonely work. "Every time I wanted to make some small adjustment I had to hike back to these damned woods. You cannot believe," she added, sincerely, "how much I hate it here."

High above us, the wind tousled the tops of the yew branches, so that the needles whispered against one another. When our children played here, they pretended it was the sound of the sea.

"So," Vivian continued, "eventually I had it milled and pulped. It wasn't easy—the wood ruined a dozen sawblades, and the first crew quit before they'd even limbed it properly. Claimed it gave them gray hairs, and arthritis." I heard the shrug in her voice. "But it was only a tree, in the end. I had the book bound, and I burned what remained. No sense taking—*ow*, you little shit!"

I tried to whip around and lost my balance, staggering back to one knee. Our daughter crouched like a fox kit between me and Vivian, snarling. Her brother stepped in front of her—your son, surely, not mine—as Vivian swore, shaking her hand. There was a bright red ring on her wrist, in the shape of small teeth. "Una didn't make much of a mother, did she?" She switched smoothly to Middle Mothertongue. "Sit down, little savages—no, farther away—and be still."

They didn't move until I asked them to. They sat, their eyes fixed on me with awful, unwavering trust, as if I hadn't already failed them. I looked away, to the ground beneath my knees. Blood had soaked through the legs of my trousers, trickling among the roots of the yew.

I remembered, for no reason, the very first time I'd gone to the grove as a child. I'd been lonely and hungry, chased by that hollow feeling that sometimes came over me, as if I'd lost something very precious but couldn't recall what it was. I'd tripped over the tangled roots of the yew and scraped both knees bloody.

When I'd looked up, there she was: the girl, bright-haired and bold, my first and only friend. Her eyes, I remembered suddenly, were the color of spring sap, and her name was ████. Like the flowers.

The realization arrived without fanfare or shock. I'd always known it was you, but I didn't understand *how* it could be you, and so I'd let myself pretend I'd made her up. But now I knew: It wasn't the book that first brought us together, or even Vivian Rolfe. It was the yew.

And it was the yew that could take me back to you, now. You were not lost to me forever. This was only one death among many, a brief and bloody pause in the endless circle of our lives. I felt myself falling toward you, slipping out of time—already I smelled frost, clean and sharp—

"Not just yet, Corporal." For the second time that day, I opened my eyes to the sound of a gun cocking. This time, it was pointed at our children.

"No—please, don't hurt them, don't." I was pleading now, beyond pride or shame. "Just let me go to her. Let me find her, and fix this—"

Vivian laughed at me. *You will beg me for it, before the end,* she'd said once. *And I will laugh.* A prophecy I'd outrun for nine years.

But how? If she'd known we would return to the yew every time we disappeared, how had we eluded her for so long? Unless—

"You let us go." I felt those nine stolen years contracting around me, shrinking inward. Everything we'd done and everything we hadn't—the price we'd paid for the freedom that wasn't even real, for a future that wouldn't last—bile burned my throat. "You let us think we were safe—I bet you even made sure the sword in the tree had no maker's mark, just to soothe us. *Why?*"

"Because you'd remembered yourselves. And after that, no threat or punishment could make you play your parts willingly. Believe me, I tried." Had she? Had we been here before? Was I a man or merely a palimpsest, scrubbed clean and rewritten so many times that my oldest memories were obscured entirely?

The bile bubbled, acidly. Vivian continued, "The stick failed me. I needed a carrot." Her eyes cut to the children. She corrected herself, "Carrots."

I looked at them—our pretty, clever son; our fierce, stubborn daughter—the sum of all our hopes, the final proof of our freedom. They were the future itself, given form. I loved them as I had never loved anything, save you.

But they were not the future, after all; they were only bait. Another link in Vivian's long, long chain of cause and effect, action and reaction.

"Oh, don't give me that look." Vivian *tsk*ed. "It's a very fine offer—a compromise, even. If you will simply return to your correct role and play your part as written, I'll give you your happy ending. Sir Una will be grievously injured when the grail is stolen. We'll spirit her away to a tower room and say she succumbed to her wounds, *Erxa Dominus,* et cetera. And then I'll let the two of you escape to the woods and play house to your heart's content. You can have your children back—a boy and a girl, fair-haired and dark. They come out the same, every time." A pause here, while my pulse rushed in my ears. "Do you hear me, Mallory? All this drama and gore—you made me cripple you, you made me kill her *myself,* in cold blood, my own—" Vivian's voice hitched oddly. In another woman, I might have thought it was a sob. "When all I wanted was to cry truce."

I didn't answer. I couldn't. I became fascinated by the small, sweet sounds of the wood: the soft crackle of needles underfoot, the endless chirp of the beck. There were no birds; the gunshot had sent them winging away.

Our daughter said: "Papa?"

I flinched from the sound of her voice. As soon as I went back through the yew—and I already knew that I would, already felt the jaws of Vivian's trap snapping neatly shut around me—she would disappear. No: A person had to exist, in order to disappear, and our daughter never would.

Unless I did as Vivian said.

"Well?" she said. "Go to them. Say goodbye."

I went to them, limping badly, clammy and cold with blood loss. They watched me come with docile, trusting eyes. All of this was frightening, but they hadn't yet encountered anything so frightening that their parents couldn't solve it. I said, "I—I have to go away," and then—only then—did their faith finally break.

Our daughter screamed for you. Our son asked *why,* over and over, his voice rising in pitch until I crushed them to me, desperately. Their bodies felt light in my arms, almost insubstantial, as if they were already fading away.

"We will—hush, listen to me—we will be together again. I swear it." I ran my hands over the sharp wings of our daughter's shoulders and the downy nape of our son's neck. *The body remembers.* "You're going to disappear for a little while. It won't hurt. It'll be like going to sleep. And one day, when your mother and I find you again, you'll wake up, and all of this will be a bad dream."

I laid them down among the roots, where I had lain as a boy. I placed our son's hand around his sister's. They curled toward one another, fetal in their fear, forming the uneven shape of a heart—mine, I thought, and yours.

I kissed them. "Wait for us," I said, and then I stood and faced the yew.

I placed my hand just above Valiance, where the bark was swollen and tumorous around the hilt you hadn't yet pulled.

Vivian Rolfe stood just behind me. She placed her chin over my shoulder, like a lover, and laid her hand over mine.

I asked, softly, "What did you say? Before you shot her."

"The truth, only." Vivian spoke in Middle Mothertongue, her breath ghosting over my cheek. "That I love her, and always have, from the very day I gave birth to her."

The chain lengthened in my mind, link upon link, receding out of sight.

Then Vivian set the barrel of her revolver against the back of her hand and pulled the trigger.

21

SEVERAL YEARS AFTER the war—what war?—during the mid-afternoon hour I generally put aside to fantasize about setting fire to my manuscript—what manuscript?—I received a book in the post.

No. It was not the affable, chap-cheeked campus postman who delivered the book. It was a handsome woman who smelled, sickeningly, of summer flowers. She was very tall; how had I never noticed how tall she was?

This time, when I saw the book, I felt no awe or terror or ambition. I felt nothing at all. How could I? I had left my heart beneath the yew.

Vivian Rolfe cleared off a corner of my desk and sat, fishing comfortably through the detritus until she found a stray cigarette and a book of matches. She did not hurry; why would she?

As she shook out the match, she said, "Welcome back to the modern age, Corporal." Her lips twisted. "More or less."

I didn't know what she meant, for a moment. But I soon discovered a brand-new set of memories stacked neatly in my skull, like towels in a guest bathroom. They unfolded all at once, a suffocating mass.

This was not the Dominion I'd left behind. It was not an empire, or even a great power of the world, but merely one fractious, troubled state among many, jostling restlessly against its neighbors. Cantford was not the pinnacle of all learned scholarship, but only a backward little college in a backward little country. There were no munitions plants spewing black smoke into the sky, no grand crusades, no processions of troops in bright Dominion red. We did not have wars, but only petty skirmishes and border disputes.

The current Chancellor was a zealous, sallow young man, who talked often of God and destiny and the days when Dominion's borders had reached from one sea to the other. I'd heard his speeches on the wireless; they were familiar. I suspected now—observing the woman sitting comfortably on my desk, looking out at the mossy green steeples of Cantford—that he hadn't written them himself.

Dominion was much diminished, but it still belonged to Vivian Rolfe.

"How did you—" I stopped. In nine years, I'd grown used to my voice, even a little vain of it: It was sweet and resonant, like a struck bell. I had sung our children to sleep with that voice, and later, in the dark, I'd used it to whisper in your ear.

Now it was my old voice that emerged, ragged as a broken fingernail. I touched my throat and found slick, puckered scars. Another memory unfolded: a burglary when I was nineteen, followed by a long fever. Random, as nothing in Dominion truly was.

I frowned, tiredly, at Vivian. "Was this really necessary?"

"No, but it was prudent. It will be easier for you if everything is as it was, before."

I swallowed, feeling the foreign-familiar pull of scar tissue, and tried again. "How did you accomplish all this? Without the book, without Una—"

"Honestly, did you think you'd dealt Dominion a death blow?" Vivian blew a neat stream of smoke from the corner of her mouth. "I still had three-quarters of a national mythology and several centuries of hard, careful work. What kind of mastermind would I be if I let the whole of my strategy rest on a pair of pawns?"

She tapped her cigarette twice on the rim of my teacup. The tea inside had long since evaporated, leaving brown stains behind like the rings of a tree. "But—and I want you to think about this, really—if it weren't me, it would be someone else. I did not single-handedly invent the crown, or the chancellorship. Where there is power, someone will wield it. Is it really so intolerable that it would be me?"

"Yes," I said, instantly. I could still hear our son's voice asking *why,* over and over.

"Oh, don't be so *myopic.* Look around!" Vivian gestured out the window. "Did you save the poor downtrodden folk of Dominion from the wicked queen—or did you ruin their favorite bedtime story? Did you strike a blow for freedom, or did you just steal a little bit for yourselves?"

I didn't know. There were too many versions of history in my head, too many chains of cause and effect—and I wasn't sure I cared about any of them, really, or if I only cared about you, and a pair of children who no longer existed.

"Well, it hardly matters." Vivian ground her cigarette into the bottom of the teacup and slid from the desk. "You'll play your part, whether you go marching or dancing. I don't think there's any need for speeches or set-dressing this time, so if you'll open the book, I can send you on your wa—"

"There you are." Harrison rounded the corner and began his usual performative slouch against the doorframe. But, as soon as he saw Vivian Rolfe, his body jerked strangely, like a puppet whose strings have gotten tangled.

"Oh," he said, and then, a little too loudly, "Jeremy Harrison, Professor of History." He extended his hand woodenly.

Vivian took it. "What an honor," she said, with the false sobriety of an adult humoring a child's game of pretend. "But I'm afraid Professor Mallory and I are rather in the middle of something."

"Of course, of course." His eyes found the book in my hands—unwrapped, your device perfectly visible—and his features twisted with pure, unadulterated avarice. But he looked back at Vivian, who gave him the faint smile of someone very important who wonders why their time is being wasted, and ducked his head. "Far be it from me to stand between a historian and his duty," he sneered, recovering his old-money unction, and scuttled away.

I waited for his steps to retreat down the hall before I observed, calmly, "He knows you."

"I should hope so. I'm the one who paid for every single cent of his education, and all those silly jackets with patches on the elbows." She took another contemplative drag. "His family are swede farmers, you know. He'd have been nothing, without me."

I thought of Harrison's pure and hateful condescension, almost comforting in its constancy. Of his desperate zeal to prove himself socially, intellectually, and sartorially superior. The product of inherited wealth, I'd thought—but actually the product of its absence.

I asked, "Why?"

"Because the only people you truly own are the ones you make. I made him—from *nothing,* from filth and obscurity—and so he's mine. Well, not *literally* mine." A sly, sidelong look here. "I was only a mother the one time."

It was bait; I declined to take it.

Vivian reeled her line back in, disappointed. "Anyway. The Harrison boy failed to fill your role, obviously, but he keeps an eye on you and your father for me, and that spiteful old woman." Sawbridge? "And there's nothing like a good sibling rivalry to keep you sharp. Una fought twice as hard once I made Ancel for her to compete with."

I thought of Ancel's face as he died, the rueful, weary expression of a man whose whole life had been spent merely to further the plot of someone else's story. I swallowed sudden sympathy. "Let Harrison translate the book, when I finish it for you." Let him have the glory and the big desk, the money and the reputation so unassailable that no one would ever inquire after his family again. "He deserves . . . something."

"Why not?" Vivian answered easily, but she had paused slightly before she said it. That pause bothered me very much, I found.

She opened the book, the wooden cover clacking hard against my desk, and drew a familiar silver knife from her hip pocket. "Your hand, Corporal."

"Wait." I kept my voice carefully innocent, unshaded by suspicion. "May I say my goodbyes?"

Vivian frowned a little. She was—and this, too, bothered me—genuinely baffled.

"To my father, and my friends, I mean." I shrugged to disguise the sudden tremor of my hands. "Since I won't be returning to this time again."

Vivian ran her tongue over her canine. "Of course. God knows we have nothing but time. Meet me here, when you're ready." She tucked the book under her arm and handed me a card printed on cheap, grayish paper. It bore no name, but only an address.

Professor Sawbridge was in her office, naturally, because she hadn't been called away to discover the tomb of Una Everlasting, because there was no tomb to discover, this time. You had died anonymously, deep in the woods, and your body had been buried by rain and rot and small, scrounging animals.

Her office was less grand than I remembered—all of Dominion was—and much cleaner. There were no architecturally unsound towers of books, no bundles of political pamphlets. There were not even any cheaply bound editions of racy novels on her shelves.

She looked up as I entered—and beamed at me. "Mr. Mallory! What can I do for my favorite protégé?"

"I—pardon?" I wasn't sure I'd ever heard her make use of an exclamation point.

Her smile was very wide, like the painted grin of a marionette. "How's the manuscript? It'll win you the endowed faculty spot if you ever finish it."

I stared at her. "But you hate my book. You called it 'Grade-A hog swill.'"

A flicker in her eyes, indecipherable. "Hate it? Why, I think it's a fine piece of scholarship. Just what the country needs."

I recalled suddenly that she'd expressed similar sentiments, many times, in this version of my life. Because this Gilda Sawbridge had undergone a sudden and thorough change of heart. She was no longer a known radical and thorn in the side of the Cantford Board of Fellows; instead, she was one of the most fervent academic voices behind the new Chancellor. She wrote editorials decrying the corruption of modern Dominion culture, and the lack of national spirit in our curriculum. She had even—and here I knew something had gone profoundly, hideously wrong—described my latest article as "something of a little triumph."

I sank slowly into the chair across from her desk, where I'd spent so many hours being bullied and berated into becoming a better scholar than I was. "Oh, Gilda." My head was aching fiercely. "What the hell did she do to you?"

"What? Who?" She blinked rapidly, as if confused. It was not an expression I'd ever seen her attempt.

I studied her soberly. "The last time we spoke—no, I know you don't remember it, just take my word for it—you told me there was something wrong with the history of Dominion. I wanted you to know you were right. It's been manufactured, all of it, in service to a woman named—"

"Is this some kind of test?" Sawbridge was chewing at her lips. They were dry and scabby, as if she did it often. "I don't know what you're talking about. I am proud to call myself a citizen of Dominion—"

"No, you don't have to—"

"And proud to serve crown and country. What more"—her voice split, like an overworked seam—"could you possibly want from me?"

It would have been an entirely baffling speech, at odds with everything I knew about Gilda Sawbridge—except that I'd seen a familiar, weary agony in her eyes. As if her heart were buried somewhere far away, and her every word and gesture was an effort to keep it safe.

Gently, I said, "It's the archivist, isn't it?" I'd remembered, in a delayed rush of images from this new version of my life, that Mistress Shaw had abruptly quit her post during my third year of study. "How did it happen?"

Professor Sawbridge seemed to collapse inward, like a punctured rubber ball. She looked, for the first time in all my lives, like what she was: an old woman. "I don't know how you could possibly . . . Well, you were always bright, when you weren't willfully stupid. Harrison caught us in the old observatory one night." She added, sounding more like herself, "Sneaking little shit stain."

"And he . . . reported you for indecency?"

"I wish he had. Sylvie and I would have lost our posts, of course, maybe spent a few months in the penitentiary, but then . . . we would've been free, wouldn't we?"

There was wistfulness to the question, as if she wanted me to tell her there was some version of her life where she was happy and safe and unshackled. I felt nothing but sympathy; it was the same foolish, childish hope that had sent me running for nine long years, and which had brought me back, here, to try again.

Sawbridge made a sound of disgust, directed inward. "No. Harrison told someone, but not the authorities. And then—they took Sylvie away."

"I'm sorry." It was almost funny, in its predictability. In all her centuries of malice and manipulation, Vivian Rolfe had only ever found one lever to push, one string to pull, over and over.

"I get postcards from her. I've seen pictures—she's well. She's taken care of." Sawbridge flashed me a guilty, resentful look. "So I'll write a thousand craven little articles. I'll dance like a goddamn bear if they ask me to. Because, for that, for her, it's—"

"Worth it." My voice cracked, falling to a jagged whisper. "Yes. I understand." I thought there was probably no one on earth who understood better. "Love makes cowards of us all."

Sawbridge flinched a little. She closed her eyes. "Yes."

"Listen," I said, "I don't know if you'll remember I said this, but things are going to get very bad, soon." Vivian had the book again, and soon she would have the story inside it. "Dominion will have a queen again. You have to get out before she takes the throne."

Sawbridge opened her eyes and propped her spectacles on top of her head. "It's that Rolfe woman, isn't it."

"It is, yes. You might think you're safe, but she's locked you up before, and she'll do it again. And the second she doesn't need you, she'll kill you."

Sawbridge absorbed this calmly, without skepticism or alarm. "Thank you, Mallory. But I think I'll stay put."

"But—"

"She has Sylvie." She said it slowly, as if she were writing out a very simple equation on the board. "If I can't run with her, then I can't run at all. And if you can't run"—she spread her hands—"then I suppose, if you'll excuse the melodrama, you stand and fight."

I sat looking at her for a while—an aging professor of history, near-sighted, slightly fat, and very, very angry—and wondered if Vivian knew what kind of enemy she'd made for herself.

I leaned across the desk and touched my lips to her cheek, as she had once kissed me. "If I don't see you again—though I'm very afraid that I will—goodbye, Professor. Thank you, for everything."

She fussed with papers on her desk, not looking at me. "Goodbye, boy."

She cleared her throat before I reached the door. "About your manuscript, Mallory." I turned to find her smiling beatifically, as if relieved of a great and awful burden. She said, with relish, "It's absolute *hog swill.*"

My father still lived in Queenswald, but he'd long since lost the narrow gray row house. Instead, he'd worked out what he called "a cordial arrangement" with both the barkeep and her husband, which—once I'd interpreted the merry waggling of his eyebrows—I'd found indecent, illegal, blasphemous, and entirely humiliating. It had been the beginning of our worst fight.

Now, as I ducked into the amber-lit tavern, I felt nothing but gratitude, and a certain embarrassed irritation with my previous selves. I'd abandoned my father over and over, in every life I'd lived, and I was about to do it again; at least I wouldn't be leaving him alone.

It was past supper, which meant my father was drifting between verb tenses, transitioning gently from *drinking* to *drunk.* I'd caught him just after the pain eased but before the weeping started, when his cheeks turned a cherubic red and his eyes crimped with goodwill. He used to sing to me, sometimes, in this mood. He had a lovely voice.

He saw me first through the bottom of his pint glass. His eye, magnified by beer, widened suddenly. The expression in it was intimately familiar to me, now: relief and irritation and joy. I'd had children of my own since the last time I'd seen him.

Thank God my heart was elsewhere; it would have hurt badly, just then.

"Well, well!" My father thumped his glass on the table. "If it isn't the pride of the Cantford Department of Propaganda!"

"Hello, Dad." He was less changed than Sawbridge had been, in this iteration of himself. I knew from my fresh-made memories that he'd still gone to war and still come back with a bad leg and a baby. He still embarrassed me; I still disappointed him; we still loved each other, however clumsily. We hadn't yet had our biggest fight, but we were about to.

My father tilted back in his chair, balancing it on two legs. "What brings you here, son?"

I couldn't even remember why I'd come, all those previous times. I'd made different excuses: I'd come to request that he stop sending his pamphlets to my campus address, for the sake of my career; I'd come to beg him to rent a flat of his own, for the sake of decency. But actually, I'd come for the same reason I always did.

"Just wanted to see you," I said, and it was the truth.

My father squinted a little, uncertainly. Then he drew a curled-up magazine from his breast pocket and slapped it on the counter. *The Journal of Middle Dominion Studies,* issue 3, volume 44. "Read your latest, of course."

The scorn in his voice had scalded me, once. I'd been proud of that article, and I'd wanted him to be proud, too, despite our differences. What an idiot I'd been: Why else, save pride, would a man who couldn't make rent subscribe to all the leading history journals? What else would make him dog-ear the pages I'd written, and carry it close to his chest?

"I tried to raise you right. Tried to teach you wrong from right." My father shook his head, dolefully. "And what have I raised? A bootlicker, it seems! A child, who still believes in fairy tales!" Here was a man who used twice the normal allotment of exclamation points.

I considered him, wondering a little. "Were you—are you *trying* to pick a fight with me?"

His squint deepened, but my father didn't abandon his script. "I don't know," he pronounced, enunciating very clearly, "how you sleep at night, with the blood of your countrymen on your hands."

He let this statement hang, full of portent. I marveled. "You *were.* God, Dad, couldn't you have found a better way to tell me about my mother?"

But I didn't think he could have. He was an ex-soldier and a lifelong radical; fighting was the only thing he knew how to do. If he had something to say, he'd shout it. If he had something to lose, he'd hide it. It occurred to me that our most honest conversation had taken place in a jail cell, across an interrogation table.

My father's mouth had fallen slightly open. "You're not—you knew?"

"Yes," I said, feeling older than myself, older than my own father. "I know everything. It's alright. You already told me."

He frowned uncertainly, but a drunk never trusts his own memory. He sat blinking absurdly, like a man who's shown up for battle on the wrong day.

I'd only come to say goodbye—and to leave things a little better than I had the previous times, perhaps—but I found myself flagging down the barkeep's daughter. She was full-grown now, and pretty in an innocent, maidenly way that made me hope she didn't know what our parents got up to in the bedroom above the bar.

I ordered two more pints and she said, "Yes, sir," in a breezy manner that made me feel a thousand years old.

I slid a glass across the table to my father when they arrived. "Can I ask you something?" He was peering hopefully down into his beer, as if it might help him make sense of this conversation. "What did you want to do with your life, before the war?"

He scratched at his cheek, which never quite managed to be clean-shaven or bearded. "I suppose I wanted to see the world. What small-town boy doesn't?" I hadn't. The woods had been world enough, for me. "I was all signed up to work a freighter, when I was drafted."

The beer was thin and flat. I wondered if the barkeep watered my father's drinks specially. "Why didn't you, after?"

"Oh, I thought about it, God knows. But . . . my leg, you know." His voice roughened. "And a ship is no place for a baby."

What happiness my father might have had, he'd sacrificed for me. As Sawbridge had sacrificed her principles for Mistress Shaw. As you had sacrificed yourself, over and over, for your queen.

I thought, despairingly, that love didn't make cowards of us, after all; it made *heroes,* and heroes usually didn't survive.

But I was no hero. I'd run from the war and I'd run from Vivian Rolfe and I was going to run again, no matter the cost. I would let the Hinterlands be invaded, twice over; I would let the Black Bastion burn. I would let my father be beaten on the steps of the capitol and my favorite professor be thrown in jail. I would hand the whole future of the world to a woman who had murdered you—more than once!—so long as I got to see my own children again.

I wasn't myopic; I was heartless.

My father was watching me, concerned. "I didn't regret it," he assured me. "Never once."

I sucked watery beer through my teeth. "Just—as an experiment. If I told you to run, now—if I told you things were about to get much worse in Dominion, very soon—would you run?"

His face creased. "Without you?"

God, he would break the heart I didn't have. "Imagine I was somewhere safe. Far away."

"Maybe," he said, not looking at me. "Sure I would."

"Really?"

He snorted. "No." He set his pint on the table. There was nothing left but yellowish foam, sliding down the glass. "If I told you everything, then you know I did something—awful, once. Something unforgivable. I think maybe I owe—"

"You did your best by me," I said, sharply. "You don't owe me penance, Dad."

"Not you. *Her.* Your . . ." I shouldn't have bought him that beer. Dampness was beginning to gather, inevitably, at the corners of his eyes. He sniffed, mightily. "And there's Melly and Bill—they're good to me, Owen, I don't care if you disapprove. And what about my Veterans for Peace boys? Half of them are class traitors, I'll grant you, but then, none of us came back right, from the war. I—I couldn't leave them behind."

He would stand and fight, then, like Gilda. Like everyone else who couldn't run.

This, I thought, was the reason Vivian needed the book so badly. Because no throne is held easily, or for long; because a nation is a story we tell about ourselves, and stories change, if you let them. Because where there is power, someone will oppose it.

She would wear the crown again—but she would have a hell of a time keeping it.

I sat with my father until the tavern was nearly empty and his words were slurring into a senseless rise-and-fall rhythm, familiar as a lullaby. I listened and thought. About heroes and cowards and the fine line between them. About you, and our son's yewberry birthmark. About freedom, which seemed to me now a lonely, foreign thing. *Who is free, who loves another?*

Eventually the barkeep and her husband came to collect my father, each of them pulling one of his arms over their shoulders, laughing a little, fond and exasperated. The barkeep caught my eye, her smile fading. "He misses you," she observed, pointedly. I said I was sorry, and thanked her for taking care of him, and of me, when I was a child. She blushed. "Oh, we don't mind, do we, Bill?" Bill agreed that they did not.

I kissed my father's forehead and told him that I loved him. He said, "There's my boy," and I knew: I couldn't run, either.

The address on the card did not take me to the capitol building this time, but to a weedy dirt track at the very edge of the city.

The cabbie leaned one elbow out of his window, frowning. His conscience appeared to be troubling him. "You sure this is the place?"

"Yes," I told him, and he almost didn't flinch from the sound of my voice. "I know where I am."

I even thought I recognized the stone by the road, though it was surrounded now by tall, slim trees. You had sat there while I combed your hair around your shoulders. I could feel it now, a white-hot brand across my palms.

It was a steep walk, and the day was already hot. I didn't mind; soon I would be very cold, and I didn't have my red service jacket anymore.

I crested the final rise and paused. I had seen Cavallon Keep in its glory, and I'd visited its graveside, nine centuries later. But I'd never seen it forgotten entirely.

There were no buses of schoolchildren or velvet ropes for visitors to form queues. There were no explanatory plaques or chattering tour guides or excavation sites. There were only the stones, tumbled and moss eaten, and the wet, warm wind, running over them.

I stood looking down at the city below me, at the shiny beads of automobiles and the zippered teeth of the train tracks. The poor downtrodden folk of Dominion, Vivian had called them, but they didn't strike me as victims. I had seen them send their sons cheerfully to war; I had seen them beaten bloody for protesting it. They had put a medal around my neck for something I hadn't done, and spit on my boots simply for being born. And they hadn't been tricked or forced into any of it—they had chosen, over and over, cruelly or kindly, selfishly or bravely.

There was a strange comfort in this, I found. Just as there was no such thing as total freedom, there was no such thing as its total absence.

I turned away from the city and into the jagged green shadows of the Keep.

None of the roofs had survived, and few of the walls. Ash and linden trees had taken root in the old halls, spindly and tall, chasing the light, so that it looked as if someone had tried to cage a forest.

It wasn't hard to find Vivian; I knew where she would be. She had never really wanted to be anywhere else.

The throne had long since rotted away, but there was still a stone plinth where it had stood. Someone had hacked through the moss and swept the leaves away, so that it shone a shocking white, like bone through skin.

Vivian waited for me there, the book in her lap, head tilted peacefully up to the light. A branch cracked beneath my shoe, and she smiled without looking at me.

"Ready, Corporal?"

"Yes," I said. There was little else to say. I was through with begging; she was through with speech-making. There would be no more squirming, looping arguments, no more grasping justifications. I would do as I was told because I had to. Because, she supposed, I had no other choice.

She handed me a spiral-bound notebook, of the kind used by court stenographers and journalists. "You'll need to make your notes here, this time, for transcription later." She tapped the wooden cover of the book in her lap. "I'll be holding on to this, for obvious reasons."

"I understand."

She handed me a holstered Saint Sinclair Mark III service revolver, three bullets, and her slim silver knife, hilt first. I took it with a hand that was perfectly steady.

Vivian said, comfortingly, "It's almost done, Owen. One last time, and it will be over forever." She was lying.

I said, "Yes, this will be the last time," and I wasn't.

I pushed the point of the knife into the pad of my finger and touched it to the page she held open. The cold, clean smell of winter came to me, and the world fell away, and then I was home.

22

I HAD BEEN afraid you wouldn't remember me, but of course you did. We've done this too many times to forget, you and me.

I stood with my hand against the yew, breath misting in the cold, heart stuttering. I waited without turning for the metal slither of sword leaving sheath, the kiss of steel against my nape.

It never came. Dry needles snapped beneath your boots as you approached. Your footsteps—always so swift and sure—were clumsy now, shuffling through the frost. At my back you paused, close enough that I could feel the heat of you. Your breath ghosted against the back of my neck, and I knew an instant of desperate, keening lust. Because you were warm and alive and with me, and they were not; because everything had been taken from us, save one another.

Then your arms came around my waist, carefully, as if you were new to your own body, unsure of its strength. You buried your face in my hair, inhaled once, raggedly, and wept. I pressed my hands over yours and held you to me until it passed, until your body slackened against mine and we stood quiet in the hasty blue twilight of midwinter.

I led you to the cottage by the hand. I wasn't sure you could find the way on your own—your steps were still uncertain, your gaze opaque.

A *whuff*ing sound greeted us in the clearing, and the stamp of a hoof. I had the sudden, implausible fear that Hen had been left waiting here for nine years, desiccating steadily, so that there would be nothing but a bad-tempered skeleton left to greet us.

But only a few minutes had passed since his master walked alone to the yew, from his perspective. He still looked exactly as I remembered him (a bad-tempered skeleton with hair).

He put his head to your chest as you approached, and you stood for a while with your cheek against his forelock. When you straightened, you looked a little less lost.

I tried to scratch beneath the point above Hen's withers, in gratitude, and he knocked his jaw so hard into mine that I bit my tongue. *Dog meat,* I whispered to him. *Leather gloves.*

By the time I'd spat the blood from my mouth and cleaned my teeth, you were standing with your back to the cottage. Your lips were pressed so hard together they formed a white seam, and your eyes were the holes moths leave behind in linen. "I can't," you said.

"That's alright. We'll sleep outside."

"It's cold." This you stated as something you observed, clinically, rather than something you felt.

I lifted one shoulder. "I'm used to it."

We didn't speak again for several hours. We only sat, feeding the fire, remembering and forgetting. In other lives, I'd talked until my throat was sore, explaining and arguing, circling, urging you to take up the quest you had abandoned. But you had not abandoned your quest this time, because you couldn't.

Eventually, you said, in a voice nearly as awful as mine, "It won't last." I was sitting with my back to your chest, a half-rotted fur wrapped around both our shoulders. Your words hummed down my spine. "Even if she keeps her word and lets us live—even if she lets us return here—it will only be for some little while. Eventually her reign will falter, and she will need this story told again, adjusted to suit some new strategy." Your voice lowered, a bitter rumble. "She'll need a different enemy to conspire against the crown. Or perhaps it's God she'll need, and Ancel will have to play his part dressed in a devil's horns and rags. Perhaps I will survive Cavallon and die in pursuit of some other damned false trinket, so she can discover it a thousand years later."

"It would be difficult." I spoke idly, without conviction. "We remember ourselves, now, and wouldn't willingly do her bidding."

"Then perhaps she will find herself a new scribe! One I don't know or can't remember. Perhaps she will make infants of us again, and have us live a dozen lives apart, until we forget each other. Perhaps she already has. Even if we get ten years, Owen, or twenty—" You choked, and when you spoke again it was less than a whisper. "It's not freedom, if it can be taken away."

I said, "No."

"Yet—we can't run."

"No." There was no freedom in running, either, if you knew one day you would be caught.

"And so, I am hers, after all." A sickly calm came into your voice as you said it, as if it comforted you. You had never liked holding the reins. "I am her weapon, her tragedy, forever."

It took so many tragedies, to make a nation. I listed them in my head like the names of the dead the papers used to print: the False Kings and their followers, the heathens and rebels; my mother, who took a bullet in the back, and my father, who put another in his own leg; the idiot boys who marched with me in the war and went home in boxes; the children who packed our shells with powder and the children we orphaned on the battlefield and our own children, who were never born.

There was not enough red paint in the world to write their names on the wall, but I supposed it didn't matter; their blood had been mixed into the mortar.

In the silence, your laugh rang too sudden and too loud. "Well, and what else could I have been? It's why I was born, after all."

"Horseshit," I said, calmly.

"Owen." You didn't want to tell me. You imagined that I would care. "Before I died, that last time, she told me—"

"She lied."

"Don't be so—we even look alike! She arranged every second of my life. Is it really so unlikely that she gave it to me in the first place?"

There was guilt in your voice, which puzzled me. Had you wished, in your starving, orphaned heart, that the queen was your own true mother, returned to you? Did you imagine it was your fault that your wish had come true?

I turned in your arms to face you, but you wouldn't look at me. You averted your face so that all I could see was your blind left eye. I had missed the shape of it, the way the pupil spilled like ink into the iris. "Yes," I said, "Vivian Rolfe gave birth to you."

You looked at me sharply. I lifted my eyebrows the way Professor Sawbridge did just before she suckered an undergraduate into saying something very stupid. "Tell me. Does that make her your mother?" You knew me well enough to suspect a trap, and stayed quiet. "Was it childbirth that made you their mother, or everything that came after? And our children—were they *yours*, to dispose of as you liked? Or were they yours to protect? Yours to raise, yours to hold, yours to love—"

"Stop." You closed your eyes. A pair of tears tracked down your cheeks and met at the end of your chin.

More gently, I said, "Both of my parents took bullets for me. You did the same, for your children. Whatever Vivian Rolfe is to you, it is not a mother."

The tears came faster then, and your lashes gathered into sharp white points. "Did—did they see me, Owen? Did they find my body on the cottage floor, as I found—"

"No, I swear they didn't."

"But they might, the next time! What is the point of me if I can't protect them? What is the point of any of this?"

"I don't know." I pulled myself gently away from you. The fire had blinded me, so that I had to crouch and run my hands over the frozen ground to find what I needed now. "You were right, though. We can't run." Boiled leather beneath my fingers, and the cold steel of a pommel. "What do you do, when you can't run?"

I drew the sword from its sheath, and your body moved before you even opened your eyes, snapping upright. I held Valiance in two hands, back braced against the weight of it. God, you were strong. "I should never have taken this from you. If I hadn't—if you'd been armed, when she found us—" I stopped, swallowing salt. "I'm sorry. I was scared, and I thought if I took away your sword and your courage, if I made you small and ordinary enough, I could keep you safe."

I had thought the same about myself. I thought if I told no more stories and asked no more questions, if I poured grease in the bright brass gears of my mind, I would survive, even if my dreams did not. Vivian must have laughed and laughed, like a general watching her enemies saw off their own limbs.

I lifted Valiance high, so that the blade caught the firelight and shone a hectic gold. "But it's not an ordinary woman that I need, now. I need a hero, Una. I need you to fight again." I met your eyes around the blade and found them huge and hungering. "But not for her."

"Owen—"

"Kneel, love." This was purest pageantry. Sawbridge had doubted whether such rituals of knighthood were ever truly practiced, or whether they were the invention of romantic poets and playwrights. But the whole of Dominion's history was an invention, a theater production which we had made real by the strength of our belief.

Still, I half expected you to laugh in my face.

You didn't laugh. Instead, the line between your brows smoothed suddenly away. You looked at me with a kind of bewildered surrender, of the kind I'd only seen before during sex, when you were very near to the edge but couldn't quite fall. You never could, until I told you to.

It didn't feel like pageantry when your knee hit the earth, or when your head bowed, so that your hair fell like dove's wings over your shoulders. Your chest was rising and falling fast, as if you didn't know whether you knelt before your executioner or your savior.

I brought Valiance down as slowly as I could, but the flat of the blade still smacked hard on your shoulder. "Do you so swear, by your good right arm, to serve with honor and with valor?"

The words came easily, by rote; I'd sworn a version of this same oath when I joined the army, while a bored recruitment officer had tapped my shoulders with a cheap tin sword, and again when I was knighted.

"I swear it."

I lowered the sword to your other shoulder. "Do you so swear, by your good left arm, to serve with faith and with constancy?"

"I swear it."

I touched the blade to the back of your skull, so the point rested on your vertebrae. "Do you so swear, by your life and death, to serve no master save—" Here my recruitment officer had said *Dominion;* you must have said *Yvanne,* when you were first knighted. I was tempted, for a long and ugly moment, to say my own name. To take you away from Vivian, like a child snatching a toy, and make you finally and fatally mine.

Your shoulders had drawn tight as you waited.

I said, rough voiced, "—to serve no master at all, ever again, save your own heart, and to fight for no cause, save the one you choose?"

I heard the air rush from your lungs, as if the words had struck you across the back. You answered, shakily, with shame, "I cannot."

A prickling embarrassment began at my scalp and moved down my spine. I felt suddenly very stupid, standing there in the freezing dark, my wrists shaking under the weight of your damn sword—

"I cannot," you said, and your voice had evened, grown stronger. "Because my heart is not my own. It belongs to you, and to our children."

My arms stopped shaking, suddenly. Valiance felt light as spun sugar in my hands. "So fight for us."

"I swear it."

"Then rise, Sir ████." Here I called you by your oldest name—the one your fathers had given you, the one I had called you before you were called anything else, back when you were only a girl running barefoot and beloved through the deep green woods. You do not want it remembered, so I have stricken it from the page.

Your face turned up to mine. You were not smiling, but your eyes were hot and bright as embers.

I held out my hand, and you took it.

We did not linger in the Queen's Wood, this time, but rode out at first light.

I fretted as we rode. We were several days ahead of schedule—would Vivian be ready? If she wasn't, would she send us through it all again, like a director whose actors have missed their cues? But you said, flatly, "She shot me in the chest and took my children from me. If she's not ready, she's a fool."

I fretted less, after that, but only watched the countryside shift from forest to scrubby woodland, from wind-scoured heather down to the low, grain-stubbled heartlands. We rode less often on the queen's roads, this time, keeping to shepherd's tracks and game trails. When I asked why, you answered, "Because, after dozens and dozens of lives, you've finally found your seat in the saddle." Hen snorted, conspicuously, and you amended, "More or less."

When, for want of fresh bread or hot baths, we passed through a township, it went differently than I remembered. I no longer pressed the townsfolk for tales of Sir Una, and no longer spent the evenings feverishly writing them down. Instead, I filled Vivian's flimsy yellow notebook with stories of my own invention. They were brief, odd tales, featuring no heroes and no great deeds, but only a place: a green and secret place, beyond the reach of crowns or gods, under the protection of a nameless knight.

I strewed these stories carefully behind us, like seeds. I knew all this work would be undone, if things went as I planned, but I hoped some sign or sentiment would linger. So I told them to the freckled girl who sold us griddle cakes and to the fishwife who smiled at us without teeth, and to the Hinterlander boys who leapt from riverboat to riverboat, wearing rags for shoes.

These boys liked my story so much they begged for another; I would trade it to them, I said, if they would teach me a few phrases in Shvalic. This they did happily, although the phrases were very specific, and puzzling to them.

It occurred to me as we rode away that I was living like one of my mother's people: on horseback, telling stories for my bread. This thought produced an anxious, overdue sort of pride in my chest. Perhaps one day, when all of this was done, I would meet a band of geweth and ask to travel with them for a season or two. Perhaps I would learn their language and some of their stories and teach them to my son and daughter.

We made good time, on our journey north. Even when we rode through towns and villages, people did not gawk or gather. They did not seem to recognize you. It was the way you held yourself, I thought: Your spine had loosened, and your face had eased. Your expression shifted easily now: You scowled at overpriced goods and smiled at small children, as anyone would.

Saint Una the Everlasting was a carven image, a figure woven in a tapestry, ageless and changeless. How could you—mobile, visibly human—be her?

It also helped that you had scraped the device from your shield with a sharp stone, leaving a pile of flaked red lacquer beside the fire one night. You would have been content to bear the shield as it was, scratched and bare, but one evening as we passed along the edge of a Gallish temple, I slid from the saddle, untied the shield, and told you to wait.

At the temple I asked after the artist of their painted alcoves and was introduced to a laughing young woman with flecks of color beneath her nails. She listened closely to my instructions, took several heavy coins from your purse, and set to work.

When I showed the device to you—a great white tree, roots and all, on a green field—you touched it once, wonderingly. The paint hadn't quite dried, so that your fingertips left two marks on the trunk of the tree, almost like the hollows of eyes.

There were still some who recognized you, of course, even with your new colors. When we passed once more through that bitter, mud-slicked village in the far north, I saw the same resentful looks, the same hateful faces. No one forgets the face of their conqueror.

You took their venom as you always did: peacefully, as your due. But this time, when that tall, scarred Hyllman man reached for your hair, you spun and caught his hand in mid-air.

"Don't," you advised him, lowly, and he spat full in your face.

I'm afraid I lost my temper, then. Forgive me—there are only so many times I can watch a man insult you. I dropped the reins and shoved the bastard hard, with both hands. His boots slid in the mud, and he landed on his back with a damp, comic slap. He floundered, swearing, and I stepped forward—

"Owen," you said, softly chiding. I discovered that my fist was raised, and that it held Vivian's slim silver knife. I lowered it, somewhat sullenly.

You knelt down beside the man, studying his haggard, hate-whittled features. One cheek was concave, where he was missing several molars, and his head was covered in glassy pink scars, as from burns.

You looked at those scars and asked, calmly, "Who did you lose, at the Bastion? A son?" The man's face warped with fresh fury, and you said, "Ah, two sons. Were I you, I would spit in my face, too."

The man's mouth worked, soundlessly. He looked suddenly less like a man than like a walking wound, still weeping.

"Would it help if I told you I, too, lost my children?" Your voice now was musing, almost disinterested. "That I, too, dream of them every night? And when I wake, I think: If I cannot have them back, then God give me revenge for the loss of them?"

A shadow seemed to pass over me as you spoke, a premonitory chill, like a sudden cloud. *But we will,* I thought, a little desperately. *We will get them back.* And if we didn't—God save the queen.

The man was staring at you, but sightlessly, without comprehension. You clucked your tongue. "Well. It's too late and too little, yet still"—you bowed your head formally—"I am sorry, sir, for the grief I brought to your house." You unhooked your purse and set it humbly by his feet. "It is not a debt that can be paid, I know, but—"

The man kicked the purse away and hissed something in Hyllish. It sounded like some variation of *Keep your fucking money, worm-feeder.*

Behind him, his wife and daughters had gathered fearfully. The coins in the bag chimed as he kicked it, and one of the women made a small, hungering sound, quickly choked.

You plucked the purse from the mud and stood, weighing it in one hand. You addressed the women. "Do you have any quilts or furs to sell, good ladies? The weather will turn soon, and he whines like a babe in the cold." You gestured at me with your chin.

I scowled at you—you would whine, too, if you'd watched your own fingers turn black—but when the women returned with a pair of matted yellow sheepskins, I rolled them gratefully beneath my arm.

You asked the oldest of the women what it would cost us. She tilted her chin and said, in accented Mothertongue, "Everything you have," and I knew she hated you just as much as her husband did.

You handed the whole purse to her and turned away, leading Hen.

I lingered. I said, loud enough that the whole of the ragged village might hear, "If you need to run, run south to the forest. They call it the Queen's Wood, now, but they won't soon." I looked toward you, and their eyes followed mine. "You will find protection there, from all comers, for as long you need it."

I followed you away from that place, and hoped fervently that I would never see it again.

Seven days later, you fought the last dragon of Dominion.

You had confessed to me, long since, that dragons were not the fell demons I knew from folklore—and yet you still tried to make me stay behind.

"Oh, for the love of God," I said, disgustedly. "Not again."

You frowned at me in obscure alarm. "Have I ever failed, in all the times I've slain this dragon?"

"No, but—"

"Have you not read the stories? Everything I do, I do alone."

I said, through gritted teeth, "Not anymore you don't. Not ever again."

You came closer to me, and I blinked rapidly, like a man staring at the sun. It was the first time in nine years I'd seen you in your full armor, and the sight of it struck me like a hammer to the skull. You were a hero stepped straight from myth, shining and true, and you were a mortal woman, scarred and weary, and God forgive me for trying so hard to separate the two.

You bowed your forehead to mine and said, softly, "Do not ask me to risk you, too." Then, more desperately, "*Stay.*"

I tilted my face upward, brushing my lips against yours, and whispered, "Make me."

In the end you made me carry your shield and ordered me to stay six paces behind you. I waited outside the shallow, stinking cavern while you ducked inside. I heard a hissing sound, the thrash of scale against stone, and then nothing. I waited for that awful, keening death cry, but it never came.

You emerged a few seconds later, bleeding freely from a scrape across your brow, grinning like a child with a stolen sweet. You tossed the grail to me, said, "Quickly, now," and we ran together back down the mountainside.

Later, as we rode away from Cloven Hill, I asked, "Why did she want them all dead, do you think? The dragons, I mean."

You snorted, cynically. "Because it kept a lot of restless young bastards busy, probably." You shrugged, plate metal moving against my back. "Or because it made my story that much grander, if it was the very last one that I killed. Or only because they were—" You hesitated, casting about for the right words. "Out of her reach, beyond any law or border. To see a dragon in flight was to see something . . . free."

I looked back at the hill once, as we made camp that evening. I thought I saw, through the shifting mist, the glint of white scales. A pair of pale wings, which arced briefly into the light and then vanished once more, beyond reach.

The weather turned on the way to Cavallon, as it always did. The high hills of the north flattened once more into low, wet farmland, the fields veiled now by scant, dirty snow. The wind slithered and bit as industriously as it ever did, chapping my lips and turning your cheeks a wild, profligate red—but this time we had the sheepskins, and each other.

On the coldest night we slept with the skins pulled over our heads. The air was black and close, and it smelled of sheep piss and sweat and the sharpening tang of arousal.

Our lovemaking had changed over those nine years in the woods, gentling into the easy, half-laughing sex of two people who know there will be a tomorrow and a tomorrow after that. But since we returned here, it had become desperate again, death-haunted, nearly violent.

I slid my hand between your thighs and pushed my fingers into you, not gently. You pulled my head back by the hair and set your teeth to my throat. There would be bruises in the morning, and raised marks left by your teeth. "Touch me," I said. I tried to make an order of it, but the word left my lips on a gasp.

You bit me, hard. "Do it yourself." You pulled my hand from between your legs and closed my wet fingers around my cock. You moved my fist up and down, mercilessly, in the rhythm I liked best, until my teeth were gritted from the effort of holding back.

"God, Una," I breathed, and your hand loosened, just a little. Enough that I could grab your wrist and twist it, forcing you onto your stomach. I had not spent nine years—more, so many more—in the battlefield of our bed without learning a few tricks. Still, I think you let me.

I moved behind you, disarranging the sheepskins and not caring. I kneed your legs apart and pushed inside you. I went slow. Cruelly slow, punishingly slow, so that it might last forever, as nothing did—until you said, with a hitch in your voice, "Please."

Neither of us lasted long after that. I bowed over your back and worked my hand beneath you and said, "Now, love, yes, that's right," and you cried out as you came.

Later, when our breathing had slowed and we were curled face to face beneath the sheepskins once more, I asked, somewhat plaintively, "Did you *really* sleep naked with your men, for warmth?"

"No." A huff of laughter against my face. "Only with Ancel and his boy."

I was jealous enough that I didn't especially like this answer, but I comforted myself with the memory of his pretty dyed-blond head smacking on the throne room floor. Then I noticed that you had fallen quiet, and that you were breathing carefully, as though to keep back a sob.

I slipped my hand over your bare hip. "You . . . miss him?"

Slowly, you answered: "When Yvanne found me, I knew nothing of court, or of fine speech, or the tourneys where knights made their names. She taught me some of it, but Ancel taught me the rest. He bullied me and mocked me, but he taught me. How to bow, how to speak, how to flirt, how to fuck." I flinched, and you said, "He was my brother, Owen, or my brother-in-arms, or something else. I hated him and I loved him, often on the same day. Of course I miss him."

I pruned the envy ruthlessly from my voice, until all that remained was grief, for your loss. "I'm sorry."

Your hip moved beneath my hand, restless, agitated. "I still don't understand it. How he could—that he would—"

"Murder you?" That came out a little too sharply; perhaps a little envy had survived. I imagined stamping it, nobly, beneath my boot. "Vivian—Yvanne—ordered him to do it. Would you have betrayed him, if she asked it of you?"

You were quiet for a long time. "No. I don't know. But then, I was her favorite, and had nothing to gain by it. And . . . I loved her—even now, the habit of love still catches me sometimes, unawares." You exhaled, began again: "I loved the queen, but I never loved her like Ancel did." You shivered as you said it. After a while you said, so softly I wasn't sure if you were speaking to me, or to yourself: "I will spare him this time, if I can."

The last of my jealousy flaked like ash and drifted away. I pulled you close to me, so that your face settled between my collar and jaw. You cried then, in the humid dark. For yourself, I thought, who had been forged like a blade for a master you no longer served, and for Ancel of Ulwin, who served her still.

Cavallon rose on the horizon as it always did: gracefully, regally, so perfectly fulfilling my expectations for a castle that it might have been cut and pasted from the pages of *The Legends of Una Everlasting: A Children's Retelling of the Classic Tragedy!* Which it had been, more or less: It was a castle as built by a woman who had only read about them in books, nine hundred years in the future.

Structurally, it was unsound. It had been constructed too hastily and too grandly, by conscripted prisoners and bewildered masons who'd never heard the words *barrel vault* in their lives. You'd told me about the cracks that formed in the mortar almost as soon as it was finished, wide enough to slip your hand inside. The curtain walls would fall well before Tilda the Younger's reign, and the cellars would collapse soon after. By the time of Lysabet I they'd abandon the Keep altogether, in favor of a new capitol in the city.

But it didn't matter. It only mattered how it had *looked:* impressive enough that bards had written of it in songs and people had spoken of it in awed whispers, and ministers and chancellors still sometimes described Dominion, poetically, as "the castle upon the hill."

You sat once more on the low stone by the road, your eyes on the Keep. I had braided your hair this time—stupid, to send you into battle with it loose—and tucked the braid neatly beneath your collar. Already the wind had worked a few tendrils loose from your temples.

I fished in my pocket for my second-to-last cigarette. I held it between my teeth as I drew my Saint Sinclair and flicked the cylinder open against my palm. "You know the signal?"

"I know the signal."

I checked the chambers carefully, spun the cylinder once and snapped it back into place. "And you'll listen for it? You'll come, no matter—"

"I swore to serve you, did I not?" Your eyes were still on the Keep, cold and yellow as the eyes of a lynx. "By my life and death."

There was such ease in your voice that I said, sharply, "Only by your life, please."

You didn't answer. You only pulled yourself back into the saddle and settled your shield on your left arm. It shone a defiant, summer green against the drab winter sky.

You turned Hen to face the gates of Cavallon, and he pawed eagerly at the earth, his hoof digging great gouges into the dirt road.

"Soon, boy," you said, and you were smiling.

23

I WALKED THROUGH the gates first, this time. You hadn't liked it much, but I simply wasn't going to watch you take another arrow. In the end I'd threatened to run in naked with a target painted on my back, and you'd thrown up your hands and said, "As you will, then!"

I strolled through the arch fully clothed, cigarette pinched in my left hand, revolver in my right. I didn't bother to hide the gun; the Hinterlanders wouldn't know what it was, even as the bullets entered their brains.

I called up to them: "The Red Knight approaches!" I spoke the words in Shvalic and sent silent, guilty thanks to the Hinterlander boys who had taught me the words. "Archers, take aim!"

I pressed my back to the curtain wall, as if I were hiding from you. There was a moment's confusion above me—they didn't recognize me and hadn't expected a warning—but my hair was dark and curling, like theirs, and I'd spoken to them in their own language. Three arrows were notched to three bows, and three men emerged from their hiding places.

They had survived the First Crusade, which meant they were cautious: Very little of their bodies were visible around the parapets. Half a face, the helmet pulled low. A right shoulder, capped in boiled leather. Small targets, even for a fine marksman. More than enough, for me.

I put my cigarette back between my teeth, cupped my left hand around my right, and let my mind fall away. My body—which had survived the same war a hundred times, which knew how to shoot in the same way it knew how to eat and drink and sleep, without thought—lifted the revolver, took aim, and pulled the trigger. My arm swung smoothly to the right, thumb on hammer, finger already tightening on the trigger again, riding that whisper-thin line just before it fired—a second target, a second shot, and a third, before the first body could hit the stones.

A weird quiet fell. I pictured the rest of the Hinterlanders crouched inside the Keep, baffled by the sound of gunfire. I pictured Vivian rising calmly from her sickbed, making her way to the throne like an actor scurrying behind the curtain.

The quiet lasted less than a second. You arrived in a clatter of hooves and steel, sword already drawn, eyes casting wildly until they found me.

I lifted one hand in greeting. "Hello, love."

You scowled. Tapped your right cheekbone. "Slow."

I touched my face and found a streak of raw, tender skin just below the wire of my spectacles. The last archer must have loosed his shot as he died.

I dropped my cigarette and stamped it just as the Keep doors crashed open. A voice shouted orders and men came swarming out, not knowing their archers were already dead, not knowing their whole brave, desperate venture was nothing but a plot device.

I nodded toward them. "One chance," I reminded you. "That's all they get."

You dipped your head to me, a ghostly imitation of the oath you'd taken, and turned to address the men marching closer. "Soldiers of the Hinterlands! Halt now, I beg you!" Their steps faltered, paused. You laid Valiance across your thighs and lifted one hand, palm out. "Only lay down your arms and let me pass, and we will shed no more blood between us. I will kill you if I must, as I have done before, but my quarrel is not with you."

At this juncture in the story, I was usually so terror ridden—so torn between duty and desire—that I had attention only for you. But now, for the first time, I studied the faces of the Hinterlanders. Young and not-young, bearded and clean-shaven, mostly men, a few women. Their armor was mismatched, ill-fitting, perhaps stolen from Yvanne's court. I recalled that this had been a diplomatic visit before it became a coup.

One of them—a somber woman with thick gray braids—answered, in perfect Mothertongue, "But ours is with you, Everlasting."

"Why?" you asked, and it occurred to me what a good question it was. Why would a group of twelve diplomats attempt to dethrone a queen?

The somber woman said, "We were shown a—vision. I cannot explain it. A scene made of light and shadows, which showed the future. The Hinterlands beneath the boot of Dominion. Our people forced to kneel to a foreign queen. Our soldiers dead or surrendered. And everywhere—your face. *Everlasting,* they will call you."

"Do you mean—did she show you a *newsreel*?" Why lie when the truth would serve her better? "God, she's efficient." Everyone in the courtyard looked at me, frowned, and looked away.

The Hinterlander leader shook her head. "We cannot let it come to pass."

You bowed your head. Here was another circle we could not break: I had killed their countrymen, and now they would kill you, to prevent it.

You hefted Valiance into the air again and said, gravely, "Then I will make it fast."

It was.

The last time you'd fought this battle, you'd relied on your strength and skill, on the sheer physical mastery that had been beaten into every atom of your body.

But this time, you also had your memories. You had seen every strike and step of this fight, every variation and surprise, and so you anticipated every blow.

A blade thrust toward your stirrup, but you'd already wheeled Hen aside. A shield lifted to stop your blow, but you'd already chosen another target. A hand caught your wrist, but you'd already tossed your hilt to your left hand. I pitied the Hinterlanders: It was frustrating, to fight an enemy that knew the future.

When it was done, and the yard was quiet once more, you had not even been unhorsed. But your head was hanging low, and your sword arm hung slackly, as if it were not your arm but only a piece of meat sewn to your shoulder. I touched your leg, just above the stirrup.

You stirred. "If—when we succeed in this—when we get the book again—we will go back to the very beginning. We will change all of this, not just the ending."

I tightened my grip on your ankle. "We will. I swear it." I had already sworn it several times on the journey here.

You fished the cup from your bags and nodded to the reins hanging loosely from Hen's withers. "Then lead on, madman."

"You don't—you're not going to dismount?"

"She had him killed, the last time I left him out here." You added, softly but with conviction, "Bitch."

So I took the reins and led you, still astride, through the great doors and into the rush-lit dark of Cavallon Keep.

The scene was set as it always was—the rustling, scurrying crowd, the stink of sweat and fine perfumes, the veiled woman on the throne and the heroes assembled at her back—save for one alteration: the book, now lying open across the queen's lap.

It was a threat as simple and effective as a knife to the throat. Should we falter or go astray—should we deviate from the script or displease her in any way—she would vanish back through time and change whatever she chose. I had anticipated it, of course, but the sight of the book still sent a sick bolt of fear through my belly.

As we entered the hall, I drew Hen to a halt (he struck, snakily, at my fingers, but somehow missed), and met your eyes. *We play it as written, then.*

As written, you agreed, silently, but you ran your tongue over your teeth. *More or less.*

"Sir Una." Vivian's voice fell weak and lovely over the hall, as it always did, but with a new, very slight tartness; she did so hate your horse.

I loosed his reins and fell back. The crowd was already parted for you, pressing uneasily against the walls. They had looked up as soon as they heard the ring of shod hooves, and they had seen you: a huge woman with a white halo of hair and the devil's own red hands, cup held in one and naked blade in the other, sitting upon a horse like death itself. You did not look like a hero, now, so much as a harbinger.

You rode slowly toward the throne, steering with your knees. Hen's shoes rang like great hammers on the stones.

At the dais, you made one of your wordless commands, and Hen halted. You did not dismount.

As I wormed and shoved my way through the crowd, I heard the queen's faint, irritated sigh. Her line, when it came, emerged through gritted teeth: "And so, you have returned to me at last."

"Yes, my queen." Delivered mechanically, by rote, while you stared down at her. Good: Let Vivian imagine this was an act of defiance. Let her imagine it would be your only one.

"And you have slain the last dragon of Dominion."

"Yes, my queen."

"And you have brought me the lost grail, which they say restores all that time takes—"

"Yes, my queen," you interrupted, and tossed the cup carelessly down to her.

She caught it—perhaps a little too quickly, for a dying woman—and I was so close now I could hear the annoyed click of her teeth.

Still, she rallied. She called, in her spring-snow voice, for wine, and lifted the cup in two tremulous hands as it was poured. She slipped the grail beneath her veil and drank.

She did not stand, this time, for the grand reveal, but made her speech while still seated, the book balanced safely on her knees. "So long have I prayed for one thing and one thing only, and now, by the grace of God and Sir Una, I am given it: *time*."

With this, Vivian drew up her veil to reveal her handsome, healthful face. While the crowd gasped and swayed, she said, through a fixed smile, "Will you not *kneel,* Sir Una, and accept my blessing?"

For a strained moment, I thought you would refuse. I thought you would kill her—kill yourself, kill our chance at a future—rather than kneel at her feet ever again.

But I had not yet given the signal, and you had given me your oath. Stiffly, as if you had grown suddenly old, you slid from Hen's back and down onto one knee.

"Will someone *please* get that animal out of here," Vivian said, tiredly, and a pair of attendants scurried, bent-backed, to take Hen's reins. I wished them luck.

An awkward beat passed, while the queen waited for your head to bow properly—but you refused to bend your neck so much as an inch, keeping your gaze insolently on hers. Pure pride, I thought, but no—you were watching the reflection in her pupils for movement at your back.

Even still, he almost had you. Ancel slipped out from the wall of the crowd, quick and graceful as a cat. Hen screamed his wild battle-scream, tossing his head while the queen's attendants clung desperately to the reins—I opened my mouth to yell a warning I knew you wouldn't hear, through the ruin of my throat—Ancel brought his sword arcing downward—

And you spun and caught it neatly on your cross guard. In the crowd, a woman screamed.

Ancel swore, disengaging, his feet falling into a perfect defensive position. He spoke, and this time I was close enough to hear the words: "*Damn*, but you're fast."

You rose smoothly, uninjured, without arrows lodged in your ribs. "Don't do this, Ancel, please." Your face was pale and frantic, a prophecy of grief. "Can't you remember? We've done this before, over and over. Don't make me do it again."

There was, perhaps, a flicker of doubt in Ancel's face. Then it passed, and he said, with a shrug, "Sorry, love."

He meant it, I thought. But he was a man who had ceded all his choices to someone else, who believed he had none left remaining to him. His motions were the motions of a wind-up doll: inevitable, preordained.

You nodded once, to show you understood, and did not blame him. Then you struck.

It was a hard blow, and fast—but not fatal. Ancel smacked it aside with the flat of his blade and turned the motion into a nasty sweep at your legs. You were forced to step back toward the dais, and the crowd inhaled like a single, many-throated animal.

You recovered before their breath was fully drawn, lunging up and under Ancel's guard—and finding nothing but air, as he slipped, eel-like, around the blow. You circled one another, guards up, and I felt my brows lowering in confusion.

I wasn't sure how many times I'd seen this duel fought, but I was sure it had never lasted longer than twenty seconds. It wasn't even a duel, really, so much as an execution with extra steps.

But this—this was the kind of fight beloved by bards and bloodthirsty young boys. The two of you came together and apart, losing advantage and then gaining it back, striking and defending with flicks and flourishes that caught the light. A slim cut appeared along Ancel's lovely cheekbone. The tip of his sword made a tiny red gouge in your jaw.

Your blade hit his and screeched upward, until your hilts were tangled and your faces were brought close. You struggled, as if you were evenly matched, as if you weren't strong enough to snap both his pretty wrists.

Ancel hissed, beneath his breath: "Finish it, damn you."

"Yield, you ass," you answered, calmly, and I understood: You didn't want to kill him, and he didn't want to survive.

Maybe he never had. Maybe he'd betrayed you because he hadn't been able to disobey his queen, and then he'd let you kill him because he hadn't wanted to live with it. Because there were always some choices remaining to us, no matter how small and bitter.

Vivian was leaning slightly forward in her seat, watching the fight with an expression of false shock. She hadn't noticed me yet. A weakness of hers—assuming that the only players on the stage were the ones she put there. I slipped my hand inside my trouser pocket.

But then Ancel swore, viciously, and I looked away to find him disarmed, sprawled at your feet. Valiance was buried in his shoulder, pinning him like a moth to the board. You drew out the blade. "*Yield.*"

His eyes cut once to the throne, then closed, as if in pain. Then he rolled desperately away, scrabbling for his fallen sword, unable to yield while his queen watched him.

You permitted yourself a brief, black grimace, and then you hamstrung him. It was a neat blow, almost clinical, drawn like a scalpel across the backs of both legs. Ancel went down, and this time he did not rise again, and never would.

It was an abrupt ending to the fight, brutal and unromantic. The court murmured uncertainly to itself. Even they felt the strangeness of the moment, like a wrong note in the middle of an old tune.

You ignored them, turning to face Vivian with something furtive and stupid in your eyes. Hope, I thought—that she had been telling the truth, after all. That she would let us both go as she'd promised.

But then, from behind the throne came a great metal slithering, as the Queen's Guard drew their weapons in perfect synchrony. Bodrow the Giant, who was even taller than you, and Carnock the Elder, who had slain the White Boar with a single spear-throw. Sir Gladwyn, with his dark skin and his winged lynx shield. You looked at them—your comrades, your friends, your fellow heroes—and the hope withered in your eyes.

Vivian had never intended to let you survive this fight. She wanted a tragedy, and she would have one. I'd known it, and so had you, and the only reason we'd played our parts at all had been to reach this very moment: when the Queen's Guard would rush out to meet you and leave the throne unguarded.

I heard the sharp clap of metal on metal, a roar of battle fury, the rising panic of the court—Hen screaming again, and the hollow pop of hooves on flesh—but I didn't look toward you. Couldn't, if I wanted to keep going. Instead, I took the last three steps to the throne, pulled Vivian's slim silver knife from my pocket, and pressed it across her windpipe.

"The book. Now."

Vivian's nostrils flared. "Goodness, Mallory! I'd almost mistake you for a protagonist. But let's not—"

"Shut up." My hand was shaking. Not with fear, but with the effort it took to keep myself from burying the knife in her neck, hilt deep. But the book was still in her lap, and all it would take was a drop of blood.

One-handed, keeping the knife to her throat, I knocked the book from her hands. The cover clacked and slid across the stones.

Vivian's eyes met mine, and I knew a moment's pure joy. We had outplayed her, at last, and now she was going to die. My hand tightened around the knife—

And a pair of arms grabbed me around the knees and bore me to the ground. My head smacked against the flagstones. My spectacles crunched into the bridge of my nose.

I twisted to look behind me, blinking through shattered lenses, and caught the glint of flowing hair, as false and yellow as fool's gold. I wanted to laugh or cry, or maybe hamstring him again. "Oh, for God's sake, man."

It was Ancel, dragging his useless legs behind him, squirming pathetically on his elbows to defend his queen. He'd left a smeary red trail behind him, and his hand was clamped, with fanatical strength, around my ankle.

"*Still?*" I kicked out and caught his injured shoulder. He screamed a little, helplessly, but didn't let go. "You still think if you're good enough and loyal enough and fucking *blond* enough, you'll be her favorite? Look at Una"—I kicked him again, harder—"*look at her* and see how the queen treats her favorite."

His eyes moved over my head, to where you fought the whole of the Queen's Guard. The best of her warriors, storied and glory ridden, against a woman who had already fought two battles today. I still hadn't looked at you, but I could hear the bellows of your lungs working hard, roughening with exhaustion, and I could see Ancel's face whitening with horror. You were not unscathed, then.

I wrenched my ankle free and dove for the book. My hands slipped sweatily on the wood, but then I had it—I *had* it—and all I needed was you. I whistled shrilly, desperately, hoping you could hear the signal over the clamor of battle.

But there was no clamor. No clash of blades, no cries of pain or anger. The hall had fallen suddenly and eerily quiet, save the heavy, ragged breathing of one person.

I turned slowly, heart seizing, fighting the urge to shut my eyes like a child afraid of the dark—but you were still standing. Your hair had been half torn from its braid, viciously enough that the roots were bloody, and your left arm hung limply at your side, but you were still alive.

There were bodies humped around you like red hills, and Hen—who had broken free of his attendants—had posted himself at your back, gore painted up to his fetlocks. You were easing Sir Gladwyn gently from the end of your blade, and there were watery pink tracks down your cheeks where your tears had slicked through the blood.

You looked up at me—at the book, clutched tight to my chest—and your face filled with longing. To go home, to go back to a time when none of this had happened. To the very beginning, you'd said.

You had taken one step toward me when Vivian said, sharply, "Alright, that's enough." Then she clapped her hands twice, and there was an odd ripple in the crowd. I looked, and saw cloaks thrown back, arms lifting, burred arrowheads pointing directly at you. I knew by your sudden and total stillness that you'd seen them, too: Archers hidden among the courtiers, holding the kind of crank-wound crossbows that could punch straight through steel. That wouldn't be invented for another two hundred years.

We had not anticipated her, after all. My limbs felt suddenly stiff and wooden.

Vivian stood from her throne, brushing irritably at her skirts. She said, in modern Mothertongue: "Well, you've fucked this one up beyond all hope of repair, haven't you?" She looked out at the frightened remnants of the crowd.

Half of them had crammed themselves through the door, and the other half were huddled against the walls, staring glassily at the dais. There was no legible story here, no playwright's careful staging to tell them who were the villains and who were the heroes. Their champion had become a devil, covered in the blood of her comrades, and their queen's white gown was turning red at the hem.

Vivian rubbed her temple, as if she had a very bad headache. "We'll have to start over. This time maybe I'll take one of the children along with me, as an incentive for good behavior. Toss me that book, please."

I didn't understand who she was speaking to until I felt the butt of a crossbow strike hard between my shoulder blades. I hadn't seen the men at my back.

One of them wrested the book from my grasp—my nails left pale, desperate scores in the wood—and the other wrenched my arms behind me. I thrashed, contriving to knock into one of them just as he made the toss. The book fell short of the dais, landing instead where Ancel lay wanly in a widening pool of his own blood.

The queen looked at the book. You looked at the queen. I looked at you.

Your face was waxen and pale, but familiar. It was the way you'd looked on your bier, I realized: Beyond fear or anger or hope. Beyond everything, save death.

Abruptly your eyes left the queen to study the archers now lined up like pallbearers at the edge of the crowd. Your expression grew a little distracted, as if you were doing sums. Could you kill the queen before the arrows killed you? Could you reach her before she reached the book, and escaped?

You nodded to yourself. *Yes.*

You wouldn't survive it, but neither would Vivian. And if you couldn't have your future or your freedom—if you would never see your children again—at least you would have your revenge. You would be a tragedy, still, but you would not be hers.

"*No!*" My scream was hoarse, shattered in my throat. "Don't do it, please, Una—I can't—" I threw myself forward against my captors, twisting my arms backward in their sockets. One of the archers cursed and drove his fist into my kidney. I doubled over, still screaming, unsure whether it was pain or grief or sheer fury that I would have to watch you die again.

Then: the *clop* of unhurried hooves. A mild, sinister whinny, which I associated with imminent injury. A rush of air above me, followed by the split-melon sound of a bone breaking.

The archers' hold loosed instantly. I staggered upright to find Hen standing nearly atop me, all four legs once again on the ground. There was something slimy and grayish on his hoof, like brain matter.

The queen was cursing at her men. "Don't waste arrows on the fucking *horse,* keep her in your sights—don't you *dare,* Mallory." She'd seen me staggering toward the book and swept up her long white skirts, ready to race for it.

Both of us stopped, abruptly, because the book was no longer on the flagstones. It was in Ancel's long, graceful hand.

Sir Ancel of Ulwin was no longer especially beautiful. His hair was sweat soaked, pressed unflatteringly to his skull, and his skin was the color of unbaked pastry. He turned the book curiously in one hand, studying the device on the cover. "This is how she does it, then." His voice wouldn't have been out of place at a dinner party, idly polite. "This is how she makes it happen again and again."

I wet my lips. "Yes."

His eyes raked over me, unimpressed. "And you must be Owen."

"How did you—"

He gestured toward you with his chin. "She talks in her sleep." This he delivered with an expression that might have been a leer, on a man who wasn't mostly exsanguinated. "Surely you've noticed." I wished, fervently and jealously, that you'd put your sword through his heart instead of his shoulder.

His attention returned to the book. He ran his thumb over the circle of the dragon, rubbing at the place where its teeth swallowed its own tail. Then he craned his neck at an awkward angle, so that he could meet Vivian's eyes. He smiled up at her, and I saw suddenly why he had been named the Knight of Hearts. It was not a rakish smile or a charming one, but a smile of pure and perfect sincerity. In Ancel's shifting, twisted character, warped by centuries spent as nothing but a sharp tool in a cold hand, this much was true: He loved Queen Yvanne the First.

"Fret not, my queen," he said, lightly. "I remain yours."

Vivian smiled sweetly back. "I know, dear boy." She held out her hand for the book.

Ancel's expression turned wry. It was the expression, I thought, of a man who has discovered he has one choice yet remaining to him, and almost wishes he didn't.

"Save me a kiss in hell, then," he said, and tossed the book—not to Vivian—but to me.

I fumbled, not expecting it, and Ancel said into that last hushed second: "Get her out of here, Owen."

Then the queen was screaming orders and I was diving sideways toward you and your arms were opening to catch me—

The book was crushed between us, the pages crumpling, sliding against your blood-soaked armor—

Ten arrows were flying from ten bows, whistling toward us—

I was grasping back through time, further back than I'd ever reached before, and the world was peeling away like old paint—

Sharp steel arrowheads were burrowing into me, lancing into my back, my right shoulder, my left ear—

And then they were passing painlessly through the air where we used to be, but no longer were—

Because we had gone away, back to the very beginning.

24

SOMETIMES, WHEN WE passed through time, it reminded me of climbing the yew with you when we were children. I felt, or imagined I felt, ghostly branches against my palms, forking and dividing and rejoining endlessly. My brain's puny attempt to make sense of the great tangle of history, I'd thought, by using a metaphor drawn from my own memory.

But it was not a metaphor. The book was the yew was time itself, and now I followed those branches down to the trunk, and then the roots, and then farther still, until I found the tiny, hard seed where everything began.

When we opened our eyes, we were not standing beneath the yew, because there was no yew. There were not even any woods, yet. It was just after daybreak, and the light poured eagerly, almost lavishly, over our faces, unobstructed.

We were lying together, face to face, upon a high, grassy knoll. The shape of the land was different—sharper, unsoftened by time—but I had walked these hills in too many centuries to fail to recognize them. In your era, they would be hidden beneath a thick green rime of trees. In mine, they would be shaved bare, sewn together by the neat stitches of railroad tracks.

Here, in the beginning of everything, there was only the long grass, rippling whitely in the wind, and the lavish yellow light, and the two of us.

I settled my head back into the pillow of the grass and looked at you. At the light which turned your armor to gold and your eyes to amber and your hair the piercing, perfect white of distant stars. In that moment you seemed to be everything at once, a series of contradictions: You were a knight with no master and a mother with no children; a manly woman and a womanly man; a hero whose name would be sung for a thousand years, and an orphan whose name had already been forgotten. You were Sir ███, who I had loved long before my birth and long after your death, in the past and the future, and here, now. Always.

Your fingers tightened around mine, and I discovered that we were holding hands, and that our hands were dug strangely into the soil. Pressed between our palms was something small and smooth and wet, like a pearl.

I drew our tangled fingers from the earth and held the pearl up to the light. You gasped, softly, beside me. It was not a pearl, of course, but the thing we had come all this way to find, and to destroy: A seed, which would grow one day into the yew.

Every night of our journey north we had discussed it. How we might not only escape the endless wheel of our story but shatter it beyond repair. How we might survive its shattering, and what it might cost us.

In the end, we had come to this. We would find the fragile beginning of the yew tree and tear it out before it could take root. We would burn the book and the seed and strand ourselves forever in the ancient past.

The seed was a strange thing: glassy and red, like a jewel. It splintered the light and threw bloody shards over our faces.

A shadow fell across us. "That's pretty."

Both of us startled. We scrambled upright, spinning to face the figure. I grabbed for the book, which had been lying between us, and you went for Valiance.

But it was only a young woman—a girl, really, tall and fleshy, with a roughly spun dress and cheeks the ruddy pink of nail beds. She regarded us without alarm, hands clasped politely behind her back.

Your grip eased on your hilt, but I said, sharply, "Who are you?"

"No one and nothing." The girl answered easily, her accent so odd to my ear it was difficult to understand the words. Then she frowned, as if remembering a dream she'd once had. "Though I think—I think I will become someone, one day. It's only that I haven't yet." Her eyes fell to my fist, where I held the red seed of the yew. "What are you going to do with it?"

"Burn it," I said, shortly. Every second it existed in the world was a second Vivian Rolfe might contrive to return to. I fumbled for a match and drew the head against the heel of my boot. The girl gasped a little as the flame caught, like a child watching a street magician.

I set the book on the tousled grass and lifted a single page. I set it carefully alight, and then another, and another, until the book was lost behind a yellow bloom of flames. It was the second time I'd burned this damn book, and I meant it to be the last.

The wind came again up the knoll, and great gray flakes of ash lifted from the book and drifted upward, away. The fire burned hotter. Into the very center of it, where the flames were tipped with blue and white, I tossed the seed.

You watched it warily, almost fearfully, breathing hard. "When it's gone, when it's done, none of it will have happened." You were holding yourself back from the very edge of hope, unwilling to feel it again. "The Black Bastion. Ancel. *My fathers*—"

I set my hand over yours, pressing silently. We would be stuck here forever. We would never see our fathers again, or anyone we had ever known. But it was worth it.

"I don't think it will burn."

I startled again. I'd forgotten the girl was standing there, watching us.

She laughed. "It would be a great jest if it did. Imagine a dragon's heart, burning!"

You said, so calmly that the question flattened into a statement, "A what."

The girl bent down and plucked the seed from the ashes. You swore. I tried, too late, to stop her.

The girl ignored us both, rolling the seed fearlessly in her palm before handing it back to me. "See? It's not even hot."

I flinched as it touched my hand, but the girl was right: It was merely warm against my skin. "How . . . did you know?" I asked. And then again, more urgently, a nameless terror clamoring in my skull, "*Who are you?*"

"No one, I already told you." The girl shrugged, and the wind carried her perfume to me. A sweet, summery smell, which I knew and refused to name. "And it was my—teacher, who taught me about dragons."

"Your . . ." I'd heard someone hesitate in just that way before they said the word *teacher.* I remembered who it had been, and in remembering, I suddenly knew what her perfume smelled like, what it had always smelled like: ulla flowers.

I grabbed you by the pauldron and hauled you abruptly backward, away from the girl. "How did you do it? How the *hell* did you—shit." I was searching for the silver knife, not finding it. Must have dropped it in the throne room. God, to have made it this far—to have the seed in my grasp and *still* not be free of her—

Your head whipped back and forth, looking for a threat. "Owen, what—"

"It's her," I spat. "*Look.*"

The girl stood watching us both with mild interest, hands still behind her back. She smiled at you—a good smile, friendly and white—and I felt a stillness fall over you. "No," you said.

But it was obvious, now that I knew. Her hair was a little lighter, but would darken eventually to metal yellow. Her jaw was hidden by baby fat, but would one day harden into a perfect right angle. Only her eyes were unchanged: zealous, relentless, entirely devoid of doubt.

The girl smiled at me. "Hello, Cor-por-al." She pronounced the word carefully, as if it were foreign to her.

My fist seized around the seed. "Hello, Vivian."

The girl—who was not yet Vivian Rolfe, but would be one day—scrunched up her nose at the sound of her name. "I suppose so. I wish I will choose a better name, but I know I don't." She paused while her verb tenses slithered and bivouacked in my mind. "I remember it all, I do, but it's a little . . . blurred. I've done it all so many times, and haven't done it yet—well, *you* know."

I did. Every time I returned to that day in my office—to my own natural lifespan—it grew worse. The memories multiplied, piling one atop the other until every voice was an echo and every gesture was familiar. The had-been and will-be converged, swallowing the present, leaving nothing but confusion.

But Vivian had never once seemed confused. I looked at her again, more sharply. She stood so comfortably in the rough-woven dress, and those odd, archaic vowels came so easily to her tongue. She was younger by far than I'd ever seen her.

"You're not from my era at all, are you? Originally, I mean." It shouldn't have taken me so long to suspect it. Vivian hadn't suffered from the same circling amnesia because she'd so rarely returned to her own lifespan. I imagined Professor Sawbridge making a pained noise at my slowness. "You're from here, from *now*."

I'd promised you we would go back to the beginning, but where was the beginning of a circle? I felt that circle tightening now around my throat, like a noose.

"Yes," said not-yet-Vivian. "Well, not *here*—I was born miles and miles away, one and twenty years past." She was older than I'd thought, then. I had been misled by the softness of her face and belly, which slumped oddly beneath her dress. She looked over my shoulder and her eyes softened. "Wilt thou kill me, then, daughter?"

I turned and discovered that your sword was braced across your forearm, the point aimed precisely toward the girl's throat—but you weren't moving. Your eyes cut once to me, and I saw turmoil in them. Here was the architect of all your misery: a sweet-faced child, defenseless and unarmed. Here was your worst enemy, before she had committed any crime against you. Here was the egg, soft and pale, that came before the asp.

You waited, and I realized you were hoping I would make an order of it and absolve you—but I wouldn't.

When you'd knelt in the woods and handed your heart to me hilt first, as if you were nothing but a weapon, I'd made an oath of my own: never to wield you like one.

Into the silence, not-yet-Vivian said, "Look at you. So grand, with your silver sword and your silver armor. And tall—even taller than me!" She laughed, but hiccuped halfway through. "Do they sing songs about you? They do, I know they do, for I made it so." There was a sudden, disconcerting sheen to her eyes.

The point of your sword wavered. "Tell it all to me, first. Tell me how—I came to be." You were buying time, perhaps. Or perhaps not—what would I ask my own mother, if I could speak to her? "I don't even know your name."

The girl blinked the sheen away. "No? But—you must know all of them, by now. Yvanne, Tilda, Lysabet, Vivi—"

"Your *true* name. The one you were born to."

"Oh." She frowned a little. "But I wasn't born to anything. My mother and father were midden-rats who lived on scraps and offal. I was Brat or Babe. I was Another-Mouth-to-Fill, before they sold me. My teacher called me other things when he bought me for his household. I was Girl and then Clever Girl and then Sweet Girl." She smiled shyly as she said it, as if she were bragging. Then her lips flattened, and her tone turned older and more world-wise. "And then, of course, I was Cunt, there at the end."

She didn't say anything further, and you didn't ask. I sighed a little. All these years together, and you still hadn't learned how to pull a story from someone. "And who was he? Your teacher."

"Oh, a great man," the girl answered eagerly, as if it mattered. As if a person might call you any name he liked, so long as he was great. "A *king*! Or at least, what passed for a king, before I came along. He conquered a pretty piece of land in his youth, and in his old age he set himself to conquer higher things. Mathematics, astronomy, history, alchemy. Life and death. Time, above all. I was only his fetch-and-sweep girl, at first, another no one in his hall—but I didn't remain so. I refused." Her chin lifted, and I could see the hard line of her jaw through the fat. "I had no letters or numbers when I came to his service, but I saw that they were precious to him, and so I learned them. Just by watching and listening and stealing scraps he abandoned. The *work* it took, the will—for years I studied late into the night, slapping myself to stay awake." She cast you an odd look, resentful and proud. "*You* had help. You had someone to make you what you are, someone to guide you, but I had to do it myself. I was alone, always."

You said, in a voice like a whetstone, "So was I." *Everything I have done, I have done alone.*

"Oh? And yet every time you die, I have to pull this man off you like a leech from a wound." There was the Vivian I knew, suddenly visible, the asp moving in its leathery egg. She ducked her head, a mere girl again. "And if you were sometimes lonely—it made you strong, as it made me strong." There was compassion in her voice, but no regret. To regret would be to doubt, and Vivian had never once doubted herself.

The wind rushed over us all, laying the grass low and pressing the girl's skirt against her legs. There was a funny-colored stain just above her knees, still damp. She continued, unprompted, "But he was a great man, as I said, and very busy. He didn't notice me until I made him. He left his slate lying on the workbench one day with a calculation unfinished. I finished it for him. He came storming into the kitchens where we slept, kicking us from our nests and asking who had meddled with his work. He was so angry—until he saw me." A memory so sweet she had to close her eyes. "He looked me over. He checked my teeth and pinched the fat of my arms. He called me clever, and I never slept in the kitchens again."

I wondered where she had slept instead. I wondered how old she had been. I swallowed, and it tasted foul. "And so, the king became your . . . teacher?"

I left the same pause before the word that she had, and the girl gave me a wary, furtive look. "He would not have called himself such. But what else should I call him? Master, though it was I who mastered him, in the end? Majesty, when I had seen him panting and stupid, brought lower than a rutting dog?" She snorted. Both you and I flinched. "No. I call him teacher, for he taught me so many things."

Your sword sagged until it pointed at her knees, rather than her throat. I glanced at your face and found it startled, almost fearful, as if Vivian was undergoing some hideous transformation, and you were no longer sure whether she was villain or victim.

I asked, "What did he teach you?"

"He taught me of the past, first. He read me holy scripture and ancient myths and showed me how to tell truth from myth. The Savior was his particular obsession: The man who died, yet lived again. The mortal who became God."

"Next, he taught me of the future. About *ambition,* which is the future on purpose." Her voice had a sing-song rhythm to it, as of a child reciting a lesson they'd learned by rote. "I had plenty of ambition, I thought. I wanted to eat the next day. I wanted to survive to see my next spring. But my teacher wanted . . . more."

She paused again, and it was you who prompted her this time. "What more could a king want?"

Not-yet-Vivian cast you a patronizing look, incongruous on her young face. "What does every king want? To *stay king.*" She looked between us and spoke in the slow, overloud voice shopkeepers sometimes used with me when they thought I was foreign. "He was old, I told you. Soon, his crown would be someone else's. His story would end. His name might be remembered for a time, but he'd studied history well enough to know that nothing that lives lasts forever." Her head tilted. Her eyes fell to my closed fist. "Save, perhaps, dragons."

The seed felt suddenly hot in my hand. I unclenched my fingers. "He made a study of them. He had them caught and staked, carved and pickled. And eventually he found . . . that." She nodded at the seed in my palm, and I saw it doubled in her eyes, like a small red spark. "A seed, hidden in the heart of every dragon, which burns on even after their death. He thought it was something to do with their life cycle—when a dragon dies, a tree grows from its heart. And one day, when the tree is grown, the dragon will be reborn, curled around the trunk. But he didn't want more dragons." A shrug. "He wanted more time."

"That's why you hunted them all down, then." I remembered, so vividly I could almost hear it, that long, keening cry as the last dragon died. "So that no one else would discover what your teacher had."

"Yes, of course, but please don't interrupt. I'm still doing my list," said not-yet-Vivian, crossly. "He taught me the past, and the future—and he taught me what it cost." One hand came out from behind her back and clutched, convulsively, at the flesh of her stomach. "We studied that seed for months and months. Then one morning he woke me with a cup of sour tea. I drank it, and he explained that he'd solved the puzzle long ago. He said all he needed was a heart—but a heart that had never been born. A soul, misplaced in time."

My eyes fell to the stain on her skirt, crusted and glossy. At the rucked fabric where her hand had fisted over her empty belly. It had been recent, I thought. Only hours ago, although she told the story like a distant memory. "I'm sorry," I said.

"You're quicker than me." Her voice had gone clipped and modern, less youthful. "I didn't understand what he meant until the bleeding started."

You asked, blankly, "The bleeding?" and I wanted to press my hands over your ears.

She ignored you. "The hell of it was, I would have drunk that tea myself. I would have drunk *arsenic* if he'd asked it of me." She laughed, blackly. "But he didn't ask, did he? He didn't have to. I wasn't his student or his daughter or his lover or even his whore, not really. I was only *his.* And he hadn't chosen me because I had wits and ambition. He'd chosen me because I had most of my teeth and a working womb."

The sun was high enough now that it was difficult to look directly at the girl who would become Vivian Rolfe. She was a shadow, a hole torn neatly in the sky, which told us a terrible story. "You were born still in the caul," said the shadow. "Tiny and curled up, like the fiddlehead of a fern. But dead, of course." At my side, you began to shake. "Remember that—you were born dead. Every breath you've drawn since then, every second you've lived, was a *gift,* which I gave you."

I stepped stupidly in front of you, as if I could shield you, as if I could catch the words before they found you. Your breath at my back was uneven, too fast.

The shadow continued. "A necessary sacrifice, he called you, in exchange for greatness. I told him I would be great, too, one day, and he couldn't imagine it. He laughed at me—laughed! While I held our little dead daughter! Then he kissed my brow and told me to go to sleep, and so"—the shadow shrugged—"I killed him."

You said, like a woman holding fast to one guiding star in thick fog, "Good."

"Yes," said the shadow. "I should have done it sooner, probably, but I loved him so. Another thing he taught me: There is nothing a person will not endure, for love." A lesson she had passed down to her daughter. *Who is free, who loves another?*

"And then?" I asked. I wasn't sure I wanted to know, but you did, and the sun was hot on my face and my legs were tired and I wanted, badly, to be through with this.

"And then I came here. It's a pretty place, and far from my teacher's holdings. I buried you and planted the seed in your chest—your heart was so small it was difficult to find, like the pit of a cherry—and then I waited." A flash of white in the shadow's face: teeth, curved in a sharp smile. "And then came the yew, and then came everything else."

Your voice, when it came, was thin and unsure. You had lost sight of your star and were drifting now in the mist. "My fathers said they found me as a baby, laid at the foot of the yew."

"Your—the woodcutter and his beau, you mean?" Odd, to hear slang from my own era on the lips of an ancient queen. "They didn't lie to you. They weren't clever enough for lies. They were simple men, but . . . good, I thought. Caring. Another gift I gave you, which no one ever gave me." Another jealous lash there, as if you owed her, as if children were born indebted to their parents.

You waited, unspeaking. Eventually Vivian—she was all Vivian, now, the asp unfurled—said, "I didn't know, when I buried you, whether I would ever see you again. But one day, when the yew was full grown, there you were among the roots. Just the same as you'd been when I buried you—except you were alive. And your hair, and your eyes . . ." A flash of teeth. "Well. I did not choose your device by accident."

"It's not her device any longer," I said. The words scraped against one another like stones on a riverbed.

I still couldn't see Vivian's features clearly, but her shadow clucked its tongue. "A sweet gesture, I'm sure, but she's worn my colors for centuries, and she'll wear them for centuries more, I promise you."

You said, suddenly sure of yourself again, "I will not."

The shadow stamped its foot. "*Ungrateful,* that's what you are. Don't you see what I've done for you? I named you. I trained you. I *loved* you. And oh, I was so patient with you! When you fell in battle, we began again. When you shattered your sword, I brought you a new one. When you were heartbroken, I brought you *him.*" In the many monologues I'd heard Vivian Rolfe deliver, I don't think she'd ever truly lost control. Every emotion she showed was a calculation, a mask presented for a purpose. But now her voice rose and fell erratically, pleading and scolding, childish and horribly ancient. "I made you—you the fetus, you the dead thing which died before it could even be named—into a knight. A champion, a hero, a saint, a legend—I made you someone who could never, ever be forgotten." She stepped sideways a little, so that the sun touched her face, and she was suddenly not a shadow but a girl, crying freely, her accent veering back toward the archaic. "Everything that was denied to me, I gave to thee."

"Yes," I drawled, purposefully dry. "Before you killed her."

Vivian's eyes narrowed at me. "*He* killed her first," she snapped. "And I couldn't save her or change it. I can't go back further than this moment, when I first buried the seed. I can't undo anything that was done to me, or that I have done up till now." How that must eat at her: To have mastery over the whole of history, but not her own. "She was sacrificed before she was born. It's what she's *for*."

She stepped closer to me. "But look what I have built in her honor." Vivian's voice turned rich and smooth. Her radio voice, which had driven men to war and children to factories. "On her altar, I built a kingdom, a nation, an empire. Though it took centuries upon centuries of work—though even my champion abandoned me, and forswore herself—still I built it, stone by stone. You're a soldier, aren't you?" That slight vagueness in her eyes, as she struggled to remember the future. "And a student of history. Who better to judge my work? Can you look at what I've made, Owen Mallory, and say truly that it was not worth the death of one woman?"

"One woman?" I asked, softly. "Are you quite sure of your math?" They assembled silently in my mind, her generations of sacrifices, so that you and I shrank and shrank, invisible among the suffering crowd.

Vivian had opened her mouth to answer, but I cut her off. "Say it's true, for the sake of argument. Say all it cost was the endless torment of one person. What is it that you have built, exactly?"

Vivian answered, in a kind of bewilderment, "Dominion."

But the Dominion I'd believed in as a boy—the castle on the hill, the ivory paradise to which I might one day ascend, if I was loyal and docile and good—was obscured to me now. Instead, I saw a throne teetering atop a stack of bones. An appetite, unslaked. A nation obsessed with a past that had never existed, in memory of a queen who had never died.

But even if Dominion had been a paradise—I stole a glance back at you, bloodied but still standing, gold limned in the rising dawn—I suspected my answer would have been the same.

"No," I said, easily. "It's not worth it." I pinched the little red seed between thumb and forefinger. "And so, I'm afraid . . . this is it. We're through." This sounded somewhat melodramatic, so I clarified, "I don't know how to destroy this thing yet, but surely you know we will not let you plant it in your daughter's heart."

"Well, no." Vivian agreed, so easily that the hairs stood up on my arms. "I gave her a decent burial, this time. I planted my favorite flower over her grave." This she said proudly, even defiantly. "My teacher says they're common, but I always loved the smell of them."

I recalled the sweet summery scent that Vivian wore in every era and felt a sick twist of pity. "Why did you bury her, this time?"

"Because I don't need her anymore. Because *you* came. You always do." Her eyes lifted from mine and found yours, and there was no doubt in them at all. Her faith in you was the faith a smith might feel for his favorite hammer, or a hunter for his best hound: pure, without flaw. "A heart that hasn't been born. A soul misplaced in time. Very soon now you're going to put that sword through your heart, and then I'm going to plant the seed in your body. And it will grow and grow, watered by your blood, fed by your rot, until one day a woodcutter finds a babe beneath the yew, and it begins again."

The words hung for a moment, spectral, prophetic, and then you said, gently, almost wonderingly, "No, I will not."

Then came the whip of metal through air, followed by a biting crunch. I flinched, but you'd only driven Valiance into the earth. You took your hand from the hilt and stepped back. "I will not be your tragedy or your sacrifice, ever again. I will not die for you."

It was then—as you stood clear-eyed, shoulders back, like a woman loosed from a long confinement, like a saint who had torn herself down from the church wall and now walked free, among the mortal—that Vivian struck.

Her motions were eerily smooth, inhumanly fast, as though she'd practiced them a thousand times. Maybe she had. Maybe we'd made it here before, over and over, and stood on the very cusp of freedom before she dragged us back down.

Vivian's foot found the back of my leg, so that I collapsed down to my knees. Her left hand fisted in my hair as I fell, and her right hand held a slim silver blade to my throat.

"I know," she said to you, conversationally. "But you'll die for him."

The knife nipped into my neck, parting the silver knots of my scars, coming to rest against the fragile sheath of my carotid. If her hand twitched, if I turned my head so much as three degrees to the left or right, I would be dead.

You hadn't moved, but I watched emotions move like seasons over your face: terror into fury into grief into vacant weariness. Had you ever truly believed we'd escaped, or had you been waiting, like a loosed hawk, for the falconer to call you back to her fist?

A trickle of blood pooled in the hollow where my clavicles met. The earth dampened the knees of my trousers. I had been here before, I thought; the body remembers.

In remembering, I discovered that I knew exactly what would happen next.

Very soon you would reach again for your sword. You would turn it awkwardly in your hands. The hilt would be too far away even for your long reach, and so you would hold it by the bare blade, pommel slanted down toward the earth. Then you would fall, and I would watch you, and in a hundred years or a thousand, in my time or in yours, we would meet again beneath the yew.

There was no such thing as fate, but this was ours.

Even if we remembered again—and we would—we would only find ourselves back here, caught in the same endless, unsolvable equation.

It would never stop because Vivian would never be satisfied. She had paid the price herself once, for a king's ambition. She had killed him, but instead of casting his crown into the mud, she had claimed it for herself. And now she wanted what any king wanted: to stay king, no matter the cost.

And it would be you who paid it, who would never stop paying it. Because you loved me, and in loving me, you would never be free.

Dizzily, sickly, in a long string of metaphors, I saw everything we could make of love: chains, debts, cages, circles. And, too, I saw everything it could make of us: tragedies, traitors, madmen, cowards.

Your hand was closing now around your hilt. Your eyes were the dull yellow of dead pine, and your limbs moved as if they had strings affixed at every joint.

I thought suddenly of my father, and of the mother I'd never met. Of Professor Sawbridge and even of Ancel, at the very end.

Vivian had made a mistake in her calculations, I thought. For sometimes—when we could not run any longer, when all our choices had been whittled down to one—love made heroes of us.

I felt my own hands resting placidly on my thighs. They were not shaking at all, because I wasn't afraid. I was only relieved, hugely and guiltily, that I wouldn't have to watch you die again—and I was sorry. For the children.

Let me write their names here, just once. They're only a dream, now, of the future that will never come to pass, but I won't have them forgotten.

Marro. Our son, named for the river where my mother died.

Thea. Our daughter, named for one of your fathers.

I smiled up at you, my neck arched unnaturally by Vivian's clawed grip. I smiled at the wild bone-white tangle of your hair—God, I would miss your hair—and at the great grim shape of your shoulders. At the age lines that puckered the corners of your eyes so sweetly, and the scar that bit through your left pupil. You had survived so much. You would survive this, too.

That deep furrow appeared between your brows. It asked, plainly: *What the hell are you doing?*

I kept my eyes on yours. I neither blinked nor flinched; I was no coward. *Setting you free, love.*

Then I turned my head, hard and fast, three degrees to the left.

THE LAST DEATH OF UNA EVERLASTING

25

OF THE TWO of us, I was the lucky one. I hadn't known that, before I watched you cut your own throat.

In all my many lives and deaths, I had never been the one left behind. I'd never been the one who lingered in the world without you, gruesome and a little absurd, like a severed limb. I'd never been the one who had to grieve and go on.

This—*this*—is what you endured, over and over?

Fuck every single person who ever called you a coward, Owen Mallory. And fuck you, for making me into one, here at the end.

I couldn't watch. Your clever black eyes had so often been the last thing I'd seen, looking into mine as if you would follow me to heaven or hell, as if there was nowhere I could go that you would not find me. Now it was my turn, and I couldn't do it. I saw that first bright spray of blood—arterial, fatal—and then I closed my eyes. I, who had watched a city burn without blinking, could not watch you die.

On the backs of my eyelids, I saw your face. The long arch of your nose, badly bruised by your spectacles. The fine bones of your cheeks, and the short silver hairs in your beard, which hadn't been there before. How old are we, Owen? How many years have we lived? Our bodies keep track, I think, even if we forget.

When I opened my eyes, all your blood was spent among the laid-over grass, and I was alone once more.

Not anymore, you had told me. *Not ever again.* Liar.

Your body slumped forward, out of the queen's grasp. For a moment she stood looking down at you, unmoving. In her right hand was a knife, still wet, and in her left were a few curled black scraps, which fluttered faintly in the wind. Your hair, I realized.

Yvanne stared down at your corpse, unmoving. Then, very slowly, she looked up at me. Her features were raw and unformed, embryonic. I had never seen her so young, or so frightened. I had never seen her do anything she had not done before.

"I can give him back to you," she said. Her voice was very high. She took a step back, and another. "The children, too, I swear. I can—*wait*—"

She stopped talking then, because Valiance was leveled at her chest, the tip tucked just below her sternum. Her tongue darted out, wetting chapped lips. "Y-you will be forsworn. You took an oath to serve me—"

"I serve no master, now." I spoke clearly and evenly, as if I were explaining to our daughter why she mustn't touch the fire.

Yvanne tried again, a puppeteer tugging desperately on slack strings. "You will be *nothing* without me. Forgotten. No one will know the name Una Everlasting—"

"That is not my name."

"You—you will be a monster. Only a monster would slay her own mother." Her voice was winding tighter and tighter, rising in pitch. She was very afraid, now. "Is that what you want? Is that what *he* would want?"

My fist tightened around the hilt. Daring of her, I thought, to make mention of you.

But I let the question hang in the air between us. It was your voice that answered: *Kneel.* You had given me back my sword and bid me to fight again. You had not wanted me by halves.

I'd been quiet long enough that Yvanne mistook it for doubt. She babbled into the silence, and her voice seemed to waver in and out of frequencies, like one of those wireless devices from your time. She was gentle, imperious, cold, warm, urgent, soothing, anything she thought I wanted to hear. "It's alright, child. We can fix this. Just do as I say."

But I never had to do as she said, ever again. This was the gift you had given me, and I would not waste it. "If I told you to leave—to go away from here, to leave the seed and the tree forever, and become no one—would you do it?"

She opened her mouth, but I spoke first. "The truth, please." My voice came thickly now, shot through with salt. "If you love me, if you ever loved me, in even the smallest measure—answer me truly. Would you stop?"

Her mouth closed. She looked at me as she had never looked at me before: uncertainly, as if I were a stranger to her. I waited.

She said, "No."

Later, I would wonder if she said it because she didn't believe I would let her live. Or because she was weary of striving and scheming and killing. Or because some part of her—the part of her that planted her favorite flower over my grave and wore its scent for a thousand years—loved me.

"No," she said again, "I would not. I never will."

It was the only gift she'd ever given me. In turn I gave her the only mercy I have ever shown: I killed her quickly.

I slid the blade up beneath her breastbone, cutting her heart into two neat halves, and withdrew it. She made a face of total astonishment, her eyes ringed in white, her mouth comically round. I tried to remember what it had felt like to die for the very first time and could not.

Her lips moved. Air passed between them, the faintest words. If I leaned close, I might have been able to hear them.

I turned away, and never looked at her again.

I knelt then, at your side. It was less hard than I'd thought it would be, to look at you. Even when you slept, your lips had twitched and tilted, your brows lifting and slanting, as if the wheel of your mind was still turning. Your face was motionless, now, and foreign to me.

I shucked my armor, stiff fingered, a little clumsy. I had been quick with this work when I was younger, but for years now it had been your hands—long fingered, ink stained, quick and fragile as wrens—which stripped my armor from me.

When I wore only my own quilted wool, I laid myself down beside you and took your hand carefully in mine. I thought: Let us lie here forever. Let us be buried as wild things are, by tooth and claw and worm. Let the grasses grow up through the sockets of our eyes. Let them find us in seven years or seventy, and let their brows furrow, because they cannot tell my bones from yours.

Everlasting, Yvanne called me. But nothing that lives lasts forever. Save, perhaps, this thing between us, which had drawn us together across a thousand years, over and over, and—my breath caught—dragons.

I turned your hand carefully and opened your fist. It was not hard; your body would not stiffen for hours yet.

The seed fell from your palm to mine, still warm. When I closed my hand around it, I felt, or thought I felt, a faint rhythm, like a distant drumbeat.

I wrapped my limbs around you and pulled you close to me. I kissed you once, hard enough that I could feel the cool shape of your teeth beneath your lips. And then I set my mouth to your ear and whispered:

"I will wait for you. Beneath the yew."

It took the whole day to bury you.

I might have gone looking for a village or croft and begged the use of a spade, but I was impatient, and I didn't want to leave you, so I used Valiance to cut the shape of your grave into the grass. It was not a small grave; damn your long legs.

I used the sharp edge of my pauldron to dig. When it hit a stone and buckled, I used the stone, and when the stone broke, I used my hands.

I did not dig a grave for Yvanne the First, Queen of Dominion. I only set my foot to her body and sent it rolling down the hill, out of sight. She would stink for a while, and then she would be bones, and then she would be forgotten entirely.

By the time the hole was dug, it was eventide, and four of my fingernails were missing. I left muddy red smears on your shoulders as I lowered you down into your grave.

It wasn't very deep, and I had no casket, but I wasn't worried; I would not leave your grave unguarded.

I unbuttoned your shirt and laid my hand briefly on your chest. I had liked to sleep just so—with your heart beating hot under my palm. It was cold now, but it was exactly what I needed: A heart that had not yet been born.

It had never occurred to Yvanne that she'd caught two people in her trap, misplaced two souls in time. I don't think she ever truly saw you at all. I was her hero, her champion, her sacrifice, and you were only the string that made me dance.

But I saw you, Owen Mallory, and swore to serve you by my right arm and my left, by my life and death. And I am not dead yet.

I had taken Yvanne's slim silver knife from her hand, and I slid it now between your ribs. I drove it into the stilled muscle of your heart, twisted it back and forth three times, and slipped it carefully from the hole. It made a slight, suppurating sound, like a boot drawn from mud.

I took the red seed between my finger and thumb and pushed it gently into your chest, nestling it down among the hollow chambers of your heart.

I left your shirt unfastened. When the seed sprouted, let it lift straight up to the light, unimpeded.

I buried you, handful by handful.

And then I lay down beside the soft earth of your grave, and I waited.

26

I DON'T KNOW how long I waited.

You would have accounted for every day, but I let them run through my fingers like water. I didn't want to know how long we'd been apart.

I know it was spring when the sapling first pushed its shoulders up through the earth, head bowed over the pale stem, like a sleeping swan. I fell asleep that night with my cheek pressed to the soil, watching it, and when I woke the first needles were outstretched, tilted toward the dawn.

I know it was summer, that year or the one after, when the first berry budded, hard and green. I touched it with my smallest finger. I thought of our son.

I know it was spring again when a storm blew in from the north, driving the swifts and small animals ahead of it. I curled my body around the yew while lightning struck so near it raised the hairs on my arms and left the taste of metal in my mouth.

I went away from the hill only when I had to, driven by thirst or hunger, and while I was away, I thought only of calamities: a stray hoof, a careless boot, a hard freeze, a hungry fawn, too young to know the needles would sting her mouth. The sapling was growing fast—strangely fast, I thought sometimes—but it was still so fragile, so small.

But I had to hunt. I had to drink at the beck. And when my red cloak finally grew so thin and rotten that it came apart in my hands, like old lace, I had to walk all the way down to Queenswald.

It was not Queenswald yet, of course, but only a handful of cob huts that had gathered like cattle in the valley below. I found the smith and traded the remains of my armor for a rough woolen blanket, a tin pot, flint and steel, and a bag of dry field peas. Then I turned back and bartered for a second blanket; it might be winter when you returned, and you hated the cold.

The smith did not protest. His eyes moved often to the hilt of Valiance, which I wore always at my hip, and which I refused to trade for any price.

Fight for us, you had said to me, and I will.

Yvanne might be gone, but a crown is a circle, too. The queen is dead, long live the queen. There will be borders drawn and redrawn, wars fought and lost. There will be strangers who come to our wood in search of rebels or deserters, timber for their warships or coal for their engines. They will find us, instead—and they will not find us undefended.

I heard whispers as I left the village. I was not surprised: I was over-tall and badly scarred, rawboned from too many seasons of game and gathered berries. I was a woman, yet I carried a sword. I carried a sword, and yet I served no lord and bore no colors, save the green grass stains on my shirt.

Perhaps she is not a woman or a knight, they whispered, *but something else, which dwells in the wastes and wild places.*

They began to leave things at the foot of the hills sometimes. A white goat kid, freshly slain. A pair of fine beeswax candles. A cup of wine, full to the brim. Offerings, I finally realized, as you might offer to a spirit or a heathen god.

I tried to repay them, feeling sorry and fraudulent. If a lamb was lost in those hills, it was found penned with the others in the morning. If a band of thieves or brigands passed nearby, they passed quickly onward, without troubling Queenswald. If a woman was chased from the village in the night, her pursuer vanished, and was not heard from again.

They were grateful, I thought, but wary. They did not till the land to the north of the village anymore or let their animals graze in the hills. Already saplings had begun to sprout among the grasses, growing tall and well.

But not as well as the yew. It seemed to bound through the seasons like a hind. Already the earth beneath it was riddled with roots, and the sky was obscured by the green tangle of branches and needles. The trunk was sturdy enough that I might lean my back against it, sometimes, and close my eyes.

Perhaps it was the magic of the yew that made it grow at five times the pace of a natural tree. Or perhaps more time was passing than I reckoned. Perhaps some nights I lay down beneath the yew and woke seven years later. It was true that sometimes when I went down into the village, I did not recognize their faces. My own face, when I saw it reflected in still water, had not changed.

I suppose time moves strangely, beneath the yew. I did not worry overmuch about it. I only waited, as I had promised I would.

Soon the yew was tall enough to cast a broad circle of shade, and the bark was furrowed and gnarled enough that I could imagine I saw shapes in the grain. There was a place halfway up the trunk that looked like a face, with a twist of wood like a long, arched nose and two knots like black eyes. I liked to put my back against the yew and rest my skull just below the face.

One day in early autumn I fell asleep there—for an hour, for a century—and when I woke, it was summer. The ulla flowers were in bloom again.

And I was not alone anymore.

I sat for a moment listening to the sound of your breath, as familiar to me as my own pulse. I had waited for a hundred lives, a thousand years—what was another few seconds?

Then I stood and circled the tree. You sat against the other side, your back to the bark, eyes closed. You were whole and alive, just as I remembered you—or nearly so.

Your hair was still curled and tousled, as if you'd just run your fingers through it, but it had turned a pure, unnatural white, like bleached bone. Like mine. We had both of us been born from the yew, as dragons are, and we were both changed by it.

Your shirt was still unfastened, as I'd left it, but on your bare chest there was now a small, silver scar, just like mine. The scar rose and fell lightly with your breath.

I looked at your face and for a moment I couldn't tell how old you were. Every version of you seemed to exist at once, overlapping.

You were the lonely, scrape-kneed boy who had found me in the green shadows between centuries. You were the scholar who had written nothing but lies and the soldier who had fled the field of battle; the bravest coward and the cleverest madman and the traitor with the truest heart; the man who had led me to my death and the man who had died for me.

You were the bastard who had left me here alone, all these years, and you were my best beloved, who always, always came back to me.

Most often I met you with a sword to your throat. This time I knelt over your sprawled legs and touched the tip of my knuckle to the hollow beneath your jaw.

Your long white lashes lifted. You looked up at me as you always did when we met beneath the yew: hungrily, wistfully, as if you didn't believe I was real but badly wished I was. But your eyes were different, this time: a dark, tawny amber, like winter honey, or spring sap.

And this time when you said my name, it was not Una Everlasting. It was the humble name of a woodcutter's daughter, the name I have stricken from these pages so that it will be known only by those who knew me.

"█████," you said, and I took your face in both my hands and kissed you, fiercely and furiously, for a long time.

When I let you go, there was blood on both our lips, and I couldn't say if it was yours or mine. I traced the fine bones of your cheeks with my thumbs, buried my fingers in your pale, pale curls. "You remember, then? Everything?" I had lain awake for so many nights, wondering what you had lost down under the earth, among the roots and worms.

"I—I don't know. Some." There was a haziness in your voice, as if you were recalling dreams you'd had as a child. You added, a little desperately, "I remember you."

"That is enough," I said, and it was.

What you have forgotten, I will tell to you; what I have forgotten, you will tell to me. We will tell our story to one another, not for crown or country, but only for ourselves.

We might even write it all down—you would like that, I think, and why shouldn't we?

We have time.

☙ UNA AND THE YEW ❧

t ends where it began: beneath the yew tree.

You might know the place I mean. If you have ever wandered west, past the village that was once called Queenswald and isn't now, then you have seen the great wood that covers the hills there. That wood has never been named, nor claimed by any king or country. There have been attempts, over the centuries, but no soldier or surveyor who has entered those woods has found much luck there.

If you have walked into those woods, and farther, to the very heart of them, then you have seen the yew. It stands like a great queen grown old, head bowed—no, there is no sword waiting to be claimed. You're thinking of a different story—a legend you heard once, or a dream you had as a child.

But it's true there is a woman who walks sometimes in that place, who wears a huge silver sword at her hip, the hilt long enough for two hands, though she holds it in one. The Keeper of the Yew, they call her, or the Green Knight.

You might have heard stories about her, but they aren't the kind of stories that are written down in books or studied in school. They're stories of the small folk, which are only ever whispered or sung. No duels are fought, no crowns are won. There are not even any heroes, really, although there are plenty of villains.

Here is a tale of the Green Knight: Once there was a dragon sighted in the skies above the wood, and a young prince gathered his men for a dragon hunt. They rode boldly into the wood, and six days later they came stumbling back out, their arrows broken, their boar spears snapped in two, their mounts set loose in the night. Dragons were still hunted sometimes—they were free things, and what is free will always be hunted—but not in those woods.

Here is another tale: Once there was a great war—there were still wars, too—and a pair of brothers fled from the front lines and ran deep into the woods, ashamed. There they came upon a tall woman with a scar through one eye and hair the color of frost.

The brothers said they sought the Green Knight, that they might learn courage. The woman smiled and told them she would bring them to the bravest man she knew. So the brothers spent the evening talking with a gangling, bespectacled man with a voice like a jackdaw and hair the same eerie, dragon-white as the woman's.

At the end of that conversation, he led the brothers to the yew and bade them prick their fingers. They fell asleep that night beneath the tree, and when they woke a hundred years had passed, and the war was over.

They are all like this: trickster tales, fairy tales, tales of great men brought low and lowly folk raised high. A lost child is found again, warm and well-fed, with a fortune in ancient gold tucked in her pockets. A hungry mother sends her sons to glean for berries, and they return with a brace of fat brown hares, some of which have tiny balls of lead in their hearts. A highwayman and his merry band hide in the wood from a wicked sheriff, and the sheriff never finds any sign of them but old firepits and arrowheads, as if their camp were abandoned years before.

You will note that the Green Knight is rarely alone, in these stories. I promised her she wouldn't be, you see.

We live in a cottage in a clearing near the yew. In winter there is smoke curling up from the thatch or, in later years, from a modern metal stovepipe. In autumn there are herbs strung between the rafters to dry, and in summer the door is propped open with a stone, so the children can flit in and out like swallows.

Yes—there are children. A son and a daughter, as before, as always. On the day her son was born the Green Knight turned his left foot in her hand. When she saw the birthmark there—as round and red as a yewberry—she cried and pressed her lips to the mark.

We even have a horse, although we rarely ride farther than the village. A huge blood-bay gelding, which the knight purchased as a colt, and which lived far longer than any natural horse should. Should you ever come across that horse, I advise you to keep your distance.

The four of us—five, if you count Hen—are not alone. There are the others—discontents and malcontents, deserters and dreamers, outlaws and foreigners—who have come to live in the wood, too. People who were driven from their homes or never had them, who lost wars or refused to win them. The hungry hearted and wistful, who believed children's stories about the wood where the crown's power ended, and the Green Knight's began.

There was a smith who refused to forge another sword; a royal falconer who set his birds free; a young woman who smashed her loom one day at the factory. Some of the Roving Folk passed through, and some of them stayed for a season or two, trading stories, teaching me a little of my mother's language. I missed them when they left, but I understood; the geweth make our homes where we will.

Once, we were visited by a young and excessively beautiful knight. He had long hair—not golden, but an astonishing shade of orange—and a lost look in his eyes, as if he were searching for someone to serve and could not find her. The Keeper of the Yew invited him to walk with her through the wood, and when they returned there were tears on both their cheeks. The beautiful knight did not stay long. Before he left, he bowed to me, somewhat ironically, and said he hoped to find a coward of his own one day. I was not wholly sorry to see him go.

More pleasant were the woodcutter and his husband, who the knight greeted by flinging her arms around their necks and kissing both their cheeks frantically. They did not understand it, and the knight never explained herself. But they built their home not far from ours, and they're fond of the children.

It's a good life, and a peaceful one. But still, the knight keeps her sword sharp, always within reach, and I carry a revolver in my coat. This is our second happily ever after, you see, and we know they only last as long as you are willing to fight for them. And no one—*no one*—fights like she does.

I wish I could tell you her name, but she doesn't want it remembered. She's seen the way names become legends become battle cries; soldiers might still go to war, but they will not do it in her name, ever again.

Even still—I don't want it forgotten. Perhaps it's the historian in me, or pure pride. Surely she wouldn't mind if I wrote it in the clumsy cipher my father ta-ught me, here on the very' last page of a book that I doubt more than one or two people will ever read.. Let me write the word) at least once.

She won't discover me; she dictated her sections of this book, but she didn't labor over it, as I did. Perhaps it soothed me, to spend my afternoons fantasizing about setting fire to my manuscript. Perhaps storytelling runs in my family, or one of my families.

Perhaps I am still so damn afraid of forgetting.

I wrote it on ordinary paper, this time—we are careful that no one harvests so much as a fallen twig or dead needle from the yew—and bound it with ordinary glue and twine. I've added a few sections from my published translation, for clarity.

Now that it's finished, I think I'm through with it. I think I will send it bobbing out through time, like a message in a bottle. There is a professor in the Cantford Department of History who told me to take good notes. Maybe I'll leave the book in a tomb or a ruin for her. When she discovers it, I hope she'll whisper *By Jove*, just for me.

And I hope—will you give this book to my father, Gilda? It might be difficult to find him—I imagine he's at sea, seeing the world. But if either of you ever wants to visit us, just go to the yew. We'll be there waiting, centuries ago.

Of course, I'll be long dead, in your time, and so will the Green Knight. Nothing that lives lasts forever.

The tales disagree on how she died. It wasn't a glorious death, for certain—there was no great battle, no grand sacrifice, no queen weeping at her bier. They say she lived happily, for a long time—a *very* long time. There are stories of the Green Knight in every era, after all. They say she died only after her children had grown and left the wood, and returned with their own children, and after those children had left, in turn.

They say one day the knight and the scholar simply laid themselves down among the tangled roots, hand in hand, and did not rise again.

They say it ends where it began: beneath the yew tree.

—Excerpted from The Life of Una Everlasting *by Owen Mallory (unpublished manuscript); supplementary materials provided by Gilda Sawbridge*

Received 8-22

Attn: Mallory

WOULD BE A HELL OF A STORY WERE IT NOT A CROCK OF SHIT WHICH OF COURSE IT IS BUT JUST IN CASE IT ISNT YOUR FATHER AND I WILL SEE YOU SOON BY WHICH I MEAN A VERY LONG TIME AGO

Gil

Received 8-22

Attn: Mallory

PS I KNOW YOU COME BACK SOMETIMES - SYLVIE SAYS YOU RENEWED YOUR LIBRARY BOOKS

Gil

ACKNOWLEDGMENTS

When my mother read the first draft of this book, she sent me—by my request, and to my gratitude—six single-spaced pages describing everything I'd gotten wrong about horses. (If you'd like to be a fantasy author, it's not absolutely necessary to have a mother who is a writing professor, falconer, archer, and horse trainer—but it doesn't hurt.)

Her notes included some fretful calculations about the amount of forage per day that would be required for a single horse carrying the combined weight of an armored rider, her gear, food, weapons, and grain. These burdens, my mother noted, would normally have been shared among a larger retinue. A knight alone—without servant, squire, baggage train, or at least a couple of good mules—struck my mother as implausible.

Which, of course, it is. The knight as a solitary hero—Gawain journeying to the Green Chapel, Galahad questing for the Grail, the Redcrosse Knight facing down the dragon—is a figment of the Western imagination. He's a fantasy of rugged individualism, a handsome piece of propaganda that obscures the actual labor that kept him fed, clothed, armed, and mounted. In this way he resembles the myth of the Lone Explorer (who is accompanied by dozens of porters and local guides), or the Lone Genius (whose notes are typed up by his wife)—or the Lone Author.

No book is written alone. Some require villages, but mine seem to take whole fiefdoms.

The Everlasting would not exist without my agent, Kate McKean, who knows every quest will take two more months than I say it will, or my editors, Kat Howard and Miriam Weinberg, who know how to turn a quest into a good story.

It took a wildly dedicated production team, including Rafal Gibek, Steven Bucsok, Dakota Griffin, Bailey Harrington, Bailey Harrington's twenty-seven-page time-loop tracking table, Katherine Kirk, and Lauren Riebs, to turn that story into a book. Heather Saunders, Shreya Gupta,

Sara Wood, and Alice Cao made it beautiful, and Isa Caban and Giselle Gonzalez championed it with stout hearts and steely nerves, even though—God forgive me—it's written in alternating second person.

There were a few (hundred) times on this quest where I doubted myself—and I was right to do so, honestly. If it wasn't for the insight and expertise of friends and colleagues like Dr. Lee Mandelo, Dr. Gerald Nachtwey, C. L. Clark, Megan E. O'Keefe, Cameron Johnston, and E. C. Tobler, this book would be so much worse. (If you'd like to be a fantasy author, it's not absolutely necessary to have friends who are gender historians, medievalists, blacksmiths, gym bros, literary critics, instructors, and far better writers than you—but it doesn't hurt.) Their advice showed me the way forward, but it was their kindness that kept me marching.

This is a book about love: defiant love, endurant love, love born in a bad world and determined to build a better one. I owe my education on this subject to the people who have loved me so well, for so long. My friends, new and old. My mom and dad. My brothers.

My children, most of all—for you, I would slay any dragon, depose any queen, learn any number of Pokémon, et cetera. And my husband, who would never let me do it alone.

ABOUT THE AUTHOR

Elora Overbey

Alix E. Harrow is the Hugo Award–winning and *New York Times* bestselling author of *The Ten Thousand Doors of January, The Once and Future Witches, Starling House,* and various short fiction. A former adjunct and Kentuckian, Harrow now lives in Virginia with her husband and their two semi-feral kids.

Black Bastion
Cloven hill
The Northern Fallows
DOMINION
The Queen's Wood
Queenswald